Praise for Christina Brooke's
Ministry of Marriage series

A DUCHESS TO REMEMBER

"Christina Brooke is a bright new star." —*RT Book Reviews*

"*A Duchess to Remember* surpasses all expectations, leaving you longing for the next installment."

—*Fresh Fiction*

"A delightful, attention-grabbing, sweetly romantic historical read you won't want to miss."

—*Night Owl Romance*

"This is a two-night, preferably one, book. Cecily and Rand's romance is a fun, deceptive, quickstep of a dance."
—*Romance Reviews Today*

MAD ABOUT THE EARL

"A true historical gem." —*Romance Junkies*

"[A] version of Beauty and the Beast . . . that readers will take to their hearts." —*RT Book Reviews*

"Captivating!" —*Night Owl Romance*

"A sweet and sexy romance." —*Dear Author*

MORE . . .

HEIRESS IN LOVE

"Each scene is more sensual and passionate than the last."
—*Publishers Weekly* (starred review)

"Riveting tale of life, loss, convenience, and heart-wrenching love! Superbly written!"   —*Fresh Fiction*

"With this delightful debut Brooke demonstrates her ability for creating a charming cast of characters who are the perfect players in the first of the Ministry of Marriage series. Marriage-of-convenience fans will rejoice and take pleasure in this enchanting read." —*RT Book Reviews*

"Clever, lush, and lovely—an amazing debut!"
—Suzanne Enoch, *New York Times* bestselling author

"A delightful confection of secrets and seduction, *Heiress in Love* will have readers craving more!"
—Tracy Anne Warren

"One of the most compelling heroes I've read in years."
—Anna Campbell

Also by
Christina Brooke

London's Last True Scoundrel

CHRISTINA BROOKE

St. Martin's Paperbacks

This is a work of fiction. All of the characters, organizations, and events portrayed in this novel are either products of the author's imagination or are used fictitiously.

LONDON'S LAST TRUE SCOUNDREL

Copyright © 2013 by Christina Brooke.
Excerpt from *The Greatest Lover Ever* copyright © 2013 by Christina Brooke.

All rights reserved.

For information address St. Martin's Press, 175 Fifth Avenue, New York, NY 10010.

ISBN: 978-1-250-02934-8

Printed in the United States of America

St. Martin's Paperbacks edition / July 2013

St. Martin's Paperbacks are published by St. Martin's Press, 175 Fifth Avenue, New York, NY 10010.

10 9 8 7 6 5 4 3 2 1

To Denise. This one's for you, Tigger!

ACKNOWLEDGMENTS

The team at St. Martin's Press never fails to amaze me with their passion and commitment to publishing. In particular I'd like to thank my editor, Monique Patterson, who pushed me beyond my comfort zone to write this book. Thanks also to the fabulous Holly Blanck and to everyone who plays a part in publishing the novels I write.

To my agent, Helen Breitwieser, my gratitude for your belief in me and for your wisdom and advice.

To Anna Campbell, Denise Rossetti, and Victoria Steele, thank you for your sterling friendship and writerly camaraderie. You make this job so much fun.

To Kim and Gil Castillo, I appreciate your attention to detail in so many aspects of the writing business.

To my dear and talented friends on the Romance Bandits blog, your friendship and support are past price. And to my readers, thank you. You make the whole thing worthwhile.

Last but by no means least, to Jamie, Allister, Adrian, Ian, Cheryl, Robin, and George, who have to suffer through deadline madness right along with me, I love you. Thank you for always being there for me.

CHAPTER ONE

Jonathon Westruther, Earl of Davenport, surveyed the three men standing over him with a jaundiced eye. They were an impressive lot, he supposed: large, well muscled, with that arrogant way of carrying themselves the Westruthers had perfected over centuries of uninterrupted rule.

"What a bunch of old sobersides you've become," he said with a lazy grin. "What've I done this time?"

Lord Beckenham, the eldest of his cousins, looked severe. More severe than usual, which was saying a lot if you knew Beckenham. "The question is not what you have done *this* time, but what you have been doing ever since your return, what you continue to do. This reckless, profligate behavior—"

"Don't read him a lecture, Becks," said Viscount Lydgate, the tall, fair-haired exquisite gentleman, whose beautifully tailored clothes concealed the ability to fight like a street ruffian. "When does any man listen to such stuff?"

He turned frosted blue eyes on Davenport. "You're the talk of London. Think of Cecily, if no one else."

"Cecily?" repeated Davenport, nonplussed.

"Your sister, old fellow, in case that drink-addled brain of yours has forgotten," snapped Lydgate. "Your behavior distresses her. That should be reason enough to mend your ways."

Cecily, who had recently become Duchess of Ashburn, was disgustingly happy, as far as Davenport could tell. But then, he'd avoided Cecily whenever possible, so he could be wrong about that.

Hmm. Distressed, was she? Davenport felt a remote twinge of . . . something. He refused to let his three cousins see it, whatever it was.

With studied insolence, he took out his watch, checked it, and gave a jaw-breaking yawn. Then he cocked his head in Steyne's direction and waited.

Steyne's face held that toplofty, sneering expression it usually wore. Xavier, Marquis of Steyne, could be a mighty unpleasant fellow. But at least he was no stranger to vice.

"Yes, I am quite aware how it must seem to you," agreed Steyne, his saturnine aspect emphasized by a deep frown. "I am scarcely one to preach propriety. But there is a difference. My sins, while legion, have never attracted vulgar scandal. *You* hover on the very brink."

"And we're going to haul you back from that brink," Beckenham ground out, "if we need to bind and gag you to do it."

Davenport's brow lightened at the prospect of physical violence. "You're welcome to try."

Despite the prospect of a good fight in the offing, he felt a nagging sense of injustice. He'd been brought back from the dead with all the drama and fanfare of one of Prinny's phantasmagoric fêtes. The irony was, Davenport no longer cared whether he lived or died. Too late, he'd discovered the price for his resurrection was too high.

Neither his cousins' threats nor Cecily's dogged expressions of love seemed capable of shaking the hold of doom upon him.

He'd lost his life's work and, with it, his purpose. Now he hunted trouble to the four corners of hell.

"No woman is safe from you," said Lydgate, his usually easygoing countenance hardened with contempt. "This business with Lady Maria must stop."

Ah. Lady Maria Shand. Davenport fingered his chin. Her duality had intrigued him. In a ballroom, she was a prim, proper miss. Get her alone in the moonlight and she lost no time shoving her delicate little hands down one's trousers.

But then, females—particularly females of his class—were so hidebound by ridiculous rules and restrictions. Forced to deny perfectly natural, biological urges and desires. The scientist in him cried out against this repression of instinctual behavior. It was his duty to liberate as many of them as possible.

However, before he'd accepted the blatant invitation to satisfy both their natural urges between the lady's elegant thighs, he'd made a shocking discovery. While he had the laudable objective of freeing Lady Maria from the chains of propriety, Lady Maria aimed to shackle *him* into holy matrimony.

It wasn't the fear of scandal that stopped him but the sudden insight that Lady Maria's enthusiastic kisses bore the sour tang of deceit.

His cousins' warning was thus belated and unnecessary. He'd kissed Lady Maria farewell the previous evening without rancor or regret—on his part, at least.

It was an entanglement that could prove uncomfortable on more than one level. Lady Maria's father, Lord Yarmouth, had been something of a mentor to Davenport at one time.

"As you said, Lydgate, lecturing will not do the job." Deliberately, Steyne placed a hand on each armrest of Davenport's chair and leaned in, his expression full of menace.

"Ruralize," he said. "Leave London and do not come back."

"What, not ever?" said Davenport, trying to be amused. What could Steyne do to him, after all? "I don't think so."

He downed the brandy he'd left untouched on the table by his elbow. The hit of alcohol seemed to sober him, rather than the reverse. What was he doing, sitting here in Steyne's library, submitting to a lecture? He wasn't a schoolboy anymore.

Ruralize. The Devil! He might as well hang himself from the nearest tree.

In the country, he'd have too much time to reflect on the wasteland his life had become. If he kept himself moving, busy, occupied, he might outrun that demon, at least for a while. He needed London, the busy stench of it, the roistering, the wenching, the endless, pointless amusements afforded to a gentleman of wealth and status.

He'd hoped his behavior would convince the doubters he had nothing more to offer the world of science he'd left behind. Yet, after all he'd done to throw dust in their eyes, someone still watched him.

Another reason to stay in London. Better to be shadowed in a busy metropolis where he might evade pursuit without appearing conscious of the mysterious figure who dogged his footsteps. In the country, there was little prospect of that.

He didn't know why he hadn't put a stop to the business. One more product of the general malaise he'd felt since returning to his old life, he supposed.

Davenport got to his feet, but the effort seemed to cost him. All those sleepless, reckless nights . . .

Tiredness swept over him, a dragging sense of fatigue. Beckenham had predicted it would all catch up with him one day, and suddenly he feared he was right.

He swayed, stretched out a hand, heard the brandy glass topple and fall to the carpet with a soft thud.

His vision slid and slipped. He narrowed his eyes, trying to bring Xavier's face into focus.

Through a woolly haze, he heard Lydgate exclaim, "Drugged? Was that really necessary?"

"I think so," came Xavier's cool reply. His hands gripped beneath Davenport's arms and lowered him back into the chair.

But Davenport didn't stop when his back hit the cushion. He was falling, falling, and try as he might, he couldn't grab hold of anything, couldn't do a damned thing to save himself.

The darkness rushed up to swamp him.

* * *

TWO WEEKS EARLIER

"Dismissed?" said Miss Hilary deVere, staring at the thin, tall woman behind the elegant little desk in mounting horror. "But—but you have always been happy with my work, Miss Tollington. I don't understand."

Miss Tollington's Academy for Young Ladies had been Hilary's life since she was fifteen years old. First as a student, now as a teacher of dancing and deportment. No girl left Miss Tollington's without a thorough, merciless grounding in courtly behavior, etiquette, and dancing from Miss Hilary deVere.

Hilary was twenty years old, an orphan under the guardianship of a man who had so many wards, he'd forgotten she existed. Which suited her very well indeed, since the last match Lord deVere had tried to make for her was with a toothless old lecher of eighty.

She'd given her all to this school. And now they no longer wanted her.

To her credit, Miss Tollington's thin, plain face worked with distress. She whisked out a flimsy lace handkerchief and pressed it to her mouth. "Lady Endicott called on me, you see."

Hilary bit her lip. Lady Endicott was a member of the Black family and very high in the instep. Relations between the deVeres and the Blacks had never been what might be called amicable.

"And what has Lady Endicott to say to anything?" Hilary knew whatever Lady Endicott had to say could not possibly be good.

"Unfortunately, Her Ladyship has a great deal to say to the running of this school." Miss Tollington blinked rapidly. The lines that pinched her mouth deepened.

She drew a long breath. "You see, Miss deVere, Lady Endicott has become our new patroness."

"Oh." Hilary clenched her hands so tightly, her fingernails dug into her palms. "Yes. Yes, I see."

No matter what she did or who she was inside, people like Lady Endicott never took the trouble to notice. In Her Ladyship's eyes, Hilary was a *dastardly deVere*. Someone from her family could not be trusted to instruct young soon-to-be debutantes in proper behavior.

And that was that.

A sense of helpless frustration threatened to choke her. She'd tried so hard to prove herself here. She didn't know how she could have done more to show that she was not one of *those* deVeres but a properly behaved, virtuous lady who didn't deserve to be judged on the sins of her forebears.

Hilary would never go so far as to slump her shoulders—good posture must always be maintained, no matter how one cringed inside—but the utter defeat she felt must have shown on her face.

Miss Tollington dabbed at the corners of her eyes with her handkerchief. In a constricted voice, she said, "I am sorry, Miss deVere. So very, very sorry. If I could find a way around it I would, but . . ."

The smile Hilary gave her mentor felt like it would crack her face. "Please, do not distress yourself, Miss Tollington. I know you would keep me if you could."

An idea occurred to her. "Perhaps there is some other task I might perform here besides teaching. I could . . . I could . . ."

How might she tell Miss Tollington she'd work as a scullery maid if only the headmistress would let her stay? The thought of returning to her tumbledown home in Lincolnshire and her horrid brothers made her give an inward shudder.

The headmistress was shaking her head. "I'm afraid that's impossible, my dear."

Hilary wondered if Lady Endicott had demanded she remove her contaminating presence from the school altogether and on the instant. The deVere men were renowned as uncouth brutes; the women, hard-riding hoydens who were loose in their morals and undiscriminating in their choices of bedmates.

A deVere female would, by her mere presence, taint the purity of the pupils at this fine establishment.

With suppressed violence, she said, "Prejudice. This is sheer prejudice."

Her emotions needed physical outlet. Hilary jumped up from her chair to pace, casting about for a solution to save her from going back to Wrotham Grange. "If Lady Endicott would only grant me an audience, I could convince her to let me stay. I know I could."

"I'm afraid not, Miss deVere," said Miss Tollington gently.

The headmistress rose, too, and came around the desk

to put her hands on Hilary's shoulders. She had never touched Hilary before, and the gesture moved Hilary more than words ever could.

"My dear girl," murmured Miss Tollington, "I am terribly sad to see you go. But Lady Endicott's command made me see that I have been selfish in allowing you to remain here so long."

"Selfish?" Hilary was incredulous. "These past five years have been the happiest of my life."

Compassion shone from the headmistress's pale blue eyes. "I know that. And that is why I have been selfish. You need to *live*, Miss deVere."

She gestured around her, at the chintzy, homey office that had always seemed so welcoming to Hilary. "I am obliged to make my living this way, and I am dedicated to the school because whenever I do something, I resolve to do it well. But do not fool yourself for a moment. If I had your connections, your fortune and advantages, I should not remain here a second longer than I had to."

The swollen feeling in Hilary's throat grew. "Forgive me, but you know very little of my situation if you think I have advantages," she forced out. "Why, my brothers would never agree to give me a London season. Even if they did, there is no respectable matron I can think of who would take me under her wing. My guardian doesn't know or care whether I live or die. My fortune is not large enough to interest him in making me an eligible match. And I don't come into my money until I am one-and-twenty, so that can't help me, either."

With a fond smile, Miss Tollington said, "And yet, these obstacles are not insurmountable. I have written to an old acquaintance of mine, Mrs. Farrington. Her two daughters are married and off her hands now. Only last month, I heard from her that she is pining for some new diversion now that her birds have all flown the nest. I cannot promise, of course, but I think she might be willing to sponsor such a decorous, genteel young lady for the coming season."

Hilary's heart gave a huge bound in her chest. An emotion between elation and panic coursed through her. She could only blink and stammer her thanks, as was proper.

A London season. Balls and routs, picnics and musicales.

"*Almack's*," she breathed.

But she had not a stitch to wear that would be suitable in London or at an Almack's subscription ball, for that matter. She could not possibly . . .

A litany of objections raised their heads, but she squared her shoulders, dismissing them. She'd grab this opportunity with both hands and refuse to let it go.

Her trustees must advance her some money from her inheritance. They'd refused her requests in the past. If she had Mrs. Farrington to help her, perhaps she might shame Lord deVere and his oily solicitor into providing for her wardrobe, at least.

She would get to London for the season or die trying.

Once she was there, she would behave with such elegance and decorum that everyone would see she did *not* belong with the deVere family. She was a rose among thorns, waiting to be plucked.

If she was very, very lucky, she might even find a husband. She squeezed her eyes shut at the thought. A quiet man, good and kind, refined, well educated. A scholar, perhaps. Nice gentry stock, comfortably situated . . . She wanted the exact opposite of her selfish, hard-drinking, womanizing brothers and that's what she would find.

She had a respectable dowry, if not a spectacular one. She might not be a beauty, but she was no antidote, either. Or, at least, she hoped not. And she knew to a nicety how to hold a household, if only she was given the chance.

The more Hilary thought about this scheme, the better she liked it. And she had Miss Tollington to thank.

Hilary threw caution to the winds. Putting her arms about the older woman, she hugged the headmistress tight.

"Thank you. Oh, thank you. I won't disappoint you, Miss Tollington."

Miss Tollington smiled down at her. "You never have, my dear Miss deVere."

There and then, Hilary made a vow. She would charm Mrs. Farrington so much, the lady would be delighted to take her to London and sponsor her debut. There she would show Lady Endicott and the rest of the ton how unfair their prejudice against her was.

She would find a husband who embodied all of the qualities she most admired.

After this season, she would never go back home to Wrotham Grange again.

Ever.

* * *

"Damnation! Bloody, bloody hell!" A string of even fouler curses issued from Davenport's lips as the pain in his head pounded into acute agony.

The torture wasn't just in his head, as he discovered from a mental scan of his body. He ached all over, too.

He lay on some kind of straw pallet in some kind of barn. He had no earthly idea where he was. For several fraught seconds in which his heart stopped and his breath suspended in his lungs he thought they'd got him. Caught up with him at last.

The mysterious, nameless *they* who had been following him for some time now.

He was unbound, at least. There was no one standing guard, ready to restrain him if he tried to escape. The door to the barn lay wide open, letting in a pale, watery light.

When his breathing calmed and his mind cleared a little, he let his head fall back against the straw and blew out a breath of relief. He remembered now. Xavier and the drugged brandy, Lydgate and Beckenham smuggling him out of London.

He'd woken, taken one look at his captors, and laid into them, fists flying.

There'd been nothing stylish or controlled about that particular fight. Wouldn't do at all in Jackson's Boxing Saloon. He grinned as he remembered a particularly nasty uppercut to Beckenham's jaw.

Witness the suffering in his right hand. He might well have broken it.

Experimentally, he flexed his fingers and swore again. Perhaps not *quite* broken.

Well, that was a blessing.

Of course they'd overpowered him. He wasn't a match for two of his cousins, though he'd given a damned good account of himself for someone who'd been drugged and tossed in the back of a farmer's cart and driven out of town.

His brow creased. Steyne hadn't been there. Left the others to do his dirty work. Typical.

And a great pity. Davenport would have taken immense pleasure in kicking the supercilious marquis in the bollocks.

Drugged. He hadn't seen that coming. But he should have known that when Westruthers make up their mind to do something, it gets done. More fool he, to let down his guard. He should have told them all to go to hell when they'd cornered him at Steyne's house that night.

What time was it, anyway? It wasn't exactly sunny, but what light there was told him it was daytime. He took out his timepiece, to discover the face had a crack in it. No doubt one more result of his set-to with Lydgate and Beckenham.

He hoped they'd suffered a fraction of his wounds. He hoped they were sore today.

He put the timepiece to his ear and heard the steady tick. Still working, then, despite the damage to the casing. He stared at the hands of the clock face. They blurred, then resolved again into a position that told him it was two o'clock. Afternoon, then.

He needed to get up, but he was reluctant to leave the dubious comfort of the sweet-smelling straw to test his body's capabilities. He ought to be thankful, he supposed, that they had not dumped him in a pigsty or a horse trough.

Too much to hope they'd be somewhere nearby, waiting for him, ready to convey him somewhere more civilized, like Cribb's Parlour, perhaps, or his town house in Mayfair.

He wondered where the hell he was.

In a moment, he'd get up and find out.

Just give him a moment. . . .

The moment in question passed all too quickly for his liking.

He closed his eyes, clenched his teeth, and defied every screaming part of his body to get to his feet.

* * *

A half hour later, Davenport rode through a light drizzle toward Stamford.

He'd borrowed a stocky big gelding from the farmer in whose barn he'd been dumped and requested directions to the nearest posting inn.

They'd left him in the middle of Lincolnshire, miles from his estate, with no funds and no means of transport. In the condition he was in, battered, bruised, and covered in bits of straw, it had taken a hell of a lot of toploftiness, charm, and persuasion to make that farmer part with his nag.

Davenport would be true to his word, however. He had a few coins in his pockets, and he'd pay some ostler or other to ride the horse back to the farm.

A cursory scan of the surrounding countryside didn't yield any glimpse of the man who had followed him in London. Maybe the fellow had been caught napping by the Westruther cousins' sudden kidnapping of his quarry. Wouldn't that be the ultimate irony?

He couldn't shake a nagging sense of unease, however. In the years since he'd disappeared from society, he'd learned to trust his instincts.

Davenport urged his horse into a canter. He'd be damned if he'd return meekly to Davenport, whether someone followed him or not. If he let his cousins interfere in his pleasures now, there'd be no getting rid of them. They'd have him sober as a judge and married to some straitlaced heiress as quick as he could stare. The mere thought of marriage to a proper English miss made him shudder.

He hadn't reached the village before he noted a figure coming toward him. Little and bedraggled, it was, on foot and lugging a pair of bandboxes.

And female. Yes, most definitely female. Slender, but rounded in all the places where a female should be round.

With a click of his tongue, he slowed his mount to a walk.

"Ho, there!" he called. "Might I be of assistance, miss?"

The rain had thickened; it dotted her face as she lifted it to peer up at him.

Woebegone little features showed beneath the soggy straw bonnet. They were finely wrought features, delicate in a way that reminded one of storybook pictures of woodland fairies. A plush, full-lipped mouth made her face oddly unbalanced, as if the mouth had come from another place entirely. *That* feature made him think of bordellos and sin.

She gave a start when she took in his face. Inwardly, he grimaced. No doubt the bruising made him look ghastly.

"No, I thank you, sir." Her voice was crisp, cultured. One of those prim females he so disliked.

Despite the pressing need to get to London, he could not leave a lady alone in this predicament.

"Let me take you where you need to go." He gestured down at his horse. "He is big enough for two, you must agree. You will still be drenched, I'm afraid, but at least you will be home in less time."

He smiled at her, wondering precisely how horrible he looked. "Don't be afraid. I met with an, er, accident, but I wouldn't harm you."

She looked at him straightly. "I know precisely what those bruises on your face mean. You were drunk and fell into a bout of fisticuffs. By the looks of you, you got the worst of it."

"Well, there *were* two of them," he murmured, after a moment of stunned surprise. What did this delicate chit know of drunken brawls?

She set her luscious little mouth in a stubborn line. "Now, if you don't mind, I'd like to get home before the storm breaks."

She stepped around him and continued trudging.

He saw no alternative but to turn his horse and follow. He called after her, "How far is your home?"

She ignored him. Trudge, trudge, trudge.

The wind had picked up, making the rain slant into their faces. Davenport shivered. He still wore his evening kit and his bloody cousins hadn't done him the courtesy of leaving him with so much as a driving coat to shield him from the elements. It was spring, but you wouldn't know it, the way the rain had turned to icy needles.

The girl's slim shoulders remained erect as a sergeant major's as she battled into the gale. Her hat drooped about her ears; her drab pelisse was dark with damp. Rats' tails of honey blond hair snaked down her back, whipped free from her tight, proper bun by the wind.

Lightning streaked across the horizon. Thunder cracked, making her halt in her tracks.

But she didn't look back. She lifted her chin, squared her shoulders, and marched on.

"This is madness," he said, pulling alongside her. "Don't be such a little fool."

He reached down to her, even though she still did not look at him. "Give me the bandboxes."

Her straight white teeth sank into the cushion of her lower lip. He became acutely conscious of a desire to soothe that beleaguered feature. Preferably with his tongue.

He blinked, cleared his throat. "Come, ma'am. Surely a short ride with me is preferable to getting caught in this storm."

She sighed. "Very well. Thank you." Reluctance showing in every line of her body, she handed the bandboxes up.

He tied them securely, then reached down a hand to her. "Put your right foot on mine," he instructed her.

She did. Her grip tightened on his hand and he hauled her up. She might be a dab of a female, but the rain weighted her skirts. The pain in his shoulder flared, but his smile didn't waver.

She didn't smile back. Her eyes flickered as she looked into his face properly for the first time, but the expression of disdain did not alter.

"Thank you," she said frigidly.

He gripped her around the waist and settled the wet, bedraggled bundle more comfortably across the saddle before him.

"You are freezing," he said.

She sat as straight as she could under the circumstances, as if she had a poker rammed down the back of her gown.

He chuckled. Really, she was absurd. "Relax. I won't bite."

Much as he'd like to.

"I am perfectly relaxed," she said stiffly.

"If you lean against me, you will be more comfortable," he murmured provocatively, his breath warming her ear. "Shared body heat does wonders against the chill."

She glanced at him suspiciously.

"I assure you, it's true. It's all to do with thermal conduction."

He went on to explain the principles of heat transference, but despite all of the obscure, multisyllabic words he threw in to impress her, she refused to participate in his proposed experiment.

"Thank you. I do not regard the cold."

She didn't regard him, either, but stared ahead. Clearly, the affront to her dignity of allowing some nameless ruffian to escort her home—and at such scandalous proximity—was insurmountable.

With a mental shrug, he set the horse into a brisk walk, enjoying the way she was forced to move against him in rhythm with the motion of their mount. Despite the icy damp of her, despite his own aches and ails, his body went on full alert for action.

At close quarters, he noticed the warm, creamy perfection of her skin. That her irises were not blue, as he'd expected from her fair coloring, but light brown, flecked with hints of gold.

She had a lovely, queenly neck, he discovered, sadly

shadowed by the high collar of her pelisse. She dressed like a spinster aunt, but she couldn't have long left her teens.

"I believe it is customary in such situations to make polite conversation with your rescuer," he said, teasing her.

She turned her head to look at him. Who knew warm brown eyes could turn so cold?

"We have not been introduced," she said. "Therefore, I cannot converse with you."

He wanted to laugh. Her bottom was so near to his groin as to make them very close acquaintances indeed. Yet she would be a stickler for the proprieties.

"Allow me to rectify that error," he said. "I am—"

"Pray, don't trouble yourself." She flicked a repelling glance at him. "I don't expect we shall meet again after today."

He did laugh then. "Oho! If you think that, you don't know much about men, Miss . . . ?" He ended on a note of inquiry.

"Persistent, aren't you?" She cocked an eyebrow but did not turn her head. She seemed quite determined not to look at him any longer than necessary. Did he present that much of an ugly spectacle?

Persistent? He thought about that. "I can be."

In the pursuit of science, he'd been dogged. Some might say obsessed. And yet, since his return, he'd found little worth his extended attention. However, he would persevere with this lady, if only to ruffle those dignified feathers of hers.

She ignored him.

"Very well, then," he said. "If you will not give me your name, I shall be obliged to make one up."

"Can your horse not go any faster?" she asked.

"Let's see, shall we?" He nudged the gelding into an easy canter, taking the opportunity to hug her in tight against him, ostensibly to save her from falling.

She squawked a furious protest. He ignored her.

"I might call you Joan," he decided. "You have a certain air of the burning martyr about you. But I daresay that is merely because you are obliged to ride in the embrace of a reprobate such as me. If you smiled, you would not look like a Joan at all. You do smile, on occasion, I trust?"

No answer. Silent outrage poured from her in waves.

"*Not* Joan, then. Hmm. Something from the Greek pantheon, perhaps. Aphrodite? Or is that wishful thinking on my part?"

"You are ridiculous!" she burst out. "Even if we were introduced, I should never give you leave to use my given name."

She'd colored up quite nicely now, torturing that poor, pretty underlip with her teeth. A sudden yearning startled him in its sharp urgency. What the Devil was wrong with him? She was not the type of woman he usually favored. He couldn't conceive of her ever sticking her hands down his trousers, moonlight or no.

The rain had eased a little, but lightning still frolicked about them. The storm was about to break around their ears and he didn't give a damn. There was something about this young lady. He couldn't put his finger on precisely what it was, but he wasn't about to let her slip from his grasp too easily.

They'd covered two miles or so before it occurred to him he could use the storm to his advantage.

"I fear we might be obliged to take shelter nearby," he commented. "It probably isn't safe to be out."

"I'd rather be struck by lightning than go anywhere private with you," she declared in a stifled voice. "Ride on, if you please. My . . . destination is just down that lane, up ahead."

He noticed the slight hesitation. Hadn't she said she

was going home before? Was she so prejudiced against him that she didn't want him to know where she lived?

He hadn't realized they were so close to the end of this delightful journey. He wanted to know more about her, to keep teasing her until he broke through all that dreadful propriety to the flesh-and-blood woman beneath.

He wondered who awaited this prickly little creature. Not a husband or a lover. For one thing, she didn't have a ring on her finger. For another, he could see she was a virgin as clearly as if it had been stamped across her forehead.

Indeed, virtue never had such a staunch defender as this young lady. Despite the danger of falling from the saddle as their speed increased, she held doggedly to the pommel rather than lean back against him and accept his embrace.

Her profile was finely wrought. Enchanting. Perhaps it was just as well she did not smile. His heart might not have stood it.

Temptation gnawed at him. He'd had many women since his return from exile, but despite the intricate games aristocratic coquettes liked to indulge in, not one had left him in any doubt that those games would end in bed.

This lady gave him no quarter. The hunter in him found her complete disinterest—indeed, her antipathy—irresistible.

He glimpsed a sprawling manor house at the end of the lane. This was it. He halted his steed and stared down at his fair passenger.

CHAPTER TWO

W "hat do we stop for?" Even now, much as she longed to do so, Hilary could not bring herself to look this dreadful man in the eye.

He presented the most shocking figure. She recognized all too well the familiar signs of a scoundrel. She'd had considerable experience of them in her own family.

But this one was a slight variation on the theme, she had to admit. He possessed a sense of humor, for one thing. Intelligence, too. He did his utmost to hide it, but there was a disquieting expression in his gaze when it rested on her, as if he saw her more clearly than he'd any right to do. She wasn't sure she liked that.

He was chivalrous in his own audacious, careless way. She was not stupid enough to believe he'd rescued her out of pure altruism, however. She knew the look in a man's eye when he wanted her. She'd dealt with plenty of those while living in her brother's house.

He was covered in bruises, but even beneath his swollen jaw and the purple contusion that flared across his cheekbone, she could tell at a glance he was a remarkably handsome man.

Liquid brown eyes framed with thick lashes, a head of dark brown hair that, even windblown and wet, fell romantically over his brow. A handsome, strong jaw that spoke of determination, perhaps even a streak of stubbornness, belied by his easygoing manner.

There was something about a man garbed in evening dress and looking utterly disheveled that awoke in her a dormant heat.

Confusion seethed in her brain. How could she find him in the least attractive? She knew his type from bitter experience. He was precisely the kind of man any lady with the least common sense would avoid.

His situation shouted a debauched personality. How on earth had he come to be riding about the countryside in his evening clothes at three in the afternoon? Perhaps he had not yet gone to bed?

Bed.

No. She ought not to think of this man in connection with a bed.

She'd tried not to notice how large his shoulders were, how strong the arm that encircled her. How broad the thigh that brushed hers now and then as he steered his horse.

He was a brute, a rogue, and most probably a libertine, too. He was everything a deVere trying her best to maintain her own standards in the face of an impossible handicap did *not* need.

But her pulse raced. Her body longed to melt against him, to draw warmth from that big, masculine form. Thermal conduction, he'd called it. Whatever the terminology, remaining aloof from him was like staying away from a roaring fire when one was frozen to the marrow.

If she could just get home without giving the fellow any hint of her disquiet, she would be safe. Not far now.

Then he stopped.

She couldn't help it. Her head whipped around. She stared up at him, her eyes widened at the intent expression on his face.

A flush scalded her cheeks. She'd been determined not to react to his teasing and succeeded for the most part. But the serious look disarmed her. She bit her lip.

"Stop that," he ordered, startling her. Gently, he traced her lower lip with his fingertip, freeing it from the anxious clutch of her teeth.

He took her chin in a decided grip, tilted her face upward.

She let him do it, entranced by the compelling power of those serious dark eyes. Her heart beat frantically, but her brain had packed its bags and gone on holiday. She couldn't have strung two thoughts together if her life depended upon it.

On a muttered oath, his mouth descended to hers and took command. His lips were hot and she was so very, very cold. His heat radiated outward, down her body, flowing through her, right to her toes.

He lifted her, pressed her more firmly against his body, warming her twice over. His arms, tight around her, his lips searching, drinking her in.

And his tongue. Oh, goodness, his tongue traced her lower lip, soothing, teasing. A gasp of shock made her lips part. Accepting an invitation she'd no notion of issuing, he licked inside, a languid, lascivious slide of his tongue that only seemed to make her heart pound harder and her knees go weak.

Finally, he raised his head. "Honey." He said it on a ragged laugh. "I shall call you Honey, because you taste so very sweet."

That made her shove away from him so hard she almost fell off his horse. "Put me down. Set me down this instant."

His arm merely tightened around her. Heat glazed his eyes.

"No."

A thrill of fearful excitement speared through her, and wasn't that the opposite reaction to the one she ought to have? She'd always known her deVere blood would get her into trouble one day. If she'd resisted him as soon as he'd tried to kiss her, she'd be free now.

To her relief—or disappointment, she didn't know which—he didn't try it again but merely urged the horse forward.

After a few moments, he asked, "Who lives in this house?"

"My brothers," she said shakily, not knowing whether to be glad or sorry for his change of subject. "They are large and ferocious. I daresay they would delight in adding a few extra bruises to your collection when I tell them what you've done."

He brightened. Not the reaction she'd hoped for. "Really? Who are they, your brothers?"

"Thomas and Benedict deVere," she said, hoping their reputations preceded them. "So you see—"

He laughed. "But I know them. At least, I know Tom. Well, well," he said, eyeing her in a way that did not bode well at all. "So you're a deVere."

He seemed to find the circumstance vastly entertaining. She was not amused.

"This does *not* constitute an introduction," she said.

"Honey, I'd say we're well past the introduction stage, wouldn't you? But that's all right. I like calling you Honey."

Casually, as if the matter wasn't anything of particular interest, he said, "I'm the Earl of Davenport, you know."

"Davenport?" She frowned. "But I thought the earl was an older man."

His lips twisted in a parody of a smile. "What? You haven't heard? Where have you been these past few months, in a convent? No, no, you are thinking of my cousin Bertram. He succeeded me."

"*Succeeded* you?" Now she was thoroughly confused.

"I was dead, you see," he explained, as if that were the most reasonable thing in the world. "My cousin inherited. But then they found I wasn't dead after all, so I am now the earl. And he is not."

"But . . ." Oh, dear Heaven, it couldn't be.

Her body went hot, then cold, then hot again. For the first time in her life, she felt as if she might faint. Hilary closed her eyes, squeezed them shut, then opened them again.

"What is your first name, my lord?"

"Jonathon," he said. Then he flashed a genuine smile. "I knew you'd come around to my way of thinking. My dear Honey, this is the start of a beautiful friendship."

He bent toward her, with that teasing lilt to his lips she utterly abhorred. He meant to *kiss* her again? He actually meant to—

"Ooh!"

For the first time in her polite, faultless life, Hilary drew back her hand and slapped her irritating companion's face.

* * *

His reflexes were nothing short of spectacular, for he dodged her flying palm, making the blow glance past him rather than connect. But Hilary had put her full force into the slap; when her palm mostly met air, there was nothing to stop her momentum. She pitched forward and tumbled off the horse.

And somehow, he was falling with her, wrapping his arms about her, shielding her body but not completely saving her from the teeth-jarring impact of the ground rushing up to meet them.

"Ooph!"

Winded, she gasped for air, sprawled out on top of the big, bruised brute. Then she laid into him with her fists, pummeling that rock-hard chest.

He chose to let her hit him this time; even through the haze of rage she knew he could subdue her easily if he wished. The confounded man didn't even flinch.

"Enough." He gripped her wrists, and a steely glint in those dark eyes told her she'd ignited his temper, too.

She tried to lift her knee to his privates, but with a buck of the hips he rolled so he was on top of her, his own knees pinning her down by her skirts, his body crushing her. She felt the wet mud squish beneath her back. Her pelisse would be ruined, but what did the Earl of Davenport care for that? Or for anything about her.

"What is *wrong* with you?" Davenport shouted down at her.

"You don't know, do you?" she fumed. "You truly do not know. The name deVere does not ring any bells with you, does it, my lord?"

"Bells?" He shook his head, and she could see his astonishment was genuine.

"Wedding bells, to be precise," she bit off. "You oaf! We were betrothed, you and I. You cannot have forgotten."

He looked first thunderstruck, then appalled. "Nonsense. I've never been betrothed in my life. We've never even met."

"Our parents arranged it, and I—I—" Her throat worked. "All these years, I thought you were dead."

"It was a mistake," he muttered, watching her warily. "Oh, no, no, don't do that. Don't cry. I'm back, you see? You needn't pine for a dead man anymore. You can go and get yourself shackled to someone else."

That cleared up any urge to weep. She freed her wrist from his slackened grasp and struck him again on the chest. "Pine for you? *Pine* for you? I was doing very well without you."

But she realized now that she had not done so very well without him. She'd marked time, waiting for . . . what? Had she known, deep down, that he'd come back from the dead? What a foolish thought.

He'd been her own private tragedy, bravely borne, a secret she'd hugged to herself.

She'd never met him, that much was true, so she hadn't felt his loss on a personal level. But she'd built up the Earl of Davenport in her head to such a god-like creature that no mere mortal could replace him. She'd grieved for him. Prayed for his soul.

The dastard.

He'd asked if she'd lived in a convent. She might as well have; Miss Tollington's was so cut off from the world that Hilary hadn't heard of Davenport's return. That must have been quite an event.

"You and I are not betrothed," asserted Davenport. "That I would remember."

"They never told you." She spoke the thought out loud.

"I'm not the marrying kind, actually," he said, watching her with distinct unease. "Deeply sorry if my parents raised expectations. They had a habit of doing that, I believe. But there it is."

The idiot thought she wanted to marry him now?

"Get off me!" she told him.

"Oh, right." He removed himself and stood. Then he held out a hand to help her up.

There was a great sucking sound as he hauled her out of the mire. The clothes were plastered to her back, wet, horridly uncomfortable. Could this day get any worse?

She stalked over to his horse, which had been standing, quiescent, while all of this went on.

Wrestling with the ties holding her bandbox in place, she said crossly, "I wouldn't marry you if you were the last man alive."

"Now *that* shows excellent judgment on your part," he said in an approving tone that made her want to hit him again.

Suddenly it occurred to her that she'd behaved abominably. No matter what the provocation, a lady should never hit a gentleman, for he could not fight back.

That was one of the many precepts she'd instilled into her young charges at Miss Tollington's. Yet here she was, covered in mud, with stinging knuckles. And she'd brought all of that on herself.

She bit her lip.

It behooved her, as a lady, to apologize.

She still wanted to scream at him, but she made herself turn and look the Earl of Davenport in the eye. She squared her shoulders, lifted her chin, girded her loins—oh, dear, ladies were *not* supposed to think of their loins. . . .

She thought of his loins instead, the ones that had been pressed against her most intimately a few seconds ago.

A sizzle of heat passed through her. She tamped it down.

Stiffly, she said, "I apologize for hitting you, my lord."

"Oh, think nothing of it." He waved her away. "People are always hitting me. I don't regard it, I assure you."

She gritted her teeth. "It was conduct unbefitting a lady."

"But the provocation *was* severe," he said in a soothing tone that made her want to fly at him again.

Hilary felt a growl rumble low in her throat. How did he bring out this violent streak in her? She had never, not once, raised a hand to her brothers, and they could try the patience of a saint.

Lord Davenport would turn a saint homicidal, she thought resentfully.

"Still, I should not have done it," she said. "I am sorry."

She made herself hold out her hand. "Now I must thank you for seeing me safely home."

She realized that the rain had all but stopped, though one could see from the black clouds on the horizon that the storm had not passed.

He grasped her hand. The wary look in his eyes had vanished. A wicked gleam took its place.

"Good-bye." She gave his hand a decided shake and tried to get free.

He held on. "But I shall see you to your door, of course. As a gentleman should."

"It's not necessary," she said.

"I insist."

"I am not getting on that horse again."

"Of course not. You'll muddy the saddle."

He smiled at her, his charm returning in full force now that the imminent danger of matrimony was past. "We'll walk."

* * *

Davenport had never heard sweeter music than Honey's voice telling him she wouldn't marry him if he were the last man on earth. For a few minutes there, she'd had him terrified.

But now that nightmare prospect had vanished, he intended to stay around and annoy her as much as possible. Annoying Honey was proving to be the best entertainment he'd had in years.

She insisted on scurrying away to change, so he left her bandboxes in the care of a manservant and took the farmer's nag around to the stables.

Grooming horses was a way to keep one's hands occupied while one cogitated on serious conundrums. He'd lived in his head most of the time as a younger man, and something about the rhythmic, mindless activity of rubbing a horse down had always assisted the thought processes.

He'd come up with his best insights not in his laboratory, but in the stables.

That was all done with now, of course. He had neither the resources nor the inclination to embark on further scientific study. That belonged to another lifetime.

Only after it had been taken away from him did he realize how greatly his work had isolated him. Only when he couldn't go back to see his family and friends did he realize how much he'd taken them for granted while he'd been in their midst.

Well, he was back now, and look what his nearest and dearest had done to him. Drugged him, beaten him, shipped him off to the country.

And all of that had led to a most entertaining afternoon.

He thought of Miss Primness forcing herself to apologize to him over her outburst and chuckled. Hadn't that just about stuck in her throat?

Worth almost breaking his neck and his leg to fall with her into the mud. He could still feel the soft roundness of her petite body beneath him, the enticing V at the juncture of her thighs . . .

Given his injuries, he ought to be crippled with agony, but when he'd stared into those fuming, sizzling golden brown eyes of hers, he'd felt no pain.

He finished with the big gelding and flipped a coin to one of the stable hands. "This horse belongs at Pruett's farm. Take him back there, will you, with the Earl of Davenport's compliments and thanks."

All but rubbing his hands in anticipation, he strode back to the house.

Wrotham Grange was a ramshackle establishment, whose primary form of decoration was moth-eaten tapestries, dark medieval-looking furniture, and dog hair. The place smelled only a few degrees better than a kennel.

There did not seem to be any female servants, which probably accounted for the pervasive sense of neglect.

How did a delicate morsel of propriety like Honey live in such a place? He was not exactly famed for his fastidiousness, but he balked at this level of slovenliness.

He heard voices coming from a room behind closed doors. Not all of them were masculine.

His brows drawing together, Davenport knocked.

A rough, slurring voice bade him enter.

The sight that met his eyes would send poor Honey into a fit of convulsions.

He'd seen more refined orgies in a brothel. A fire roared in the hearth, no doubt to warm the many acres of bare flesh that quivered and jounced about the place in wild abandon.

At second glance, he realized there were fewer present than he'd thought. Four females and two men. The men, mercifully, were still fully clothed. The women appeared to be performing some sort of peep show for their entertainment and cavorted about in various states of undress.

He recognized Tom deVere from their time together at Eton. DeVere was a big man, stockier than he'd been at school, a hard rider to hounds with dirty blond hair and a broken nose. His younger brother, Benedict, was even larger. Both of them sprawled in overstuffed chairs in their shirtsleeves, guzzling wine straight from the bottle and calling out lewd instructions to their female companions.

Ah, yes. Brothers who whore together . . .

"Good God! 'S Davenport," said Tom, peering up at him owlishly.

"Who?" grunted Benedict, without taking his gaze from the tarts.

Davenport felt something cold and wet nudge his hand. He turned to see a spaniel gazing up at him imploringly. He held the door open and the canine shot out of the drawing room, as if released from prison.

One of the girls, a dark-haired plump and rosy morsel with enormous breasts, sashayed toward him.

"Hello, lover," she purred in a husky, low voice. "Fancy a bit of the other, then?"

Lord Davenport looked down at her and smiled.

* * *

A chorus of high-pitched, excited barks greeted Hilary as she walked into the hall. The muted thunder of dog paws grew louder. Hilary braced herself to be mobbed by a multitude of furry bodies that wriggled in delight.

Laughing, Hilary pushed inquisitive muzzles from her skirts, distributing pats and ear scratches among her brothers' many hunting dogs and receiving slobbery licks and a liberal covering of dog hair into the bargain.

She ought to have more care for her clothing, but her pelisse was so dirty and disheveled, the dog hair scarcely mattered. Besides, this was all the welcome home she was likely to get.

"There you are, Lucy." Her favorite pointer was too old to go hunting now and leaned against Hilary's thigh, waiting patiently for her turn. Hilary gently pulled on the pointer's velvety ear.

Their grizzled old manservant emerged from the dark corridor, glaring at her balefully. His sharp, "Out!" sent the dogs careering off again, Lucy loping gently at the rear.

"Hello, Hodgins," said Hilary, peeling off her wet gloves. "Are my brothers at home?"

"Uh, yes, miss. In a manner of speaking." He took her gloves and received the sodden mass of bonnet gingerly.

"I fear you will have to dispose of the hat. I, er, met with an accident."

An accident by the name of Davenport.

She pressed fingertips to her lips, remembering the kiss that had preceded her fall into the mud. Thinking of it made her hot and uncomfortable, even a little dizzy, as if she were falling from that big horse all over again.

Heavens, she needed to get hold of herself. "Ask Trixie to look at the gloves and see what she can do, will you?" she said to Hodgins. "Perhaps they might be saved. I shall go up and change. Would you have a bath drawn for me, please?"

"Aye, miss."

Hodgins's grizzled head jerked up, as if he heard a noise. His beetling brows lowered in dudgeon.

"Carriage," he grunted.

He nodded toward the potholed drive, where a smart barouche drew up outside the open front door. Hodgins was never happy about visitors. They meant more work.

"Good gracious," said Hilary, peering out. "Who on earth could be calling when I've only just returned?" Her brothers rarely entertained company at this hour of the day.

A fashionably dressed lady of middling years alighted from the vehicle. Hilary frowned. A lady who looked like that would not be calling on her brothers. She must be here to see Hilary. But how could that be?

Before Hilary could collect her wits enough to scuttle out of sight, a dazzlingly liveried footman appeared at the door. With a bow, he handed Hodgins a snowy white card.

"Mrs. Farrington to see Miss deVere."

CHAPTER THREE

Blood drained from Hilary's face. *Mrs. Farrington.* The lady on whose good opinion she depended to sponsor her London debut.

Hilary glanced around wildly for an avenue of escape. How could this happen? How had the lady been so swift to respond to Miss Tollington's appeal? Why couldn't she have waited until Hilary was at least clean, for pity's sake?

She caught sight of herself in the looking glass and gave a faint scream. Her hair was dripping wet, flattened where her bonnet had hugged it, straggling down everywhere else. Her clothes were soaked and covered in mud. Grime streaked her face.

The wonder was that Davenport had wanted to kiss such a specimen. It showed a dismal lack of discrimination on his part.

Don't think about that now—

There was no time to run upstairs. She searched for something to hide behind, but she was too late. Her unwanted guest swept into the vestibule.

Mrs. Farrington was a comfortably rounded lady of about fifty years, with improbable black hair and bright blue eyes. She had a bird-like way of tilting her head as she surveyed her surroundings.

The blue eyes widened to astonishment when they saw Hilary.

"Heavens, dear child! What happened to you?"

Hilary lifted her chin. "A trifling accident, ma'am," she replied, modulating her voice to a semblance of calm. "I was caught in the storm and—and took a tumble from my horse."

She curtsied with all the grace she could muster, conscious of the small pool of muddy water in which she now stood. "Thank you for calling. I, er, believe you are acquainted with my former employer, Miss Tollington."

"Oh, the dear creature. Yes, indeed I am, for we were at school together, you know. Ha! To think of Clarissa as headmistress of the academy." Mrs. Farrington's eyes twinkled. "We were quite naughty when we were girls together, you know. Oh, nothing too dreadful, you know. Just pranks."

That surprised Hilary. She'd always regarded the headmistress of Miss Tollington's Academy for Young Ladies as the epitome of decorum. Hilary couldn't imagine her former employer putting a frog in a teacher's bed or dipping other girls' pigtails in an inkwell.

Despite her frozen body, Hilary warmed to Mrs. Farrington. Miss Tollington had not let her down. If only Mrs. Farrington hadn't responded to the headmistress's plea with quite so much alacrity.

With a twinge of unease, Hilary wondered where Lord Davenport had taken himself off to. It would be too much to hope he'd left for good.

"It is very kind of you to come," she said, impulsively stretching out her hand to her guest.

If Mrs. Farrington hadn't been disgusted by Hilary's state of dress, then the lady was unlikely to be deterred by prejudice over Hilary's family. Indeed, if she were not predisposed to take Hilary under her wing she would not be here.

"Oh, as soon as Tolly wrote, I knew I had to help you," said Mrs. Farrington, removing her gloves and taking Hilary's proffered hand in hers.

"Such an unfortunate situation for you. I would have helped Tolly, too, you know, but she is of a very independent disposition. Stubborn?" She clicked her tongue and shook her head, glossy sausage curls fluttering. "As a *mule*, my dear. Tolly always would go her own way."

When she'd imagined the lady who would take her to London, Hilary had conjured up a proud, haughty middle-aged matron. Not this lively bundle of wry humor.

Jubilation danced a jig in her breast. She beamed at her guest, then recollected her duties as a hostess. "Oh, but what am I about to keep you standing here? Tea in the drawing room, please, Hodgins."

Hilary glanced at her manservant, who hovered nearby. His gnarled old face made several grimaces and his mouth worked strangely. She gave him a decisive nod to reinforce her order, wishing that for once Hodgins would do as he was asked without argument.

"*Not* the drawing room, miss," he muttered.

Her irritation spiked. Hodgins was far too accustomed to having everything his own way. Well, she would not let Mrs. Farrington see that she couldn't manage a servant properly.

"Of course the drawing room," she said impatiently. "Where else would we go, pray?"

At least the drawing room was safe, situated in the relatively new part of the house. One never knew one's luck in the older wing; the ceiling could fall in at any moment.

She ignored Hodgins's mutterings. If the drawing room hadn't been dusted since she was last here, that couldn't be helped. At least Mrs. Farrington did not appear to be the sort to stand upon ceremony.

Hilary experienced a heady rush of confidence. She felt she could tell this comfortable little matron anything. When she explained about her brothers, Mrs. Farrington would see precisely how it was.

"I am just returned from the school myself, practically this minute," Hilary said as she led Mrs. Farrington down the corridor. "So I'm afraid I cannot vouch for the state of the house. It is mainly a bachelor establishment, you know."

"My dear, I have sons," said Mrs. Farrington. "I know all about that, I assure you. They never entertain me in their town lodgings, and believe me, I am glad of it."

She chuckled. "Men, even the best of them, need ladies to civilize them."

Better and better. Hilary was almost delirious with glee. Almack's, such a far-off mirage at Miss Tollington's, now seemed to loom before her, solidly within her grasp.

But before she reached the double doors that led to the drawing room, Hodgins nipped around in front of her to bar her way, arms outstretched. His face was the picture of agonized entreaty.

"Believe me, miss, you do *not* want to go in there."

A feminine shriek of laughter punctuated this sentence. It came from inside the drawing room.

Oh.

Hilary's mind blanked. At the most inopportune moment, her happy aplomb deserted her completely.

She couldn't think. She knew what those shrieks meant, and she couldn't think. All she could bring to mind was that her brothers were hosting an orgy *inside* the drawing room and she had the one lady whose good opinion meant the world to her, standing here, with her, *outside* the drawing room and . . .

Where? Where could they go? A falling ceiling would be preferable to what she suspected awaited them in the room at whose pocket doors she stood.

Why, oh, why hadn't she listened to Hodgins?

Hilary had a sudden vision of Almack's, shimmering on the horizon, fading slowly into the night.

Pull yourself together, Hilary. You're made of sterner stuff than this.

Another shriek, followed by a chorus of giggles and dirty masculine laughter.

She jumped, darted a glance at Mrs. Farrington, whose blue eyes were wide with surprise, and hurried into speech. "Oh! I did not realize, my brothers must have taken over the drawing room to rehearse a—a play." She stammered over the ridiculous fable.

"I'm surprised you didn't mention it, Hodgins," she added.

The manservant coughed. "Sorry, miss. I tried."

The astonished Mrs. Farrington glanced curiously at the closed doors.

"Come, ma'am," said Hilary, desperate to escape. "We won't disturb them." She addressed the manservant. "We'll go to the south parlor instead, Hodgins."

She nodded at him that she understood, belatedly, the message he'd intended to convey. With a lugubrious sigh, Hodgins stomped off to order tea.

On an ingratiating, apologetic smile Hilary said, "So sorry, ma'am. Shall we?"

They turned to go.

The doors to the drawing room were flung wide.

"Ah," said a familiar, irritating voice. "There you are, Honey."

All the hairs stood up on the back of Hilary's neck.

Horror flooding her senses, she turned, to see that her imagination had not played her false. The drawing room resembled a bordello—or, at least, what she imagined a bordello must look like.

Half-naked women, mostly clothed men, empty wine bottles strewn about, articles of clothing festooned over the furniture . . .

And in the doorway that big, gorgeous ruffian of an earl, standing solid and tall as the trunk of a tree, with two females—*two!*—twining around him like vines.

He grinned down at her. "Care to join us?"

Hilary would never know if she could have saved that situation.

Perhaps Mrs. Farrington, that broad-minded mother of sons, might have comprehended that Hilary did not ordinarily live in this den of sin, that the most unfortunate combination of circumstances had conspired against her this afternoon.

Maybe, just maybe, a lady with that decided twinkle in her eye could have been brought to understand.

And if the Earl of Davenport had not been standing there, dripping in whores, grinning at her and calling her *Honey,* that is undoubtedly the outcome Hilary would have worked her utmost toward.

But.

The image of Almack's winked out, replaced by that grinning, disreputably handsome face.

Hilary gave a bloodcurdling cry of berserker-style rage and launched herself at the Earl of Davenport.

* * *

Even cold, wet, furious, and fighting like a wildcat, an armful of Honey beat two armfuls of blowsy bits of muslin any day.

"Excuse us." With an apologetic glance at the stunned faces of his cohorts, Davenport disentangled himself from the two girls, picked up the raging mass of mud and wet wool, and put both himself and her outside the drawing room.

As she rained blows on his back and shoulders, he turned and shut the drawing-room doors behind them.

"Now, now, Honey," he said soothingly. "What seems to be the problem? I'm sure we can sort this out."

"Sort this out?" She launched herself at him again.

Suddenly he noticed that tears streamed down her face. She was genuinely distressed.

That made him feel a twinge of . . . something.

But he did not want to search for the nearest exit as he usually did when a female had a fit of the vapors. He wanted to know what was wrong.

Surely her brothers' habits were known to her. He couldn't be brought to believe she'd never witnessed a scene like that one before.

Then he remembered. There'd been someone with her. Who was, now, conspicuous by her absence. "Where did your friend run off to?"

Honey stopped hitting him and whirled around to stare down the empty corridor.

Moments ticked by, with only her heavy, ragged pants breaking the silence.

Then she wailed, "Oh, dear Heaven, what have I done?"

She slumped against the wall, covering her face with her hands.

He gathered her into his arms. "There, there," he said, kissing the top of her head. "I'm sure we can—ooph!"

She'd punched him in the solar plexus.

"Was that necessary?" he wheezed.

"Keep your hands off me." She spoke viciously, through her teeth, and he caught a glimpse of her deVere ancestry.

She was a virago in tiny, fragile, fairy form.

Conscious of an absurd pleasure that he'd managed to

irritate her until the tears dried on her cheeks and those pretty eyes flashed with fire, he said, "What's wrong? Who was that female?"

"*That female* was the one chance I had to get to London. She called to satisfy herself that I was a genteel, virtuous young lady. And look what happened," she cried. "I was so close. So. Close." She pinched her forefinger and thumb together, held them up near her narrowed eyes. "*This* close, to achieving my heart's desire."

He blinked at her.

"Almack's!" she wailed. "I could have danced at Almack's. I could have found a decent, gentlemanly husband. And *you* ruined it."

He tilted his head. "Do you know what you need? A nice hot bath and a change of clothes. You're frozen."

"The only thing I need right now is to skin you alive!"

She raged on about what a cretin and a dastard he was, but that wasn't exactly news, so he didn't listen. He was too busy applying his mind to the problem of her heart's desire.

They both wanted the same thing: to go to London.

"I'll take you to Town," he said.

What could be better? He'd made up his mind to make a nuisance of himself around Wrotham Grange until the novelty of baiting Miss deVere palled. But truthfully, he wouldn't vouch for the bed linen in this establishment and the whores were a distraction he didn't need.

If he took Honey to London, he'd kill two birds with one stone.

She hadn't heard him. "I only hope I may not be ruined," she was saying miserably. "I should be obliged to marry you after all, and then I'd likely murder you before the wedding breakfast was over."

"Steady on," he protested. "I said I'd take you to London, not take you to wife."

She stared up at him, deflated. "I would rather drown myself than go anywhere with you."

"Bath," he said, taking her by the shoulders and turning her about. "Hot bath, dry clothes. Then we'll talk."

He propelled her down the corridor. She let him, suddenly listless, as if the catastrophes that had befallen her today had crushed her spirit.

He didn't like that, so he said hopefully, "Come to think of it, I'm cold and wet, too."

She didn't answer.

"We could save your servants the bother and pool our resources, so to speak—"

"I know what you are trying to do, but it won't work," she said dully. "I will have a bath. *Alone.* I will put on dry clothes. And when I come back downstairs, Lord Davenport, I expect you to be gone."

CHAPTER FOUR

The bath helped calm Hilary to the point where she ceased imagining various and original forms of torture for a certain peer of the realm.

There was no use casting all of the blame on him. She was responsible for her own fate. If only she'd listened to Hodgins. If only she hadn't flown into such a dreadfully unbecoming rage with Davenport.

Looking back, she wasn't sure why she'd done it. If it had been any other of her brothers' loutish friends standing there, inviting her to an orgy, she would have coldly requested him to leave and then ushered her guest to a different room.

She would not have flown at him and tried to scratch his eyes out.

Seeing Davenport with those women had set her alight. Why, ten minutes before he'd been kissing *her*.

She suspected such behavior was entirely typical for the Earl of Davenport. Thank goodness, once again, that she'd never married him as her mother had planned.

She slid down in the tub, tilting her head back to wash her hair, and grimaced at the new spiderweb of cracks in the ceiling. Dry rot, wet rot, death watch beetle, they had it all here. The place was falling down around their ears and her brothers did nothing to stop it.

She had to leave. She simply must get out of this shameful situation. She'd give anything for a London season, but until Miss Tollington had arranged an introduction to Mrs. Farrington, her prospects of making a London debut had been zero.

She'd made friends at the academy when she'd been a boarder there, but all of her friends were married now, comfortably settled in the country, and disinclined to participate in the fashionable whirl of the season.

Why hadn't she the sense to cultivate more useful friendships? She sighed. All of the more fashionable, aristocratic girls thought her a bore and a prude. Or else, they'd looked down their noses at her family.

She'd been content at the academy, but now that the promise of more had been dangled before her she couldn't simply let her dream go. She would have to find another way to get to London this season.

She'd been *so close* to leaving all this behind. To enjoying the myriad delights of a London season—dancing and balls and dinners, trips to the theater, the opera. To finding a quiet, kind, gentlemanly husband who would never embarrass her or make her lose her temper. A man with whom she could live a contented life and bear sweet, contented children . . .

"More hot water, miss." Trixie, the lone female servant in the house, lugged a bucket over to the tub and heaved.

A gush of steaming water poured down Hilary's back. "Ahh, thank you, Trix."

Warmth spread through her limbs. Her toes felt hot needles prick them to life.

She ducked her head under again.

"Has Lord Davenport left yet?" she asked the maid,

who was busy unpacking Hilary's meager wardrobe and putting it away.

"No, Miss Hilary. The master ordered a chamber to be made up for him."

Hilary ground her teeth. She ought to have expected that.

Again, she wondered what on earth had come over her to launch herself at a man she hardly knew. Well, if it killed her, she would be civil to him for the remainder of his stay.

She would consider it a test of her will and determination. If she could manage not to lose her temper with Lord Davenport, she could accomplish anything London society had to throw at her.

But no, she was not going to London, was she?

The mere notion of remaining one more night at the Grange depressed her, but the rest of her life? Anything would be better than living in a house that was falling down around her ears, where orgies took place in broad daylight.

Remaining under the Grange's leaky roof after the debacle that afternoon was likely to injure her reputation past redemption. If Mrs. Farrington spread word of the disgraceful scene she'd witnessed in the drawing room . . .

Hilary squeezed her eyes shut. She didn't want to think about it.

"Ever so handsome, he is," Trixie was saying as she laid out a clean gown and underthings. She'd been rattling on in her usual way while Hilary was lost in thought.

"Who?" she asked, knowing full well.

"Lord Davenport, of course." Trixie opened her eyes wide. "I wouldn't mind some o' that, I can tell you."

Hilary forbore to chastise the maid for her ribaldry. It was almost impossible to persuade any female servants to remain in this house, so one had to take what one could get. She suspected Trixie spread her favors equally between Hilary's brothers and any gentlemen who visited and took her fancy, but there was nothing Hilary could do about that, either.

Besides, Hilary found herself curious about precisely what "some o' that" might entail.

In an airy voice of studied unconcern, she said, "How can you tell? He is covered in bruises. Do you think him handsome?"

"Aye, as handsome as he can stare. But that arse, miss, begging your pardon. Seldom seen a finer pair o' buttocks on a gentleman." Trixie cupped her hands as if to squeeze the body parts in question. "What I wouldn't give for a feel o' them beauties."

The open look of relish on Trixie's pretty features caused Hilary to submerge herself again.

Gracious! She'd noticed almost everything else about Lord Davenport, but his buttocks had been covered by the tails of his evening coat.

Which made her wonder how Trixie knew what they looked like. . . .

No, she would *not* think about Lord Davenport and his spectacular hindquarters.

"I wish you would not talk in such a vulgar fashion," she said belatedly, and quite unreasonably, since she'd encouraged the maid to expand on the subject.

Living at the academy all her adult life with only brief sojourns home, Hilary was woefully ignorant of what went on between men and women.

She knew the sorts of advances she was *not* supposed to encourage. But she wasn't terribly certain of what it was she was guarding so vigilantly against.

Oh, she knew the theory and she'd caught glimpses of her brothers' raucous goings-on here and there. But theory and glimpses didn't begin to explain anything. And how would she know if she didn't find out from Trixie? Hilary could hardly ask her brothers, and Miss Tollington would have been no help, even if she had been inclined to discuss such matters.

Trixie seemed to enjoy the act of procreation; that much was clear.

Would Hilary enjoy it? Would she long to squeeze her quiet, gentle husband's buttocks? It seemed unlikely, but one never knew. The particulars of the marriage bed were a mystery she suspected she wouldn't solve until the moment was upon her, so to speak.

Her experience of men thus far ought to have put her off the male of the species for life. And yet there was something compelling about the idea of having one of them for her very own. Surely there were nice gentlemen in the world. Men of taste and refinement and morals.

All of her dreams flooded her senses, luring her to follow them, no matter what the cost. How paltry of her to be so cast down at this one small setback. Mrs. Farrington might have seen the worst of her, but here was Davenport offering to take her to London.

He was neither so irresistible nor so persistent that she couldn't hold him off for the duration of a day. They would not even be obliged to stay overnight somewhere if they left at dawn. They could take the old coach. Her brothers wouldn't have any need of it.

That way, no one would see her traveling in Davenport's company. And if it would be scandalous to go on her own with Davenport in a closed carriage, she could take Trixie with her, couldn't she?

She sat up so quickly, water slopped over the sides of the tub. "Help me, Trix. I need to get dressed."

* * *

"I mean to say, dear fellow, it isn't done," said Davenport confidentially to Tom deVere. "Even *I* know that. Must cherish one's womenfolk, you know."

He'd cleaned himself up as best he could with the assistance of a pert little maid named Trixie and returned to the scene of debauchery that had so shocked Honey and her companion.

Davenport regretted the devilish impulse that had made him confront Honey with the whores at his side. This was what got him into trouble more often than not—devilish impulse. She was a gently bred lady, despite her tendency to hit people.

He was now endeavoring to explain that fact to her brothers.

"If m'sister don't like it, she can go back to that school she came from," slurred Tom, giving his companion's fleshy breast a hearty squeeze.

She shrieked, whether with pain or laughter Davenport couldn't quite tell.

"She can't go back; she's been 'smissed," said Benedict, the younger of the two. "We're stuck with her. But we won't be changing our ways for any naggy dab of a female. She'll mind us or she can hire herself out as a guv'ness for all I care."

"She is a lady," said Davenport. "She is your sister. She deserves respect and consideration."

"She's a prune-faced little bitch," said Benedict.

That did it. Despite Benedict's bulk, he came easily out of his chair when Davenport bunched his fist in the fellow's grubby shirt and hauled him up.

Nose to nose, Davenport spoke clearly. "Pay the girls off. Get rid of them. Now."

"Who's going to make me? You?" Benedict wheezed a laugh. The strength of his wine-soaked breath could have knocked a man down.

Davenport answered that question with his fist. He smashed it into Benedict's face and watched him sprawl back against the armchair with blood streaming from his nose. Then he turned to shoot a glaring challenge at Tom.

Tom swung the tart off his lap and bore in. Davenport sidestepped, turned, and booted Tom's backside, sending him sprawling.

He looked at the women. "You've been paid?"

Wide-eyed, they nodded.

"Then you can go," he said, and turned to face both brothers.

That there were two of them evened the odds a little. He could easily dispatch one drunken bully, but two made the challenge more interesting.

Davenport's body screamed in pain when a ham fist collided with the region of his kidney, but he didn't suffer too many blows before he'd knocked both men down.

This time, they stayed down.

He was considering what to do with them when Honey burst in.

"What on earth is going on here?" she demanded, looking wildly from her brothers to Davenport. "What did you do to them?"

He inspected his knuckles. "Oh, just a friendly bout. Must keep my hand in, you know."

"You floored both of them?" she squeaked, betraying a most unladylike knowledge of boxing cant. She ran to bend over Tom, patting his stubbled cheeks.

Her hair was still wet from her bath—and hadn't he enjoyed a few fantasies about that activity? The golden tresses were darkened with damp, tied back in a thick braid. Unfortunate, that. He wanted to unbind it, run his hands through it, cloud it around that piquant little face.

She was calling her brothers' names, to no avail. The

combination of liquor and a Westruther right had done for them.

"Throw a bucket of water over them," recommended Davenport. "That'll wake them up. Though I daresay they wouldn't thank you for it."

She straightened, surveying him coldly. "You cause trouble wherever you go. I asked you to leave before. Why are you still here?"

"I thought you might need me," he explained.

She gave an incredulous laugh. "The last thing I need is for you to brawl with my brothers."

"That was not planned," he admitted.

"Then why did it happen?"

"I told the lovely impures to leave. Your brothers took exception." He thought it best not to mention the insult to Honey. No good could come of that.

She sighed and shook her head. "There'll be more where they came from. And now that you've goaded my brothers, they'll behave even worse tomorrow."

She was probably right about that, but he didn't regret punching Tom and Benedict deVere. The two of them needed a lesson.

"Honey," he declared, "you cannot stay here."

She stared up at him. "No," she said. "That is just what I was thinking myself."

Again, she surprised him. A speculative expression gathered in those lovely eyes of hers. "You offered to take me to London."

Was it going to be this easy? He suppressed a wolfish grin. "Of course. It's the least I can do."

"Yes," she said crisply. "It is."

"Well, that settles it. We'll be off, shall we? I daresay there's a carriage in your stables we can borrow."

"We cannot go now," she said, glancing at the clock.

"If we leave at first light, we can reach London before evening. That way, we shall not be obliged to put up at an inn overnight, which would be most improper."

Not so much of a greenhorn as he'd like. Well, it wasn't as if he'd never managed to be amorous in a carriage before. "All right. But you'll have to protect me from your brothers until morning."

Honey eyed them with a raised eyebrow. "I should have said you were capable of taking care of yourself." She squared her shoulders. "There are conditions."

"But of course." He tilted his head, trying to appear interested.

"First, you must stop calling me Honey."

"I'll try. But the thing is, you see, that it keeps popping out of my mouth. Look at you. You're all gold and cream, and that color of your eyes . . . I've never seen that color before. You make me think of honey. And then before I know it, out it pops again."

She made a frustrated kitten sound, a cross between a "harrumph," a choke, and a spurt of unwilling laughter.

He smiled at her.

She scowled back. "I am Miss deVere to you. I will not entertain any other appellation. Next. You will not brawl while in my company. I do not wish to draw attention to our journey. We must try to remain inconspicuous."

Honey eyed him doubtfully. "Do you think you can manage that?"

He bowed. "I'll do my poor best."

She pointed a finger at him. "Do you promise you will not punch anyone?"

Briefly he thought of his shadow. But if the man hadn't harmed him in the past few months, he wasn't likely to do so now.

He held up one of the weapons in question in a gesture of taking an oath. "I promise."

She nodded. "Third, and most importantly, is our destination. I have been thinking, and it seems to me that you and I have a mutual connection."

Manfully he denied himself the opportunity to turn that statement into sly innuendo. "Indeed?"

"Yes, your cousin Lady Rosamund Westruther married my cousin Griffin deVere, Lord Tregarth. I have never met Lord Tregarth, but you could introduce us."

His own plan had been vague about their destination. He'd just wanted to get her away from this place and keep her with him for as long as possible.

Rosamund . . . Yes, by Jove. It might very well be the answer.

"That is a very good plan," he said. "Exactly what I was thinking myself."

"Lady Tregarth might put me in the way of a family to whom I can be of service," said Honey with a brave squaring of her shoulders. "I daresay with the season coming up, many young ladies require a final polish to set them on the right path."

A governess? What a terrible waste that would be. But he didn't argue. He simply nodded.

"Excellent." He rubbed his hands together. "Any other conditions? If there are, I shall be obliged to write them down. Can't keep more than a couple of things in my head at once, you know."

She took a step toward him. "Yes, there is another condition. You must not kiss me again, or try any . . . funny business."

"Funny business. Hmm." He contemplated her for a moment. "No, I'm afraid I can't promise that."

Her eyes snapped wide. "What?" The word came out as a squawk of outrage.

He spread his hands in a helpless gesture. "When I give my word, I don't break it. And I fear that you, my dear Honey, are too much temptation for a man like me to resist."

She tried to appear outraged and haughty but only managed to look sweetly discombobulated. "But—but—" she sputtered. "You would force yourself on me, even though I have asked you not to?"

"Ah, come now," he said easily. "Who said anything about force?"

* * *

The man was a devil in rake's clothing. Now he'd put her in an intolerable position. If she went with him, it would be tantamount to *asking* for his improper advances.

She couldn't afford to refuse him and he knew it. The dastard.

London.

Even if she could not take part in the season or obtain those coveted Almack's vouchers, being in London might be enough. Perhaps her cousin Griffin might take pity on her and intercede with her guardian on her behalf.

Oliver, Lord deVere, had routinely ignored her pleas for an advance on her inheritance to fund her come-out. Her persistence had finally been rewarded by a threat to marry her off to a toothless octogenarian marquis, so she'd given up.

But Lord deVere would have to listen to Griffin, wouldn't he?

The price was to suffer the rakish advances of Lord Davenport for the space of a day.

"I have hat pins," she warned him. "And I'm not afraid to use them."

He winced. "There will be no need for hat pins, Honey, I assure you."

"Miss deVere to you."

"When we are in public," he agreed, "I shall call you Miss deVere."

She supposed she had to be satisfied with that.

He pursed his lips. "What shall we do about your brothers?"

Her resolve hardened. "We won't tell them. They'll still be sleeping off their excesses when we slip away tomorrow morning. We'll send the carriage back with a message that I'm staying with Lady Tregarth."

"So that's settled then," he said, matching her decisive tone.

His face was grave, but a wicked twinkle lurked in those dark eyes as he came toward her. "Shall we shake hands on the bargain?"

Feeling absurdly daring, she stuck out her hand. He took it in his, and time shuddered to a halt.

So much heat in his palm, so much strength in the clasp of his fingers. His hand was so large that it all but swallowed hers. The effect was electrifying; she felt it all the way down her spine.

She started, pulled away.

"I—I'd better see to dinner." Her tone was all fluttery and breathless. *Ugh.* She could have kicked herself for sounding like such a dunce.

He gave her a smile so full of amused understanding that she regretted her former vow to remain civil to him.

With a scowl, she hurried away to the kitchens.

CHAPTER FIVE

B y virtue of judicious dousing with cold water, Davenport sobered up the brothers deVere enough to sit down to dine with their sister and guest.

Honey had been astonished at Tom and Benedict's easy acceptance of Davenport after he'd trounced them. For his part, Davenport soon saw that her brothers weren't quite as bad as their earlier behavior might have suggested. Once they were a few degrees more sober, they admitted the impropriety of their behavior.

It was clear, however, that they did not intend to change their ways for their sister and would find any means they could to be rid of her.

That finally decided Davenport, had he needed persuasion in the matter, to abide by Honey's wishes and keep their departure on the morrow secret.

By the time Honey had retired to bed, the deVere brothers were well on their way to oblivion once more. They wouldn't wake before noon, he'd wager. By then, he and Honey would be long gone.

The surly manservant had shown Davenport to his room with bad grace, informing him that if he wanted something in the night not to bother calling, for there was no one but the mistress to hear him in this wing. With a belligerent stare at the broken bellpull as if daring it to resurrect itself, Hodgins stomped out, slamming the door behind him.

Davenport looked around. If the bedchamber they'd chosen for him was the best they had, he shuddered to think of the state the rest of the house must be in.

Plaster had cracked and fallen away in some places; curtains and hangings that once might have been green were moth-eaten and faded to the color of sludge. Dust lay thick on every surface, gathering in the grooves of the intricate, heavy carving on the bedposts. The canopy above his head bore so many holes it resembled a cobweb.

He lay on the most uncomfortable mattress he'd ever had the displeasure to encounter—and that was saying something for a man who'd been dumped in a barn the night before.

It didn't help that he couldn't stop thinking about Honey and the one promise he'd refused to make. He didn't believe in cloaking his wicked intentions in virtue. She had to know he'd do everything he could to seduce her on the way to Town.

She'd informed him loftily that her maid would travel with her, for propriety's sake. If the maid in question was the redoubtable Trixie, he foresaw few problems there.

His body pulsed in anticipation. Honey, with her top-lofty manner and her tightly wound virtue. She was a challenge, and the uncertainty of success merely added spice to the chase.

Fantasies of a rocking carriage and a pliant Honey danced through his head.

He smiled into the darkness. Who needed sleep?

There was a loud, splitting crack.

Then the world fell in on top of him.

* * *

Hilary couldn't sleep. She'd tried warm milk, counting sheep, reciting the litany of social rules she'd instructed her students to repeat by rote.

Drat the man! Nothing worked when she could see his smiling face, those sensual lips telling her he would most definitely *not* promise to keep his hands off her person on the way to London.

She recalled, all too vividly, the feel of those lips on hers, the warmth and hardness of him as his arm encircled her frozen body on that horse.

What would it have been like to be married to such a man?

Hilary shuddered to think of it. She'd wager he was a constant subject of gossip among the ton. With that cheerfully roving eye, he'd cut a swath through the ladies of London, whether he was a married man or no.

She didn't regret that their betrothal had come to nothing. Indeed, the whole notion seemed to have been a figment of her mother's imagination. That could well be the case. Marigold deVere had always harbored illusions of grandeur.

Ethereally pretty but dowerless, Hilary's mother had come from a minor branch of an aristocratic family. Her notions had never fallen into step with those of her brutish husband, however, and her spirits had slowly declined until there was nothing left.

Marigold had given up, but her daughter wouldn't. She would find a way to attain her dream if she had to brave all of Davenport's attempts to ravish her.

Ravish. The word held an illicit thrill, particularly in the context of Lord Davenport.

She did not want to think about that.

The threatened storm had not eventuated, leaving the air oddly sultry. Or perhaps it was the fire she'd ordered, so she could dry her hair at its heat before she went to bed.

She threw off the covers, tossed and turned a bit, pounded her pillow with the flat of her hand.

Double drat the man!

His face kept swimming up in her mind's eye. That smiling, disreputably bruised, extraordinarily compelling face. And she'd still not caught a glimpse of his remarkable buttocks. . . .

A sound like the rumble of thunder made her start awake from her drowse. Disoriented, she glanced toward the window. A masculine shout made her realize that the thunder had come from inside the house.

"Oh, no!"

She leaped out of bed and flew into the corridor. The commotion had come from the guest bedchamber.

She hurried toward it and wrenched open the door.

There, stark naked with his back to her, in the midst of a pile of ceiling plaster and debris, stood Lord Davenport.

Hilary's jaw dropped.

He was covered from head to toe in grayish-white plaster dust. He looked like a statue of a Greek god as he surveyed the wreckage, one hip negligently cocked. A David, a colossus still standing proud and tall through the sacking of Rome, with wide, muscled shoulders, a slim, tapered waist, and firm, taut buttocks.

Buttocks.

Hilary swallowed hard. Now she understood.

Her mind filled with understanding, in fact. She couldn't seem to move or speak for understanding. Her thought processes ground to a complete halt.

He turned and saw her. "Oh, hello there."

Her eyes popped. She opened her mouth. Closed it. David was *nothing* like it.

Gracious, but she'd never dreamed . . .

How on earth did he manage to walk around all day with *that* dangling between his legs? Flushing, she tore her gaze from his groin, only to fix on that imposing chest.

As easy in his nudity as he was in his clothes, Davenport gestured at the carnage behind him. "As you can see, there's been a slight accident."

From somewhere, she dredged up the ability to speak. "Put . . . some . . . clothes . . . on!"

He glanced about him, as if the notion had only just occurred. "Afraid I can't. Your maid took my things away to see if she could get the mud out."

Sheets. She thought of sheets, but the bedclothes were buried under the rubble.

"Ah." He turned and reached up to yank down the bed curtain from a post that leaned drunkenly toward the bed.

The ripple of musculature in his back and buttocks as he fully extended his arm to pull down the threadbare damask made Hilary feel a little faint.

He took his time about arranging the curtain around his waist and securing it.

Dark eyes glinted at her through the mask of plaster dust as he put up his hand to brush some flakes of ceiling from his hair. He ought to appear ridiculous, she thought.

He was, in a word, magnificent.

Oh, dear.

Far too late, she averted her gaze. "You are not hurt?" she inquired, staring at the bedpost.

"No, I was lucky. I hadn't managed to fall asleep yet, so I leaped from the bed in time."

There was a taut silence while she wondered if the cause for his insomnia might mirror hers.

"You cannot stay here," she declared. Talk about the obvious!

"No, I suspect you're right about that."

She tried to think of where else to put him. She'd have

to make up another bed. And somehow draw a bath for him so he could wash all that plaster dust off.

"I apologize," she said, though the words scraped in her throat. "It must have been a shock."

"I'm still trembling," he said. He held out his arms. "Hold me?"

That did not deserve a response. "I'll order a bath, and while you're . . ." She gestured with a flap of her hand, trying not to imagine that body of his, wet and naked in the tub. . . .

She cleared her throat. "While you do that, I'll see to another bedchamber for you."

She didn't wait for his answer or look at him in the eye again. She hurried away, fighting the firework thrills of awareness his teasing request had set off inside her.

An agony of confusion dogged her as she went to fetch Trixie. Traversing corridors, climbing stairs, she scolded herself for her prurience. How much she'd wanted to stay right where she was and simply gawk at him. What a wicked temptation it had been to obey him when he'd asked her to hold him, plaster dust and all.

Ridiculous man. And she was worse, allowing herself to be caught up in his nonsense.

Even more mortifying than his nakedness was the reason behind it. Shame washed through her. What must he think of a family who let their house fall down around their ears? Her brothers refused to spend money on repairs to the old redbrick building, lavishing their income on their stables instead. Their living quarters shrank with every passing year as more rooms were shut up, abandoned to rot and decay.

Despite the need to distance herself from Lord Davenport, the desperation to get away from the Grange was greater.

Hilary lifted her chin. She could handle Lord Davenport. Once he had his clothes on again.

She scratched on the door of her maid's attic room. She must treat Lord Davenport as a trial and a test of her good sense and self-restraint. If she could come through a journey to London with the greatest scoundrel in the country without allowing him the liberties he so clearly craved, it would be a triumph of virtue over sin.

But the clear memory emblazoned on her brain of him standing amongst the rubble in all his naked glory made her doubly thankful that Trixie was going with them.

As if in answer, the maid's tremendous snore greeted Hilary as she opened the door.

She smiled wryly at the notion of Trixie lending her either propriety or moral support. Ah, well, she was better than nothing, Hilary supposed.

* * *

Davenport was vaguely embarrassed at all the fuss. But he was covered with plaster and he couldn't see himself retiring to bed again in this state.

He said, "Please, do not trouble yourself further, Miss deVere. You ought to be in bed."

She dismissed his objections. Clearly, she was humiliated by what had happened and determined to set all to rights.

So he let Honey and the saucy little maid bustle about. They roused one of the stable hands to boil water and carry it up.

All the while, Davenport tried to catch Honey's eye, to draw her aside, but she was having none of it.

He even flexed his muscles a few times in an experimental manner, just to see if she was covertly watching him, but she had firmly averted her gaze. She didn't speak to him the rest of the night.

The bath seemed to take an inordinate amount of time to fill, with the sullen stable hand rubbing his eyes and slinking backward and forward with bucket after bucket of steaming water. They'd brought him to another bedchamber, this one more decrepit than the last.

Honey made up the bed with her own fair hands, shooing away his attempts to help.

He watched her, all wifely efficiency, and thought of the excellent meal she had conjured from nothing that evening. She would make some fellow a good helpmeet.

That led him to wonder what she looked like naked, a place all stray thoughts seemed to lead him at the moment, much as all roads led to Rome.

Sooner or later, he was going to find out. Sooner, rather than later, if he had his way.

Whether it was a scientific theorem or seducing a woman, when Davenport found a matter worthy of his attention and effort, he did not give up until he'd achieved his aim.

Honey thought the trip to London would be the end of their acquaintance. He knew it was only the beginning.

When all was ready, he took her aside and said in a low voice, "You go to a lot of trouble on my behalf. Thank you."

"It is no trouble," she said, addressing his left ear. "I must apolog—"

"Never mind that." His mouth kicked up at the corner. "I'd have ten ceilings fall on my head for the privilege of seeing you in that night rail."

Despite her icy demeanor, a delicious blush stole into her cheeks. She crossed her arms in front of her pretty bosom.

That was better. He'd prefer a blush of sexually aware embarrassment to one of painful mortification. She was a proud little thing. It was no easy matter for her to suffer the indignities her brothers inflicted on her.

One more reason to take her away from all of this.

"You'll adore Rosamund, you know," he said. "Everyone does."

She bit her lip, and he endured a kind of sweet pain that he could not, at this moment, do anything about the way she mangled that poor feature when she was anxious.

"I hope she likes me," she said in a quiet voice.

"Of course she will," Davenport responded. "Now, much as I should wish to keep you here, that would be selfish. You must go to bed, my dear. We have a tiring journey ahead of us."

He couldn't stop himself. He chose a moment when the servants had temporarily left the room, grasped her by the shoulders, and swiftly, softly kissed her forehead.

He heard her gasp, felt her stiffen. He drew back and gazed down at her.

For an instant, her eyes remained closed. Then they fluttered open, gleaming pools of brandy lit by candle flame. Confusion warred with a smoky sensuality that sent hot blood rushing about in his body.

She came to herself and darted a quick look around.

"I wish you would not touch me," she said, though her tone lacked all conviction.

"I can't help it," he said. "You have this dreadful effect on me. My brain closes down completely."

"If I didn't think I must be one of legions who have that effect on you, I might be flattered."

He didn't think it wise to explain to her just how different she was from those legions. He gave a helpless shrug.

Her gaze fixed on his chest with the movement and he

laughed in silent enjoyment. She was endlessly entertaining. His delighted anticipation of their journey to London increased with every moment.

"Ought you not be going now?" he suggested. The final bucket of water had been disgorged into his bath. "Or would you like to stay and scrub my back?"

A series of expressions flitted across her face, all of them conflicting.

"Good night, my lord."

The words were pronounced in her most withering tone.

By contrast, he remained quite alarmingly *un*withered long after she left. So unwithered, in fact, that he declined assistance from either servant with his bath. He'd be obliged to scrub his own back, for his genitals did not seem to be taking Honey's no for an answer.

The silhouette of her lovely, lithe little body beneath that worn night rail had him worked up into a fine state.

When the servants departed, he dropped his makeshift covering. Sinking into the steaming water, he began to scrub vigorously at his chest.

Before he'd finished removing the plaster dust from his torso, the redoubtable Trixie popped her head around the door again. "Beg pardon, my lord, but I was wondering if you be needful of anything else." She said it with a wink that left him in no doubt of her meaning.

His parts had withered quite nicely until her avid stare stirred them up again.

Davenport dropped a washcloth on top of his privates and sat up.

"Actually, Trixie my girl, there *is* something you can do for me."

He smiled his most charming smile.

* * *

This was not a household in which servants were up before dawn, lighting fires, drawing curtains, dusting, and making ready for the day. Hilary was reasonably certain she and Davenport had another hour or so, at least, to be gone.

She dressed and ordered Trixie to pack her meager belongings, then lay and light the kitchen fire.

While Trixie tended to the kitchen hearth, Hilary raided the larder and packed a hamper for the journey, then hurried down to the stables. There she found Billy the stable hand already putting the horses to the ancient traveling coach.

"Do you think it will run?" she said, eyeing the vehicle dubiously.

"Should do, miss." The boy showed not the slightest curiosity about where his mistress might be going at this hour and why she'd need to resurrect this ancient coach to do it.

She supposed she'd have to take his word for it. Really, there was no other alternative. Hiring a chaise in the village would cause gossip, and neither she nor Davenport had the funds to do it, in any event. If she could just get to London without anyone seeing her in Davenport's company, she'd be safe.

Thus, the hamper. They must change horses, of course, and have this pair sent back to the Grange. But she need not alight from the carriage for that. She'd chosen a hat with a veil, and since she was not at all known on the road to London, she was reasonably certain of passing unnoticed. If only Lord Davenport kept to his promise not to punch anyone on the way.

She hurried back to the house, to find that her escort still had not risen. The fire burned brightly in the kitchen hearth, but Trixie hadn't reappeared. Perhaps she was seeing to her own packing.

Impatience gnawed at Hilary. She glanced at the clock.

If his lordship didn't make haste, her plans to get to London within daylight hours might be ruined.

Unable to stand the delay, she raced upstairs to his bedchamber and scratched on the door.

No answer.

Unwilling to knock more loudly in case someone might hear, she turned the knob and slipped into the room.

He slept.

Thankfully, the big body that had kept her awake far into the wee hours was covered this time by sheet and coverlet. Only one arm, strong and muscular, was flung carelessly free.

He looked . . . sensual in repose. Abandoned, as if he'd thrown himself into the arms of sleep.

She supposed he'd had a rough time of it over the past twenty-four hours. A kind woman would let him slumber on.

But Hilary was not kind. She was desperate.

"My lord," she said. "Lord Davenport. Wake up."

He did not stir.

She took one step toward the bed.

"*Please* wake up." She said it as loudly as she dared but got no response.

He was dead to the world.

Hilary ventured as far as the bedside. His hair was still damp from his bath. She noticed he had not managed to remove quite all of the bits of plaster from the dark tangle. Her fingers itched to do it for him, but she forced herself to hold back.

As if he were made of hot coals, she poked him, a quick jab to the shoulder with her index finger. His skin was smooth; the muscle beneath it, hard.

Still no response.

She glanced toward the tub by the fireplace and saw that the water in his bath was a cloudy gray. He ought to have had a change of water, but the lateness of the hour had made that impossible. Considerate of him to dismiss the servants as soon as the bath was drawn.

Her eye alighted on a ewer on the washstand. Upon peering inside, she saw that it contained clean water. A fresh towel hung over the washstand rail, ready for use. At least he could finish his ablutions before they set out.

She slid a quick glance at him in the looking glass.

And caught him watching her.

The gleam of dark irises was so quick, she might have missed it if her attention had not been so narrowly focused on him.

The blackguard had been feigning sleep.

"Lord Davenport," she said imperiously. "You must get up. We must be away."

Her only answer was a soft sigh. He rolled over, muttering something as if in the midst of slumber. The covers twisted, slipping down to reveal the solid, beautifully drawn line of his back, a hint of the crevice at the top of his backside. A strategic maneuver, she thought.

He rolled again, onto his back, the covers winding low around his hips.

Lord, but the man was a peacock!

Ire rose, crowding her chest. This was all a game to him, wasn't it?

Well, it wasn't to her.

With a grim set to her mouth, she picked up the ewer and marched over to the bed.

Without hesitation or mercy, she upended the ewer over his head.

Icy water gushed forth, splashing, soaking the pillow, all but drowning him.

He made a sound that was half gasp, half roar, and bolted upright, the covers pooling around his waist.

"You baggage!" he sputtered.

"You were awake the whole time." She slammed the ewer down on the bedside table. "You were watching me."

"If I'd thought you'd bloody well—," he began, wiping water from his eyes. Suddenly he broke off as if struck by the absurd picture he must present. He began to laugh.

"Keep your voice down," she hissed.

She saw too late, moved too slowly. One arm snaked out to catch her around the waist. He pulled her down with him on the bed, making her wet, too.

The next thing she knew, he'd flipped her to her back and was looming over her, the water from his sodden hair dripping in her face.

He brought up one hand to shove the wet tangle out of his face. The laughter died out of those dark eyes and the intent look that had so undone her on the road outside replaced it.

With his thumb, gently, he wiped a droplet of water that had settled, cool, against her lips.

Her breath caught. Her brain seized.

He lowered his mouth to kiss her.

"Stop!" She bucked and pushed at him, but it was like trying to move a solid wall.

He halted the downward swoop, his lips hovering a mere breath away from hers. But he didn't move away.

Frantic, Hilary wriggled, trying to get out from beneath his big, beautiful body, desperately casting about for a reason to deny herself what she most longed for at this particular moment.

Almack's . . .

Almack's and all it stood for—respectability, opportunity—rose up to give her strength.

"Get off me," she panted. "You oaf, get off!"

For a telling moment, he hesitated, dark eyes searching hers, as if to divine her true desire. She glared stonily up at him. He sighed and rolled away.

Hilary sprang up. "I told you I'll have none of your boorish advances, my lord."

"Sorry," he said, not looking at all apologetic. "My memory does not function well at this hour. I forgot."

She curled her lip. "I suppose the response is automatic. You would have done the same to any woman who happened to be here, I daresay."

"Any *pretty* woman who happened to be here," he corrected. "Well, why wouldn't I? Pretty women are invariably in one's bedchamber at this hour for precisely that reason."

The notion of all the other pretty women—other pretty, accommodating women—he'd enjoyed in such a manner made her unaccountably furious.

Frostily, she said, "Perhaps I didn't make myself clear yesterday."

He looked up at her, not a bit repentant. "My dear Honey, if you enter a man's bedchamber for any reason other than that his ceiling has just fallen in, you must be prepared for the consequences."

That arrested her righteous anger. "Ordinarily I would never do so," she said, on the defensive. "But we need to leave, and we need to keep it a secret, and I couldn't find Trixie to wake you."

"I told you what I am," he said, ignoring her justifications. "I told you I will do my level best to seduce you. In the face of those warnings, your presence in my bedchamber is clear provocation. Don't come near me if you don't want me to put my hands on you."

Davenport sounded distinctly irritated now. He rearranged the bedclothes across his lap. Which of course drew her attention to that very area.

"Ah," she said, nodding wisely. "I see that you are like most men, grumpy as a bear with a sore head in the morning."

His jaw turned to granite. "My dear Miss deVere, I have an erection between my legs the approximate size and hardness of a flagpole. If you don't want me to use it on you, go away."

For a moment, Hilary actually thought it was possible that her head might explode. She choked, gasped, turned, and scampered for the door.

CHAPTER SIX

A flagpole?

A giggle rose up in Hilary's throat as she put the finishing touches to breakfast. She rather wished she had someone with whom she could share that tidbit.

Trixie would split her sides over it. . . . Hilary frowned. Where *was* Trixie? She should be down here by now.

Davenport sauntered in, seemingly recovered from his bad temper. "Ah," he said, sniffing the air appreciatively. "An Englishman's breakfast. Food of the gods."

He strolled over to where she scrambled eggs in a skillet and stood behind her, peering over her shoulder. "You really can cook."

He sounded surprised. Of course, most ladies of her station did not know how to boil an egg.

He did not touch her, but he stood close enough that she felt him, all the same. She was hot from the blaze of the kitchen fire, but her body temperature rose again now, several degrees. She even felt a little light-headed.

"I—y-yes," she stammered. "I learned from the cook at Miss Tollington's."

He reached over to nick a piece of bacon and pop it in his mouth, brushing her arm as he did so.

Hilary swallowed hard. It was all quite deliberate; she was sure of that.

She kept thinking of flagpoles. Tall ones, straight and hard.

No.

"Take care; this is hot," she warned. Hilary turned with the sizzling skillet in her hands, so he was obliged to make room or be scalded.

She maneuvered past Davenport to slide the bacon onto their plates. Ordinarily, she would not have troubled to make such a breakfast for herself, but she wanted to fill her companion's stomach so they wouldn't have to stop too often for sustenance on the way to London.

They sat down to bacon, toast, and scrambled eggs. "Not your usual fare, I don't doubt," she said. "But I gave you a large serving."

"Delicious," he asserted. "Best breakfast I've ever tasted."

She doubted that, but he ate every morsel and accepted a second helping.

Hilary felt absurdly pleased. It was only bacon and eggs, of course, but she enjoyed cooking and feeding people. Something most true ladies never turned their hands to, of course. Well, she wouldn't have, either, but her brothers could never keep a decent cook for long. The choice had been to live on bread and cheese or learn to cook herself.

Davenport was a sensual creature, she thought now, watching him savor the simple meal. The easy domesticity of this scene suddenly struck her as amusing. She and the scandalous Earl of Davenport, sitting down to breakfast at a kitchen table.

Passing the last twenty-four hours under review, she marveled at what a transformation her life had undergone. All because of this man.

"What were you doing yesterday, riding about the countryside in your evening clothes?" she asked. A question that had occurred to her many times, only to be supplanted by shock at his next outrageous exploit.

He grimaced. "My cousins, bless them, thought I could benefit from some country air. They drugged me, bound me, and threw me in a farmer's cart, then drove me out here and dumped me in a barn."

She gasped. "But that's terrible. These cousins of yours sound like brutes."

"Oh, no," he said cheerfully. "I daresay I deserved it."

"Was that how you got those bruises?" Even now, the contusions had not faded but turned mottled purple and yellow. The lurid markings on his face ought to lessen his appeal.

They didn't.

"Yes, I gave quite a good account of myself, as I recall, but there were two of them." He shrugged. "I think they would have taken me as far as my estate near Peterborough, but I gave them too much trouble. Hence the barn."

She regarded him doubtfully. "You seem to bear them no grudge."

"I don't." He cut into the bacon. "If they hadn't brought me to the middle of nowhere I wouldn't have met you, Honey."

A melting feeling in her insides threatened to overpower her good sense. Yet she couldn't help but reflect that if his cousins had not served him such a turn, she might be on her way to a London season with Mrs. Farrington at this moment.

Well, perhaps not. Her brothers' escapade would have been difficult to explain away. Still, without Davenport, she'd not have made that outrageous display of fury that was utterly foreign to her nature. Looking back, she couldn't believe she'd behaved in such a disgraceful manner. He had the most maddening effect on her. She'd never met anyone quite like the Earl of Davenport.

She braced her shoulders as she cleared the plates. No use crying over spilled milk, was there? She'd simply have to make the best of the situation. At least, she would get away from the Grange.

"What is Lady Tregarth like?" she asked him.

"Rosamund? Oh, she's the beauty of the family," he said.

"How does she go on with her husband?" she asked. "I saw him once, years ago, and he terrified me."

"Wraps him 'round her little finger," said Davenport with a laugh. "But you'll see for yourself."

He drained his tankard of ale, then said, "Thank you. That was excellent. I don't know when I've enjoyed a meal more."

"You're welcome." She glanced at the clock. "We should make haste. Hodgins will be up soon."

She frowned. "Where is that Trixie?"

He rose from the table, took his tankard over to the bench where she'd stacked the plates, and set it down. "I haven't seen her."

He put a hand up to feel his jaw as he accompanied her out of the kitchen. "Come to think of it, she promised me hot water and a shaving kit this morning, but it didn't materialize. Perhaps she slept in."

"No, she was up betimes this morning." Raising the skirts of her plain cambric gown, Hilary mounted the narrow staircase to the upper floor.

After much searching, they went up to the attics to see if Trixie was in her room. A faint cry reached them as they came to the final set of stairs.

"Trixie!" Hilary rushed to the landing, where the maid sat all of a heap, whimpering with pain. "What happened? Did you fall down the stairs?"

"My ankle!" wailed Trixie, sticking out her left foot for Hilary's inspection. "Ooh, but it hurts so much, miss. I was just getting me bags and I tumbled arse over—"

"Yes, I see that," interrupted Hilary hastily. She took Trixie's leg in her hands. "Let me look."

"Ow! Ooh, it hurts," sobbed Trixie, snatching the affected limb away from her hold. "Don't touch it. I can't bear you to touch it, miss."

"I have plenty of experience with my brothers injuring themselves," she assured the maid. "I'll be able to tell if it's broken or not."

"Perhaps I might be of assistance here," said Davenport from behind her. The suave note in his voice made Hilary frown, but Trixie's face lit up like a candle.

"Oh, my lord," she breathed, pain apparently forgotten for the moment.

Hilary suspected Davenport merely wanted to get his hands on a pretty ankle, but he made no move to crouch down to examine Trixie's injury.

"Try to move your foot from side to side," he instructed the maid. "Like this."

He demonstrated with his own foot.

Cautiously, but with determination, Trixie did as he said. She winced. "It hurts, but I can move it."

"Right," said Davenport. "Try this." He pointed his toe, then flexed his heel.

Trixie did the same, with a wince and a sharp cry of pain.

"It's not broken, I don't think," Davenport said. "Perhaps a bad sprain. Do you think you could walk with my support?"

The maid's face lifted to his like a flower lifted to the sun. "I—I'll try," she said bravely.

With his assistance, she hobbled a couple of steps on the landing, but the stairs proved too much for her. He swept her into his arms and carried her to her room, then laid her gently on her narrow cot.

In a low voice, Davenport said to Hilary, "It would be cruel to make her travel with us."

"Oh, do you think so?" said Hilary anxiously.

"Do not be concerned for me, miss," said Trixie, blinking back tears. "You must go to London without me."

Guilt sliced through Hilary. "But I cannot leave you here with only Hodgins to care for you. You could die of starvation up here and no one would notice."

"He'd notice fast enough if I weren't at my duties, miss," said Trixie with a sniff. "Besides, it will be better in a day or so, I expect."

Hilary bit her lip. Could she spare a day or so? What other disasters might befall her if they waited that long?

"No," she declared. "You must come with us."

"*Eh?*" Davenport and Trixie chorused.

"I need you for propriety more than anything else, Trix," said Hilary reasonably. "The journey is but a day. We can set you up nicely in the carriage with a cushion to rest your foot upon. It's not as if you'll be obliged to *walk* anywhere. His lordship will carry you where you need to go."

She smiled at her companions. "You see? Problem solved. Now, we'd best be going or Hodgins is sure to give the game away. Will you take Trixie down to the carriage, please, my lord? I shall get our things, and then we can be gone."

* * *

Davenport bent a stern gaze on Trixie, willing her to say nothing until Honey was out of earshot.

She held her tongue until her mistress's footsteps died away. Then she collapsed into giggles.

He frowned at her. "This is not funny. Do you think she rumbled us?"

"Bless you, no," said Trixie, wiping her eyes. "My lord, the look on your face! Hoo, I thought I'd split my sides, I did. Serve you right, sirrah, having such designs on a virtuous lady."

The reproach glanced off his armor. "Let's get moving, then. If she won't be parted from you over a sprained ankle, I daresay I shall think of something else."

He should have chosen a contagious fever. But he'd thought it likely Honey would insist on remaining behind to nurse the wench.

Clearly, his skills at the game of seduction were a little rusty. He needed to hone his strategy if he was going to lure the virtuous Miss deVere to his bed.

So close . . . Ah, he could still feel the heady rush of having her beneath him on that damnably uncomfortable bed this morning. He hadn't been fully awake or he'd have handled that encounter with more finesse.

He shook his head. He needed to keep his wits about him, stop allowing her the advantage. She was attracted to him; he could smell it on her, the sweet scent of desire. When he'd kissed her, she'd responded with a helpless, innocent passion that was like a revelation, the mere taste of an addictive drug.

But the mere taste was all it had taken to get him intoxicated to make him crave more.

And now his hopes of having her to himself in a closed carriage had been dashed. Not by any awareness on her part of just how dastardly he could be, but by her laudable compassion for her maid.

Well, there would be many opportunities in Town. He'd make sure of that.

He began to stalk off when Trixie spoke. "My lord?"

"Yes, what is it?" He turned impatiently.

She pouted and lifted her dimpled arms. "Aren't you going to carry me down?"

* * *

They were finally ready to leave as dawn got a good orange glow on the landscape. Having deposited Trixie in the coach with slightly less gentleness than her invalid status warranted, Davenport eyed the equipage critically.

"Is this the best you could do?" he said to Honey, who stepped away from her conversation with the pimply-faced youth on the box.

"Sadly, yes. Billy assures me it is serviceable, but I can't be certain. No one has used it since my parents were alive."

She regarded him. "Thank you for taking such good care of Trixie."

"My pleasure," he lied. "Are you certain she is better off with us than here? I cannot help thinking it is cruel to subject her to such a journey."

Honey's brow furrowed. "It would be callous in the extreme to leave her behind. No one would care for her. You don't think we should stay until she gets better?"

No, that he certainly did not. "If I have to sleep one more night in that house, I'll murder someone. Preferably, your brothers."

"Not if I get to them first," she said, grim faced.

With a mental sigh of resignation, he offered his arm, "Shall we?"

On a last look at the life she left behind, Honey nodded and let him hand her into the coach.

CHAPTER SEVEN

A s he helped Honey up, Davenport sent a swift glance around. A glint of light caught his attention. It came from the stand of trees that grew in wild disorder beside the rutted drive.

Honey must have felt him tense beneath her hand, for she turned back and studied him curiously. "Is something wrong?"

He resisted the urge to bundle her into the coach, willynilly.

"Not a thing in the world," he said, climbing up after her.

His shadow had found him. Or, more accurately, his shadow had never lost sight of him, even though he'd been smuggled out of London in the dead of night, then arrived at the Grange by circuitous means.

Someone was extremely persistent.

Davenport seated himself beside Honey on the lumpy, threadbare banquette opposite the maid and stretched his legs as far as they'd go. Once, the squabs had been royal blue velvet, but they weren't anymore. Damn, but it must be depressing to live amid all this decay.

His irritation with the deVere brothers flared anew.

Davenport slid a sidelong glance at the enchanting profile of his companion, so delicately drawn, culminating in the prettiest mouth he'd ever seen. He experienced a powerful urge to shower her with every imaginable luxury. She should bathe in champagne, wear diamonds in her hair, silk on her body.

Nothing at all when she lay there in his bed, ready and waiting for him.

He wondered what she looked like naked.

As if aware of his regard, she blushed prettily and turned away, staring unseeing out the window. He repressed the impulse to lean past her to pull down the shade. If someone was out there waiting to put a bullet through him, so be it, but he'd die before he'd let Honey be hurt.

Common sense told him that whoever followed him didn't mean to kill him or he'd already be dead. He couldn't remain vigilant every moment of the day, and they—whoever they were—had been following him around London for the better part of six months.

He hadn't taken much more than a cursory interest until now. He hadn't taken more than a cursory interest in anything besides women and liquor since he'd returned to Town.

So. What did they want?

If they followed him because they expected him to resume his former path of scientific inquiry, they'd be doomed to disappointment. He was done with all that.

Someone kept track of his every move. Someone who was damned good at hunting men.

"Can't this thing go any faster?" he said.

Honey replied, "No, I don't think it can. I ordered the coachman to spring the horses, so I daresay this is the outer limit of their speed."

Staring out the window at the passing countryside, she said wonderingly, "I cannot believe I am truly going to London."

Turning to him, she stretched out a hand impulsively to brush his wrist. "Thank you for agreeing to take me." For once, she beamed up at him with unalloyed friendliness.

Davenport sucked in a breath.

He'd seen her disdainful, frustrated, furious, cold-eyed, exasperated, defeated, mortified, shocked. . . . Now that he thought about it, in the past twenty-four hours she'd fairly run the gamut of emotions—mostly provoked, he must admit, by him.

He had not yet seen her smile.

It was like sunshine, that smile, pouring over him, through him, filling his senses with light. He fell into the glow of it, stretched out like a cat to bask.

Puzzlement soon dimmed the gleam in her eyes.

"What is it?" she asked. "You seem distracted, my lord."

"Your beauty would drive any man to distraction," he murmured, without the least premeditation or guile.

"Beauty!" She snorted, all trace of her former warmth gone. "Do not think to empty the butter boat over me, my lord. I am passable, that is all."

Passable? Davenport would have argued that point but halted the vehement denial that sprang to his lips. He refused to make a cake of himself over her. Particularly with Trixie's bright, inquisitive gaze upon him.

Then, too, the strength of his need to convince Honey how wrong she was about her delightful appearance bothered him.

He'd known this slip of a girl rather less than a day. He'd take pleasure with her if he could, but he made it a rule to keep his affairs light and uncomplicated. Not for any woman would he change his ways. Not even for a woman who smiled up at him like a sunburst.

He turned the subject. "Did you leave word for your brothers? They will worry about you."

"No, they won't worry," she said. "But you may be easy. I did write them a note, saying that I had left for Town with Mrs. Farrington to accompany me."

"Won't they find out soon enough you're not with her?"

"Oh, no," she said. "They won't mind what I do, as long as I am out of their house and I'm not asking them for money."

He wished now that he'd made those brothers of hers hurt more when he'd had the chance. "You are such an innocent," he said, shaking his head. "What if I had evil designs on you?"

She gave him a severe look. "You do have evil designs on me."

"And yet, here you are, traveling with me to London, with only an incapacitated maid for protection."

He glanced over at Trixie, who had fallen asleep. As if on cue, the maid emitted a gentle snore. "You are too trusting, Honey, my dear."

"I believe I have your measure, my lord," she said, smoothing out her skirts.

"You are perhaps unaware of my reputation with women," he murmured provocatively.

"I do not need to listen to gossip. I can see for myself that you are a scoundrel," she said. "But if you did not assault me this morning when I was in such a vulnerable position, I do not believe you will assault me now."

"Perhaps I merely waited until your brothers were not here to help you," he said. "Did you think of that?"

Her eyes widened. She had not thought of that. But she recovered. "I was in your bedchamber. It would not have been difficult to convince them I had solicited your advances."

He tilted his head. "True. I wonder why that didn't occur to me."

"Perhaps," she said with an almost condescending smile, "because you are not quite as black as you wish to paint yourself, my lord."

He considered. "No, that can't be it. Must have been that my wits are a little slow first thing in the morning."

And again, her smile had that gallingly knowing quality to it. "I think your wits are far sharper than you would have me believe."

He regarded the toes of his evening shoes, which had been ruined by mud. All the asinine phrases he might have uttered to disprove her claim deserted him.

Again, he changed the subject. "Do you think Trixie needs medical attention? Perhaps we ought to take her to a doctor."

"For a wrenched ankle?" she said, diverted. "I doubt there is much the doctor would recommend that we are not already doing. Perhaps when we get to London . . ."

She trailed off and frowned, as if an unwelcome thought had occurred to her.

Ah. He'd wondered when she'd consider the practicalities of her stay. Finances being one of them.

He waited to see if she'd mention the problem to him. He had his own plans to fund her little sojourn in the metropolis, but he'd have to go about it in a subtle manner. Honey would never accept charity from him.

Besides, while he fully intended to entice her to his bed, he had no plans to ruin her. She was a gently bred lady and he did not want to scuttle her chances on the Marriage Mart. In such an affair, discretion was called for. He could be discreet when he set his mind to it; it was just that ordinarily he didn't see the need.

She tilted her head, and a sliver of sun slanting through

the window burnished those lovely eyes to gold. "Do you think, my lord, that your cousin will put me in the way of work while I am with her? I could offer my services to a genteel family whose daughters require instruction in dancing and deportment."

"Hire yourself out as a governess?" He shook his head. "My dear Honey, that would never do."

"Why not?" she demanded. "It's a respectable occupation for a lady. It's what I've been doing for the past four years."

"Not under my cousin's care," he said firmly. "Rosamund would be mortified at the idea of a guest in her house obliged to earn her keep."

Not to mention that if Honey tutored these girls, she'd likely be asked to live in their household. She'd be chaperoning girls at balls and parties and thus inaccessible to *him*. He didn't like that idea at all.

She opened those luscious lips to argue. "But—"

"Do you *wish* to make your hostess a laughingstock?" he demanded in a tone of righteous indignation.

And, damn it, he *was* indignant, if not in a righteous cause. She was a mulish little thing when she got the bit between her teeth. What if she ruined his plans? He'd be obliged to steal her away somehow and that would take a lot of effort, besides creating a scandal of epic proportions.

She seemed to see the force of his argument, because she subsided back against the threadbare squabs. "Perhaps I might be of assistance to Lady Tregarth, then. Does she have children?"

"One on the way," he said. "But don't let that concern you. She's as fit as a flea. I daresay she will ask you to sew something or do some tatting or whatnot," he added vaguely. "She is always making something for those charities of hers. And then there will be invitations to write for parties, that sort of thing. But you're not a servant. You're a guest. Rosamund won't ask you to do anything she wouldn't ask her cousin or her friend."

* * *

The very idea of Rosamund, Lady Tregarth, considering Hilary a friend filled her with a bittersweet longing. She'd seen all her own friends drift away from Miss Tollington's to become wives and mothers elsewhere. Fully occupied with their families and households, they'd largely forgotten her, though she made a point of continuing to correspond with them.

The other teachers at Miss Tollington's were pleasant but considerably older than Hilary. Then, too, living in such close quarters had made them all guard their privacy to such an extent that she didn't know any of them in the intimate way one knew one's bosom bows.

A baby . . . How lucky Lady Tregarth was. Hilary had seldom thought beyond the gentle, kind husband of her dreams. But now the idea of children of her own filled her heart with longing.

"When is Lady Tregarth's baby due?" she asked.

He looked at her as if she were mad. "I haven't the foggiest notion. Poor Tregarth is beside himself with worry over her. He dotes on her, you know."

A deVere who doted on his wife? This Hilary must see.

"She must be very beautiful," she said.

"Oh, she is. A diamond of the first water," said Davenport. "But you'll meet her yourself."

A flutter of nerves seized her chest. "Are you certain Lady Tregarth will be prepared to have me to stay? Perhaps it is not a good time."

"Well, if it isn't, I'll take you to my sister, the Duchess of Ashburn," said Davenport cheerfully. "Although I'll say this: You'd be far better off with Rosamund. Cecily can be a mite prickly."

"Particularly where females who might have designs on her brother are concerned," observed Hilary, nodding.

He cleared his throat, as if that idea made him uncomfortable. "We shall concoct a story to explain our meeting."

He considered for a moment. "I have it. I rescued you from some deadly peril and escorted you to town. I shall beg my cousin to take pity on a poor, desperate young lady."

She sniffed. "We are in my carriage, my lord. And given the state of your, er, person . . ." She gestured at his rough appearance. ". . . I should think it more likely that *I* rescued *you*."

"That's good," he said, after a thoughtful pause. "And my cousins will believe it, because they will feel great remorse over leaving me in that barn. Did a ferocious bull trample me into the hay? Or perhaps the owner of the barn took to me with his shotgun. Was I on death's door? Did you nurse me back to health? Did the tender touch of your dear, sweet little hands bring me back from the brink?"

"You do have a flare for the dramatic, don't you, my lord?" said Hilary dryly.

"Indeed," he said. His mouth set into a faintly grim line. "Generally speaking, I don't have to embellish on the true state of affairs."

She waved a hand. "Most likely, you got drunk, had a bout of fisticuffs, and fell down in a ditch somewhere, from which I, in my infinite mercy, retrieved you."

He chuckled. "Now that is just plain uncharitable. Unlikely, too, for I can hold my liquor."

"Every man thinks he can hold his liquor," said Hilary. "It is a great pity so few of them are correct on that point."

He didn't take offense at her observation, merely saying, "Never mind. I shall think of something to satisfy them."

"As long as your tale doesn't cast aspersions on my honor, I don't much care what you tell them. But I ought to know, so that I can play along."

He cocked an eyebrow. "You are prepared to lie to my nearest and dearest? That's encouraging."

Hilary frowned, conscious of a slimy feeling of guilt.

It wasn't as if she liked lying. Sadly, it had become second nature to her, however. When she'd possessed friends, there'd been the awkward question of why she never invited them back to Wrotham Grange with her for the summer. No, she always went to other girls' homes, or if there weren't any invitations in the offing, she would slink away to the Grange alone.

She wished, on occasion, that there was someone with whom she might share the ramshackle deVere side of her life, someone who would understand.

But the specter of her friends turning away from her when they discovered how she lived, with the house falling down around her ears and two debauched, loutish brothers who did not have a genteel bone in their bodies, loomed too large.

In the end, she'd lost those friends anyway. When one's only common ground is an institution and that common ground disappears, it becomes well nigh impossible to maintain the connection.

As if he followed her train of thought, Davenport said, "Do you have friends in London? Will you enjoy picking up those threads again?"

"Oh, yes. Indeed," she murmured. "There are many ladies who have at one time or another been students at Miss Tollington's Academy. I daresay I shall find a delightful circle of acquaintances when I reach London."

She tried to infuse her tone with enthusiasm, but it was hard. What if they shunned her because she'd accepted a post as teacher at Miss Tollington's school? Or what if

Mrs. Farrington spread tales about her horrible experience at the Grange yesterday?

That did not bear thinking about.

Hilary straightened her spine. She'd managed to get this far. Why let such trifling social difficulties stop her embracing the opportunity?

"We are making good time," Davenport commented. "We should reach London tonight." He glanced out of the window, up at the sky. "Assuming the weather holds."

This hopeful prediction was immediately followed by a great lurch that threw Hilary against Davenport and caused the half-reclining Trixie to tumble from her seat.

Davenport's arm instantly closed around Hilary as he braced his back against the wall of the coach. The world went topsy-turvy as the carriage crashed onto its side.

"Damnation! Are you all right?" Davenport took her face between his large hands and surveyed her keenly. He lay beneath her on the wall of the coach that had now become its floor.

"I'm perfectly well," gasped Hilary. Pushing away from him, she turned to check on her maid. "Trixie, are you hurt?"

"No, miss," said the maid, straightening her bonnet. "Not but what I'll give John the coachman a piece of my mind for this! Took a corner too fast, I'll wager."

"I don't think there was a corner," said Davenport. Having laid Hilary gently aside, he was now on his feet, head and shoulders poking out of the open carriage door above them.

He climbed out of the conveyance, then reached down to help Hilary.

She gripped his arms above the elbows and he did the same for her, swinging her up, out of the tumbled carriage as if she weighed no more than a child. Her stomach swooped as she hovered for a moment in midair. Then he caught her to his chest before swinging her down to the ground.

As he performed the same office for Trixie, Hilary rounded the vehicle to find the coachman scratching his head over the damage to the wheel, while Billy quieted the horses and unhitched them from the mangled traces.

"What on earth happened?" demanded Hilary.

The coachman shook his head. "Axle's broke."

"Can you fix it?" she said.

He eyed her. "The *axle's* broke, miss," he repeated patiently. "Need a smithy for that job."

Davenport came around and inspected the damage. "There's a village farther down the road, about two miles or so, where we can arrange to get the coach repaired. You two can ride the horses. We'll walk."

"But how long will that take?" Hilary almost wailed with frustration.

The coachman rubbed his chin. "Hard to say, miss. It's pretty bad and not the work of a moment to mend. I doubt we'll get the carriage back on the road today."

* * *

Davenport knelt down beside the coach. He ran his hand over the bent axle and found the damage was just as bad as the dour coachman had said.

Had the wheel been tampered with? There was no way to tell. One couldn't assume anything except that the vehicle had been in a poor state of repair to begin with.

The circumstance didn't quiet the edgy sensation prickling at the nape of his neck.

He surveyed their surroundings but didn't catch any sign of his shadow.

"We'll have to walk to the inn," he told Honey. "I'll be able to hire another conveyance there."

"But what about Trixie's ankle?" said Honey. "She could not possibly walk two miles."

Davenport mentally kicked himself for instigating that foolish deception. There was no way in hell he was carrying the plump maid all that way.

"Sorry, I'd forgotten Trixie's ankle." He drew a breath through his teeth. "Billy, can you take Trixie up before you?"

Billy grinned down at the maid. "Aye, that I can."

Trixie gave a disdainful sniff but condescended to allow herself to be lifted up before Billy. There was no saddle, of course, but the steeds were accustomed to being ridden by postillions and docilely accepted their burdens.

"Come on," said Davenport to Honey when he'd tied her bandboxes to the horses' harness. "We might as well take a shortcut cross-country if we must go on foot."

* * *

Hilary wasn't certain how it came about that she ended up alone with Davenport and without her having the least say in directing her own servants. Despite his seeming nonchalance, he displayed the qualities of a man who was born to command.

Unable to think of a better scheme, she picked up her skirts and climbed a stile after him.

"The broken axle is most unfortunate," she panted, hurrying to keep up with Davenport's long, easy stride. "Do you think it was an accident?"

His head snapped around. For the first time, he looked at her. "Why? What else could it be?"

She halted, taken aback by his taut expression. Real concern shadowed his eyes.

Now she began to feel uneasy. "I don't know. I thought

perhaps Billy had thought of a scheme to slow me down until my brothers catch up with me." She shrugged. "Which is nonsensical, for Tom and Benedict wouldn't follow me anyway."

Relief sketched across his features.

She narrowed her eyes. "There's something you're not telling me, isn't there?"

A shot rang out.

The next moment she was flat on her back on the ground beneath the hedgerow, with Davenport on top of her.

The breath crushed out of her lungs. She was afraid, but most of all, she was acutely aware of him, sprawled over her. His body, so big and heavy, but heavy in a way that was not at all unpleasant.

"Was that a—"

"Gun. Yes," he gritted the words between his teeth. Then he let out a stream of vicious invective that shocked her to the marrow.

"Someone is trying to *kill* you?" she squeaked.

"I didn't think so," he said. "But I wouldn't put money on it at this juncture."

He shifted so that he supported his weight on his elbows. His body was hot and hard and his breathing came fast, but he was all business now. That teasing light had died from his eyes.

"Just what is happening here?" she hissed. "You know something about this. You must. People don't just go shooting at other people for no reason."

"I am not at all sure the shot was for us. It's probably someone out for a day's sport, shooting wood pigeons."

"Then why," Hilary managed, "are we lying here like this?"

"Better to be safe than riddled with holes." He gazed down at her, and a hint of his customary good humor returned. "Why, Miss deVere," he said, his piratical mouth curling at the edges. "We really must stop meeting like this."

* * *

Another shot sounded. Farther away, this time. Probably a couple of local lads out bagging fowl, just as he'd told Honey.

Davenport cursed himself. He'd overreacted. If the man who followed him had wanted him dead, he'd have had ample opportunity well before now.

He was so keyed up, he hadn't taken the time to enjoy the feel of Honey beneath him. Now that the perceived danger turned out not to be danger at all, he did.

She must have seen some change in his expression, for she squirmed a little in an attempt to get up. The action sent deliciously tantalizing sensations through his body.

Truly, he must stop torturing himself like this when he knew nothing would come of it. They needed to get to that inn and make sure nothing else happened to slow their journey.

"Is it safe now?" Honey said, pushing at his shoulders with her palms. "That shot seemed farther away."

"You smell of violets," he said, drawing a deep, appreciative breath.

"You are making that up," she said impatiently. "Is it safe to be on our way, do you think?"

He cocked his head to listen but heard no more shots. "We'll wait five more minutes. That should do it."

And then he set about *not* kissing her. He brushed a long, curling tendril of deep gold from her face, tucked it behind her ear. As if he wished to clear a path for his mouth to follow.

He imagined pressing his lips to the pulse point in her graceful neck, feeling her responsive shiver. He thought about taking her pretty, lush mouth, possessing it in the same way he burned to posses her body, plunging deep.

She could scarcely mistake precisely what he wanted. The size and hardness of him pressing against her stomach must be impossible to ignore.

Something heated and softened in those brown eyes. "Don't look at me like that," she breathed.

"Like what?" Stupid question, but all of the blood had deserted his brain. Stringing more than two words together was beyond him.

"Like you want to, oh, to devour me." She gave a choking gasp and thrashed a little. "For pity's sake, let me up."

To his regret, another faint sound of a distant shot finally settled the matter. He let her push him away and wriggle out from beneath him.

After a moment or two, he rose and followed her as she marched off toward the village.

"You are incorrigible," she complained, increasing her pace. "I believe you knew they were hunters all along."

He hadn't, but he now felt foolish for his overreaction, so he said, "You can't blame a scoundrel for trying, Honey."

"Stop calling me Honey!" she yelled.

He grinned. "But it suits you so well."

She made a noise between a cry and a growl and stalked off, even faster this time. He had no trouble keeping up with her, of course, with his longer stride. That seemed to infuriate her more.

They soon reached the inn. Too soon for his liking.

The establishment was a small one and the only carriage available for hire that day was a gig, so he hired it and ordered the horses put to.

He didn't find the servants in the stables or the yard, but the carriage horses were there, so Trixie, Billy, and the coachman must have made it here and be somewhere on the premises. He ordered Honey's bandboxes to be transferred from the horses to the gig.

"The servants are probably in the taproom," he told Honey, heading for the inn. "At least Trixie won't have gone far." He hoped not, or the game would be up and Honey would be furious with him.

There was no private parlor at this small commercial establishment, so he commanded Honey to wait in the vestibule of the shadowy, dark-paneled inn while he went to the taproom to find Trixie and the men.

When she protested, he pointed out to her that ladies did not frequent taprooms and besides, she'd wanted to maintain her anonymity, hadn't she? Wouldn't it draw attention if she went in there with him?

For once, she did as she was told, pulling her veil down over her face while she waited for him. The entrance hall to the inn was dim and full of bustle. He didn't think anyone would notice her there.

The hostelry clearly did a roaring trade in merchants and prosperous farmers passing through on their way to the metropolis and back. Even at this hour, the taproom was full to bursting, noisy with good cheer. The scent of spilled ale, sweat, and dung filled his nostrils.

Davenport's presence garnered a few startled and curious looks. They were not accustomed to seeing noblemen in full evening kit at a little after three in the afternoon, it seemed.

Well, and who could blame them for staring? Honey was right to avoid appearing in his company. He looked what he was, a wealthy scoundrel out for a spree. One that lasted days, not just one evening.

A swift reconnaissance told him Billy and the coachman weren't present. As a sop to expectation, he ordered an ale and asked the landlord if he'd seen men of their description and a woman of Trixie's. "Too busy to notice," was the answer he'd expected and the answer he received.

If they weren't here or in the stables, where were they? If he was to keep his promise to Honey to get her to London tonight, they needed to get moving. He'd leave the men to wait for the carriage to be fixed and return it to the Grange, but Honey wouldn't go anywhere without Trixie.

Only, where was the chit?

CHAPTER EIGHT

The most peculiar sense of apprehension overtook Hilary when Davenport left her. When he was around, she was by turns exasperated, shocked, and infuriated. But there was no doubting the fact that having a big, strong man at one's side made one feel safe from the rest of the world.

She marveled at the way Davenport had taken command back in the stables, giving orders and demanding a vehicle and a horse with utter assurance, despite having no more than a few coins in his pocket.

His manner alone was enough to convince staff that he was, indeed, the Earl of Davenport, an aristocrat whose credit was good anywhere. No matter that his face was bruised like a prizefighter's, nor that even Trixie's ministrations could not make his evening dress pristine again.

There was an air about him, a force of personality that could only spring from a background of privilege and ease. But more than that, a bone-deep confidence and a knack for command, when he chose to exercise it, brought him instant obedience.

Hilary perched on a little wooden stool against the wall and looked about her. She'd never been in such an establishment as this bustling inn. It was not a hostelry that catered to ladies, or females of any description, for that matter. Commercial men—tradesmen and farmers, bankers and city clerks—seemed to frequent the place.

The noise that spilled from the taproom was loud and often punctuated by obscenity. She winced every time another raucous burst of laughter rang out.

She supposed she ought to be glad it was laughter she heard and not a brawl. One guess who'd be at the hub of any fight that came his way. Though she had made Davenport promise not to punch anyone during their journey, she wasn't confident he'd keep his word if it came down to an affray.

She recalled how he'd looked, standing over her two enormous brothers, fists clenched, feet planted wide. The fierce light in his eyes had faded as soon as he realized she stood there, but she'd caught sight of it for all that. And she'd known then, if she hadn't suspected all along, that the Earl of Davenport was not a man to be trifled with, however easygoing his general demeanor.

Hilary sat in the corner at the edge of a row of chairs against the wainscoted wall, trying to look inconspicuous and succeeding fairly well, she thought. She folded her hands in her lap, cast down her gaze, and waited.

Some time passed before she felt someone's attention upon her. No mistaking that feeling, although she'd be hard-pressed to explain or justify it.

Much as she wanted to, she couldn't resist looking up.

That was a mistake. A big, florid-faced man with a mustard waistcoat gave her a knowing grin that had a cruel edge to it.

"Well, now, and ain't you a pretty little thing?" The words were loud, slightly slurred.

Hilary darted a look around, hoping the man did not address her. But of course, that was a vain hope.

According to the rules of etiquette, no gentleman would

dare approach a lady to whom he'd not been introduced. Not unless he wished to be snubbed, that was.

But those rules only applied to gentlemen, not to men of this man's ilk. Nor to scandalous earls, she thought dryly. And being herself without a maid or chaperone to lend her respectability she was fair game.

"Oh, come on now, love. Give us a smile."

Unease dripped down her spine like cold molasses. She ought to give the man a blistering set-down. He was probably some ordinary merchant, a bit full of himself, hopeful of setting up a flirtation with a young woman who appeared to have no one near to protect her.

To him the encounter was a harmless distraction, but it wasn't to her.

She kept her gaze lowered, regarding the man's mud-splashed boots, willing him not to come any closer.

Another pair of boots joined the loud waistcoated man's. "Cor blimey, what have we here? You all alone, sweetheart? Need some company, eh?"

Now there were two of them! The second man was even larger than the other, with a bushy black beard that seemed to emphasize his wet-mouthed leer.

Refusing to answer their rude questions, Hilary sat up straighter. She disliked feeling cowed. She wanted to give the men a piece of her mind. Yet, she reminded herself, to engage in any manner with these strangers would draw attention and she needed to avoid that at all costs. Besides, if she reprimanded them, they'd read it as either a challenge or an invitation. She wished to give them neither.

Cravenly she longed for Davenport to return. He might be an unprincipled oaf, but he'd dispatch these fellows in the blink of an eye.

She lowered her gaze again, staring at the men's boots, doing her best to ignore their jibes, until one of the men muttered, "Toplofty bit o' muslin, ain't she?" and came several steps closer.

She was about to spring up when another set of feet— these clad in battered evening shoes—fetched up in front of her gaze and Davenport's rich voice accosted her.

"Here you are, Honey. Just where I left you," he said cheerfully, having no notion of her predicament or how her stomach churned.

She lifted her gaze to his impossibly handsome, lividly marked face and relief broke over her like a king tide. She shot out of her seat and only the good breeding she had drummed into herself restrained her from casting herself upon his broad, manly chest.

I could kiss you, she thought recklessly. *I could throw my arms around those big shoulders and . . .*

But of course she didn't, because well-bred ladies never kissed a man to whom they were not related, married, or betrothed. And certainly not in a crowded inn.

A big hand clapped Davenport on the shoulder. "'Ere, I was talkin' ter the lady first."

A diamond-bright hardness entered Davenport's eyes. He turned, shrugging off the meaty paw. Ranging himself beside Hilary, he faced the two men.

"The lady is with me," he said in a mild voice that belied his expression. "Now, if you two gentlemen will step aside, we'll be on our way."

Hilary glanced at Davenport, impressed with how civilized he sounded.

The look on his face was anything but civilized, however. She'd never seen him like this before. When he'd fought her brothers, there'd been a hard light of excitement, enjoyment, in his eyes. Now there was cold fury.

The other men scented a fight. Ignoring his request, they stood their ground, alert and ready. The bearded man went so far as to cross his arms over his barrel chest, making it clear he wasn't going to budge.

Davenport sighed and turned to her. "Would you mind stepping aside, my dear?"

She needed no further persuasion, scuttling back into her corner like a mouse. She knew from bitter experience she'd be in the way if she stayed and that Davenport might be distracted if she tried to help.

Davenport's elbow shot out, clipping the bearded man on his furry chin, sending him reeling back. A swift strike of his heel connected with the other man's knee.

With a howl, the fellow crumpled on the spot.

The bearded man recovered quickly, boring in again.

Davenport leaned forward, picked up a chair, pivoted, and crashed it down on the bearded man's head. The chair was flimsy. It splintered and cracked and flew into pieces. The big man shook himself like a dog and kept coming.

"Honey," Davenport panted, "I'm doing my best not to use my fists, but it's getting damned difficult."

That stupid promise! How could he think she would hold him to it?

"Never mind that," cried Hilary. "Hit him!"

The florid man had screamed with pain over his knee, but he was even now staggering to his feet with murder in his face.

It was two against one, but without his hands tied by his promise to her, Davenport fought like a god, with strength, power, and a strange fluid beauty. Other men, drawn by the commotion, took sides and came in swinging.

From what Hilary could see from her place flattened against the wall, things turned riotous from there. More men piled into the fray and soon these respectable farmers and merchants were a teeming melee, rolling and crashing about and punching one another with no earthly idea why.

Davenport fought on, all the while wading through the roiling mass of bodies toward the yard entrance. Hilary abandoned her post and darted to the doorway, ready to escape with him into the yard.

Then she saw them. Her brothers, Tom and Benedict, entering the inn from the other door. They'd followed her. Not only that, they'd very nearly caught her, too.

"Davenport!" she yelled over the din. "Look!"

He ducked a flying fist, then glanced around. When he saw her brothers, who were even now piling onto the fight with their customary gusto, he muscled through the mass of flailing limbs to her.

"Hurry!" Gripping her hand, he pulled her out to the stable yard.

She stumbled a little as she tried to keep up with him. That cold, hard look had not left his face.

"Did you have any luck in the taproom?" she asked, belatedly recalling the reason he'd left her alone in the first place.

He shook his head. "They probably went to the smithy. No time to find out. We have to get out of here before your brothers see us."

"I can't believe they've followed me," said Hilary, running to keep up. They wouldn't have troubled themselves just for her. There must be some other reason.

Davenport practically threw her into the seat of the gig that stood, ready and waiting for them. Climbing up beside her, he flipped a coin to the ostler who held the horse's head. "I'll need someone to find a broken-down coach about two miles from here on the north road, repair the broken axle, and return the coach to Wrotham Grange, hard by Stamford."

If the ostler thought this an odd request, he didn't dare argue, just tipped his hat and said, "Aye, your lordship."

"What about Trixie?" Hilary clutched his arm as he set off at a spanking pace, weaving around other carriages and pedestrians in the yard.

He waved off that objection. "I'll send someone for her when we get to London."

"But—"

"Do you want your brothers to catch up with us and drag you home?" he demanded.

"Of course not. Only—"

He glanced at the enormous stable yard clock. "And you want to be in town tonight, don't you?"

"Well, ye—"

"Then we must be off. We've lost far too much time."

She didn't know what to do. "But I feel awful leaving Trixie with her sore ankle."

"Well, it's either look for her and risk running into your brothers or press on." He shot her a glance that was full of challenge. "What's it to be?"

Her desperation to get away from the Grange overcame her fears for Trixie. The other servants were with her, after all. Besides, Trixie, of all people, would understand the urgency of Hilary's flight. "Yes. All right, let's go."

But Davenport treated her answer as a foregone conclusion. They left the inn and her brothers in their dust.

Or at least, that's what she hoped. They'd traveled many miles before Hilary stopped casting wary glances over her shoulder.

As the immediacy of her fear faded, Hilary became acutely aware of Davenport. The gig was no slender sporting vehicle. It could seat three people quite easily. Yet Davenport's muscular thigh continually pressed against Hilary's as he drove the equipage as fast as the hired horse could go.

Davenport's touch made her edgy and hot. She didn't like it one bit.

"I wish you would stop doing that," she said crossly, drawing herself farther to the edge of the seat. "Really, this is exactly the sort of thing I wanted to guard against when I insisted on bringing Trixie."

He grinned. "You're not afraid of being alone with me in an open carriage in broad daylight, are you? Honey, even my superior skills with the ribbons wouldn't permit me to make love to you and drive at the same time. *Although* . . ." He trailed off, tilting his head as if imagining ways of accomplishing both tasks at once.

Her stifled gasp made his smile broaden.

"Besides," he added, lowering his voice, "when I make love to you, I intend to give it my full, undivided attention."

Why did she keep blushing like this? She ought to be accustomed to his outrageous remarks by now.

She managed a *humph* of disapproval. "You are not chivalrous."

"This is what I keep telling you," he said. "I am London's most notorious scoundrel. As such, it is my job to seduce you. As a virtuous lady bent on establishing her pristine reputation, it is *your* job to stop me."

He looked down at her and shook his head. The wicked gleam in his eyes invited her to share the joke. "I should not have to explain these things to you."

He was right, she realized. Clearly, she'd lost her grip on reality if she trusted this cheerful blackguard to do the honorable thing. He might protect her from *other* wolves, but she must not forget that Jonathon, Lord Davenport, was the most dangerous predator of them all.

Only one thing bothered her. Would a true scoundrel keep reminding her of the fact?

"It is not proper for me to drive all this way alone with

you, even if it is in an open carriage," she managed stiffly. "How shall I look Lady Tregarth in the eye, arriving in such a state?"

"You needn't worry. I'll think of some explanation to satisfy her." He returned his attention to his horse. "Rosamund might be a countess, but she's not nearly as high in the instep as you are."

"I daresay," she said tartly, "that being a Westruther, your cousin might walk down St. James's stark naked and no one would turn a hair. Whereas *I*—"

"Whereas if *you* walked down St. James's stark naked, Honey, you would cause a riot."

The gleam in his eye made her all too conscious of his intentions to see her stark naked as soon as possible. As if she'd needed reminding.

Her fault for mentioning that "naked" word. What devil prompted her to invite these lewd speculations? Perhaps there was more deVere in her than she'd thought.

No. She was forced to admit that her companion addled her wits with his handsome looks and his audacious swagger. Few women could resist the Earl of Davenport, she was sure.

Well, *she* would resist him. Everything depended upon her doing so. She must show the world a deVere could behave with the utmost taste and propriety. She must convince a good, respectable man that a deVere lady could be a good, respectable wife.

"What I am trying to say," she continued with forced patience, "is that as a deVere, I cannot be too careful of my reputation. I am at a disadvantage to begin with, thanks to my rotten family."

"You know," he said after a while, "I shouldn't think your family matters as much as you expect. The best strategy with society is to act as if you don't care what people think."

"I suppose that works for someone like you," she muttered, feeling waspish.

He rubbed his stubbled jaw with the flat of his hand as he considered that. "No, I cannot truly say anything much works for me, or that I've ever cared to win the ton's good opinion. I am beyond the pale. Or I would be if I wasn't an earl and disgustingly rich into the bargain. Of course, I *don't* care what people think. Being dead for nigh on six years puts such stuff into perspective."

Hilary had wondered about that extraordinary circumstance before, but so much had happened since their first, inauspicious meeting that the question had gone clear out of her head.

She would have probed further, but he added, "No, this is what I've observed among ladies of the ton. Even the greatest scandal can be overcome if only one has the brass to face down the gossip."

Hilary didn't believe it. As a deVere, she couldn't let one tiny chink in her armor show. Look what had happened to her at Miss Tollington's. Even when she'd behaved impeccably, her family had weighed against her. Ultimately, the deVere reputation had tipped the scales.

The utter shock of the moment Miss Tollington had dismissed her still resonated through her soul like the after-tremors of an earthquake. More than two weeks had passed since that fateful decision had rocked her to her foundations and she was yet to recover.

When she'd let fly at Davenport in front of Mrs. Farrington . . . She shuddered to think of it. That had been more than a chink in her armor. She'd stripped herself bare.

The provocation had been impossible to withstand, of course. But now that she had Davenport's measure, she could deal with his audacity. Or at least, she could deflect his attempts to seduce and embarrass her with her temper and her virtue intact.

Davenport looped a rein to slow the horse when they rounded a bend. His hands were bare, she noticed. If he'd ever worn gloves with his evening rig, they would have been white, and quite ruined by now.

For some reason, those naked hands held her spellbound. The backs of them were slightly more tanned than the rest, with a sprinkling of dark hair that caught the light as they moved. Large hands, capable and strong. They tempted a lady to place her trust in them.

She remembered the feel of those hands gripping her shoulders when he'd kissed her and barely suppressed a shiver.

From there, her thoughts skipped to the sight of him, forever emblazoned on her memory, standing like a statue of Apollo among the ruins of his bedchamber ceiling.

Naked.

She yanked the check string on that runaway thought.

What was wrong with her? One minute, she solemnly vowed to follow the path of rectitude; the next, she was picturing the worst libertine in the country without his clothes.

It was Davenport. *He* was what ailed her. No other man had ever incited such violent and conflicting emotions in her breast. It was his fault and his alone that she now appreciated the joys of a perfect pair of male buttocks.

Oh, dear. She recalled many instances of her delicate mama attempting to wash her brothers' mouths out with soap. Hilary wished she could do the same to her mind.

"Penny for them," said Davenport idly, interrupting her brain's wild meandering.

She started. "What?"

"Penny for your thoughts," he said on a deep chuckle.

"Although I daresay I could be persuaded to pay a lot more for thoughts that make your color fluctuate so delightfully. You really do have the most exquisite skin, you know. Translucent, like my sister's finest Chinese porcelain. Like a white rose with the faintest blush of pink at the center."

The soulful way he uttered the last sentence made her laugh in spite of herself. "You are the most complete hand, Lord Davenport. Why can you not be serious, even when you are trying to flatter a lady into your . . . er . . . arms?"

He shrugged. "You are too clever to succumb to such stuff. No matter how genuine the sentiment."

He did not know her as well as he thought if that was his opinion. Thank goodness he did not try such stuff in earnest. She imagined it would be impossible to resist.

That was the danger of him. Even though one knew he talked nonsense, one wanted so desperately to believe . . .

"I am glad you understand me so well," she said, primly folding her hands in her lap.

He drew rein and turned to her, his voice very low and graveled. "As long as *you* understand *me,* my dear. I mean to have you. I mean to have you every way a man can have a woman and some others not even I've thought of yet. I give you fair warning of that, for I don't lie when it comes to my intentions. I don't flatter and I don't deceive and I *do not commit myself to anyone.*"

She stared into that suddenly serious face and her heart pounded hard. Each word he uttered sent spears of delicious heat arrowing down to her belly, and lower.

He'd awakened unprecedented sensations within her. Longing. Desire. Need. He'd told her explicitly that he intended to use her body and that his use would not lead him to any kind of emotional attachment. Certainly not to marriage.

In that moment, the easygoing charm she was accustomed to from him vanished. Yet she was not afraid. Not of him, at any rate.

On a sudden insight, she realized he sought to place some distance between them on an emotional plane, while he maneuvered closer to her on a physical level.

As if she might encroach on the emotional well-being of the notorious Earl of Davenport. As if she, Hilary de-Vere, had the power to touch him or make a claim on his affections.

Something twanged at the edge of her mind. Something that restored her equilibrium just enough to reply, "There is a saying, my lord. 'Save your breath to cool your porridge.' Which essentially means, 'Don't talk about a thing. Just do it. Or do not.'"

There was an arrested expression in his dark eyes. Then he spoke softly. "Is that an invitation?"

"Yes," Hilary said. "An invitation to stop talking nonsense. Now," she added, refusing to preen at the astounded look that had replaced the arrested one, "do tell me what story you have concocted that will explain away this hare-brained journey."

CHAPTER NINE

S everal moments passed before Davenport could collect himself to answer her. How had the mood passed from hotly, heavily carnal to clipped and prosaic in the blink of an eye?

One short reproof from her and he felt like a schoolboy reprimanded by his governess for pulling his sister's hair. Not that he'd ever pulled Cecily's hair, of course, but still . . .

He recovered his aplomb, but only after a rather awkward pause. "Oh, that's easy," he said. "I'll tell Lady Tregarth the truth."

"What?" Honey went white as a virgin's night rail.

"Why not?" he said, suppressing a satisfied grin. "Rosamund has become well acquainted with the deVeres by now. She will understand. More than that, she will sympathize."

Honey stared at him, blinked. "I see you will be no help at all. I must concoct some tale or other on my own."

He shrugged. "Suit yourself."

The conversation had so engrossed him, he'd momentarily forgotten to keep an eye out for Honey's brothers. He hadn't seen anyone thus far, but that didn't mean anything. Tom and Benedict must have a fair idea of their destination by now.

He'd taken care to leave the main road, following a more circuitous path to London. That would make it more difficult for the brothers to get wind of them and perhaps give his shadow some trouble, too. With any luck, they'd be confused and charge off in a different direction when Davenport failed to take the expected route.

He kept a weather eye cocked at the deep charcoal clouds that gathered on the horizon. The wind had picked up; he was almost certain they wouldn't make it to London before the heavens opened.

The fresh breeze dampened. He halted the horse and handed Honey the reins so he could pull up the gig's hood. It was hardly adequate shelter against a squalling storm, but it was the best he could do. He wished he'd had the presence of mind to fetch the rug from the coach before they'd abandoned it.

He climbed back into the gig. "I fear we are in for a thorough soaking," he said cheerfully. He *was* cheerful. They'd be obliged to stop somewhere for the night, during which time all kinds of interesting activity might ensue.

Honey bit her poor lip anxiously as she handed back the reins. "We must make it to London this evening. I do not care if we are both drenched to the skin in the process. We *will* get to London tonight."

Gad, but she was a determined little thing. He admired her spirit. But as the wind blew ever colder and the rain drenched his breeches, he grew slightly less enchanted with her stout refusal to consider the comforts of a dry bedchamber and a roaring fire.

Not to mention a big, manly body between the sheets to warm her chilly flesh.

Just imagining it sent his own flesh into all kinds of torment. It seemed his destiny was to be wet and cold on the outside while aflame for this woman within.

Two days. Two days they'd known each other, yet he felt as if he'd suffered from this thwarted lust for a month.

He had to hand it to her; she didn't whine. Her delicate features formed a mask of grim determination to face down the elements; that gorgeous peach of a mouth was pressed in a stubborn line. Her bonnet drooped; her pelisse grew steadily more sodden. They no longer spoke because neither of them could be heard over the howling of the wind.

The sky had darkened to pitch, even though it was only four in the afternoon. Honey was right; if they raced to get there, they could reach London late this evening. *If* the weather was fine and they had a chaise and four with a friendly moon shining above them, that was.

This gig had not been built for nighttime travel, that was clear. It did not even boast lamps to light the immediate path ahead.

Lightning splintered the sky. The nervous horse shied with a high-pitched whinny. "Damnation!" Davenport swore, quickly bringing the poor beast under control.

He turned to Hilary. "My dear, this has gone far enough. We will have to stop somewhere, at least until the storm passes. I'm afraid of injury to the horse if we stumble along in the dark."

That lower lip of hers had taken an awful lot of punishment since the start of their acquaintance. Her shoulders drooped and the crestfallen expression on her face made him wish he could halt the storm for her.

"Very well," she said. "Let us seek shelter at the first place we find."

* * *

Almost an hour passed before they found a suitable place to stop. The cottage was a neat establishment owned, as it turned out, by a prosperous farmer and his wife. Hilary warmed immediately to Mrs. Potter, a comfortably rounded matron of middling years. She had a no-nonsense way about her and cried out in dismay at the sight of the two sodden travelers dripping on her doorstep.

"Come in, come in." She shepherded the two of them inside the small vestibule and divested Hilary of her sodden bonnet and pelisse. Hilary's bandboxes had been exposed to the worst of the elements. They were now a soggy, bedraggled mess of cardboard, and the contents were in no better state.

"What a dreadful evening to be caught out on the road."

"Thank you, ma'am, you are very kind," said Hilary, turning with relish toward the fire.

"We apologize for trespassing on your hospitality," said Davenport with that devilish twinkle in his eye she'd come to mistrust. "My wife and I are indebted to you, Mrs. Potter."

Hilary's eyes narrowed. *Wife??*

At least he'd endeavored to safeguard her reputation, she supposed. But couldn't he have said she was his sister? She ought to have thought of that. She ought to have made him promise to behave. Strangely enough, he seemed to be a man of his word, if one could get him to give his word in the first place.

"Nonsense, nonsense," said the lady, all smiles. "I was only just saying to Mr. Potter, now that our only chick has left the nest we are lonely these nights. Married very well, did our Daisy. Only now she lives all the way down in Kent and we never see her."

Mrs. Potter sighed gustily, then seemed to recollect herself. "We were just finishing our dinner, but there is plenty if you'd care for some raised mutton pie. It's not what Quality like you is used to, but—"

"Not at all, Mrs. Potter," said Davenport. "I must admit I'm famished and pie sounds just the ticket."

"You must come upstairs and get dry first," the lady said, her gaze flicking over Hilary's sodden garments. "Daisy's bedchamber is all I've got, but you are much of a size with my girl, my lady, if you'll pardon my saying so. I'll find some things of hers for you to wear."

"You are so kind," murmured Hilary. "But I couldn't wear your daughter's gowns and we must be on our way once the storm passes—"

"But surely you must stay," said Mrs. Potter, flinging up her strong, weathered hands. "That storm is only just getting started, and how can you travel in a night as black as pitch?"

"I'm afraid she's right, my dear," murmured Davenport. "It is a wild night."

Before Hilary could answer, their hostess took Davenport's endorsement as consent. "I'll make up the bed and search out some clothes for my lady."

Hilary's heart plummeted. No matter her desperate need to get to London, she was forced to admit that it was impossible. They couldn't risk laming the horse by letting it stumble into a pothole or endangering themselves by riding through an electrical storm.

If she'd had a horse of her own, if there'd been the slightest possibility of moonlight to guide them . . . but the clouds had amassed against her. There was no help for it. She must stay in this cottage tonight.

At least she could do so anonymously. Somehow, Davenport had managed not to give their names and it was clear Mrs. Potter was too diffident or too polite to ask.

She looked Davenport up and down. "My Jebediah is a big man, Your Honor, but not big enough for his clothes to fit you."

"Oh, that's quite all right," said Davenport. "With your permission, I'll remove my coat, which I believe got the worst of it. The rest will dry off in front of the fire overnight."

As Mrs. Potter bustled off, Davenport appeared solicitous. "Shall I play lady's maid for you, my dear?"

"That won't be necessary," said Hilary between her teeth. "I'm sure Mrs. Potter will be good enough to oblige me."

At the lady's request, Hilary followed Mrs. Potter to Daisy's bedchamber. As she was an only child, it seemed Daisy had been given every comfort the Potters could afford. The dominant color of the chamber was a pretty, feminine pink.

While the furnishings were a trifle too frilly for Hilary's taste, she suffered a burst of envy that surprised her. Clearly, the Potters doted on their little girl. What would it have been like to have grown up surrounded by such love?

Against her hopes, a tester bed easily large enough for two dominated the room. She tried very hard *not* to think about that bed.

From her cursory inspection of the cottage on her way to the bedchamber, she realized that Daisy's was the only spare chamber with a bed in it. Even if she'd known how to do so without being thought odd, she could not have asked for sleeping quarters separate from her "husband."

Well, Davenport could sleep on the floor for all she cared. She was not sharing a bed with him, that was certain. Even fatigued as she was, she'd surely not sleep a wink all night unless she might put some distance between them.

Hilary peeled off her wet garments and gave herself a vigorous towel dry, before donning the chemise and petticoat Mrs. Potter provided. The corset was a little too large for her, but after lacing it as tightly as she could,

Mrs. Potter helped her into a pretty muslin gown sprigged with primroses and a matching shawl.

The muslin gown gaped a little at the bosom. Clearly, young Daisy possessed more in that department than Hilary did.

Mrs. Potter clicked her tongue and pinned the bodice so that it clung a little more snugly, but she couldn't do anything about the neckline, which skimmed low across Hilary's breasts. Not so low that there was danger of a nipple showing, of course, but lower than anything Hilary had ever worn.

You'll have to get used to this, she told herself. She would behave with irreproachable propriety in London, but she had no intention of being a dowdy. She was perfectly well aware that ladies of the first consideration wore gowns that plunged much lower. It was just that she felt rather . . . exposed. And that was not the best frame of mind in which to fend off the advances of a certain roguish earl.

Mrs. Potter insisted on arranging Hilary's hair in a becoming style. It would have been churlish to refuse; the lady clearly missed her daughter and enjoyed having a proxy tonight.

Hilary was outfitted in dry clothes and longing for sleep when she came down to join her hosts and Davenport at the table. A welcoming fire blazed in the hearth and the fragrance of mutton pie met her appreciative senses.

She saw Davenport's tall figure standing close to the fire. His coat and waistcoat were gone and the fine lawn of his dress shirt was still wet, plastered to his chest.

He really ought to take it off, she thought, then blushed as the desire rose in her to see those wondrously muscled shoulders again. This time, not covered in plaster dust. This time, slathered in golden licks of firelight.

His evening trousers were mostly dry—or at least, the backs of them were, as far as she could tell. Of course, thinking of his trousers led to thinking of his buttocks, and the tester bed upstairs, and all that pink—

Madness. She shook off such lurid imaginings and moved to the table, smiling at Mrs. Potter, who had not stopped talking all the while.

Hilary shook hands with the quieter Mr. Potter, a stocky man with an impressive head of chestnut hair, who looked rather bewildered by their invasion but too respectful to object.

Davenport's dark gaze took her in, from the top of her damp, piled-up curls to the toes of her slippers, and an expression that was half smile, half anticipation lit his eyes. Resting his elbow on the mantelpiece and setting the heel of his shoe on the fender, he rubbed his jaw with his thumb, contemplating her in silence as Mrs. Potter rattled on.

Heat rushed up Hilary's throat to her cheeks. *Drat the man!* The way he looked at her made her feel giddy, as if rival flocks of butterflies staged a pitched battle in her stomach.

The meal, which had smelled so enticing before, hardly tempted her to sit down. She had that sick, excited feeling that she was coming to recognize as bound up with . . . with . . .

Desire.

The word, sinful, tantalizing, hovered at the edge of her mind.

Her eyes widened. She wanted to shove the notion aside, but it merely grew larger the harder she tried to block it out.

She wanted the Earl of Davenport. She wanted him in a way no gently bred, virtuous young lady of impeccable birth and breeding ought to want a man.

In this, she was far more like Trixie than the bloodless ideal into which she'd tried to mold her students at Miss Tollington's.

Dear God, he hadn't even touched her and she was burning up.

But his eyes . . . they smoldered now, as if he'd caught the scent of her desire on the wind and reacted to it instinctively.

The breath seized in her lungs. Her heart pounded. Mrs. Potter said something; Davenport took several moments to respond.

Then he broke the spell, cutting his gaze away. With a distant, charming smile, he started toward the table.

"By all means, ma'am. I confess, I find myself suddenly ravenous."

* * *

Davenport's mouth watered, but it was not for his hostess's raised mutton pie.

Who would have thought Honey could look like that?

Hitherto, he'd seen her in dark, drab, unflattering colors and hard-wearing, serviceable fabrics. With the exception of the night rail she'd worn when his ceiling had fallen in, she'd been covered virtually from head to toe.

Now, gowned in borrowed muslin, she stole his breath.

The style of her dark gold hair, piled high on her head, seemed to emphasize the delicate turn of her features, the slender enticement of her throat.

And her bosom in that gown . . . Ah, how magnificent to be a man when sights like that were to be had. He could spend days lavishing attention on those sweet, plump little breasts.

He ached to see her nipples, to discover their color and shape. He wanted them in his hands, in his mouth.

He wanted to see her breasts move as he moved with her, over her, inside her.

Fortunate for him that the table concealed his growing impatience to sling her over his shoulder and make for the stairs.

Thank God for this night. For the storm, for the circumstance that made it impossible for them to have separate rooms. For his own insistence that they were a married couple.

He hadn't lied earlier when he'd told his host he could eat a horse; he had been famished. But that was before Honey had looked at him in such a way.

He hadn't known. How could he have guessed? Even with his scientist's insistence that women were creatures with sexual instincts just as men were—even the most repressed of them—the look she had given him when she came down to dine rocked his preconceived notions about this particular woman to the core.

Beneath that prim exterior beat the heart of a passionate, desirous woman. If only he could draw that woman out. If only Honey would let her escape from that prison of propriety in which she'd caged her.

Tonight. Tonight was his chance to see if that female would come out and play.

The anticipation built until his stomach churned with it. He forced himself to do justice to his hostess's cooking, but each mouthful was an effort. He took a long swallow of his host's raw red claret and waited until they could decently retire for the evening.

A hand of cards was suggested. He said, more abruptly than he ought, "No, I thank you. It's been a delightful evening, but my wife is fatigued. We ought to retire."

He rose, giving Honey no chance to demur, and bowed to Mrs. Potter. "The best mutton pie I've ever tasted. Thank you, ma'am. Good night."

He took Honey's hand to help her rise.

Hot currents started where their fingers met and raced up his arm, arrowing south to pool deliciously in his loins.

He glanced down at her as they left the dining parlor. "What's wrong?" he said a trifle testily. "You look like a lamb to the slaughter."

"And you, my lord," responded Honey, "look like a wolf who has just spied its dinner."

He didn't reply to that, just hauled her up the stairs with more haste than grace. "Which room? This one?"

He flung open the door, pulled her inside, and shut it behind them.

* * *

With a determined tug, Hilary slipped free of Davenport's hold and hurried to the dressing table, saying breathlessly, "I am so tired. I think I shall go straight to bed."

Her fingers trembled; she reached up to take the pins from her hair, but she couldn't seem to steady her hands enough to accomplish the task.

Heavy footsteps sounded behind her. She whirled, to see Davenport land with a flying leap on his back on the big tester bed. He'd removed his shoes, but otherwise he was fully clad.

Thank goodness for small mercies.

He grinned at her and patted the space beside him. "Most comfortable bed I've slept in for days. Why don't you come up here and try it?"

"No, thank you," she said, placing two pins in a pretty little dish on the dressing table. "And I'm sorry to tell you this, but you are *not* sleeping in that bed with me tonight."

"Oh, but I am," said Davenport, clasping his hands behind his head with the air of a man who intended to stay put. "After two nights sleeping under what can only be described as primitive conditions, you cannot expect me to take the floor on this one."

Despite her hard-hearted resolve, she saw the force of this argument. The memory of the night he'd spent at the Grange, of his ceiling falling in, still covered her with hot, prickly embarrassment.

She glanced around. "Very well, then. You take the bed. I'll take that armchair by the fire."

He looked outraged. "Don't be ridiculous. A gentleman can't let a lady sleep in an armchair while he takes his ease in a bed."

"But you are not a gentleman," she pointed out. "You are the greatest scoundrel in all the land."

He tilted his head to consider that. "All right. You take the chair."

She blinked at his quick acquiescence, but she was forced to say stiffly, "I'm sure it will be most comfortable."

"Perhaps it will be if you're accustomed to sleeping at the Grange," he agreed, with less tact than truth. "I do wish you'd be sensible, though. This bed is big enough for four people. It's a crime for you to get a crick in your neck sleeping upright."

"My lord, I am so tired, I believe I could sleep standing up," she said lightly.

And that was the truth, for besides the fatigue from an eventful day, not to mention rising at such an early hour, she'd drunk far too much of her hostess's cowslip wine at dinner. If she didn't keep her wits about her, she'd end by agreeing to one of Davenport's outrageous suggestions. He was the sort of man who could beguile one into sin before one knew what was happening. She needed to be on her guard, but she was so very tired. . . .

She turned back to the looking glass mounted on the dressing table and took out the last pin from her hair.

With fumbling fingers, she braided her tresses into one long tail.

She rummaged about the elegant little drawers in the dressing table, but there were no ribbons, so she was obliged to leave the braid loose.

"Shall I assist you to undress?" The voice came from directly behind her.

Hilary gave a nervous start. She hadn't realized he'd risen from the bed. He'd moved as silently as a cat.

She lifted her chin. "That won't be necessary."

She'd sleep in Daisy's corset if that's what it took. However, it had been quite loose, so perhaps she could wiggle the garment around to the front somehow and unlace it from there.

She really ought to have had the presence of mind to ask Mrs. Potter to help her once more. But this man had addled her wits to such an extent, she was barely keeping her head above water.

He smiled at her. "Come now, Honey. It will be easier if I unlace your stays. You are not the first female I've seen in her shift, you know."

Grimly aware of that fact, she said, "I'll manage for myself. Thank you."

"I can do it in the dark. With my eyes shut, if that would make you feel better."

"I'll just bet you can," muttered Hilary. "Turn your back while I change."

Mrs. Potter had laid out a pretty embroidered lawn night rail for her guest to wear. Hilary eyed it, wishing she could wave a wand and thereby transfer it to her magically unclad body. She had the feeling undressing with Davenport in the room would prove too much temptation to resist. For whom she did not know, precisely.

With a shrug, he turned and walked toward the fireplace. "If you don't need assistance, you won't mind if I get out of these wet things, will you?" And without waiting for an answer, he stripped off his shirt and spread it over a chair before the fire.

She tried, she really did *try*, not to look at the play of his muscles as he moved.

His hands went to the buttons of his evening trousers and she gave a squawk of protest. "Do *not* remove your trousers."

He sighed. "My dear Honey, they are soaked. If I take a chill we will never get to London."

She saw the force of this argument—not that she was quite so heartless as to want him healthy only to further her own scheme. He must have been suffering all through dinner, wearing those sodden garments.

Compassion won over modesty. "We must extinguish the lights, then," she said.

With a shrug that clearly stated she made far too much of the whole business of nudity, Davenport did as she asked, turning down lamps and snuffing candles with that schoolboy trick of pinching them out between finger and thumb. They went out with a sizzle and hiss—a sound that seemed to echo in her own body at the thought of him, bare skinned in the same room as she, once more.

At last, there was only the fire to light the chamber.

She turned her back and heard the rustle of fabric. Footsteps, and then another, lengthier bout of shushing of bedclothes.

"There," he said. "I'm all covered up in bed now. Never fear."

She could not help looking. True to his word, he lay under the bedcovers and they were pulled very properly up to his chin. He looked like the wickedest schoolboy she'd ever seen.

As she watched, the gleam in his eyes transformed to something altogether darker, smoky with intent.

"Your turn," he said softly. "I'll shut my eyes." His tone was husky, like the scrape of a boot on gravel.

She narrowed her gaze. "I don't trust you to keep your eyes closed."

"Smart woman," he said. "I wouldn't trust me, either, if I were you."

For some reason, it was an effort to drag her gaze away from his, but she summoned all of her flagging will and managed it.

In fulminating silence, she looked for something she could use as a screen. But of course. The tester bed had curtains. They were made of swathes of muslin, not as sheer as gauze but not opaque, either.

Still, with the lack of light, she didn't think he'd be able to see anything. She drew the curtains all the way around the bed, ignoring his laughing protest.

"My dear Honey, you think of everything, don't you?" He sighed. "I was so looking forward to watching."

"My heart bleeds," she said, swiftly unpinning her bodice.

* * *

Davenport chuckled to himself. What Honey did not know was that with the fire behind her, she was silhouetted quite magnificently against the curtains of the tester bed. He was quite content to lie back against the frilly pillows and watch the show.

She bent and fiddled with her bodice, then reached out to the dressing table. He heard the soft tap of pins dropped into a china dish.

Working more quickly than he liked, she shoved the puffed sleeves of the gown down her arms and pushed the rest of the dress down until she could step out of it.

Carefully, she laid the gown over a chair.

Then the awkward business of the corset. She tried to reach up over her head—slender arms silhouetted like a dancer's against the bed curtains. Davenport felt a distinct twitch in his genitalia at the sight. But the shoulder straps of her corset restricted her movements too much to allow her to reach the ties at the back that way.

A muffled sound of frustration, then her hands dropped and came around behind her from the waist. She'd need to be a contortionist to reach the ties from there.

She even tried pulling her arms out of the straps, then gripping the corset at the top and twisting it around her torso. Davenport's mouth watered at the way her body shimmied and strained.

His mind slid to the way her thumbs hooked inside the corset, brushing her breasts. He imagined putting his own thumbs there, lifting her breasts free from restraint, and his arousal ratcheted up another notch.

Another sound of frustration, an angry little feminine snort.

He waited for her to ask. Waited in the ticking silence. He could almost hear the violent debate that raged in her mind.

In the end, she didn't ask at all.

Apparently giving up the struggle with her stays, she set one foot on the chair and rucked up her petticoat above her thigh, exposing her legs. Beautiful legs they were, if he was any judge—and of course he was. The shadows clearly delineated her delicate hands fumbling at the garter on her thigh, smoothing the stocking down, down, over her knee, down her shapely calf. Then, the other leg.

He all but groaned. He wanted to kiss along the path her hands traveled, down, down, and then up, up, up. His body ached for her and he wondered if he'd ever have such a grand opportunity to act on the promptings of his own sinful desires.

But she had to want him, burn for him, as much as he burned for her.

She put up her arms one more time and chivvied the night rail over her head. So now she wore a night rail, shift, and petticoat. At least she had sense to undo the tapes of the petticoat and let it fall to the floor.

But what a performance! He could not imagine the discomfort of trying to sleep with stays on, but if she wanted to be a martyr, who was he to stop her? Still . . .

He made one last attempt. "There is more than enough room to spare if you wish to sleep in the bed here," he offered. "Truly, you could leave a space between us that a stagecoach could drive through."

"No, thank you." Her voice was clipped, but he heard the note of frustration and smiled.

"Hand me the coverlet, will you?" she said.

He stripped the warm quilt from the bed and leaned out to give it to her. "Can we dispense with the bed curtains now?" he said. "They feel like a shroud."

"Oh, I think we are better off with them where they are." She snatched the coverlet from him and scampered over to the armchair she'd chosen.

"At least move the armchair away from the fire," he said. "You don't want stray sparks alighting on you while you sleep."

She seemed to see the force of this, for before he could offer to haul furniture for her she jumped up and did as he said. Then, she retreated again under the obscuring folds of the quilt and tucked her feet up under her.

"Pillow?" he offered hopefully.

"No, thank you. There is a bolster here that will serve."

They lapsed into silence.

He raised himself on one elbow. "Honey, I cannot help thinking—"

"No."

"But you didn't even hear what—"

"*No!*" She gave an exasperated sigh. "You are just going to come up with one more excuse to get me into that bed and I'm not going to listen."

"Pity," he said, lying back again, putting his hands behind his head. "This ranks among the most comfortable beds I've ever lain in. I daresay I shall sleep like a babe tonight."

"Then I suggest you stop talking and do so."

He smiled at the pettish note in her voice.

"Good night, Honey."

"Good *night*." She said it more as a command than a good wish.

Obediently, Davenport lapsed into silence.

He waited for what seemed like an age to his tired, sore body. Finally, he was rewarded with the soft sound of Honey's deepened breathing.

With panther-like stealth, he slipped out of bed.

CHAPTER TEN

Hilary drifted slowly into consciousness from an exquisite dream. She did not open her eyes immediately but savored the warmth and softness cocooning her. Nestling her head a little farther into the pillow, she gave a gentle murmur of appreciation.

She'd dreamed of a god fighting a stormy battle, shielding her from the tempest with his body, beating back the lightning with his mighty sword. Now, in the quiet calm of breaking dawn, the god cradled her in his arms as they floated together among the clouds.

The arm circling her waist felt strong, powerful, unyielding. The chest against her back was armor plated, solid and hard, but not cold to the touch as she might have expected metal to be. Warm. So very warm . . .

She felt utterly possessed. Protected. Safe.

The god sighed, his breath flowing hot over her ear. With a pleasurable shiver, she nestled back farther into him. She wanted to stay in this dream forever, secure and content.

The god muttered something and nuzzled her, tickling the tiny hairs at her nape. More thrills skittered down her spine.

His palm flexed against her abdomen; then his hand slid upward to close over her . . . her—

Her eyes snapped open. *"Davenport!"*

With a shriek, Hilary exploded from the bed in a flurry of linen and blankets and flailing limbs. The bed curtains tangled her up. She couldn't seem to locate a break in them.

In her haste to get away from the dastard who had taken such gross advantage of her, she tumbled off the mattress, through the bed curtains, and onto the floor.

"Ooph!"

With a confused exclamation, Davenport wrenched the bed curtain aside. "The Devil! Are you hurt?"

She glared up at him, winded and gasping for breath. He knelt on the bed with his hands on his hips, naked as the day he was born.

She wanted to yell at him to cover himself, but she couldn't speak. Her tumble had knocked the breath out of her. All she could do was wheeze and pant.

And stare.

The magnificence of Lord Davenport in daylight was a sight to behold. And to her utter astonishment, his . . . male member seemed to grow larger and more—*oh, Heavens!*— erect, even as she watched.

Her face burned, but she couldn't drag her gaze from the sight of that strange collection of implements between Davenport's legs.

He *was* a god. One of those reprobate deities who came down to earth and ravished unsuspecting maidens in their sl—

Her hands flew to her bosom. "Where is my corset?"

Her gaze sought wildly about the room. Davenport turned, giving her an excellent view of his spectacular hindquarters, and hunted through the bedclothes.

Oh, dear. She actually felt faint.

He came up with the corset and held it out, strings dangling limply. "Here."

Hilary made no move to take it from him. "What happened in that bed last night?"

She wanted quite desperately to check her body, to make sure he had not done anything untoward. More untoward than removing her corset, that was. But she couldn't do it while he watched.

That reminded her that she ought to object to his state of undress.

"Pray, cover yourself, my lord," she said in a stifled voice.

Too late, she looked away. Good Lord, he was having a definite negative effect on her morals. She ought not to have stared at his masculine form like that. But it was so amazingly fascinating to look at, how could she resist?

He sighed. "If we're not to have any fun this morning, I suppose I might as well dress. If you'd be so good as to hand me my garments?"

"Certainly," she managed in a stifled tone.

He'd retreated beneath the bedclothes again when she returned with his clothes, dry now from the fire.

"Nothing at all happened last night," he offered, reaching out for his garments. "Nothing, that is, except that I removed your corset—blindfolded, I do assure you—and deposited you on the bed before I myself went to sleep."

She regarded him with a hostile glare, but inwardly she was vastly relieved. "I told you, I didn't want—"

"Yes, well, you must blame my upbringing," he said, throwing the shirt over his head to cover the chest that had so recently been pressed up against her. "I could not allow a lady to suffer discomfort while I slept in luxury. It wasn't right."

"But this morning, I was . . . You were . . ." She really

ought to finish her sentences. She didn't like the way she was so often at a loss for words when confronted with the outrageous things he did.

Yet, despite any ulterior motives, it had been kind of him to make sure she slept comfortably. She didn't *think* she'd been violated. She'd heard the first time for a maiden was dreadfully painful, and considering the length and thickness of that thing between Davenport's legs, she rather thought they were likely right.

She wasn't sore *down there*. And in her heart of hearts, she knew Davenport wouldn't stoop so low as to molest her while she slept. No fun in that, he'd say.

No, the diabolical man wanted her complete, fully conscious surrender.

But he wouldn't get it.

Still, she was just the tiniest bit disappointed she hadn't been fully awake most of the time he'd been touching her that morning. If she'd had the least presence of mind, she would have pretended to be asleep for longer. . . .

Hilary frowned, annoyed at the tenor of her thoughts. Davenport was corrupting her. The sooner she parted ways with him, the better for her virtue and her peace of mind.

Her gaze slid to his hands as he tied his cravat before the mirror. She thought about where one of those hands had been only minutes before, watched with some fascination as he deftly manipulated the cloth into the semblance of a fashionable style.

It was a black cravat, no doubt one of Mr. Potter's finest. Somehow, the black neck cloth seemed more in keeping with Davenport's general air of disreputableness. He hadn't shaven in two days (at least), and while his bruises were fading, they were still clearly discernible, even beneath the two-day stubble that shadowed his jaw.

He looked like a highwayman or a pirate. Not that she'd

ever seen either species of male in the flesh. But there was a swashbuckling arrogance to him that grew more pronounced the more disheveled his appearance became.

He did not look like a man who had lain beside a female all night and innocently kept his hands to himself.

That was when she decided she didn't actually want to know more about what he'd done to her, if anything.

He'd been looking at her intently while she lost herself in unfinished sentences. "Honey, there is no need for outrage over a bit of innocent fondling. A man cannot help what he does in his sleep, you know."

She bristled. "I daresay you thought I was someone else."

"Quite likely," was his cool response. "You did not seem to mind. Not at first, anyway."

"That's because I thought you were—" She clamped her mouth shut. She couldn't possibly tell him she'd dreamed him into a god. That would give him an altogether too puffed-up sense of his own importance.

"Never mind," she muttered.

He stared at her, eyes gleaming with speculation. "Interesting."

To head off any more questions at the pass, she reverted to her schoolteacher manner and sent Davenport downstairs to fetch their hostess. She needed help with the dratted corset.

Davenport did not even open his mouth to tease her or offer to play lady's maid.

She wondered why she felt an odd sense of disappointment at his forbearance.

* * *

By the time they reached the hallowed streets of Mayfair at a little after ten o'clock that evening, Honey was sagging where once she had sat bolt upright and prim. Davenport was tempted to encourage her head to rest upon his shoulder, but they were almost there, after all, and he was fatigued, too, and amorous stratagems could wait.

They had slept much later than Honey could have wished in that pink, frilly bedchamber at Mrs. Potter's cottage. Then it had taken the better part of the day to arrange for the horse to be re-shod, after discovering it had cast a shoe during the confusion of the storm.

Despite the day's frustrations and sundry other unavoidable delays, he'd managed to be true to his word and Honey had not been obliged to spend yet another night on the road in his company.

Despite the significant amount of time she'd had to devise one, she had not come up with a plausible explanation for her journey to London alone, in the company of the devilish Lord Davenport.

Finally, she agreed to tell Rosamund an expurgated version of the truth. Rosamund was bound to understand and take pity on the poor female who'd been forced to endure so many undeserved misfortunes—not least of which was having to deal with him for the past two days.

Davenport looked forward to a quiet evening getting Honey settled at Tregarth House, before bathing and changing his clothes. His coat was dusty from the road, his shoes muddied, and his borrowed cravat limp. After tonight, he never wanted to wear evening dress again.

But he was doomed to disappointment. Upon reaching Rosamund's London home, Davenport was obliged to jockey for position with a press of other conveyances.

Honey blinked sleepily. "Are we there?"

"We will be, if I can just—" He shot the gig toward a gap in the traffic, scraping the wheels of a barouche going the other way.

A coachman shook his fist and yelled abuse after them,

but Davenport ignored him. He maneuvered the smaller vehicle, weaving in and out until he finally pulled up outside Tregarth House.

Lights blazed, both inside and out. Footmen lined the pavement, ready to assist guests up the stairs. Linkboys loitered, their torches at the ready, while they traded insults with coachmen and burly bearers of sedan chairs. A thick, roiling stream of guests in feathers and silks, black coats and pristine dove-gray pantaloons flowed into his cousin's house.

"Well," said Davenport. "This is unexpected."

* * *

Fatigue threatened to crush Hilary. Her bones were shattered by the constant jogging of the horse and the motion of the badly sprung gig. Her head pounded and felt strangely light at the same time. They hadn't eaten since breakfast. She'd refused to let Davenport stop for sustenance because she couldn't bear the thought of staying another night with him somewhere on the road.

And they'd made it. They'd reached their destination.

For some moments, she did not quite comprehend the noise and bother. Drowsing by Davenport's side, she'd half-hoped that once they reached Tregarth House her hosts would be from home. All she wanted—longed for—was a simple supper and a wash and a nice, soft bed to sleep in. Alone.

That would not be possible, of course. The forthcoming confrontation was perhaps the most important of her life. If only she could persuade Griffin deVere, Earl of Tregarth, to champion her cause with her guardian, she might enjoy the season she so desperately craved. And if she might also coax Lady Tregarth to sponsor her, she'd have her wish come true.

But—

"A ball?" She shot upright and turned an accusing gaze on Davenport. "Your cousin is holding a ball tonight and you did not remember?"

He shrugged. "Slipped my mind, what with all the drugging and kidnapping and ceilings falling in."

There was a touch of asperity in his tone. Far from chastening her, his clipped answer touched her on the raw. "Only think how we must appear," she said. "How are we going to get in there without anyone seeing us?"

He looked down his nose at her, and now she saw the Westruther in him, the inbred arrogance that did not give a fig for anyone else's opinion.

"Why, through the front door, of course, like everyone else."

But Hilary's wild survey of the grand terrace house had borne fruit. "The area steps. We'll go down through the kitchens."

"That we certainly shall not." He bent a severe gaze on her. "You need to stop bowing and scraping and scuttling around like a brown mouse, hoping no one notices you. You are not a servant."

"But look at me," she cried. "Any self-respecting servant would rather die than appear like this. Besides, I'm not dressed for a *ball*."

He gave her person a cursory inspection. "You look perfectly proper to me. And of course you're not dressed for a ball, but—"

"You promised no one but your cousin would know you'd escorted me to London without chaperonage," she hissed. "You promised my arrival would be inconspicuous."

She clutched her reticule and swung her legs to the side. "I'm getting down here."

They were still some distance from the front door.

"You will not," said Davenport calmly. "You'll wait until I've handed the reins to a footman and you will enter through the front door with me. Damn it, if I can carry off a bruised phiz and an evening rig I've worn for the past two days you can carry off a neat little traveling costume, even if it does belong to Mrs. Potter's Daisy."

But the last sentence was spoken to her back as she nimbly hopped down from the gig.

"Honey!" Davenport called after her, in a warning tone.

She ignored him and stepped her way through the carriage wheels, horses, and piles of manure to the pavement, making a beeline for the area steps.

The kitchens were a maelstrom of activity, in the center of which dwelled a temperamental Frenchman, the very cliché of continental chefs. He had a haughty air and pinched nostrils and a habit of abusing everyone who came within a three-foot radius of his person in a torrent of idiomatic French.

Hilary had no idea what to do, now that she'd breached the castle walls, so to speak.

Would Davenport come to find her? Or would he wash his hands of her, disgusted with her lack of backbone?

It was typical of an aristocratic male like Davenport that he wouldn't consider other people's opinions. He could do anything, the more outrageous the better, and still people would clamor for his notice. He was a belted earl with prosperous estates at his command, after all. He had no idea what it was like to be a poor dab of a female with no style or connections, and to be a deVere on top of that.

There was little time to be resentful or to stand about wondering where she ought to wait for him. A bustling cook maid thrust an apron into her hand.

"From the agency are you?" she said briskly. "You're late. Not but what we can do with every pair o' hands we can get down here."

Before Hilary could protest or explain herself, she was holding a paring knife and a potato and adjured to peel that lot quick smart or Monsieur would have her head.

With only the smallest sigh, Hilary set to work.

CHAPTER ELEVEN

Davenport was accustomed to startled looks and speculative stares wherever he went. Coming back from the dead seemed to have that effect on people, so he didn't pay too much heed to the crowd's reaction as he moved inexorably toward his goal.

He resisted the urge to bark at them to take themselves off out of his way. Instead, he smiled his devil-may-care smile. That, together with his raffish appearance, did much the same job.

He fought a path to the top of the stairs and entered the ballroom, where the butler gave him a slightly harried look when he refused to be announced. "Need to speak with her ladyship. Won't be a moment," he said as he sighted his quarry.

Rosamund, blond, exquisite, and heavy with child, stood in the receiving line, looking radiant. Her husband was nowhere to be seen, but her former guardian, the Duke of Montford, was by her side. With him, Lady Arden, matchmaker extraordinaire, smiled graciously on the guests.

"*Jonathon!* I'd no notion you'd be here tonight." Rosamund's deep blue eyes showed first delighted surprise, then doubt as she absorbed his appearance. "But what happened to you?"

He clasped her outstretched hands in his and said in a low, urgent tone, "I need to speak with you, Rosie. When can you get free?"

Consternation sketched across her porcelain features. "As you can see, I am somewhat in the middle of things, but . . . I know. Why don't you lead me out for the first waltz?"

He grimaced. Waltzing. His idea of a hot bath, a brandy (or three), and bed seemed to recede farther into the distance.

"In the meantime, go up and ask Dearlove to see to your clothes," Rosamund said in a lowered tone as more guests approached. "You look disgraceful, even for you, my dear."

She nodded and smiled her society smile in firm dismissal and he was forced to move on to the head of the Westruther family, the Duke of Montford.

"Your Grace." Davenport made an elegant, deeply respectful bow, allowing only the expression in his eyes to mock the courtesy. Montford had become his sister Cecily's guardian when Davenport had been thought dead.

Unlike his Westruther cousins, Davenport had never been obliged to submit to the duke's rule. That did not mean, however, that the duke refrained from meddling in Davenport's affairs.

Montford had not been a party to that kidnapping the other evening, though. Of that Davenport was almost certain. The episode lacked a certain finesse that characterized the duke's dealings. Besides, Xavier, Marquis of Steyne, would boil himself in oil before he'd do the duke's bidding.

His Grace smiled his thin smile. "Davenport, you have outdone yourself tonight, I think."

The suave comment was not meant as a compliment and Davenport didn't take it as such. "This time, it was not my doing. Ask Steyne if you don't believe me."

The duke's brows drew together. "It seems we must talk, you and I," said His Grace.

Ah. So Davenport's surmise had been correct. Montford didn't know of the kidnapping scheme. It occurred to Davenport that in the duke he might have a powerful ally in engineering Honey's successful debut, so he murmured assent and moved on.

"Lady Arden, a pleasure," murmured Davenport, bowing over her extended hand.

"I wish I could say the same," said Lady Arden, her brilliant gaze inspecting him from head to toe.

The lady was a beauty, but in the vein of Athena, rather than Aphrodite. Chiseled cheekbones and chestnut hair, a generous bosom and a queenly stature. She was generally thought to be the duke's mistress, though if that was the case, they were both preternaturally discreet.

The two of them were renowned for making brilliant matches, strategic alliances between their respective families and other highborn young ladies and gentlemen. In her way, Lady Arden was every bit as ruthless as the duke. A woman not to be underestimated. A woman who might also be useful to Honey, should the need arise.

Davenport was not ordinarily one for the proprieties, but he knew better than to introduce the subject of Honey with either the duke or Lady Arden in the midst of a receiving line at a ball. Besides, he needed to get Rosamund on side first.

Lady Arden tapped him with her fan. "Yarmouth is here tonight with his rapacious daughter in tow. Watch yourself, Davenport, or you will end in the briars. I hear he has plans for you."

"If he does, they are destined to remain unfulfilled,"

said Davenport. He'd almost forgotten about Lady Maria and her ambitious papa. He'd been hot for the girl, hot enough to overlook certain deficiencies in her character. Now he wondered at himself.

Lady Arden waved her fan languidly to and fro. "If you'll take my advice, you'd best make yourself scarce for a month or so, until she gets her greedy little talons stuck in some other poor man. But then," she said, almost to herself, "when have you ever taken good advice?"

He didn't believe in discussing any lady he'd been intimate with, so he managed to extricate himself from that conversation without comment. Still, how was it that Lady Arden had seen through the girl's ploy when he himself had only twigged to it the night before his kidnap? A shrewd judge of character, Lady Arden.

A wise one, too. But he couldn't take her well-meaning advice. He had to see Honey succeed with the ton.

With the aim of keeping in his cousin's good books, he dutifully went upstairs to get Tregarth's magician of a valet to see what he might do with his evening raiment.

He did pause to wonder what had become of Honey below stairs but decided to leave her to fend for herself for a while. If she insisted on shrinking into the background, there was no way she'd survive a London season. That was a lesson she needed to learn on her own.

Presumably, Honey wished to marry. Consigning oneself to wallflower status from the beginning was not the way to attract an eligible husband.

The notion of her finding a husband made him a trifle . . . *something;* he didn't know what.

Hardly surprising, he supposed, that the idea of Honey courting another man should displease him. He might not be the most devoted fellow on the planet, but once he fixed his interest on one woman, he didn't cheat. The idea of the reverse happening to him was not a palatable one.

Ah, well. Best not to jump that fence until he came to it.

He paused outside the dressing-room belonging to Griffin deVere, now Lord Tregarth. A yell of pure rage burst from within.

Wincing, Davenport knocked.

Tregarth's voice growled, "I'm *coming,* damn it."

The door opened, and a neat gentleman's gentleman peered out. "Lord Davenport."

The valet's black eyes traveled quickly over Davenport's person. He pursed his lips.

"Dearlove, I need you," said Davenport, spreading his arms wide. "As you can see. But it seems you are otherwise occupied."

"Davenport, is that you?" barked Tregarth. "Let him in."

That order was succeeded by another series of oaths.

"Your ball is going on without you," remarked Davenport, strolling in to observe his cousin Rosamund's husband standing at the looking glass, wrestling with his cravat.

"I . . . *will* . . . get this . . . right." Tregarth spoke between his teeth, lips drawn back in a feral grimace.

He was a huge man, no taller than Davenport but bulkier. Hairier, too. Tregarth's big hands fumbled with the recalcitrant neck cloth until he gave a disgusted snort and threw it down on the knee-high pile of crumpled linen beside his feet.

"Well, be quick about it, there, Tregarth," said Davenport. "I need Dearlove and I don't want to loll about here all evening watching you fume over your neckwear."

"You may take him and all his works to Hell with you," said Tregarth, snatching another neck cloth from the pile at his elbow. "I'll get this bloody noose around my neck if it kills me," he muttered, as he tied the first knot.

"If I may be of assistance, my lord," murmured the little valet to Davenport.

"Seems you have your work cut out," said Davenport, cocking an eyebrow in Tregarth's direction.

A gleam in the man's eye was all the answer he made to that comment.

"A new suit of clothes." Dearlove tapped his lips, surveying Davenport with close attention. "Evening pumps, linen, stockings. Obviously I have nothing in your size, my lord, or the task should be of the moment. However, if you care to take some brandy and remain at your ease a quarter of an hour or so, I shall endeavor."

He grinned. "That, Dearlove, is music to my ears."

"Very good, my lord."

An oath, louder than the rest, punctuated Dearlove's departure. Another cravat went by the way of its fellows.

"I can see why you keep brandy in your dressing room," commented Davenport as he poured himself a glass. "Having you as master would drive any valet to drink."

Tregarth growled. "He won't leave me. Says I'm an interesting challenge, if you please."

"I must say, he does an excellent job of keeping you in trim. Why won't you let him tie your cravat for you?"

"Because this time, I decided to do for myself. I've watched him wrangle the thing on countless occasions. But his damned finicky fingers are so quick. And mine . . ." Tregarth held up hands the size of hams with big, thick digits. "Ah, what's the use?"

"Pretend it's a woman," suggested Davenport. "Be gentle with it. Caress it into beautiful compliance."

Then he realized Tregarth only touched one woman like this: Cousin Rosamund, and fell silent.

There was an awkward pause.

Reddening slightly, Tregarth said, "Now you've done it." He sighed. "Suppose I'll have to wait for Dearlove."

He stomped over and poured himself a drink. "What are you doing back so soon?"

Davenport quirked an eyebrow. "So you heard about Steyne's plot, did you?"

He ought to have guessed. Tregarth and Davenport's cousin Lydgate were as thick as thieves. Obviously Lydgate had not known about the drugging part. That was all Steyne's doing. But Lydgate had gone along with it once the deed was done.

Davenport grimaced. He'd punished Lydgate with his fists, and Beckenham, too. But Steyne required more subtle handling.

There would be a reckoning between them, however, and soon.

Tregarth nodded. "Told Lydgate to mind his own business. That's the trouble with the Westruthers. So damned toplofty, they can't stand to see their name besmirched."

His eyes met Davenport's over the rim of his glass. "What brings you here tonight, looking like that?"

"Just got back from my rustication," said Davenport.

Tregarth grunted. "Shortest rustication in history."

Davenport tilted his head in acknowledgment. "Brief though it was, my stay was thoroughly delightful. I did not get as far as Davenport, however. The journey took an interesting turn."

"You mean you beat the living daylights out of Beckenham and Lydgate, and they dumped you in a barn to fend for yourself."

"As you see, I bore the brunt of their ire, too," said Davenport, passing a hand over his jaw.

He felt stubble. "I'll get your man to shave me while I'm here."

"Why bother? You look like a pirate. Ladies love that

sort of thing. Or so I'm told," added Tregarth hastily, reddening again.

Hmm. Another place his mind refused to dwell, given Tregarth's marriage to Rosamund.

"Be that as it may," Davenport said, "I met a young lady in my travels."

"Pretty?"

Davenport frowned. "What has that to say to anything?"

"A great deal, I imagine."

"All right, very pretty. Exceedingly so. She's a relative of yours. A Miss Hilary deVere."

He'd discovered her name by questioning Trixie. He wouldn't tell Honey that, however, and spoil the fun of annoying her with his pet name.

Tregarth looked blank.

"Sister to Benedict and Tom deVere. They have a rundown property in Lincolnshire, near Stamford. You must know them."

The big man's brow lowered. "Pair of wastrels, and I daresay their sister is no better."

"But she is," insisted Davenport. "And she's here. I've brought her to stay with you."

"You've *what*? Are you out of your mind? I don't want any blasted deVere female in my house—"

Davenport held up a hand to stop him. "If you say anything that might lead me to plant you a facer, I shall break my hand, and I've got too great a sense of self-preservation to start a fight with you, in any case. Forget about the stable she comes from. This girl is as virtuous and pure as the driven snow. Which is why I had to take her away from that place."

Seriously, he said, "She is your kin, deVere. She needs your help."

"I won't have her," blustered Tregarth. "Rosamund is in a delicate situation. I won't have anyone upsetting her."

"So delicate, in fact, that she is downstairs as we speak, playing hostess to four hundred guests and in the pink of health, too. Look," said Davenport. "I'm as fond of Rosamund as I could be. Do you think I'd bring trouble on her head?"

"You're besotted," ranted Tregarth. "Deceived. All the deVere women are the same. Trouble, with a capital *T*."

"Just as all deVere *men* are the same, I suppose," Davenport said smoothly, keeping a rein on his temper, but only just. "Uncouth brutes full of low cunning but without any of the finer feelings. Including compassion for a defenseless female, it seems."

Tregarth sent him a blazing glare. "If she is virtuous and defenseless and all you claim, what are *you* doing with her?"

Trying his best to free Miss deVere from that very same virtue, was the answer.

An answer Davenport could not give. The need to possess Honey in the physical sense operated on a different level from the need to make sure she received her due: a London season. Right now, he focused on winning Tregarth's approval of his scheme to the exclusion of all else.

Without a blink, he said, "I saved her from intolerable circumstances in her brother's house. She had nowhere to go, so I brought her here. If you turn her away, she will be obliged to try to earn her keep. I daresay you know what that would mean."

"Take her as your mistress," recommended Tregarth. "That's the best you can do to help her."

"Ruin her, you mean." Fury surged through Davenport at such callousness. The very idea of turning his Honey into a woman who had no choice but to move from one protector to the next was unthinkable.

A discreet and altogether delightful affair was one thing. Openly taking Honey as mistress was quite another.

He felt a twinge of dissatisfaction with that reasoning, but he didn't pause to examine it too closely.

"Please," he said to Tregarth. "Just meet her. As soon as you lay eyes on the girl, you'll see what I mean."

Tregarth threw up his hands. "Aye, I'll meet her. But I can tell you right now, my answer will be no. And if you upset my wife over this, I will cut out your liver and feed it to the dogs."

CHAPTER TWELVE

When Davenport went downstairs again, he was freshly washed, shaven, groomed, and dressed to the hilt in his own evening clothes, which Dearlove had procured with lightning speed from his town house a short distance away.

Davenport went in search of Honey, confident that she would have found somewhere below stairs to remain until he could fetch her again. He hoped she'd be a mite chastened by the time she'd spent there. He was still irritated with her for scuttling off in that craven fashion.

He found her, not cowering in a corner waiting for him as he'd expected but in the kitchens, of all places. Holding a rolling pin in one hand and gesturing emphatically toward the hearth with the other, she was at the hub of activity like a queen bee in her hive. Indeed, she had several drones running to do her bidding. Even the temperamental French chef seemed to treat her with flattering deference.

There was a smut of flour on her nose, and wasn't that just adorable?

How had she managed it? He stood there, watching her, until he realized the room had fallen silent, and that everyone in it was watching him.

"Ah. There you are, Miss deVere," he said.

Her gaze snapped to him. She dropped the rolling pin with a noisy clatter.

Someone opened the lid of a mighty cauldron and steam billowed around him. But he didn't need the steam to feel a sudden, unmistakable heat. All she had to do was meet his gaze to make his insides sizzle.

Damn it, not now. He needed to set aside his lust for ten minutes and have a sensible conversation with the girl.

As her gaze took him in, a series of expressions flitted across her face. They resolved into a fierce glare.

"Excuse me," she said to him, her lips thinning dangerously. "The staff are shorthanded, and I must—"

"Certainly, you must not," said Davenport. He pointed at the chef. "You. Send to Davenport House for more staff if you need them. I cannot imagine what you are about not to have solved the problem earlier."

The butler arrived on the scene then and spoke up. "Indeed, my lord, it will be attended to, I assure you. An accident to one of the cook maids had only just occurred when Miss deVere walked in or we'd never have accepted her assistance."

"Do not blame them," said Honey. "I gave them no choice but to allow me to help."

"I am not blaming them," said Davenport. He knew precisely who was responsible for this state of affairs. He knew also that servants weren't likely to respect Honey for her generosity.

Honey's chin jutted in mulish determination, but even she would not argue with him in front of the staff in a strange house.

"If you please, Miss deVere," said Davenport, bowing. He did not wait to see whether she followed him but turned to lead her from the kitchens.

At the foot of the stairs, he took her elbow and hustled

her into a deserted corner. "Just what did you think you were doing, mucking in with the servants like that?" he demanded.

"Take your hands off me," she hissed. "You'll soil your beautiful white gloves."

* * *

Hilary stared doggedly up at Davenport, unable to keep the shrewish note from her voice.

"What?" The big, stupid oaf had the gall to knit his brows in a puzzled and slightly hurt expression.

Oh, she could have snatched up the nearest carving knife and stabbed him through his oh-so-elegant coat! How dare he leave her to fend for herself in this place while he went and dressed and groomed himself with an elegance that would rival Beau Brummell in his prime?

When she'd first laid eyes on him, lounging in the doorway to the kitchen, she'd thought him a dream come to life.

Then steam had billowed around him, like the clouds in heaven—or rather, the heat from another place entirely. He looked like a dark angel from the underworld, come to steal her away to his torrid lair.

Then, it hit her. He'd left her to grub about in the kitchens while he had turned himself into a confounded fashion plate.

"No doubt you are to attend the ball, my lord," she said with a slight curtsy. "Do not let me detain you."

She'd simply curl up in a corner with the spiders and die.

"Don't be such a little fool." He grimaced. "Do you think I want to go to the deuced ball? Rosamund won't talk to me unless I do. I have to get her approval to the scheme, because I can tell you Tregarth is adamant he won't have you."

Though she'd half-expected to be turned away, the blow was severe.

"Oh." She swallowed. "Well, then, I . . ."

Utterly at a loss, she passed a floury hand over her eyes. It wasn't as if she'd placed her faith in Davenport, for goodness' sake. Was it? Surely she'd not been fool enough to trust *him* to carry this off.

And yet she had.

The horrid sensation of being cast adrift in a huge city where she knew absolutely no one threatened to engulf her.

"I ought to look for somewhere else to sleep tonight, but . . ."

Good God, she'd not thought beyond her arrival, had she? What sort of idiot would not have foreseen this possibility, planned for it?

No, she'd been too desperate to escape from her brothers' house. And far too trusting of this most untrustworthy scoundrel.

"My dear Honey, do try not to talk nonsense," said Davenport. "I am togged up like this so I can dance the waltz with my cousin and convince her to let you stay. She is the softest touch imaginable *and* she can make Tregarth do whatever she wants. You will not have to go anywhere else tonight; you'll see."

He smiled down at her, and her heart gave a hard, slow flip.

She wished with all of her being that she could match him for ease and confidence. Most of all, she wished that she could wear a beautiful gown and glide into that ball on his arm. See him regard her with admiration—awe, even—instead of amused tolerance, as he did now.

If only she could make Lady Tregarth like her. If only she could persuade her guardian to part with some of the interest on her capital so that she might fund her debut.

She was in London, but that wouldn't do her much good if Lord deVere exercised his powers as guardian and shipped her back to the Grange. Her brothers might well be scouring London for her by morning.

"Are you sure you'll be able to convince Lady Tregarth to have me?" she said.

His teeth gleamed as the smile turned to a devilish grin. "My dear, any woman who waltzes with me is putty in my arms."

She snorted.

"So sure am I, in fact," he added, ignoring the interjection, "that I am now going to put you in the hands of the housekeeper. She'll find a chamber for you and make you comfortable while I work my wiles on my cousin."

When they emerged into better light, she noticed that his stubble was gone and that the bruising on his face now contrasted starkly with his bare, unmarked skin. His hair was brushed in gleaming dark waves but not puffed up and pomaded like many gentlemen's coiffures. She liked that it still appeared natural, if tidier than she'd seen it hitherto.

Oh, but she was glad he hadn't looked like this when she'd first met him. She would have been too shy to fight with him or even speak to him, come to that.

Now she said, "You will tell Lady Tregarth what we agreed upon, won't you? No outrageous falsehoods or, or—"

"Never fret, my dear. I have this under control."

He bent to kiss her forehead, as he would to a child. "Sleep well. We shall face them together in the morning. Tonight, you must get some rest."

She felt unaccountably irritated with this benign, paternal dismissal. But she went with the kindly housekeeper, who did not turn a hair at being ordered to prepare a suitable bedchamber for an unexpected guest in the middle of a ball.

In fact, Mrs. Faithful seemed to accept Hilary's kinship with the master as reason enough to welcome her. If only she knew.

"This suite belonged to the master's sister, Lady Jacqueline," said the housekeeper, showing her in. "Married now, and living in the country."

The chamber was elegantly appointed and furnished with excellent taste. Hilary blinked, unable to imagine any deVere living in such exquisite luxury.

"It is beautiful," she breathed.

"The mistress refurbished the entire house when she married the master," said the housekeeper. "Lady Jacqueline is not one for frills and furbelows, as you might know. The fights they had, those two! But the mistress won her way in the end, and Lady Jacqueline loved the chamber in spite of herself."

How could she not have loved it? thought Hilary. Every square inch?

Hilary wanted to lie on the thick carpet and make snow angels in the deep, luscious pile. She wanted to throw herself into the tester bed and sink and sink into the plump mattress. She wanted to swathe herself in the apple green curtains and waltz.

Not a speck of dust clung to any surface. Not a rent or a moth hole could be seen. No spiderweb of cracks crazed the intricately plastered ceiling.

Hilary felt as if she'd died and gone to Heaven.

And she resolved, then and there, that whatever she had to do to stay in this house, she would do it. Even if that meant bargaining with the Devil himself.

* * *

As luck would have it, Davenport returned to the ball-room just in time to claim his dance.

Rosamund's blue eyes shot sparks. "I thought you were going to leave me without a partner," she said. "What have you been about, all this time, hmm? Some flighty matron took your fancy, I daresay."

"Not a bit of it," said Davenport. "And if marriage has turned you into a naggy shrew, Rosie, then I wish you were still a maid. Without a partner, indeed." He frowned down at her shattering beauty. "I'd wager you've never sat out a dance in your life."

He thought of Honey and vowed to ensure she didn't suffer the fate of a wallflower, either. But he had to see that there was a season and a ball to attend, before he worried about who would dance with her.

"That does *not* excuse your tardiness," said Rosamund.

He eyed her severely, and a dimple peeked out beside her mouth. "Oh, do forgive me." She sighed. "I *am* being a shrew. It's just that I am so tired and out of sorts tonight. I cannot imagine why I thought it was a good idea to hold a ball when I look and feel like one of Mr. Simpkins's hot-air balloons. Only not so light on my feet."

He swept her into a turn and smiled down at her. "You are feeling cross and unappreciated. I know precisely how that might be remedied."

He leaned down and whispered in her ear. She gurgled a laugh and somehow managed to rap his wrist with her fan while never missing a step. "Flatterer!"

But he had put her in a better frame of mind with his outrageous and inappropriate remarks; he could see that. She beamed up at him, and he wondered why the laughter of a dazzling diamond such as Rosamund should have so little effect on him. When the rare smile of a certain other young lady twisted his guts in a disconcerting and unfamiliar way.

He didn't dwell on the matter but let Rosamund turn the conversation in the direction he wished it to go.

"Griffin tells me you have a favor to ask," she said bluntly.

"Did he? Is that all he told you?"

She rolled her eyes. "No, of course he told me everything. You know he can never keep anything from me when I'm determined to get it out of him. Where is she? And how on earth did you come to be responsible for her?"

"She is, at present, upstairs in bed," he answered, choosing the easiest question to answer first. "As for the rest, I met her by chance, rescued her from a storm, and escorted her home. Her name's Miss Hilary deVere. Some sort of relation of Griffin's, you know."

"Yes, so he said. But that doesn't precisely recommend her, as you are very well aware." Rosamund pursed her lips. "The deVeres are at best ramshackle, and at worst . . . Well, it is improper of me to speak thus of my husband's family, but I daresay you know."

"I know. But she's different."

Rosamund regarded him doubtfully. "Griffin said she was likely your fancy-piece. *Is* she your fancy-piece, Jonathon? For if you dared bring such a creature to me—"

Annoyed, Davenport frowned down at her. "Is it likely I'd do such a thing?"

"That's just the problem," said Rosamund. "The old Jonathon wouldn't have dreamed of it. The man you are now . . ."

The trouble in her expression caught him off guard. Hell, he might be a scoundrel in any number of ways, but he'd never even contemplated corrupting the innocence of his female cousins.

"Well, dismiss the idea, Rosie. Not only would it be vulgar to bring my mistress to your house, but why would

I? If she were my fancy-piece, as you call her, I'd set her up, snug as you please, in a little house in Kensington. No need to find a respectable female to chaperone her for the season."

Her face froze. "The *season*? Are you mad?"

Really, this was coming out all wrong. He hadn't much experience of asking favors of anyone. He'd always been self-sufficient to a fault. Then, too, he'd been alone for far too many years.

Uneasily he said, "Perhaps this wasn't the best time to mention the subject."

"I should think not," said Rosamund with unwonted asperity. "You've gone and gotten yourself into a scrape, haven't you, Jonathon?"

"I'm not a grubby schoolboy, you know."

"You could have fooled me," Rosamund muttered. "And what Cecily will say to this I dread to think."

His dear sister would have plenty to say, he was sure. He knew Rosamund wouldn't keep this to herself. He only hoped he might avoid a scold from Cecily while at the ball.

"I'll explain everything to you tomorrow, when you've recovered from this evening," he promised. "Please, let her stay tonight. You can throw her out tomorrow if that's your inclination once you've met her, but I assure you, it won't be."

"She is so very different from the rest of her kin, then?" said Rosamund skeptically.

Davenport smiled. "She is a sweetheart. You'll see."

* * *

As soon as the waltz ended, Davenport tried to make good his escape from the ballroom, but a shift in the crowd brought him face-to-face with Cecily, who was talking with her husband, the Duke of Ashburn, and another couple. The second man of the party was young, auburn haired, with a nervous air, as if he was poised on the brink of running from the ballroom. The unknown lady was clearly his sister, with similar coloring and an equally nervous demeanor.

"By all that's wonderful," said Davenport. "Gerry Mason! What are you doing down from Cambridge?"

He leaned forward to shake his old friend's hand and clap him on the shoulder.

Too late, he remembered. The slight stiffening of the usually pleasant fellow's face, the perceptible pause before his hand gripped Davenport's, told him that Gerald hadn't forgotten anything.

Davenport made himself give an unconcerned grin. "Thought you never did the season, old fellow. Isn't your microscope missing you?"

If Gerry were more socially adept he might have cut Davenport, but then again, he'd be a brave man to try it while Cecily and Ashburn formed part of the group.

Mason flushed and seemed about to stammer an answer, but Cecily threw herself into the breach. "Why, Mr. Mason is being a good brother, escorting Miss Mason about town for the season, are you not?" With a smile, she turned to Gerry's companion. "Miss Mason, may I present my brother, the Earl of Davenport? I don't think you've met."

The lady was so timid she barely squeaked a greeting before falling silent, with a scared look at her brother from her big blue eyes.

Ordinarily, Davenport wouldn't have spared another thought for Miss Mason, but with Honey's debut in the forefront of his mind he felt a twinge of sympathy for the awkward girl. She was all gangling limbs and freckles. Painfully shy, too.

Before he could check them, the words were out of his mouth. "Would you care to dance the next set, Miss Mason?"

Without allowing the lady herself to answer, Gerald cut in. "I should think not, Davenport."

Very slowly, Davenport turned his head to look at Gerald.

The man swallowed hard, but he stood his ground. Brave of him.

With an unconcerned laugh, Cecily said, "I'm sure I can find you a better partner than my dull old brother, Miss Mason. Come with me and we'll see who might be interesting."

With a minatory look at Davenport that sent a silent command to behave himself, she led Miss Mason away, leaving him with Ashburn and Gerald.

Cecily needn't have worried. Davenport's anger was directed at himself, not Gerald. For a few moments, he'd forgotten he was considered to be a libertine and a rotter. He was the kind of fellow a gentleman like Gerald wouldn't let breathe the same pure air as his virginal sister. Who could blame him? Certainly not Davenport.

Yet, when he'd seen Gerald, the years had slid back. He'd been at Cambridge again and the world was an endlessly intricate puzzle he'd set out to solve. But he couldn't return to the innocence of those days. He ought to thank his old cohort for the reminder.

Ashburn, smoothly debonair as usual, engaged Gerald in a conversation about the younger man's latest attempts to isolate the active ingredient in the Cinchona tree to help treat malaria. While Davenport had often staged theatrical experiments at the Royal Institution and routinely set fire to things, Gerald quietly went about finding ways to save people's lives.

Commercially minded as usual, Ashburn was urging

Gerald to patent his discoveries, but Gerald was adamant that his research should be available to all.

"At the least, you must be quicker to publish your findings," said Ashburn, his sleek black brows drawing together. "Those damned Frenchmen keep taking all the credit."

Gerald shrugged. "I don't set much store by such things. The race to publication has never interested me."

"The Institution would view you more seriously if you did take an interest in it," said Ashburn.

Gerald's gaze darkened. "The Royal Institution lauds all kinds of charlatans."

Ashburn glanced at Davenport. "Quite so."

Unreasonable to feel a gut-clenching sense of betrayal at Ashburn's agreement. Well, what could he expect, after all?

"Good evening, gentlemen." From behind him, a silvery feminine voice broke like the chiming of bells into their very masculine group.

A lady with glossy jet-black hair and bright blue eyes approached them on her father's arm.

She was a vision of loveliness, from the tasteful diadem in her elegant coiffure to her satin dancing slippers. Her bosom was generous for such a slender woman, her height on the tall side, her bearing regal.

There was a cold fire in her eyes when her gaze rested on him. She'd taken their parting badly, but she was too well-bred to make a scene. Still, the night was young.

Damn. He'd meant to escape the ballroom before he encountered her again. Too late. And not only Lady Maria but her urbanely smiling papa as well. It never rained but it poured.

Davenport said, "Lady Maria. Lord Yarmouth. You know the Duke of Ashburn, I believe."

Ashburn bowed.

"And Mr. Mason."

"Yes, yes, of course," said Yarmouth in his silkiest voice. "We've known Gerald forever, haven't we, my love?"

Yarmouth was a large man with a balding egg-shaped head. What was left of his hair was black as his daughter's. The man always smiled, even when humiliating his pupils for some error or transgression.

It had been Yarmouth's passion for chemistry that had originally infected Davenport. Gerald, too, had been a protégé of Yarmouth's at one time.

Lady Maria's cheeks pinked as she greeted Davenport's companions. She hadn't taken her attention from Davenport for an instant. He found her steady regard unnerving. She looked like a cat deciding how it would play with a mouse before the kill.

Which was ridiculous, of course.

"Lady Maria." Gerald's voice had the bite of a whiplash as he snapped out a bow.

Her gaze flickered to him and back to Davenport. The flush on her cheeks deepened. She lifted her chin, as if in challenge.

She ought to know better than to think such tricks could reanimate Davenport's regard. He couldn't summon so much as a spark of interest.

The musicians struck up in the preliminary strains of a lively country dance.

"Ah," said Lady Maria. "The set is about to form."

Her wide blue eyes with their thick, sooty lashes took on an expectant gleam, and he knew that any gentleman worth his salt would pick up this cue.

Clearly, he wasn't worth his salt, or any other form of seasoning, come to that. Dancing with the chit would only fuel her father's ambitions and give credence to whatever amorphous rumors had gathered about London's famous scoundrel and the virtuous Lady Maria Shand.

Stubbornly Davenport remained silent until Lady Maria was forced to include the other gentlemen in her faint smile.

Ashburn had developed an alarmingly keen interest in polishing his quizzing glass with his handkerchief. Rightly so. Cecily would skin him if she saw him dancing with the enemy.

Gerald reddened and took a jerky step forward. "If you'd care to dance, my lady, I should be honored."

Poor Gerald. He'd always been awkward around females, particularly pretty ones.

A momentary tightening of her bow-shaped lips indicated her displeasure at this turn of events but she was intelligent enough to realize she'd lost this round..

With a smile that could have cut glass, Lady Maria made a curtsy and placed her hand lightly on Gerald's proffered arm. Sparing a glance for her hapless dancing partner, she said, "Thank you, Mr. Mason."

Gerald led Lady Maria away.

Ashburn excused himself and Davenport would have made good his escape also, but Yarmouth stayed him with an uplifted hand. "Davenport, my dear fellow. We must talk."

"Must we?" muttered Davenport. He knew what Yarmouth would say. Since Davenport's resurrection, his former mentor had been his greatest supporter. And thus his greatest danger.

They both watched Gerald and Lady Maria take their places in the set. The couple seemed to be having some sort of heated discussion. Oh, Maria would not even hint at such a thing by her demeanor, but Gerald's face flamed almost as brightly as his hair.

"Poor Gerald," murmured Yarmouth, as if reading Davenport's thoughts. "Was he being self-righteous just now?"

"I don't blame him," said Davenport. "What I did was unforgivable."

"Hmm." Yarmouth slid a sideways glance at him. "You seem to be taking all the slings and arrows with remarkable grace. I don't know how you stand it."

Davenport shrugged. He wasn't sure which was his less favorite topic: his scientific disgrace or the prospect of marrying Yarmouth's daughter.

"I could help you clear your name," said Yarmouth.

"Oh?" This ought to be good. "How so?"

"I have influence in many quarters. Some of them beyond even Ashburn's reach."

And the price for using that influence would be . . . wedding Lady Maria, no doubt.

Davenport switched on a smirk as genial as Yarmouth's. "You are generous."

"Not at all." Somehow, the man's relentless smile increased in brightness. "I daresay you know the favor I'd ask in return."

Now the gloves came off. "My dear sir, I'm flattered. But let me assure you, the rumors about me are most definitely true. I'm not the youth you knew years ago." He paused, looking down at his hands for a moment. Then he raised his gaze to look directly into Yarmouth's eyes. "And I would make the devil of a husband."

"You have made my daughter the object of your attentions," said Yarmouth, a hint of steel showing beneath the smooth demeanor.

"Rest assured, I have seen the error of my ways, sir," said Davenport, bowing. "I mean to cut her dead when next we meet."

Davenport escaped from the ballroom as soon as he

could. Cards couldn't possibly hold his attention tonight, so he was left with the choice of going home or finding some other amusement on the town.

The contempt twisting Gerald's face as he'd referred to Davenport's fall from grace kept rising before his mind's eye. They'd been friends and fierce competitors once, driving each other to new heights of discovery.

Now Davenport was a laughingstock, banned from the Royal Institution. His former cohort resented him for it, counting his demise as a personal betrayal. Another price Davenport paid for freedom.

His encounter with Lady Maria had left a sour taste in his mouth. It was as if he'd been drinking of cool spring water for the past two days, only to chase it with a dose of vinegar. The urge to see Honey again, to cleanse his palate, grew too insistent to ignore.

Ah, but he was edgy, out of sorts. He needed to get this matter of Honey's debut settled and move on to the far more stimulating task of seducing her.

He'd talk Rosamund into chaperoning Honey; he had no doubt that he'd succeed with his softhearted cousin. There was the tricky question of persuading Honey's guardian to go along with the scheme, but Davenport was confident that if he presented his plans as a fait accompli, deVere would have no choice but to acquiesce.

He'd be a fool not to. Honey was of no use to her guardian moldering away at the Grange. With a London season, she'd have the chance to make an alliance that would do credit to her family and take her off her brothers' hands into the bargain.

DeVere might be rough around the edges, but he wasn't stupid. He'd see the advantages of having Rosamund present the girl.

Before he knew it, Davenport was standing in the

corridor near Jacqueline's bedchamber, where he'd heard the housekeeper mention she was taking Honey.

Poor little thing. She was exhausted. She'd be asleep by now, no doubt.

He wouldn't wake her. He'd just see . . .

With a quick glance around, he turned the handle of her door and slipped into the silent chamber.

CHAPTER THIRTEEN

D avenport eased the door shut. The room was dim, lit only by the fire, and he waited a moment or two for his eyes to adjust.

Silence greeted him, save for the tick of the mantel clock. He couldn't hear her soft, even breathing the way he'd heard it last night. For a moment, he thought he must have the wrong room, but then he realized the curtains around the tester bed were drawn.

He moved softly to the bed and eased open the velvet drapes.

There she was, sound asleep. He couldn't make out the particulars of her body in the darkness. She was just an amorphous mass of bedclothes. All covered up, wrapped in the sleep of the innocent.

He knew from experience how deeply she slept. Last night, he'd lifted her from the chair, carried her over to the bed, and laid her on her side so he could get at those corset laces. To preserve her sense of modesty, he'd even done it blind, with his hands sliding up underneath the borrowed night rail she wore.

That wasn't to say he hadn't enjoyed touching her, nor that he'd been able to resist certain "accidental" touches that weren't strictly necessary for the removal of a lady's corset. His body warmed at the memory.

Sliding the unlaced stays out from under her sleeping form had been the trickiest part. He'd been convinced she'd wake. She hadn't. But she'd spent an extremely trying and tiring day, after all.

Davenport took a taper from the spill jar on the mantel and touched it to the fire, then lit a candle with it. He carried the candle over to the bed, confident that a herd of elephants wouldn't wake her. If, by chance, she did wake . . . would that be a bad thing? They ought to plan their strategy for tomorrow.

And if that led to something more interesting, who was he to complain?

She'd omitted to braid her hair, he noticed. The soft golden glow from the candle picked highlights from her tumbling dark gold locks. In sleep, with her expression serene, her lips parted slightly in the faintest hint of a smile, she looked ravishingly fresh, and somehow very dear.

The breath caught in his chest.

He wanted her to wake up so he could talk to her about her future, about what had happened in the ballroom tonight. He wanted—burned—to awaken her in the metaphorical sense, too. When had innocence been so alluring, so compelling?

Yet it wasn't her innocence alone that drew him. It was her courage in pursuing what she wanted so doggedly, her ability to see through his banter and his rakish façade. The adorable way she became so utterly befuddled by her own desire. She probably didn't even realize that all of those heated flutterings inside her were the product of good old-fashioned lust.

Yes, the upright Miss deVere was capable of great passion. Her temper alone told him that. What a pity it would be if she married some dull dog who didn't know how to kindle that passion to life.

He believed devoutly in the right of every woman to her own pleasure. He'd bedded enough married women to know they wouldn't seek him out if their husbands satisfied them in the bedchamber. What a crime to keep them all so ignorant. Most didn't even know what they were missing.

Suddenly he wondered if he was doing the right thing, aiding Honey in her quest for a husband. Knowing how much she disapproved of him, her brothers, and all their ilk, he could imagine the kind of dry old sobersides she'd favor as a spouse. Someone like Beckenham, for pity's sake.

He blinked. Beckenham would be utterly perfect for her.

The notion made him want to punch something. Preferably his cousin's granite-like jaw.

But no. With relief, he remembered that although the Earl of Beckenham did his duty by sitting in the Lords whenever Parliament was in session, he never took part in the season. Besides, Becks would probably turn his nose up at the idea of marrying a deVere. Davenport refused to see her married to a man who despised her family. That would be even worse than wedding the aforementioned dull dog.

Hot wax dripped onto his gloved hand. He hurriedly set it down in the candlestick on the bedside table with a click.

On a restless murmur, Honey turned her head toward the light, as if seeking something. A prolonged flutter of eyelids and she opened her eyes, squinting against the candle's glow.

"Don't be alarmed; it's me," he said softly. "Davenport."

"Hmm?" She wasn't really awake or she'd set up a screech.

He smiled, laughing at himself. He was randy as a spotted youth, yet she was totally oblivious. Here was one female quite capable of resisting his fabled charm. And just what did he think he was doing, waking her in the middle of the night after a hard day's travel? He ought to know better.

A pity the cock-stand in his trousers wasn't as reasonable and logical as his brain.

"Go back to sleep," he told her with a wry twist to his mouth.

"Mmm." She sighed and closed her eyes again.

He pulled the coverlet over her shoulder and collected his candle. With a silent prayer for strength, he made himself back away from the bed.

A brief, furtive reconnaissance told him the dimly lit corridor was empty. He emerged from the bedchamber, turned, and slowly eased the door closed with as little noise as possible.

His fingers had just left the doorknob when Rosamund rounded the corner toward him. "Jonathon! I might have known."

Damnation. A litany of curses ran through his mind as he desperately tried to come up with a plausible excuse for being there.

He'd faced cutthroats and bullies and ruffians, not to mention his own cousins, but he'd feared none of them as much as he feared the fury on this beautiful pregnant lady's face.

Her guinea gold tendrils bobbed emphatically as she marched up to him, a look of bloody murder in her celestial blue eyes.

He held up his hands in the gesture of surrender. "Rosie, I can explain."

Her hand clamped on his wrist. In an emphatic whisper, she said, "I want that girl out of here this instant."

He laid a hand on hers. "No, Rosie, you don't understand. I didn't touch her. She's had a long journey and she's among strangers. I only came up to see if she needed anything."

"You should have inquired of the housekeeper," hissed Rosamund, tightening her grip. "*Gentlemen* do not enter ladies' bedchambers at any time for any reason. Certainly not in my house."

She wrenched open the door, no doubt expecting to behold a scene of debauchery. He held the candle up to illuminate the darkened room. Anyone could see Hilary was fast asleep. Not a sign of frenzied lovemaking anywhere.

Recalling what he'd left undone, he moved to the bed and carefully tugged the drapes shut so the morning sunshine wouldn't wake her.

Then he stepped back and turned, to see Rosamund gazing at him oddly.

With a finger to his lips, he took his cousin's hand and led her from the room.

"She's worn to the bone," he said. "Let her sleep."

Outside again, with the door shut, Rosamund said in a low voice, "I accept that nothing happened between you tonight, but I do *not* like it, Jonathon. That you think you have license to enter that girl's bedchamber tells me one of two things: she is your mistress—"

"*I told you she's n—*"

"—*Or*," said Rosamund with a frown at him for interrupting her, "she is a virtuous girl who is in grave danger of being corrupted by you. What if Mrs. Faithful or one of the maids had seen you? You'd be obliged to marry the girl, and a pretty mess that would make."

An odd twist in the region of his chest made anger

spark. "You were not always so starched up, Rosie. I seem to recall you mentioning one or two exploits—"

"They were with *Griffin,* you dolt! We were in love. We were betrothed, and now we're *married.*" She threw up her hands. "What does it take to get it through that thick head of yours that you cannot go around trifling with women in this thoughtless, selfish manner? Particularly women of *that* family."

Her face set. "I'm sending for Lord deVere in the morning."

He groaned. "Don't do that, Rosie, not yet. Not until you get to know her. She's—"

"Clearly, you don't yet understand how society works," said Rosamund with terrible patience. "If you ruin the girl in my household, everyone will hold me to blame, and they'd be right."

Her eyes grew suspiciously moist. "I trusted you, Jonathon. When you told me she was not your fancy-piece—"

"She's *not* my—"

"But you want her to be," she said bluntly. "You would never take this trouble out of altruism. No man would." She thought for a moment. "Except, perhaps, Beckenham."

"Oh, yes, Becks is the model of propriety, isn't he?" He all but snarled the words, causing Rosamund to step back.

He didn't care. She had to listen. "I brought Miss deVere to you because she has been oppressed all her life by her male relatives, forced to grub for her living as a governess. She's never had a season like other girls of her station. The school didn't want her anymore because she's a deVere, and she was forced to go home. Rosie, her brother's house stinks like the kennels and when we arrived there the place was full of whores. It was clear as day those louts had no intention of changing their ways simply because their sister was in the house. Can you imagine yourself or Cecily in such a situation?"

She flinched.

"But go ahead," he said bitterly. "Send her back there. Hilary deVere is as much of an innocent as any of you girls were when you debuted. She was so desperate to get out of that place, she accepted *my* escort, and you may be sure that she had my measure from the outset. *I* was the lesser of two evils."

Rosamund blinked. Some of the tautness left her frame. Suddenly her eyes widened. She stared at him as if a novel thought had occurred to her.

That look gave him hope until she seemed to shake off whatever notion had entered her brain. "It is out of the question. I cannot keep her here without informing her guardian, no matter how innocent she might be."

He ran his hand through his hair and turned away so she wouldn't see the disappointment in his face. He was care-for-nothing Davenport. He ought to brush this off with no more than a shrug of regret for the lost opportunity of bedding a woman he was hot for. But he couldn't bear the thought of Honey back there in that hovel, subjected to all kinds of indignities, with no means of escape.

He blew out a breath. He'd never wanted to shake a woman before, but he was coming close to it with Rosamund. He couldn't look at her but gazed up at the plasterwork on the corridor ceiling. "It was all for nothing, then."

He must think of something. He couldn't let Honey go back there.

There was a long pause before Rosamund spoke. "If— *if*—I find the girl to be all you say, I shall invite her to stay with me for the season. And I shall prevail upon Montford to use his influence with her guardian to agree."

He turned back, eager as a damned puppy and unable to hide it. "You will?"

"Y-yes." She took a deep breath. "Yes, Jonathon. I will."

"Thank you, Rosie." Grinning, he caught her hands up in his, pulled her to him, and gave her a big, smacking kiss, full on the lips.

Laughing, blushing, she pushed him away. "Good Heavens, if Griffin saw us, he'd cut out your liver. Now we must go down. I've been away from my guests too long already."

* * * *

Hilary woke to the panicked sensation of not knowing where she was. The curtains around her bed were drawn, blocking out the light as well as any detail that might have oriented her.

Even more bewildering, the bed beneath her back was soft as a cloud. The linen smelled of lavender and rare, precious sunshine and the coverlet gave a luxurious, papery rustle whenever she moved. As her eyes adjusted to the darkness, she saw that the draperies surrounding her were made of rich swags of sumptuous velvet.

Recollection flooded back. Good gracious! What time was it?

Hilary hauled back the heavy drapes and swung her legs over the side of the bed.

Sunlight filtered through another set of drapes at the window. These were fashioned of silk taffeta, fine as a lady's ball gown.

Not wishing anyone to see her from below, she opened the curtains a crack and peeked out.

London!

Outside, there was bustle, even at this hour: maids and

errand boys, men delivering all manner of provisions to the grand houses in the street.

She glanced at the clock and realized the hour was far more advanced than she'd guessed. Eleven o'clock and no one had come to wake her.

She must dress, but she couldn't find her clothes. Had the housekeeper murmured something about sending a maid to unpack for her? She'd been too fatigued to raise any kind of protest.

She flushed. By now, the entire household would know how meager her wardrobe was, how worn with laundering her undergarments were.

Well, either she could remain here, trapped by her own fears, or she could ring for a maid to bring her water and help her dress.

She walked over to the bellpull and gave it a firm tug.

As if by magic, a maid appeared, carrying a breakfast tray. "The mistress ordered this brought to you, miss. If you'll be so kind as to get back in bed, I'll set it down. Or would you like to eat at the table?"

The maid gestured toward the small table by the window.

This was an unexpected honor. Ordinarily, the unmarried ladies in a household did not receive breakfast in bed.

"In bed, if you please." Suppressing a squeal of delight, Hilary slipped back between the sheets, determined to savor the experience. "Thank you," she murmured, sniffing the delicious, savory scents appreciatively.

The maid bobbed a curtsy. "Ring when you are ready to dress, miss, and I'll help you."

Thanking her again, Hilary twitched the napkin from the tray and spread it over her knees. She'd been too nervous to think about eating last night. Now her stomach growled in anticipation.

When at last she emerged from her allotted bedchamber some time later, Hilary wore a neatly pressed gown of fine navy cambric, which had been a gift from Miss Tollington, and a serviceable shawl. By some miracle, all of her gowns had been laundered and pressed overnight.

The maid had wished to style her hair in a pretty confection of curls around her face, but Hilary balked. She couldn't afford to present a frivolous or vulgar appearance. Her usual neat bun at the nape of the neck would suffice.

Time enough for frivolity when she'd convinced her hostess to let her stay.

She wondered where Trixie was and whether her brothers had caught up with the girl. Trixie could talk her way out of most trouble, but this particular exploit might be difficult to explain away. She only hoped the girl had received Davenport's message.

Once dressed and groomed, Hilary found her own way to the drawing room. Though luxurious, Lord Tregarth's town abode wasn't so large that one might become lost.

She took her time to look about her, drinking in the sight of her ancestors' portraits as she traversed the long gallery on her way to the stairs.

"Bunch of ruffians, aren't they?" commented a deep voice behind her. "Warriors and thieves and pirates, every one."

She gave a start and whipped around. "Lord Davenport. Don't creep up on me like that."

"Sorry. I thought you'd hear me coming, but you were lost in a brown study, I gather."

He took her elbow and guided her to the next portrait. As if she couldn't very well walk a few paces without his assistance.

His voice was a trifle husky, but that was the only trace of evidence that he'd spent a dissipated night.

"Worse for wear this morning, are you?" she asked, wishing she might keep the waspish note from her tone.

But she couldn't help it. He was so stomach-clenchingly handsome. Women must trip over their own feet to throw themselves at him. He'd probably forgotten her name by the time he'd danced with all those elegant ladies at the ball last night.

"I am not accustomed to rising at this hour, but I needed to speak with you before we face the others." His gaze narrowed on her. "You seem out of sorts yourself."

"Oh, not in the least. Whatever gave you that idea?" She moved on to a likeness of Catherine deVere, a daughter of the house whose formidable eyebrows hinted at an equally formidable temper.

"I trust you were comfortable last night?" he said. "No lumpy mattress, no ceilings falling in, that kind of thing?"

"You are hilarious," she said. "Everything was perfect. Thank you."

"I am delighted to hear it."

He hesitated, making her look up at him in mute inquiry. "I have some news that you will not like."

Her voice scraped. "Oh?"

But there was no time for him to tell her this news. At that moment, the most exquisitely lovely lady Hilary had ever seen walked into the gallery. Her palm rested lightly on her stomach in that universal, protective gesture of expectant mothers.

The newcomer did not wait for Davenport to make the introductions. "Good morning," she said. "You must be Miss deVere. I'm Lady Tregarth, you know."

She shook hands with Hilary, enveloping her in the golden warmth of her smile.

Lady Tregarth was not so much older than Hilary herself, which made her less of an imposing figure than Hilary had imagined. There was a decided twinkle in those deep blue eyes. Hilary liked her immediately.

"It's a pleasure to make your acquaintance, Lady Tregarth." Hilary made a curtsy so elegant, it would have served as a model for every other curtsy ever made, but Lady Tregarth chided her for her formality, took her hands, and drew her up.

Giving her fingers a small squeeze, she said, "You must call me Rosamund. And I shall call you Hilary, yes?"

Hilary nodded, scarce able to believe she was being received with such affability. For a bare, frightening instant she wanted to weep.

Releasing her, Rosamund bent a minatory gaze on Davenport. "My husband has a cracking sore head this morning and refuses to leave his bed. You had a pretty batch of it last night, I hear. *After* you'd turned the head of every female in the vicinity." She rolled her eyes. "I cannot tell you how many supposedly idle inquiries I received about the source of those bruises on your face. The silly chits are determined to make a romance of you, but I keep telling them it is nothing of the kind."

Davenport gave a slightly contemptuous snort. "I'm obliged to you. Now, listen, Rosie. We need to discuss Miss deVere's stay in London."

"Yes," said Rosamund. She turned to Hilary. "I'm afraid, my dear, that I was obliged to send for your guardian this morning."

A sick feeling churned in Hilary's stomach. "Oh, no," she whispered. Her stay would be cut short immediately if deVere had any say in it.

"Hilary, you are still a minor and neither Griffin nor I can reconcile it with our consciences to keep your presence here from your guardian."

Disappointment soured Hilary's stomach and put a metallic taste in her mouth. She managed a smile. "My lady, of course I understand. You were right to inform Lord deVere. He would learn of my presence in Town soon enough, in any event."

Once her brothers arrived in London, deVere would be the first person they told about her escapade.

She tried to quell the queasy pitching of her stomach. She loathed deVere's mode of communication, which mainly consisted of strung-together insults and shouting.

Rosamund nodded her approval. "I hoped you would be sensible. Come along, both of you, to the drawing room. The family is here as well. We are having a council of war."

"Wait." Davenport laid a hand on her arm. "Who is there, precisely? And what does the rest of the family have to say to anything?"

Rosamund opened her eyes wide. "Cecily is here, of course, and Montford." A small frown creased her brow. "I don't know how the duke heard about the matter, for I did not tell him and Cecily didn't, either, I'm sure. But he accompanied Lord deVere."

"Damn," muttered Davenport.

Hilary's heart plummeted to the soles of her half boots. Being raked over the coals by her guardian, Oliver, Lord deVere, was one thing. Having him harangue her in front of all of these strangers—a duke, for goodness' sake!—was another. Lord deVere would be sure to humiliate her.

"And Lady Arden, too," added Rosamund serenely.

"What?" Davenport threw up his hands. "Suddenly, a matter requiring the utmost discretion has become public knowledge."

"Not public, dear boy," said Rosamund. "None of those present has a reason or an inclination to gossip. And you must admit, Montford and Lady Arden always exercise a civilizing effect on Lord deVere. Come, we must discuss what is to be done."

She sailed out of the gallery, much in the manner of a captain leading a charge.

Hilary's steps dragged. Davenport caught her elbow and turned her to face him. "You don't have to go in there, you know."

"Yes, I do," she said. "I need Lord deVere's support to make my come-out. He's my guardian. Besides having the power to order me back to the Grange, he holds the purse strings."

Davenport frowned, opened his mouth as if to argue, then shut it again. "Very well."

He took her hand and drew it through his arm as they followed Rosamund. "But you are not to stand any nonsense from any of them. They can be . . . formidable."

She suspected that was an understatement.

"I'm well accustomed to bluster from the likes of Lord deVere," she replied.

His lips pressed together in a grim line. "Hmm, yes. What you're not accustomed to is—"

He was obliged to break off, for here they were on the threshold of the drawing room.

The soaring proportions of this scarlet and gold salon had been arranged to inspire awe. They certainly inspired awe in Hilary. No less did the assembled personages daunt her.

For some reason, all of them were standing in a cluster by the fireplace at the far wall as she and Davenport followed Rosamund in. The three of them were thus obliged to traverse the entire length of the room to reach the group.

No one spoke. They all stared at the interloper in their midst. She felt their gazes like hot needles pricking her flesh. All that could be heard was her own heels and those of Rosamund and Davenport clicking on the parquetry floor, echoing through the silence, *click, click, click.*

Hilary strove for a calm demeanor. She might be nervous on the inside, but she refused to show them how intimidated she was.

Davenport found her hand and gave it a surreptitious squeeze.

No doubt he meant it to be comforting. Hilary nearly shot out of her skin. A mix of sensual shock, embarrassment, and fury surged through her.

She snatched her hand away. What did he mean to do? Show them all that he and she were on much more intimate terms than was proper? Such a display would sink her chances from the outset.

When they finally reached the group of dignitaries awaiting them, Rosamund made the introductions. Hilary swiftly gauged the mood of each member of this party.

She saw immediately the likeness between Cecily, Duchess of Ashburn, and her brother. Cecily had the same dark coloring as Davenport and the same-shaped eyes. Snapping dark eyes they were, full of animation and intelligence.

And hostility. Yes, Hilary knew precisely how the duchess viewed her: as a scheming wench bent on ensnaring her brother. The sooner she was disabused of that notion, the better.

"Your Grace," said Hilary, making a curtsy even deeper and more elegant than the one she'd bestowed on Rosamund.

There was no invitation to call Cecily by her given name.

The duchess said, "I'd say I'm pleased to make your acquaintance, but we'd know that for the social lie it is. Suffice it to say I'm reserving judgment on you, Miss deVere. You are not what I expected."

Hilary smiled. "While Your Grace, if you don't mind

my saying so, is precisely as Lord Davenport described you. I have been looking forward to making your acquaintance."

Cecily blinked in surprise; then her gaze took on a hint of speculation.

Hilary lifted her chin.

"Bravo, Miss deVere." The suave, cool comment came from an older gentleman, whom Rosamund introduced as His Grace, the Duke of Montford.

He was somewhere between forty and fifty, Hilary supposed. Yet he possessed the lithe, languid grace of a younger man. His eyes were as cold and sharp as icicles. They seemed to drill down into her innermost thoughts.

Hilary sank into a deep, deferential curtsy. She only wished the duke *could* read her mind. Surely then he'd realize she had no designs on Davenport. Heavens, hadn't she said time and again that she couldn't imagine a worse fate than to be married to him?

Lady Arden, by contrast, bestowed on Hilary a genuine smile. "How very interesting." She threw an amused glance at Davenport. "Not at all in your usual style, my dear."

A woman of mature years, Lady Arden was strikingly handsome, with a magnificent figure. Her comment and the amused familiarity that tinged her words made Hilary bristle. Had Davenport and Lady Arden . . . ? Surely, she was much too old for him.

At least Davenport did not seem to share the lady's amusement. "As you say."

A deep growl emanated from the armchair in the corner. The small group parted, and all turned to look at Hilary's guardian.

Lord deVere's was not a handsome face, but it was arresting in a swarthy, rough-hewn way. A very different cast of man from the elegant Duke of Montford, but about the same vintage, she would guess.

"Come here, my girl," he rumbled.

Bracing her shoulders, Hilary moved toward him and dipped a curtsy. "Lord deVere, perhaps we might meet in private. We have much to discuss."

"Discuss?" DeVere looked around him, as if inviting the company to share his incredulity. "*Discuss?* There is nothing to discuss. *I* am going to tell you what you will do and *you*, my precious ward, will do it! Understand me? What the Devil d'you mean by coming to London, eh?"

"I wrote to you that I intended to travel to Town, my lord, for the same purpose most young ladies of my age and situation visit during the season. As you did not write to reject the proposal, I assumed you agreed with it."

She had not written to him, in point of fact, but since she knew very well that all of her careful missives found their way directly into deVere's fire, she was reasonably certain he wouldn't catch her in the falsehood.

He gazed at her through half-lowered lids. "Come to catch yourself a husband, eh? Well, now, let me have a look at you."

He eyed her up and down as if he inspected a heifer at market. She suffered his scrutiny without comment because he held her future in the palm of his big, meaty hand. She itched to box his ears, however.

"Turn around," he ordered.

"That's enough, I think." Davenport ranged himself beside her. "Accord Miss deVere some respect, sir."

"Respect?" spat deVere. "Filly runs off alone with the worst rake in Christendom and you say she's worthy of *respect*? How many times did you *respect* her on the way to London, eh, boy?"

Hilary gasped at the implication. She sensed the tension in Davenport and was ready when he took a hasty step forward, fists clenched. She grabbed his arm and hung on.

"Don't, my lord," she said. "Please. Such accusations are beneath contempt."

To deVere, she said, "Lord Davenport is innocent of these charges, sir, but you are right to reproach me. I behaved rashly by going with Lord Davenport, but the circumstances were such that I had no choice. Perhaps, if we might discuss this in private—"

"*Damn* me, but you're an impertinent wench," said deVere, slapping his massive thigh. "I'm here to control the damage you've caused with your flighty ways and you're giving me a lesson on propriety?

"And *you*," he purred like a big jungle cat, turning his head to glare at Davenport. "Even if this silly chit didn't know better, *you* did."

Between his teeth, Davenport said, "I rescued Miss deVere from an intolerable situation. A situation she might not have been placed in if her guardian had done a better job of protecting her."

"And you brought her to London," said deVere, stroking his chin. One eyebrow jerked up. "For what purpose?"

"Miss deVere must have a season," Davenport responded. "It is her due as a gentlewoman and a daughter of your noble house."

Hilary could not help but stare to hear Davenport speak with such a haughty air. A glance at the younger members of his family told her they were equally astonished.

"Be damned to you, sir," said deVere. "That she will not. She'll go straight back to that infernal school and stay there until I'm ready to find a husband for her."

"That infernal school dismissed her, or didn't you know?" said Davenport. "For no fault on her part other than having the misfortune to be born a deVere. I discovered poor Miss deVere on the road, trudging alone through a storm. Upon escorting her home, I found her brothers engaged in an activity I cannot mention in front of ladies."

"Oh, don't mind us," put in Cecily. "Were they having an orgy, Jonathon? I wonder that you didn't join in."

The goading sting in Cecily's tone made Hilary cast a quick glance at her. Cecily's dark eyes smoldered. There was something wrong here beyond the present crisis, but Hilary couldn't fathom what.

"Cecily, do not be vulgar," said Montford calmly. "But this is abominable, Davenport." He turned his wide-eyed gaze to deVere. "Really, I don't see what else my cousin could have done, do you? It appears he acted out of the purest sense of chivalry."

Davenport narrowed his eyes at the duke, as if unsure whether to trust this unruffled declaration of support. He turned back to deVere. "The reality is that only her brothers and the people in this room know anything of the matter. If Miss deVere is seen to be in company with Lady Tregarth for the season, all will be well. It will be as if Miss deVere and I never met."

At these words, Hilary felt the oddest sensation in the pit of her stomach. A heavy, sinking feeling she didn't wish to examine too closely.

How many times since she'd made his acquaintance had she wished she'd never met him? And yet—

"I won't have it," roared deVere. He jabbed a finger in Montford's direction, baring his teeth. "And I won't have you encouraging the chit to defy me, either."

"I wouldn't do that for the world, deVere," said Montford. "You may act as you wish regarding Miss deVere. She is your ward, after all, and wholly your concern. *My* concern is that my relative does not figure as the villainous debaucher of innocents in this piece."

"Protecting the good name of the Westruthers, as usual," muttered deVere.

"Precisely."

Fear and disappointment clenched around Hilary's heart. For a moment, she'd hoped Montford might support her. But His Grace only acted to save Davenport from an entanglement with a penniless, good-for-nothing deVere.

Once more, she was alone, at the mercy of her heritage. And of her horrid guardian.

"I don't believe it," rumbled deVere, glaring at Davenport from beneath lowered brows. "When did you say you made my ward's acquaintance?"

"The day before yesterday," lied Davenport.

"You spent the night where?" barked deVere.

Davenport looked arrogantly down his nose at deVere. "In her brother's house."

"While this orgy took place?"

"No, my lord. I ejected the brothers', er, companions from the house immediately."

DeVere's brows lowered. "So you, the most notorious rogue in London, were alone with my ward in a house where her drunken sots of brothers were her only chaperones."

"Yes," said Davenport between gritted teeth.

"Overnight, you say."

"That is correct."

Hilary was ready to sink into the Aubusson carpet with humiliation. When deVere shot the Duke of Montford a blazingly triumphant glance, she knew the conclusion everyone must draw.

Davenport's voice sliced through the air, "I did not lay a hand on Miss deVere, either then or on our journey to London."

Lady Arden frowned. "No one will believe that." She turned to address Hilary. "My dear child, what on earth were you about to let this rapscallion escort you to London? Didn't you know what must come of such behavior?"

"I . . . I . . ." Hilary gulped for air. This could not be happening. She was ruined. All of her dreams turned to dust.

In that moment, she hated Lord deVere with a white-hot passion. Why must he force the issue? What sort of man kept pushing and pushing until he brought the dishonor of his own ward out into the open?

She would never have her season now. Never meet that kind, gentle man of her dreams, never hold their dear, sweet babies in her arms.

She would be exiled, sent back to her brother's house to stew in the filth and degradation of the place until she could no longer remember what proper conduct was. She'd turn into her brothers' drudge and become a dried-up old maid or, worse, finally succumb to her fate and become the fallen woman these people clearly thought her already.

She couldn't face it. She simply couldn't.

Incipient tears burned at the backs of her eyes, but she'd die before she broke down and wept in front of this array of coldhearted strangers. Of them all, only Rosamund showed her any true sympathy.

After a struggle, she said, "You must not blame Lord Davenport. He has acted with the utmost nobility throughout our association. But I quite see how it might look to the outside world. I was so desperate to get to London, I did not consider all of the ramifications of the journey."

She lifted her chin. "If it were not for your neglect, Lord deVere, and that of my brothers, I should not have been driven to this pass. No doubt you think I did wrong to travel to London with Lord Davenport. I can only say that remaining at Wrotham Grange would have been worse."

She caught Davenport's eye and held his gaze. "I cannot be sorry for my actions, foolhardy though they might seem in retrospect. Thank you, my lord, for your efforts on my behalf. I only regret the trouble I have caused you and your family."

* * * *

Fury descended before Davenport's vision like a red haze. How *dare* deVere make such filthy accusations against Honey?

He'd thought he had himself well under control, but the valiant speech she made tore at what passed for his heart.

The words came out of his mouth before he could stop them. "My dear Miss deVere, there is no need for such tragedy. If my relations and yours are convinced I have compromised you, there is only one way to make amends. We must set a date."

There was a collective gasp. Everyone pinned their attention on Honey, who stood frozen in place.

She eyed him as if he'd run mad. On the contrary, now that he'd committed himself he enjoyed a moment of sheer, blinding clarity. This was the only way to keep her in London. They'd pretend to be engaged.

"A—a date?" said Honey, all at sea.

He took no offense at her bewilderment. His own nearest and dearest seemed rather befuddled by this sudden attack of decency. Cecily and Rosamund regarded him with their eyes wide and their jaws slightly dropped. Even Montford appeared a little more pinched around his aristocratic nostrils than usual.

"For the wedding," Davenport explained, beginning to rather enjoy himself. "In fact, there is quite a romantic story to all of this." He smiled down at Honey. "Why don't you tell them, my dear?"

The girl's eyelids fluttered as if she might faint. In a

wavering voice, she said, "Oh. Well . . ." She swallowed hard. "But my lord, you relate the circumstances so much better than I ever could."

"Never say the two of you are engaged!" Rosamund exclaimed.

"But this is too fantastical," said Lady Arden. "How comes this about?"

Honey gasped like a landed salmon and flapped her hands a little, so he manfully threw himself into the breach once more.

"You see, Miss deVere's mother and mine were bosom bows. They arranged the match between them long ago."

He couldn't recall what the Devil Honey's mother's name was, but it made no odds. He was quite likely to forget such details even if the tale were true.

Fortunately, Lady Arden directed the obvious question to Honey herself. "Who *is* your mama, child?"

"Marigold Waterstone is—was—my mother's maiden name," faltered Honey, her eyes wild. "She . . . she died. Almost ten years ago, now."

"Marigold Waterstone," repeated Lady Arden slowly. "Yes, now I recall. You have the look of her, my dear."

"So I'm told," said Honey with an agonized glance at Davenport.

He took her hand, which lay, unresisting and cold, in his. Her creamy skin had turned pale. He trusted she wouldn't faint. "My mother and Miss deVere's mama settled it between them that we should be betrothed when we were older."

"Why have I never heard anything about this?" demanded Cecily, who had at last found her voice.

Montford tilted his head. "Nothing in your parents' effects suggested such an alliance had been made."

However, Montford knew as well as Davenport that the former earl and his countess were prone to making unilateral arrangements for their progeny without documenting them, as in Cecily's case.

Davenport smiled. "I knew of the arrangement from my earliest years. But then, of course, my parents were killed in a carriage accident before the betrothal could be formalized."

Suddenly Hilary's hand tugged and whisked from his clasp. She took a deep, shaky breath and he waited with a delicious kind of anticipation to see if she'd throw cold water on his ruse.

She gave a tremulous smile. "W-when Lord Davenport and I met by chance, it was as if Fate had brought us together, and I—*we*—realized our union was meant to be. We wished to keep our engagement secret while I came to know him a little and enjoyed my come-out, but now . . ."

She spread her hands and said brightly, "Surprise!"

CHAPTER FOURTEEN

The company was quite dazed by the end of this thrilling recital. Davenport thought they'd brushed through it remarkably well. Now he needed to get Honey alone without delay so he could make it clear to her he had no intention of actually going through with the marriage itself.

He'd taken a drastic measure to save her from returning to the Grange, but what else could he have done? DeVere had as good as called Honey a trollop, accusing them of fornicating all the way to London.

If he had any sense of chivalry, he'd have thought of this before. He'd known as soon as they were obliged to spend the night on the road without Trixie they were taking a risk.

Still, he was damned if he'd marry any lady purely to satisfy deVere's overweening ambition. Once Honey had enjoyed her month in Town, they'd call the whole thing off. By then, she was sure to have cut a swath through the eligible bachelors of the ton.

The thought gave him pause. He wasn't entirely sure he liked the notion of her pursuing other gentlemen while supposedly engaged to him. He'd have to warn her to be discreet.

"One thing I ought to mention," he said, "is that we

agreed the betrothal should be kept secret for the time being."

He essayed a fond look at his new betrothed. "I want Miss deVere to enjoy her season to the full while we become rather better acquainted. Should she decide that we don't suit, or if she receives a more advantageous offer—"

Cecily snorted. "More advantageous than the Earl of Davenport?"

"Ah. You flatter me, dear sister." Thank God Hilary deVere's notions of eligibility were not the same as the rest of society's.

He continued. "Regardless, I wish you all to keep this strictly to yourselves. As you have no doubt observed, we were wholly unacquainted before two days ago. It might be that Miss deVere will change her mind when presented with the choices a London season has to offer."

"Then she'd be a fool," said Cecily, narrowing her eyes. "She does not look like a fool to me."

Before he could defend her, Hilary spoke up, her cheeks a trifle flushed. "I agree with Lord Davenport. I would also like the betrothal to be kept secret. In fact, I insist upon it."

And wasn't that the greatest compliment he'd ever received? Despite her untenable position, Hilary deVere didn't wish to marry him any more than he wished to marry her. Regardless of his desperate desire to remain disentangled, her eagerness for secrecy struck him as just plain insulting.

"Bollocks," said deVere, slapping his thigh. "You're betrothed or you're not. This business of keeping it secret won't wash."

"My dear sir," drawled Lady Arden. "I beg leave to tell you that your language belongs in the gutter. Along," she added, "with your linen and that coat."

DeVere muttered something under his breath, but under Lady Arden's haughty stare he subsided.

Hilary said, "Yes, we will keep it secret, and if anyone asks me if it's true that we're engaged, I'll certainly tell them it's no such thing."

She turned to Cecily. "So you needn't fear your brother has been trapped, Your Grace. I know it must seem like that, but I assure you it is not."

"My dear Miss deVere, I cannot imagine what you think I have to say in the matter of your marriage to my brother," said Cecily with the kind of cool indifference that made Davenport want to turn her over his knee.

"Quite a lot, I imagine," responded Honey quietly. "I can see you are fond of each other."

"Fond? Of this termagant?" Davenport shook his head. "Must have me confused with someone else."

The Duchess of Ashburn most improperly stuck her tongue out at him and then they both broke into laughter. Her eyes twinkling merrily up at him, she said softly, "What a cawker you are, my dear."

"Children, children! Behave." Rosamund, ever the peacemaker, steered them back on course, and soon the conversation turned to preparing Miss deVere for the season.

Stars sparkled in Honey's eyes as the discussion moved deeper into the waters of fashion and balls and the myriad delights of the ton. Watching her drinking in the glittering world Rosamund revealed, ably assisted by Lady Arden, Davenport struggled to harden his heart.

Honey could have her season, but he needed her promise that she'd break off the engagement before the wedding was due to take place. There was no way he'd actually marry her.

While the other ladies probed his betrothed for more

information about this whirlwind courtship, his sister drew him aside.

With a gleam of humor, she said, "You got yourself into this, dear brother. Now how are you going to get yourself out?"

He lifted an eyebrow at her. "What in the world makes you think I wish to get out?"

"You might play your cards close to your chest, but I know you. You'd no notion of changing your ways and settling down when you left London. You cannot have altered that much in a matter of days."

"But weren't you telling me only recently about love's transformative effect?" murmured Davenport.

"And that's another thing," said Cecily, ignoring the frivolous interjection. "Only one night is accounted for in your romantic tale of rescue. But you were gone for two."

His mouth quirked in a cynical smile. "So you were in on the kidnapping plot, were you?"

"It was my idea. I needed help with the execution, of course." Cecily threw up her hands. "We had to do something, or you would have been forced to marry Lady Maria. Yarmouth was making all sorts of veiled insinuations in that odiously unctuous, smiling way of his until Montford stepped in. Whatever else she may be, Lady Maria is not some round-heeled tavern wench, Jonathon. She's a lady and Lord Yarmouth is a powerful man. You ought not to have seduced her. And now, just when we'd saved you from that catastrophe, you've gone and landed yourself in the suds again."

"I didn't seduce Lady Maria," he said. "And it doesn't become you in the least to talk that way, Cec, let me tell you."

He hadn't succeeded in seducing Lady Maria when he'd been shipped off to the country willy-nilly. Or rather, she hadn't succeeded in seducing him. Despite her gentle birth and her demure demeanor, the girl was a consummate tease, with far more experience in dalliance than her adoring father knew.

Well, she could forget her ambitions to snare a tarnished earl.

At this moment, he could not quite remember what the point had been to chasing Lady Maria. Last night, he'd realized he'd never even liked her very much.

Not that any of it was Cecily's business. "Stay out of my affairs, sister mine."

"Yes, I see you brought me fit punishment for my meddling." She flicked a glance at Honey.

He frowned down at her. "You are quite wrong about her, you know. Miss deVere is a woman after your own heart."

That caught her attention. "How do you mean?"

"In the course of our acquaintance, she has pushed me off a horse, dumped water over my head, and punched me in the jaw."

He passed a hand over the jaw in question, which had now lost its tenderness from his cousins' pummeling. Honey's slap had more fury than power behind it and she'd missed, but still, the sentiment was the same.

Cecily gave a ladylike snort of laughter and her dark eyes gleamed. "Did she, indeed? Well, it appears there is more to this Miss deVere than meets the eye. I reserve judgment on her character, but I still do not believe you wish for this marriage."

That he most certainly did not.

While he exchanged a few words with Montford and Lady Arden, he wondered if Honey understood why he'd stipulated that the betrothal be kept secret. Though he'd tried to get her alone so he could make his stance clear on the point of their eventual nuptials, he couldn't get near her once the announcement was made. The women corralled her between them.

The conversation had turned to fashion as it so often did when Cecily and Rosamund put their heads together. They deemed it vital to cart Hilary off to Bond Street without delay.

And didn't deVere look like the cat in the cream pot? This was what he'd been angling for all along with those accusations of illicit behavior, the old Devil.

DeVere's rumbling growl cut through the female twittering. "Miss deVere will not be staying here, so you can forget about your plans for this afternoon."

Rosamund turned to him with a supercilious lift of her brows. "I assure you, sir, I am more than happy to accommodate my cousin's future bride."

Keep her under scrutiny, more like, thought Davenport, eyeing his female relatives warily.

That was the trouble with women. They were so mercurial. One minute, they looked daggers at the girl; the next, they were bound and determined to take her shopping.

"Don't make no odds if *you're* happy," grunted deVere, heaving his big frame out of the chair. "I am the girl's guardian and *I* say who chaperones her while she's in London."

He jabbed a finger at Hilary. "The wedding will be one month from today. One month is all you get for your precious season, my girl. Then you'll be shackled to his lordship all right and tight."

The light in Honey's eyes dimmed a little, but she bowed her head submissively and made a dutiful curtsy. "Yes, my lord."

She was a bundle of suppressed excitement. Even this setback did not seem to bother her unduly.

"*Yes, my lord,*" mimicked deVere nastily. "You'll stay with Mrs. Henry Walker. She's a deVere by birth, some sort of cousin of mine. She will bring you out in society."

"Yes, sir."

Tenderhearted Rosamund was clearly troubled by this exchange. She addressed deVere, her tone frigid. "May we not entertain Miss deVere to tea today, at least?"

DeVere folded his arms. "No. I'm taking her to Mrs. Walker directly."

Rosamund looked to the Duke of Montford, but he made no move to intervene in this scheme. He watched Honey intently. The Devil only knew what conclusions he drew about her and the reasons for this betrothal.

Davenport might have argued with deVere's high-handedness, but he didn't. He wasn't acquainted with Mrs. Walker. He'd have to find out how suitable the lady was to act as Hilary's chaperone—and how he might circumvent that matron's watchful eye. He needed to get Honey alone, and Rosamund had proven herself far too vigilant a chaperone for his liking.

Seeing no help forthcoming from her male relatives, Rosamund took Honey's hands and squeezed them. "You'll come to us often, won't you? Do not look so downcast, my dear. You will have a wonderful time in London. We'll see to it that you are invited everywhere, won't we, Cecily?"

"Yes, indeed," Cecily murmured with a glance at deVere that signaled a clear challenge.

Amazing how little it had taken for Cecily to change her mind about Miss deVere. No sooner had she heard about Honey's mistreatment of Davenport than she'd formed a favorable, if tentative, opinion of the chit.

He needed to speak with Honey before this all went too far. "I'll call on you when you're settled," he told her as he took his leave.

After the cornucopia of delights the ladies had laid out for her, not even the prospect of Mrs. Walker's dubious chaperonage could dampen Honey's enthusiasm.

"I'll look forward to it," she said, smiling, giving him her hand.

She glowed up at him as if he'd hung the moon and stars for her, and a curious warmth spread through his chest. Her expression was so much in the manner of a lady regarding her sweetheart that he had to get a firm grip on himself to stop from falling into those honey brown eyes.

If anything had put that look on her face, he reminded himself, it was the prospect of a London season, not him.

The syrupy warmth turned to a burn of chagrin. His resolve hardened as he bowed over her hand.

Honey. His Honey was getting the dearest wish of her heart, just as he'd promised. Now, he would claim his reward. It was time to take all of that sweetness and softness and make it his own.

* * *

When Davenport reached his own house that afternoon, his cousins were waiting for him in his book room. Obviously, they'd caught wind of the news. At this rate, the whole of London would know about his fake betrothal by the evening.

"Davenport." Beckenham nodded a greeting. Absentmindedly he passed his palm over a series of contusions that mirrored Davenport's own, then ran his fingers through his closely cropped black hair.

Lydgate, impeccably attired in blue superfine, high shirt points, and snowy cravat, lounged elegantly in a deep overstuffed armchair. His classical features were marred by bruising around one of his startlingly blue eyes.

"But how remiss of me, Lydgate," Davenport drawled. "You need another black eye to go with the one I gave you. I know how you like everything to match."

"Pax," said Lydgate, holding up a well-manicured hand in a gesture of peace. "I haven't been able to show my phiz abroad since you rearranged it, Cousin. I'm in no mind to spill any more blood on your account."

"We hear you are to be congratulated," said Xavier, emerging from the shadows. The only one of them without a mark on his face.

He crossed to the brandy decanter that reposed on the gleaming sideboard. "Drink?"

Davenport eyed it suspiciously. "Only if it's not doctored like the last one."

"Drug your own brandy?" Xavier's sneering smile tilted his lips. "My dear fellow, I wouldn't dream of it."

He poured two glasses, handed one to Davenport. After he saw Xavier take a sip of the beverage, Davenport followed suit.

"Suspicious, aren't you?" murmured Xavier.

"I've reason, haven't I?" said Davenport. "That was a scurvy trick to play on me, Steyne, and you know it. Left Becks and Lydgate to do your dirty work for you, too."

"I did not think it would require three of us to subdue you."

Xavier glanced at his two cohorts, whose faces appeared every bit as worse for wear as did Davenport's. "Perhaps I was wrong." He held his arms wide. "Do you want to have a go at me now? I'm at your disposal."

He spoke in that maddeningly emotionless tone Davenport loathed. The urge to hit someone had passed, however. Davenport gave him a blank stare, then leaned against the mantel and savored his drink.

"We hear you're engaged to be married," said Beckenham.

"Straight to the point, as usual," murmured Xavier.

Ignoring him, Beckenham said, "What is this, Davenport? Did you pick up the first wench you saw and propose? Is this some sort of joke?"

"Is she hopelessly ineligible?" Xavier looked interested. "An opera dancer, for example?"

"She's a deVere," snapped Davenport.

Lydgate slapped his palm to his forehead, wincing. "Not another one in the family. Wasn't Tregarth bad enough?"

Since Rosamund's husband was possibly Lydgate's closest friend, no one paid that comment any heed.

"I cannot conceive how you could be dumped in a barn one day and engaged to be married the next," said Beckenham, his brow furrowing.

"Well, of course you couldn't," said Lydgate. "A man like you never does anything without due care and consideration. But this is Davenport we're talking about. He ain't like you, Becks."

"More's the pity," commented Xavier. "What are you going to do about her?" he asked, his gaze keen and incisive.

"Do about her?" Davenport blinked. He had no intention of sharing his (as yet rather hazy) plans with his cousins, or the true reason for the engagement.

"Well, obviously the two of you can't marry," said Lydgate. "A deVere female? Who ever heard of a Westruther heir marrying a deVere?"

This was precisely the sort of prejudice Hilary continually faced. It was on the tip of Davenport's tongue to say he *would* marry Hilary deVere and be damned to the lot of them, but he caught himself in the nick of time.

"My dear fellows, I appreciate your concern, but the fact of the matter is, it's none of your damned business. Now, shall we drink together in harmony or shall we strip and settle the matter with our fists?"

They opted for the former, which suited him very well. He needed a drink or three to stave off the panic that rose in his chest at the mere thought of marriage.

A more immediate problem occurred to him. "She wants to go to Almack's."

"What woman doesn't?" was Xavier's cynical reply.

"Suppose I'll have to take her there, though." He stared at the dregs of his glass

"Weren't you banned from Almack's?" said Lydgate idly.

Davenport straightened. "Was I? What for?"

He hadn't paid much attention to such things. What would he want with Almack's? You couldn't drink, you couldn't game for high stakes, and you certainly couldn't get your leg over a willing wench or two.

"Flooring the porter when he turned you away for arriving after eleven o'clock, I expect," said Beckenham.

"No, I don't think that was it." Davenport frowned. He might be an idiot, but he didn't go around hitting innocent employees who were only obeying orders.

"Kissed some girl behind a potted plant?" suggested Lydgate.

No, that didn't ring a bell. Until Lady Maria had made such a bold play for him, he'd restricted himself to bored married ladies and women of another class entirely. He'd never needed to skulk around snatching kisses at a subscription ball.

He shook his head. "No, it's gone. I simply do not recall."

"I shall start a betting book on the subject." Lydgate took out a notebook he used for the purpose and began to scribble away. "My money is on propositioning Mrs. Drummond-Burrell."

"Ugh! Give me some credit for taste."

"You were probably castaway," said Beckenham, tossing

back his brandy. "I'll put a hundred on it. When do we meet this paragon of yours?" He rose, as if ready to depart now that he'd delivered various measured words of censure on Davenport's conduct.

Davenport rubbed his nose. "Montford will decide that. What's the bet he'll want us all together around his table so he can intimidate the poor girl into submission?"

"What *does* the noble head of our house think of the match?" inquired Xavier, watching Davenport closely.

"Doesn't like it," said Davenport. "He'll probably enlist your help to break up the engagement, only it looks like you've taken on the task all by yourselves."

"Not at all," said Xavier. "I rarely do anything to assist Montford's schemes if I can help it."

"Well, I don't like it," said Lydgate. "First, all the girls go off and get happily married, bang, bang, bang, one after another. And now you, Davenport. *You!* Where will all this falling in love end? is what I ask myself. It's a damned epidemic, so it is."

Beckenham looked back from the doorway. "I think you can safely say it will stop at me," he said, and went out.

Davenport sighed. He ought to have predicted that if he offered marriage, his irritating cousins would leap to the conclusion that he was in love.

Perish the thought! His only consolation in the entire business was that Honey was equally horrified at the notion of their marriage. As for love, she'd laugh herself sick over the mere suggestion she'd fallen in love with a scoundrel like Davenport. No, Miss Hilary deVere would scour ballrooms of Mayfair and beyond for suitors to avoid marrying him.

The notion ought to have comforted him, but it didn't. Not in the least.

*   *   *

As Lord deVere hustled her out of the carriage and up the steps to Mrs. Walker's door, Hilary cast a critical eye about her. She had the gravest misgivings about the lady deVere had chosen to be her duenna.

She'd labeled society's condemnation of her family as prejudice, but the truth was most deVere men *were* brutes. That's if her father, her brothers, and Lord deVere were anything to judge by.

She hadn't met Lord Tregarth, but from what little she'd seen and heard, she suspected he was somewhat of a brute, too. Goodness knew why a refined lady like Rosamund should love such a man, but there was no accounting for taste.

Hilary was largely unacquainted with the female members of her clan. DeVeres did not generally gather together for cozy family celebrations.

She ought to keep an open mind about Mrs. Walker, just as Hilary longed for people to keep an open mind about her. But with every yard they traveled, she could not help wishing she were back at Tregarth House.

She was so consumed by her thoughts that she did not take in her surroundings on their short journey, though she'd yearned for the city sights as long as she could remember.

She wondered if Mrs. Walker knew she was about to have a guest thrust upon her for the space of a month. Not only a guest, but a young lady who required strict chaperonage into the bargain. Hilary thought it unlikely. Surely deVere would not have had the opportunity to arrange the matter with her before his call at Lord Tregarth's house.

Her prospective duenna's residence was situated in Half Moon Street, an address Hilary knew must be respectable because one of her students from Miss Tollington's lived there.

That was a good sign, wasn't it? Her tension eased a little.

"DeVere to see Mrs. Walker," said her guardian.

The butler mutely held out his salver and DeVere patted his coat in a fruitless search for his card case. After some fumbling and muttering, he gave up.

He glared at the butler beneath lowering brows as if daring him to ask for his calling card. "Well, come on, man. Don't keep us standing here like dolts."

"Very good, my lord." The imperturbable butler must have had experience with deVere, for he didn't turn a hair at such treatment. He ushered them in, then bowed and went in search of his mistress.

The salon they entered was an ornate drawing room, gilded and decorated in the Oriental style in an alarming combination of salmon pink, gold, and puce.

Hilary barely repressed a shudder at the décor, but at least the ceiling appeared to be in good repair. Clearly, Mrs. Walker didn't begrudge money spent on maintenance, unlike Hilary's brothers. That was a somewhat promising start.

"Don't stand there gawping, girl!" DeVere gave her a shove between the shoulder blades that made her stumble farther into the room. "Sit down over there."

Their hostess kept them waiting for so long, Hilary wondered if she was at home. She and Lord deVere sat staring glumly at each other until a trilling voice broke the silence.

"*Oliver?* Is that you?"

Mrs. Walker paused on the threshold as if to pose for a portrait. One hand was stretched slightly above her head, caressing the doorframe, while the other fiddled with the strings of a truly scandalous robe.

The lady had red hair and brown eyes and a plump,

curvaceous figure—easily discernible beneath the filmy layers of gauze that did very little to cover them.

Hilary blinked, then blushingly averted her gaze. Clearly, Lord deVere and Mrs. Walker were closer than most distant relations. Hilary wished she could make herself invisible or liquefy and melt into the floor.

DeVere launched to his feet with a muttered oath, but before he could do much more than say, "Now, Dolly, don't—," she hurried forward and flung her arms around him, practically scaling his large body like a buxom, red-haired monkey.

He pushed her away from him—but not before he'd had a friendly grope of her rounded bottom—and said, "Put some clothes on, m'dear. I'm not here for . . . ah . . ." He cleared his throat. "I've brought a lady with me."

"What?" she demanded, her cooing turning to a scold. "I told you before I don't like that sort of thing. If that's what you want, sirrah, you can take yourself off."

"Be damned to you, you harridan!" shouted deVere. "Look at her. She's my ward. Name's Hilary deVere, daughter of Nathaniel."

"What?" said the lady, staring hard at Hilary. "Never say— Ah, but she has the look of her hoity-toity mama, don't she? Well, what do you expect *me* to do with her?"

"Bring her out. Take her on the town. Chaperone her to parties. You know the style of thing."

"Chaperone? Me?" She gave a great belly laugh. "You're cracked, you are."

Lord deVere's beetling brows lowered and his bottom lip stuck out. Hastily the lady backtracked. "What I mean is, delighted, I'm sure. Er, how long am I to have the, ah, pleasure of Miss Hilary's company?"

"A month. Maybe less. Tell 'em to make up a room for her. Everything at my expense, of course."

Mrs. Walker's eyes brightened at that. With a quick, shrewd glance at Hilary, she rang the bell, and the housekeeper came in answer.

"I have a young relative come to stay, Mrs. Harbury. Make up the yellow bedchamber, will you? And take Miss deVere to the upstairs parlor while I talk to his lordship."

With a disapproving sniff, the housekeeper did as she was told. "This way, miss."

Glad of an opportunity to escape, Hilary followed the servant upstairs. Mrs. Walker was just as she'd feared. Worse. For she was quite obviously Lord deVere's mistress, which showed not only loose morals but also a total lack of discrimination.

Imagine being kissed and . . . and . . . *fondled* by Lord deVere!

Was this Mrs. Walker truly a deVere or was she merely some random mistress deVere thought would make a good chaperone?

Whatever the case, she doubted Mrs. Walker had ever darkened the doors of Almack's.

Some time later, when deVere had left without saying farewell or giving Hilary the least notion of his plans for her—if, indeed, he had any—Hilary was once again called down to the drawing room.

Her hostess was clothed respectably now, in a dark cambric gown with a striped spencer and shawl. She looked like any other society matron, save for the beacon red hair. Hilary thanked Heaven for small mercies.

Now that she was able to look Mrs. Walker full in the face, she noticed the lady was somewhat older than she'd first appeared. In her bone structure Hilary detected the low brow and pugnacious chin that showed unmistakably she was a deVere.

So that, at least, was true. Hilary could only hope the

lady was discreet enough in her affaires to still remain in good standing with the ton.

"Come. Sit by me, dearie," said Mrs. Walker, patting the couch next to her. "Lord deVere has told me all about you. What an exciting time you've had, to be sure."

Hilary would rather describe it as by turns frustrating, infuriating, harrowing, and humiliating, but she said cautiously, "Just so, ma'am."

"And betrothed to the Earl of Davenport. Quick work, my girl. Clever work, too, if you got him on your hook after only one night."

"It's not like that," Hilary protested.

"Oh, now, lovey, we're family," said Mrs. Walker with a wink. "You don't have to pretend with me."

"No, I mean, I truly didn't *hook* him, ma'am. Lord Davenport is honoring a family obligation. But as I explained to Lord deVere, the earl wants me to make sure there is no other gentleman I would prefer to marry before we settle down together. That is why he wanted me to have a season."

"Honor? Obligation?" Mrs. Walker laughed. "For a minute there I thought you were talking of Davenport. The greatest rogue in London, my dear. You'll need to do better than rely on honor and obligation if you want him firmly tied to your apron strings."

"But I don't—"

"Come now, dearie, you can't tell me you were on the road with the rogue all that time and he never had you. I've never heard of a woman—whore or lady or parson's daughter—who could resist the Earl of Davenport."

The dreamy look in her eye told Hilary that if Davenport's taste ever ran to vulgar redheads past their prime there'd be a willing conquest waiting for him right here in Half Moon Street.

"Well, you have now," said Hilary with dignity. "For

your information, Lord Davenport behaved like a gentleman the entire time."

She could not stop the betraying blush that rose to her cheeks. The heat came in waves as she recalled each and every instance where Davenport had most certainly *not* behaved as a gentleman should.

"If you say so," said Mrs. Walker with a knowing and blatantly envious smile. "All I'm saying is, now you have the chance to snare him good and proper, you must use it. You need only tell the truth and let Lord deVere do the rest."

Hilary argued herself hoarse, but nothing she said could shift Mrs. Walker's stance on the issue.

The lady waved away her objections with a flick of her heavily beringed hand. "We shall ask Davenport to escort us shopping tomorrow. That ought to get him hot and bothered."

"Good gracious, why?" said Hilary, genuinely curious.

Mrs. Walker rolled her eyes. "Saints preserve us, how did a deVere grow up so innocent? While you're being measured and fitted, he'll be looking at your body, of course. Imagining what you're like naked. Get him primed in all the right places, that will."

Heat rushed into Hilary's face once more. "Then I beg you will not request Davenport's escort, ma'am. I should be covered with shame to know the direction of his mind."

Mrs. Walker shrugged. "Men are all the same, dearie. Not a one of them meets a woman without imagining her with her clothes off, mark my words."

The notion made Hilary's stomach flutter wildly. The shopping expedition she'd so looked forward to when Rosamund had proposed it now made her exceedingly nervous.

She was obliged to sit docilely as Mrs. Walker went through all of the invitations in her fancy card holder, revising her plans for the next month. "For the sorts of entertainments that suit me wouldn't be right for a debutante, my duck. I shall have to send acceptances to all manner of balls I had no notion of attending."

"I'm sorry to cause you so much trouble, ma'am," said Hilary.

Sternly she reminded herself that Mrs. Walker had not asked for a debutante to be thrust upon her. She ought to be grateful the lady was willing to put herself out for a virtual stranger with no claim on her except a distant kinship.

"Well, I daresay that when you're a countess you won't forget," said Mrs. Walker comfortably.

Hilary refrained from disabusing the lady about her future status. "Indeed, I shall never forget you, ma'am," she said, with perfect truth.

Mrs. Walker glanced at the clock. "Now, if you'll excuse me, I must rest for the evening's engagements. You'll be tired, I daresay, and quite happy to spend a quiet night at home."

When the rigid housekeeper showed her to her bedchamber, Hilary found herself in a room decorated in a mixture of the Egyptian and the Chinoiserie styles made popular by the Prince Regent. Four painted and gilded palm trees formed the bedposts, while faux bamboo trellises full of birds of paradise and exotic flowers decorated the walls.

The chaise longue by the window sported crocodile feet. She hoped they were faux, too, although she rather suspected they might be real.

The room might hurt the eyes with all of its clashing splashes of color, but it was a large step up from the Grange in terms of comfort and repair, so she ought not to complain. She tried very hard not to long for the sumptuous elegance of Lady Tregarth's home.

No, she must simply make the best of her situation. She'd evade both Lord Davenport's attempts at seduction and her guardian and chaperone's attempts to trap him into marriage. She would rise above the handicap of Mrs. Walker's vulgarity and conduct herself with elegant aplomb in the hope of establishing herself and attracting an eligible suitor.

While her London season would not be the glittering debut of her dreams, she had much for which to be grateful. She owed Lord Davenport a debt she could never repay.

She remembered the warm-enough-to-burst feeling in her chest when Davenport had announced they were engaged. For a crazy instant, she'd believed he genuinely wanted to marry her. How foolish. More, for an instant, she'd longed for it to be true. That was more foolish than anything.

The last thing a sensible woman wanted was to be married to a profligate, no matter how handsome and charming he might be. Why, he was probably visiting some woman even now, doing with her what he'd wanted to do with Hilary.

Denial beat within her, but she must face the truth about him. Jonathon, Lord Davenport, was every bit as black as he was painted.

Even his loving family—and they did love him; that much was evident—did not believe him capable of honorable conduct or fidelity.

A strange ache settled in her chest.

He'd said he'd call on her but the hours ticked by with no sign of him. Mrs. Walker bade her farewell and rustled out to an engagement, trailing a cloud of pungent perfume behind her. Hilary dined alone on cold meat and cheese.

Waiting for Davenport to come, she felt jumpy, impatient, frustrated. She needed to have a private conversation with him, to assure him she did not intend to make him honor his engagement, to reassure herself that they both understood the rules of this mad-brained scheme.

If only she might send for him to attend her now. But a proper lady did not receive a gentleman alone, and certainly not at this hour.

"There you are, miss." Trixie bustled in. "What a job I've had getting here. His lordship said as how I must come to you directly. Did you have to stop on the road? Did you get your hands on his—"

"Oh, Trixie!" Hilary put her arms around the girl and hugged her, hot tears springing to her eyes.

The maid rubbed her shoulder, then drew back to look into her face. "Why, Miss Hilary, whatever is the matter? Ain't you in London about to have your debut, just like you always wanted?"

"You haven't met our hostess," said Hilary darkly. She turned away to dash the salty liquid from her eyes.

"Oh, she's all right," said Trixie. "No better than she should be, according to her servants, but that's no surprise. Most of the highborn ladies in London change lovers faster'n' they change their linen, mark my words."

"Yes, but, she's so . . . so . . . vulgar," said Hilary, wringing her hands. "I know it doesn't become me to speak of her that way when she has been so kind as to sponsor me, but I did hope . . ."

She plumped down on the bed, watching Trixie rearrange the clothing Mrs. Walker's maid had put away to her own liking. "Oh, Trix. You should have seen the bedchamber they gave me at Tregarth House. And Lady Tregarth is so very beautiful and elegant and . . . and everything I've ever dreamed—"

She broke off, as a thought occurred to her. "Your ankle. You're not limping anymore."

Trixie widened her eyes. "My ankle's ever so much better now, miss, thank you kindly for asking."

"You went from being unable to walk at all to this in one day?" Hilary narrowed her eyes. She set her hands on her hips. "You weren't hurt at all, were you?"

The maid turned away to fuss with Hilary's underthings, as if unable to hold her gaze.

Hilary's ire grew. "Davenport put you up to it!"

Trixie sniffed, unrepentant. "I did it for you, if you must know, Miss Hilary. You deserve a bit of fun and his lordship is just about the best fun there is, if I'm any judge of the matter."

"Then please, do me no more favors," said Hilary bitterly. "My guardian says I've been compromised. I am now engaged to Lord Davenport. It's temporary," she said hurriedly, before Trixie could speak. "It's also a secret, so don't go telling all and sundry."

"Lawks," breathed Trixie, her jaw dropping. "Never say he proposed."

"Of course not."

The maid's brow furrowed. "Then how—"

"Well, he had to say something, didn't he?" said Hilary, throwing up her hands. "Lord deVere painted me as the veriest trollop, and they were all staring down their noses at me as if I were a—a smudge on the carpet. It was awful, Trix. So when he told them we were engaged, I agreed," she added lamely.

"Bless my soul," breathed Trixie. "And how did his family take it?"

Hilary swallowed. "Not well."

Trixie sat down next to her on the bed and sighed. "You're in the suds now, Miss Hilary, and no mistake."

Hilary nodded. "I know. But if we can only keep the betrothal secret, we might brush through it all right."

A faint hope. Too many people knew of the engagement already, and deVere had every reason to make it public. However, coming to London at all had been but a faint hope three weeks ago.

Now that she was here with those prized Almack's vouchers dancing just beyond her grasp, she was even more determined to achieve the dream she'd harbored secretly all her life.

It wasn't as if she asked for a palace or a prince, or even a wealthy, fashionable existence. All she'd ever wanted was security, stability. A kind, calm man she might settle down with and be happy.

She merely needed a way to be rid of her gorgeous, rakish, infuriating secret fiancé first. Her only consolation was that he would be equally eager to be rid of her.

Ignoring the hollow feeling in her chest, Hilary lifted her chin. There was no cause for despair. Davenport might not want her, but perhaps some other gentleman might.

She smiled warmly at her maid. "I'm so glad you're here, Trix. You cannot imagine how your presence has lifted my spirits."

"It was a near-run thing, miss, I don't mind telling you," said Trixie, shaking out clothes and folding them, as if the maids in Mrs. Walker's establishment didn't know their work. "We was coming back from the smithy, John the coachman and Billy and me, when who should rumble out of the inn, fuming and swearing, but the master and Mr. Benedict?"

Hilary feigned shock. "Do you mean my brothers followed us?"

"That they did, miss. They'd got into a fight, goodness

knows how, and then there they were, bleeding and cursing and staggering about. If they hadn't been so worse for wear, they would have tanned Billy's hide for running out on them like that."

"Oh, no," said Hilary, stricken. "How thoughtless of me. I expected them to blame me. Are you all right, Trixie?"

"Of course," she scoffed. "If I don't know how to handle the master by now, you can call me a ninny."

"They must have been furious about the carriage," said Hilary.

"Not a bit. They never use it anyway, do they? And Lord Davenport ordered the repairs to be done at his expense, so that's all right."

"Are—are they coming after me?" She didn't know whether to hope for it or pray they'd turn around and go home.

"Bless you, no," said Trixie. "All they cared about was getting their horses back. And John and Billy, too. Only, somewhere along the line they decided a spree in London would be a fine idea. But they told me to tell you they wash their hands of you and if you expect them to squire you about to parties and such, you can think again."

Hilary digested this and tried to identify her reaction. Relief, certainly. She wasn't disappointed or even saddened by this evidence of her brothers' priorities. Her brothers had never cared a button for her. She'd known that for many years.

She only very occasionally wished they'd prove her wrong.

"What about you, Trixie?" she said. "Did they try to force you to return to the Grange?"

Trixie avoided her gaze. "Oh, no, miss. Besides, Lord Davenport offered me a handsome sum if I came with you to London, so I'm sticking to my side of the bargain."

Her gaze flickered to Hilary and away again. "I'm doing it for the money o'course. A girl has to look out for herself, you know."

Hilary flew up to hug her maid, startling her so much she dropped the petticoat she held.

"Thank you," whispered Hilary. "I shall never forget it."

Trixie had no sooner left for the night when Hilary heard a soft tapping. She rose from her dressing table to open the door.

No one there.

The tapping grew more insistent, and went for longer this time. Hilary whirled around to see a figure at the window. A muffled shriek escaped her before she realized who it was.

Davenport.

She hurried over and threw up the sash. "How on earth did you get up here? Come inside, before someone sees you."

He climbed over the sill, ducking his head as he folded his big body almost double to fit through the open window. As soon as he'd cleared the sill, Hilary darted forward to pull down the window and yank the curtains shut.

"Fortunately, I'm adept at climbing into ladies' windows," said Davenport, brushing a cobweb off his shoulder. He cast a glance around him. "Good God!"

He prowled around the room, inspecting it, curling his lip with aristocratic disdain at the mishmash of exotic styles.

"What are you *doing* here?" she whispered.

She'd waited forever for him to come, but now it was far too late for him to be paying calls and most improper to do it in her bedchamber, of all places.

If he was found here, there would be hell to pay. Thank goodness Mrs. Walker had gone out for the evening or they'd be forced to marry as soon as the special license could be fetched.

He went to the door and closed it with a soft click. Then he turned and regarded her. "I've come to visit my betrothed, as I promised I would."

The heat in his usually merry dark eyes made Hilary nervous. She retreated behind a spindly little chair. As if *that* would stop him, but still, she had to do something.

"I—I must express my gratitude for your chivalry today," she said, her voice shaking a little. "Needless to say, I wouldn't dream of holding you to the arrangement."

"Gratitude is unnecessary," he told her. "I had my reasons for giving them the lie, and those reasons had nothing to do with chivalry."

So, it was all meant to be a fabrication. Good. Excellent. At least she knew for certain now where she stood.

Her brow furrowed. "Why, what do you have to gain by it?"

He opened his mouth as if he would tell her, then shut it. "Never mind. But don't go casting me as some prince in a fairy tale. My motives are rarely pure."

She thought he protested too much, but she didn't argue the point.

A sudden smile lit his features. "That's a fetching ensemble you're barely wearing."

She glanced down at herself. In the heat of the moment, she hadn't even grabbed a wrapper.

He crossed the floor to her, picked up the chair behind which she'd retreated, and set it aside.

Then he stood looking down at her, a smiling question in his eyes.

Hilary swallowed. He crowded her vision with those wide shoulders and that deep, muscular chest. She inhaled his scent, clean and somehow spicy.

Something deeply feminine within her responded to all this patent masculinity. In spite of every precept she held dear, a yearning unfurled within her, wrapped its fine tendrils around her vitals, and tugged.

Nervously she faltered, "We might be betrothed, but it's a sham, as you said. It certainly doesn't give you the right to enter my bedchamber, or—or, take liberties. . . ." She trailed off.

He remained silent, looking down at her. She felt his heat. He was so close, she could smell the starch in his cravat.

"Of *course* I won't hold you to the engagement," she faltered. "I don't want to marry you any more than you want me."

"But I *do* want you," he said, swiftly capitalizing on her slip of the tongue. He reached out to brush the backs of his fingers down her cheek. In a low, soft tone he added, "I thought I made that clear at the outset."

Resisting the urge to lean into his stroking like a cat being petted, she pleated her fingers together. "You said that to tease me. I know it is difficult for you when people insist on believing the worst, but—"

"You see, when it comes to me," he said, reaching out to set his hand on her waist, "*people* are so often right."

He drew her toward him so that their torsos almost touched.

Hilary was breathing hard now, almost whimpering with the effort of restraint. She wanted to throw herself into his arms, to seek shelter and comfort after the trials of the day. How strange that in a world she'd longed for since she was seventeen her only ally should be this man, this scoundrel.

She didn't believe his denial of chivalry. He'd saved her, hadn't he? She'd been trapped like a fox surrounded by baying hounds, and he'd come to her rescue in the nick of time.

Her insides melted at the recollection. The relief of his intervention had threatened to overwhelm her.

There it was again, that intent, searching look, glazed with heat. It burned into her, made her insides clench and her hand tremble in his.

"I am going to prove them right about us," he said. "I want you, Honey. I want to be inside you, to pleasure you."

Sinful words, but they made her shudder a little in places she rarely thought about. In the pit of her belly, between her legs.

His arm stole around her while one fingertip traced her mouth. So gentle, so beguiling, she lost the thread of her thoughts. Though his breath came as easily as his smile, she sensed tension in him, too, as if he held himself on a tight rein.

Yet all he did was brush the slightly rough pad of one finger over her lower lip, over and over.

Her lips parted on a gasp.

He dipped the fingertip inside a small way, moistening it on her tongue. Then he gave a soft groan, as if restraining himself was too much agony to bear.

"By Jupiter, Honey, you'll be the death of me."

* * *

The urgency hadn't left Davenport's body, much as he'd willed it away. When the wetness of her mouth surrounded the tip of his finger, the hot thrill of it jolted like lightning, straight down to his cock.

And then he was reversing their positions, pushing her up against the wall, leaning in, palms against the silk hangings either side of her head.

Her beautiful breasts rose and fell rapidly, drawing his

attention. It was a dilemma to know which part of her to feast on first.

He must remember that she was new to lovemaking. He must not rush her.

Damn, but that was going to be difficult.

"My lord, you must stop this," she breathed, but her tone lacked conviction. Her breathing was ragged with desire.

"I know. But I can't."

Her eyes went wide. Her teeth worried at her lower lip and he knew now where he ought to begin.

"Stop that," he said, and sank his mouth into heaven.

How had he refrained from kissing her all this time? It seemed like years since he'd last sampled those luscious lips. Her taste was every bit as sweet as he remembered, the texture soft, moist, delicate, and yet powerfully feminine. Her essence drew him in, until all thought of technique and caution and coaxing a virgin slowly and surely to fever pitch was forgotten.

He deepened the kiss, molding his mouth to hers, probing with his tongue. Her head pressed against the wall, holding her steady against his passionate assault.

And wonder of wonders, she kissed him back. Tentatively at first, then fiercely, her slender fingers plunging through his hair.

Heat surged through him. Blood pounded. He caught her to him, swung her away from the wall, wrapped his arms around her and feasted.

She uttered an incoherent moan of half pleasure, half helpless plea. He slid his hand to her waist, and lower. Caressing her lovely bottom, he urged her against him, wanting her to understand what she did to him, what tonight would mean to them both. Her gasp told him she felt his urgency, understood it, too.

He let his lips slide down her throat to sip at the junction between neck and shoulder. Gently, no biting. He didn't want to frighten her, even though his instinct was to sink his teeth into the pulse point at her neck.

She threw her head back, and he supported her as her knees buckled.

The creamy swells of her breasts enticed him. Reverently, he kissed each one as it plumped up above the line of her night rail, delved his tongue into the soft valley between.

"I could die a happy man right here," he murmured into her cleavage. But that was only half the truth. He could only die happy when he finally got inside her.

His cock stood to attention and saluted at the thought.

CHAPTER FIFTEEN

O h, dear Heaven," murmured Hilary. She knew she'd let matters go too far. This was dangerous, sinful and wrong.

He was so large and overwhelming and . . . and male. For once, she reveled in the simple directness of Davenport. His utter certainty was a relief after the torture of her own warring emotions.

So when he kissed her with such command and mastery, she surrendered to the blaze that flared inside her. Just for a little while, she told herself. For a few moments, she could be free.

No one would ever know that she'd let her inner deVere come out just this once. No one but Davenport, of course.

He kissed as if he might consume her. The plunge of his tongue was lascivious, drugging, wildly exciting. She experimented, responding to him in a way she'd never dreamed of doing only two days before.

His hands roamed her body, taking liberties that shocked her but intrigued her, too. When his hand stroked her bottom, the startled recognition of her own wicked longing made her too confused to pull away.

She'd done nothing much with her own hands, unsure what she was supposed to do, what might be acceptable or appropriate. The image of Davenport's naked buttocks flashed in her mind's eye, and Trixie's grasping little fingers flexing in the air.

Did she dare? Her own fingers flexed, then stilled. No, she didn't.

She felt the hard press of his member against her belly and thought of flagpoles straight and proud and somehow dangerous and she would have pulled away, but he was nibbling at her throat in a manner that made her weak-kneed and turned her brain to mush.

A spasm of thrills shot through her body each time his mouth pressed and sucked. She'd never dreamed her neck could be so exquisitely sensitive. She'd never dreamed a man could reduce her to a quivering mass of incoherent need.

By the time he nuzzled at her breasts, she was limp with bliss and his sorties over her body no longer shocked her. She simply wanted more.

He was a devil, no doubt about it, to corrupt her so thoroughly in the space of a few minutes. Or days. She supposed this seduction had begun the instant they'd met.

No one will ever know.

Equally devilish, the deVere in her whispered through her mind.

Growling with impatience, Davenport slid the shoulders of her night rail down and lifted her breasts free. The cool air caressed their tips, hardening them to points.

"Pink." His husky, low voice was tinged with satisfaction. "I thought so."

And then his mouth was on her nipple, teasing sensations from it with his tongue, sucking with increasing pressure as his tongue flicked back and forth. His hand covered her other breast, stroking, weighing, squeezing gently, rolling his thumb over its hardened peak.

The pleasure was so intense, she almost couldn't bear it. Now she knew what all the fuss was about, why women flung away their reputations, their very lives, for *this*. This was sublime.

Hilary swayed and before she knew it he'd swept her up in his arms and laid her on the bed.

Her legs dangled over the side and he knelt down between them to remove her slippers. Then he took hold of her skirts and pushed them up, sliding his hands up her legs as he went.

"Wh-what are you doing?" she said, a little more alert now that he'd left off tormenting her breasts. Her body felt as if it had melted into the mattress, but the cool rush of air against her thighs made her suddenly aware of how vulnerable she was.

She sat up a little, supported by her elbows, her person disarranged in the most wanton fashion. The neckline of her night rail hugged beneath her bare breasts, lifting them. Her skirts were rucked up to her thighs—

And Davenport's head was rapidly disappearing beneath them.

"*Davenport!* What—"

"My dear Honey, I have been wanting to do this since I first laid eyes on you. Just lie back and enjoy."

The words were murmured, scarcely audible, against her thigh. His mouth brushed her sensitive skin, then pressed a kiss there, right there, on her thigh. He murmured words that she supposed he meant to be soothing, but she couldn't relax for the ripples of sensation that spasmed through her at his touch.

She protested again, but suddenly his mouth was on her, between her legs, and she nearly jumped out of her skin. She tried to wriggle away from him, but his hands clamped down on her thighs, his thumbs spreading her, opening her to him. His wicked tongue delved and swirled and made mockery of her shocked protests.

"Oh, that's . . . that's . . ."

His only response was to tongue the bud of flesh above the opening to her sex and she was in danger of losing her mind as well as the power of speech.

With a soft groan, he sucked hard on that sensitive part of her and all of the building sensations seemed to gather in tight. Her mind spun away, her spirit floated on bliss for several moments. Then she exploded, convulsing against his mouth in helpless, racking shudders that overtook every muscle in her body.

In a daze, she returned to herself slowly. Oh, *oh*. Surely that was the end of it? But no, he wasn't done with her yet.

His head emerged from beneath her night rail, but his hand took over where his lips and tongue left off. Wicked dark eyes caught hers and held them as he explored her with his fingers.

She wanted to close her eyes, shut out the directness of his stare. The excitement that pounded through her seemed to increase tenfold when their gazes locked like that. She couldn't hide what she felt, couldn't escape the knowledge that it was he, Davenport, who stroked her so intimately.

The quirk of his lips told her he knew it. Part of her wanted to deny her own desires. How could any true lady gain such pleasure from all this wantonness?

"Honey," he murmured, moving over her. He leaned down to kiss her. Languidly, gently, exploring her mouth with his tongue. Bliss flooded her in a warm, syrupy rush.

Gently, he traced the moist folds of flesh at her sex. She became increasingly aware of the pressure of one finger, easing into her.

What followed would be another, more significant intrusion.

Shockingly, she wanted it, wanted *him* there. "Please," she heard herself beg. "Please, Jonathon."

His gaze became hotly, fiercely triumphant. Not in a smug way, but in the manner a conquering hero might greet a hard-won victory.

He took her mouth again. Still trembling with the aftermath of her body's strange and wonderful convulsions, she wrapped her arms around his neck and pulled him down to her.

He was fully clothed, right down to his boots. She wanted to see him, but she was too shy to express the need.

He kissed her deeply, and this time her own kiss flared with passionate abandon. He didn't waste time with his clothing but quickly freed his member and stroked her with it, just as his fingers had stroked her moments before.

"*Oh,*" she said, alarmed at the memory of this part of him, his size. "Oh, I don't think—"

But his hand skimmed up her body and found her breast, and the words died on her lips as his mouth took possession of hers again.

The tip of his erection nudged at her opening and her doubts slipped away. She wanted that—him—inside her with a desperation that increased with every touch.

He gave a muted groan. "So wet," he breathed in her ear. "So hot. So very, very sweet."

Then he pushed into her. She felt the burn, a stinging pinch of pain, and gasped.

She stared up at him, and the look on his face was stripped bare of his usual flippant humor. It was stark with a beautiful agony. His eyes were closed now, dark lashes thick and spiky against high cheekbones, as if he wanted to feel everything about this moment without the distraction of sight.

He stayed still, buried inside her, until she began to adjust around his thick, hard length. The strong arms braced either side of her trembled, just a little. He sucked in a breath and thrust farther inside, longer and deeper, until surely there was nowhere left to go.

She remembered the amazing dimensions of his male apparatus and found herself hoping he'd reached his limit—or hers—in that regard.

After the initial sting of his entry, the pain had dissipated. She was only conscious of being stretched and filled to her limit, of her inner walls shifting to accommodate him.

He opened his eyes and began to move, slowly. A long pause, then a deep surge into her and out, then a long pause. In the pauses, her body grew to crave his return so much she was nearly sobbing with it. She lifted her hips, mutely urging him to go faster.

He thrust deeper still, so deep he seemed to hit something inside her that twisted through her body, a pleasure bordering on pain.

The slow, delicious slide of him became a tingly, warm sensation spreading through her blood, fizzing like champagne. Fireworks bloomed inside her, a quieter, less centered explosion than the one she'd experienced earlier, but somehow lovelier, more intimate.

She sighed, feeling a closeness with Davenport that she'd never felt with anyone else. She surrendered to it, for just this moment, just this night.

She lifted her hips to urge him on, tentatively ran her hands down his back and down, down to fleetingly caress the bare skin at the top of one buttock where his shirt had worked free of his trousers.

At that quick, furtive touch, he gasped and stiffened all over, muscles bunching tight. With a muttered exclamation, he gripped her hips and plunged into her, thrusting ever faster, until he pulled free with a hoarse cry.

His seed spurted onto her belly, warm and moist and filling the air with musky, salty scent. She watched him, wondering at such violent pleasure, that her body had been the cause of it. If his bliss had approached the strength of hers, he must feel every bit as elated as she did now.

Chest heaving, he rolled to lie next to her. They both lay on their backs, staring up at the ceiling. The occasional shudder moved through him still.

He turned his head to look at her, his gaze troubled. "I hurt you. I'm sorry, Honey."

He reached out to tuck a tendril of her hair behind her ear.

She shook her head. "It was but a moment of pain. After that—" She blushed. "But we cannot do that again," she added belatedly.

His fingertips trailed down her throat, tiptoeing along her breast until they reached her nipple.

"That would be a shame," he said gravely, dark eyes dancing as he touched her with consummate skill. "For you know that a woman's capacity for pleasure is infinite, whereas a man must recover himself before he can, er, find his pleasure again."

"Mm?" She'd stopped listening to what he said beyond the first few words. Even after all they'd done, her body flooded with pleasure as he paid exquisite and detailed attention to her nipples. Her tender sex throbbed in anticipation.

His voice thickened as he kissed the place between her breasts. "But, if you'd rather we didn't . . ."

He knew his own power and made sure she knew it now, too. He set his mouth to her body and she writhed, helpless beneath his merciless assault. Her blood pulsed. Her breath quickened. Fire raced in her veins.

Madness. She was mad for him. Insane.

"Honey, let me," he whispered urgently into her navel. There was no longer any amusement in his tone. "Please." *Let* him? She barely restrained herself from begging.

"Oh! Well . . ." She squirmed as he moved lower still. "Perhaps . . . perhaps just one more time."

CHAPTER SIXTEEN

The following morning, Hilary couldn't stop the blushes that rose to her cheeks every time she thought of the night just gone. The sensations Davenport had evoked in her, the things he had done . . . she shivered.

He was wicked and incorrigible and wholly immoral. And yet last night he'd made her feel so utterly sated, so excited and possessed, as if he'd taken control of her body, played it like an instrument in a sweet song as old as time.

Last night, she would have let him do anything he wanted to her.

She'd even let him wash her *down there,* removing all traces of their lovemaking before he'd left.

He'd taken her and she'd trusted him with her body, with her innocence. Why, when Lord Davenport posed the greatest of all threats to her well-being, did he make her feel so safe?

In his own careless, unconventional way, he kept rescuing her. From the storm, from her brothers' house, from those horrid men in the inn, from the condemnation of her relatives and his.

The realization unsettled her. He was scarcely her idea

of a Sir Galahad. Indeed, if she accused him of it, he'd be revolted.

And yet, when one looked at bare facts without prejudice, one could not but conclude that Lord Davenport was every inch the hero.

Her hero, at least.

Confusion teemed in her brain. She ought to feel ashamed at having lost a woman's most precious possession to him last night. But all she felt was a deep, heated longing for him to do it all over again.

What about that quiet, kind gentleman of your dreams? The country squire, the scholar, the parson?

Those dreams paled beside the reality of Lord Davenport.

Her rational self chastised her. She could never have him. They would break the engagement when her month in Town was over and that would be that. Davenport would move on to another woman—*other women*—and forget her as soon as she was out of his sight. In fact, he might well tire of her before their month was over.

She was a fool if she didn't try to make some eligible connection while she was in London. Davenport might take her to his bed, but he would never take her as his wife.

A strange ache wrapped around her chest. Well, she couldn't waste time in regret. She'd have to deal with that trouble when it came.

She reached the morning room to discover her hostess in a frothy vermilion negligee, a lace cap perched slightly askew on her fiery locks. The lady had crumbs down her front and a mountainous stack of what looked like invitations piled up before her.

Mrs. Walker was muttering to herself, sorting through the cards.

At Hilary's approach, she looked up. "Ah, there you

are, dearie. What do you suppose all this is? We are invited everywhere."

Hilary's brow wrinkled. "But I don't understand. No one knows me in London."

"Mark my words, Lord deVere has seen to that." Mrs. Walker chortled in delight, waving one card in the air. "This one's from Lady Arden for a soiree tonight. A very high stickler indeed, Lady Arden."

Yes, Hilary was well aware of that. "I made her ladyship's acquaintance yesterday."

Stunned, she sat down at the breakfast table and watched her hostess go through card after card of cream stock.

"You needn't be so shocked, Hilary," said Mrs. Walker. "As Davenport's future countess you'll be sought after, mark my words."

"But no one is to know of the engagement," said Hilary, though the circle of those who did know seemed to widen with every passing hour.

"This secrecy business is harebrained," said Mrs. Walker. "Where do you think you'll find a better catch than a belted earl, my duck? And not one of those pauper lords, either. You may be sure Davenport is plump in the pocket. All the Westruthers are."

"Still, we might decide we do not suit," said Hilary.

The lady scoffed. "You'd best resign yourself to marrying Lord Davenport. The secret will be out soon enough and then you'll have no choice."

She couldn't marry him, not even if the betrothal became common knowledge. Not when he didn't care for her in the least.

Mrs. Walker gave a huff of exasperation. "I can't imagine what ails you, child. He might be a wicked young man, but you cannot deny he's sinfully handsome. Rich, titled, what more could a young lady want?"

Only love, thought Hilary.

The notion startled her. She'd never articulated a need for love before, not even to herself. She'd never dreamed of receiving such a precious gift. Contentment, stability, yes. Those she'd longed for. Love? Situated as she was, the mere idea of a man to love her had been an unimaginable luxury.

What a time to realize love was what she'd wanted—needed—all along.

Desperation shortened her breath, made her pulse race. Dear Heaven, she'd kill herself if she was in love with Lord Davenport. She must not allow herself to harbor tender feelings for a rogue like him. Not when she was so close to attaining her lifelong dream.

But she wasn't given the opportunity to dwell on the notion. Mrs. Walker declared she must obtain a wardrobe appropriate for the season without delay.

"I'll take you to my own modiste," said Mrs. Walker. "She's got a real eye for color, Madame Perrier. Knows just what I like."

If the modiste's eye for color coincided with Mrs. Walker's, Hilary suspected she was in dire trouble.

She wished with all her being that Rosamund and Cecily had managed to prevail upon Lord deVere to let them assist her with her wardrobe, but she couldn't very well express such disloyal sentiments to Mrs. Walker.

The prospect of shopping in London could not entirely distract her from the larger problem of Davenport and the evening she'd spent with him. He'd taken possession of her body in the most intimate ways imaginable and she'd let him. More, she'd reveled in it. Why would she have done such a terrible, irrevocable thing if she wasn't in love with him?

No, she *couldn't* be that stupid. Fall in love with a rake

like Davenport? She might as well watch for the sky to fall as wait for him to love her in return.

"Come along, dear," said Mrs. Walker. "We have much to do today."

Obediently Hilary climbed into the carriage and tried to put her mind to the task at hand as Mrs. Walker rattled on about the latest fashions.

Hilary rarely purchased new clothes, and when she did, they were made of durable, serviceable stuffs suitable for everyday wear at the school. A clever seamstress in the village made them, and while Hilary knew they were sadly countrified, their lack of modishness scarcely seemed to matter. Besides, she couldn't afford to purchase clothing in the exclusive shops in Bath. Her brothers were distressingly clutch-fisted when it came to pin money and Lord deVere was worse.

She was relieved when, despite Mrs. Walker's summons, Lord Davenport did not appear to escort them to Bond Street. She couldn't possibly discuss her apparel with him looking on, especially after last night. The mere notion made her stomach go all hot and fluttery. She'd be sure to give herself away and everyone would know that she and Davenport had been intimate.

Oh, she was a sad case indeed. She'd heard Trixie say that once a man got what he wanted from a girl he lost interest. The notion made something twist painfully in her chest. Last night she'd done more than give Davenport her body; she'd laid herself wide open, made herself vulnerable. Until last night she'd been the one doing the rejecting.

Now . . .

Suddenly her wish for a nice, quiet gentleman seemed like a shiny soap bubble that had burst.

She didn't want a nice, quiet gentleman. She wanted an

infuriating rogue, a deliciously handsome scoundrel. She wanted Davenport.

The shock of that revelation nearly made her trip as she descended the carriage steps.

Oh, she was deranged, surely? The physical act of loving him must have addled her brain.

As they entered the sumptuous showroom of Mrs. Walker's favorite modiste, Hilary was startled out of her reverie. She looked about her and swallowed hard.

She had no experience of London dressmakers, it was true, but she'd expected something a little more genteel than the establishment they entered.

She'd imagined walking into a showroom filled with colorful, sumptuous fabrics and stacks of the latest fashion magazines, like *La Belle Assemblée*. This shop was furnished in gaudy brilliance of purple and gold, with a plush velvet chaise longue at one end and a massive chandelier looming overhead. The walls were such a violent color, they seemed to pulse around her.

"Madame Perrier has a style that is utterly unique," whispered Mrs. Walker.

Hilary could well believe it.

"Besides being dagger cheap, my dear," added Mrs. Walker. She beamed at the emaciated little woman who emerged from the back of the shop.

"Madame Walker, how lovely to see you," said Madame Perrier. Hilary detected an undercurrent of East London in Madame's "French" accent.

Madame had dark hair and snapping dark eyes and wore black bombazine, which made her look like an undernourished crow. Altogether an unprepossessing aspect. And this woman was a wizard at dressmaking? Hilary found it difficult to believe.

Equally difficult was associating the eye-watering color

of Madame's establishment with the funereal sobriety of her gown.

The dressmaker gave Hilary a quick, hard, assessing stare before directing a look of inquiry at her patroness.

"I've brought you my kinswoman, Miss deVere," said Mrs. Walker, taking Hilary's hand and patting it. "She is making her come-out this season and requires dressing. An entire wardrobe, madame. Her guardian insists upon it."

A thin eyebrow quirked. Calculation gleamed in the woman's black eyes. Then she clicked her fingers and another woman appeared—equally thin and dressed in the same manner as her mistress but tall as a beanpole.

"If Mademoiselle will step on the plinth?" said the tall woman in a sepulchral tone that made Hilary feel as if she were being led to the scaffold.

The experience went downhill from there.

The assistant brought forth several bolts of cloth, each shade more lurid than the last, and instructed Hilary to hold them against herself so Madame could judge the appropriate shades for her complexion.

Aghast, Hilary said, "But I ought to wear pale colors, don't you think, Mrs. Walker?"

Debutantes always wore white or pastels or sprigged muslins. She didn't even want to touch a bilious shade of chartreuse Madame insisted would be exactly the thing for her complexion.

Mrs. Walker waved away her tentative bid for independence. "My dear, you are pretty but not enough of a beauty to outshine the other gels. You must be different—and what better way to stand out than to wear bright colors? I assure you, *my* unique sense of style was what caught the late Mr. Walker's eye. Bless his soul."

"I know it is terribly tame of me, but I don't mind

dressing like all the other debutantes," ventured Hilary. "Indeed, I don't wish to stand out, particularly."

All she'd ever wanted was to take her place among the fresh-faced daughters of the ton at Almack's. How often she'd heard the pupils at Miss Tollington's bemoan all of the rules of society. Hilary relished every one. She positively yearned to show how well she'd learned them, how modest and quiet and elegant a deVere could be.

How on earth could one appear modest and quiet—not to mention elegant—in eye-watering burnt orange?

What would Davenport think?

The doubt crept into her mind before she could stop it. Oh, she was a sad case indeed to crave his admiration.

Disappointment curdled Hilary's stomach as she surveyed her reflection in the gilt-edged looking glass. She'd dreamed of appearing exquisitely gowned before Davenport, of seeing awe in his eyes instead of that amused gleam. If she wore a gown made of fuchsia pink silk he'd either roll on the floor laughing or cast up his accounts.

She shuddered. What gentleman would want a girl who dressed like a Chinese lantern?

Hilary argued her case, her tone polite but firm, to no avail. She bit her lip, desperate to come up with a way to foil Mrs. Walker's plans without criticizing her chaperone's taste.

The shop bell tinkled, startling her. She turned her head, to see Lord Davenport's tall form in the doorway.

"My lord!" said Mrs. Walker, beaming at him. "You found us."

"Lord Davenport," said Hilary, her voice scraping slightly.

There was an intense, smoldering look in his eyes when they alighted on her that sent a spear of heat to the pit of her belly. She all but melted on the spot.

By now, he'd assimilated the horrors of the décor.

"Good God," he said, looking about him. "It's like being trapped inside a sore throat."

"Good morning, ma'am," he said, bowing to Mrs. Walker, ignoring the dressmaker completely. "Honey, where the Devil have you been?"

He looked aggrieved, which was rich, considering Mrs. Walker had invited him on this jaunt and he'd failed to appear at the appointed time.

"Here," she answered. "As you see, I am being measured for gowns."

"In *this* place?" He took another glance around. "Looks more like a brothel than a dressmaker's shop. You can't buy gowns here."

A muted squawk of fury burst from Mrs. Walker's lips.

Hilary nearly choked on a spurt of laughter but did her best to frown him down. "Mrs. Walker patronizes this shop. She recommends Madame Perrier's services highly."

Davenport eyed Hilary's chaperone, who today wore a mustard yellow ensemble, edged with bottle green. "I daresay."

The dressmaker herself stood openmouthed with shocked fury at his outrageous comments. Hilary noted that the emotion colored the lady's cheeks nicely. She looked a little less like an effigy now.

"Cancel the order, Mrs. Walker," said Davenport. "Honey, come with me."

He held the door open for her and bowed. Nearly skipping with relief, Hilary tossed the bolt of fuchsia silk into the scrawny arms of Madame's assistant and hurried to join him.

Ignoring Mrs. Walker's squawking protests, Davenport calmly drew Hilary's arm through his and strode up Bond Street.

"Oh, I could kiss you!" she whispered. So utterly thankful to have been spared the humiliation of wearing

Madame Perrier's creations, she really could have kissed him, right there on Bond Street in full view of all onlookers.

He glanced down at her with a glint in his eye. "Make your apologies to Mrs. Walker and we'll find somewhere for you to have your wish."

Vignettes of the previous night rose in her mind's eye, making heat pool in her belly. Coloring, she shook her head. No matter how often and severely she castigated herself for her behavior, she couldn't bring herself to regret it.

Now her tarnished hero had saved her from sartorial suicide. "You are becoming a white knight, you know, Davenport. You are forever rescuing me from something."

The notion made him stop short. He was silent for a moment, with an odd look on his face. Then he said, "Don't be ridiculous," and kept walking.

"Ah. Here we are." He stopped outside a shop with an elegant bow window that did not have a shingle out the front or any indication of the owner's name or the shop's purpose. He ushered Hilary through.

With a soft gasp of wonder, Hilary stepped into an establishment that was as different from Madame Perrier's as champagne from small beer.

* * *

"Come along, Mrs. Walker," Davenport called as the irate matron puffed her way up the street toward him. "Don't dawdle."

"My lord," she panted as she caught up with him. "This is Madame Giselle's. Lord deVere has given me a strict budget and I assure you, it don't stretch to that woman's prices."

"Don't give it a thought," said Davenport, who'd expected nothing less. He let the door close with Honey on the other side of it so she couldn't hear them. "You may send the bills to me."

The blowsy matron's shrewd face turned calculating. "Now that's what I call gentlemanly."

"On two conditions, ma'am," said Davenport. "First, you must have a wardrobe for the season from Giselle also, and place yourself completely in her hands."

"Well, I don't know," said Mrs. Walker, glancing dubiously at the shop window.

"At my expense, of course," murmured Davenport.

The lady's face lit up, and Davenport saw that she could be attractive if not for the dreadful garments she wore. And the hair, of course.

Her eyes narrowed. "What's the second condition?"

"You must leave all sartorial decisions about Miss deVere's gowns to Miss deVere and Madame Giselle."

Mrs. Walker sniffed with affront. "Well, I'm most happy to, I'm sure."

Looking anything but happy, she barged ahead of him into the sumptuous salon.

He didn't think she'd give them any trouble, however. The prospect of a season's worth of new gowns from London's most exclusive modiste ought to keep her quiescent.

Once he'd delivered Honey into Giselle's capable hands, he intended to leave everything to the women. The only thing he knew about ladies' clothing was how to remove it, an accomplishment in which he took simple pride.

However, his sister patronized Giselle and that was enough to recommend her. Cecily was accounted the most stylish woman in London, so it made sense that he'd bring Honey here.

Honey looked at him askance when the exotically dark Giselle greeted him with purely Gallic enthusiasm. When Madame mentioned the Duchess of Ashburn, however, the slight stiffness that had entered Honey's manner vanished.

So Honey wasn't quite as innocent of the world's ways as she liked to appear. She suspected he brought his mistresses here. Or that Giselle had been his mistress. Not a bit of it. He could behave himself when he wanted to, as his false betrothed would see.

"Miss deVere requires a gown to wear to a soiree this evening," said Davenport. "In addition to a wardrobe for the season, of course."

Madame ooh-la-laed and tsked and shook her head, no doubt trying to drive up the price. "Tonight? But that is impossible. You expect me to work the miracle, milor'."

He slapped his gloves on his palm. "Impossible, eh? Pity, that. Well, we'll just have to go elsewhere, won't we, Miss deVere? Good day, madame."

With a slight smile at Honey's crestfallen air, he turned to go.

"Mais non, pas de quoi! Ah, you are teasing me, Lord Davenport." Giselle wagged a slender finger at him. "You would not go anywhere else, for Giselle's creations, they are the best."

She put her fingertip to her lips. "I do not normally do this, you understand, but if Mademoiselle does not object, I have a sprigged muslin that might do very well." She waved a hand. "Young ladies, they are capricious. Mademoiselle decided she wanted pink silk, not white muslin, and so we have my so beautiful creation languishing."

"What do you say, Miss deVere?" said Davenport.

Giselle tried to appear nonchalant, but her gaze darted between Davenport and Honey. She'd taken a risk telling them the gown had been another lady's leavings. Most women of his acquaintance would never accept another woman's castoffs, even if that lady had never worn the gown.

But what was the alternative? He wanted Honey to shine and tonight was the perfect opportunity to attend a party on friendly territory. That was, he *hoped* Lady Arden's house proved to be friendly territory. He wouldn't place money on it after yesterday.

"Indeed, I should like to try the gown," said Honey. "I daresay it will require alterations—"

"They will be of a moment." Madame waved away that consideration, and the gown was fetched.

His warning to Mrs. Walker had been unnecessary. With barely a glance at the chaperone's hideous attire, Giselle expertly ejected her from the proceedings until it was her turn to be measured. With flattering deference, she served the lady champagne and offered her several fashion periodicals to choose from.

Davenport selected a sofa somewhat removed from the chair on which Mrs. Walker perched. Sinking down into the comfortable cushions, Davenport sat back and watched the show.

He wished he might join Honey in the small dressing room where Giselle took her to change into the spurned sprigged muslin. His imagination ran wild over the things he could do to her in that confined space while everything went on as usual in the dressmaking shop outside.

"Charming," he said when she emerged from the dressing room to stand on the raised platform for Madame to fit the garment to her slender form.

She blushed prettily at his praise, but she kept her gaze lowered, as if suddenly shy.

Who would have thought that little virago who had abused him and pummeled him with her fists only days before would now color up and regard her toes when he praised her?

He eagerly anticipated the day when she was no longer shy of him or ashamed of her own desires. As he watched her, his own need seemed to become even more powerful and urgent.

The gown was simple, virginal even, but it transformed her. Without all of the coverings she usually wore to mask her assets, he noticed her in excruciating detail. The elegant turn of her neck, the neck he'd so recently nuzzled and kissed to make her sigh and shiver. Her breasts, modestly covered but enticingly framed by a scalloped bodice. The lush lips he had traced with his tongue now curved in a smile. Her eyes shone with delighted anticipation.

Those eyes had been glazed with passion last night.

He couldn't wait to have that slender, lithe body beneath him again. Last night had been like taking one sip from a glass of the finest wine, only to have it whisked from his grasp. He wanted to savor her, drink deep of her, until he was intoxicated, castaway.

The need grew uncomfortable as he watched Giselle's fingers flutter around Honey's form, measuring, draping, turning her this way and that. Here the line of the bodice was discussed, there the skirt pinned tighter around Honey's trim waist.

Soon Honey floated in a whirl of silks and furbelows. He felt a warm sense of achievement at having been the cause of that animated expression on her face, even if indirectly. He couldn't deny a feeling of satisfaction that he and no other man had paid for the clothes on her body. A wave of possessiveness struck him so hard, it would have knocked him down if he weren't seated already.

The feeling was new to him. Hilary deVere was an innocent in both nature and experience, unlike any woman he'd bedded before. Perhaps that was the reason. She was naïve and thus he felt doubly obliged to keep her and protect her.

From everyone but himself.

He was no knight-errant—quite the reverse where she

was concerned—but having brought her to London, it was his responsibility to shelter her from the spite of the ton. He wouldn't let anyone belittle her or shun her because she was a deVere.

Giselle assisted Honey down from the platform and indicated it was Mrs. Walker's turn to be accoutred.

Hilary crossed the lavishly carpeted floor and sank down beside him on the sofa.

"Thank you," she whispered, impulsively placing her hand on his wrist. "Oh, thank you, my lord. You cannot know—"

Moisture glistened in her eyes, and instead of wishing himself elsewhere at the sight of feminine tears, he wished them both away from this place. Somewhere private so he could take her into his arms.

He waved away her gratitude, for his part thankful Mrs. Walker hadn't mentioned his offer to foot the bill. Honey would have killed him if she knew he was paying for it all.

"Do you attend Lady Arden's soiree this evening?" she asked when she finally realized he wasn't interested in basking in her effusions of gratitude. "It seems Mrs. Walker and I are to go."

"I'll be there," he said. "In fact, I'll escort you."

Her shoulders relaxed, as if in relief. "Thank you. I admit, I am in a quake over my first appearance in society. It has all happened so fast."

He was already calculating ways and means to detach her from the rest of the company. He knew Lady Arden's house fairly well. "The good thing about soirees is you don't have to dance," he said. "Perfect way to ease into things."

But the tenor of his thoughts must have shown in his face, for she blushed delightfully and glanced toward Mrs. Walker.

"You must not look at me like that," she breathed.

"How do I look?" he murmured, so low, only the two of them could hear. "Like I want to kiss you from your topmost curl to your toes? Like I want to spill this champagne all over your naked body and lick it off?"

He reached across her for the bottle he'd left on the table and she gave a nervous start.

Grinning, he filled an empty glass with the fizzing gold liquid. "Decent stuff, this."

Davenport offered the glass to her, but she shook her head, frowning at him, with that twitch to her lips that showed she was trying to suppress a smile.

Stupid to feel so triumphant at this small victory. He set down the glass and fell to considering ways and means to have her again tonight.

When all was settled, his newly fakely betrothed fairly danced out of Giselle's shop. Her chaperone was equally frisky, having ordered as many gowns as Giselle judged he could stand without being bankrupted. The glowing look Honey cast him was worth every penny.

"Until tonight, then, Lord Davenport," she said, giving him her hand. "We ladies have more shopping to do." She patted her reticule. "Madame Giselle has given me a list of the best establishments to patronize."

"Ah, then you must do so, and spare *no* expense," he said, with a glance at Mrs. Walker.

Honey looked at him oddly, but Mrs. Walker took his meaning. He trusted Honey now had the gumption to order what she liked without allowing her chaperone an opinion.

In fact, a newfound confidence radiated from Honey like sunshine. She looked elegant and at ease, her naturally graceful carriage making her plain gown and pelisse appear elegant, if not fashionable.

Something struck him full force in the chest. A warm

burst of energy that had everything to do with how Honey looked at that precise moment. It was such an alien feeling, he couldn't place it at first.

He continued to stare down at her, puzzling it out. He'd spent so long—years, really—numbing his emotions. Now that he experienced one so powerful and unexpected, it set him back on his heels.

"Why, what is it, my lord?" Honey said, her brow wrinkling in concern.

Then he realized. The feeling was pride.

CHAPTER SEVENTEEN

An invitation from the Duke of Montford arrived in Half Moon Street that afternoon to an impromptu family dinner before Lady Arden's soiree.

This was a surprise. Hilary's impression of the Duke of Montford was that he never did anything in a casual or impromptu fashion.

Thank Heaven for the sprigged muslin Giselle had delivered late that afternoon, perfectly altered to fit. The sprigs were tiny peach-colored blossoms that warmed the white background enough to complement Hilary's skin tone.

The peach satin sash around her waist matched her slippers. A reticule in striped silk accompanied the gown with Madame's compliments, and a light paisley shawl completed the arrangement. Hilary's coiffure was too fussy for her liking, but Mrs. Walker's maid assured her the style was all the crack.

Hilary would have preferred Trixie to dress her hair, but her maid didn't know the current styles in London.

"I'll precious soon learn," she promised, eyeing the tight coils that snaked over Hilary's head with contempt. "And not from that sour-faced fussock, neither. Beg pardon for saying this, but you look like you're wearing your brains on the outside of your head, miss."

Hilary observed her reflection in horror. Trixie was right. Oh, to have her plain, uncomplicated bun back. At least she'd look like herself.

Was it better to be fashionable even if the fashion didn't suit her at all? She suspected that in the ton it was. However, given her chaperone's taste she couldn't be at all certain that the Medusa style truly was fashionable.

"Is there anything so lowering as unattractive hair?" she cried. Particularly when the rest of her looked so fine. "Well, there is no time to change it. This will simply have to do."

Davenport called for them, and he was alarmingly punctual. A glance at her monstrous hairstyle had a slight frown pinching his brow.

"I know," she muttered as she took his arm. "I look like a Gorgon, and not in an attractive way."

"I've never seen such glorious hair so badly dressed," he said frankly. "Even so, you'll be the prettiest girl at the soiree tonight."

She knew he flattered her, but she couldn't help gleaning a small amount of comfort from his words. Halting on the steps outside the house, she said seriously, "Thank you, Lord Davenport."

She wanted to thank him for the compliment but, more than that, for all he'd done for her to bring her to this point. Only she couldn't say everything that was in her heart in front of her chaperone.

"Not at all." He glanced down at her and his expression became arrested. A slight frown gathered in his eyes. He opened his mouth as if to say something, shut it again.

"Come along, Mrs. Walker." He tossed the words over

his shoulder, drawing Hilary along with him. "If we want to turn the duke up sweet, we must not be late."

"Can this be the greatest scoundrel in all of London talking?" Hilary teased, trying not to feel rebuffed.

He grimaced. "I can't say that punctuality has ever been my strong point, but then I've never wanted a favor from His High-and-mightiness before. Montford can open all sorts of doors for you that I, the aforementioned scoundrel, cannot."

He lowered his voice. "He is particularly adept at finding husbands for the ladies in his charge."

Experiencing a stab of betrayal that was quite ridiculous under the circumstances, Hilary let him assist her into the carriage. She sank into the plush, velvet-covered squabs beside her chaperone and tried to forget her disquiet in her appreciation for the carriage's luxurious appointments. A far cry from the moth-eaten, ratty old coach they'd taken from the Grange.

She didn't want to dwell on Davenport's determination to find her a husband. She was beginning to doubt she'd ever feel the same way about another man as she felt about him.

Foolish to entertain such thoughts, but there it was. Other men seemed to fade beside Davenport's vibrant energy.

Then again, how many gentlemen had she met, besides the men of her own family? She ought to try to keep an open mind. That would be the sensible thing to do, not pin her hopes on a rogue like Davenport when he was obviously so eager to be rid of her.

The thought caused a hard squeeze of pain around her heart.

To take her mind off these troubles, she asked about the Westruthers, who seemed so large a part of Davenport's history. "Rosamund mentioned that she and the

Duchess of Ashburn were the duke's wards," said Hilary. "But you were not?"

"No, I was of age when our parents died, so I was spared that honor," he said. "When I was presumed dead, Cecily was left alone in the world."

His face was in shadow, so she couldn't make out his expression, but she thought she detected a grim note in his voice.

When she said nothing, he continued. "I trusted my heir and his wife would care for her, but it turned out that they were small-minded and mercenary."

"What happened to them?" said Hilary. "It must have been difficult for your cousin to be demoted to heir presumptive after holding the title all that time."

"My cousin and his wife have the use and management of my estate in Wales." Again the grim note.

"Were they unkind to Cecily?" she ventured.

"She never speaks of unkindness, so I can only guess. Fortunately, the Duke of Montford had been nominated as guardian in the case of my death and he removed Cecily from their care. He took her to live with his other wards, some of whom you will meet tonight."

She wanted to know why he had disappeared, what he'd done in the meantime, and the reason for his return. However, this was not the time or place to drag those details out of him, so she asked, "Was your sister happy with the duke?"

There was a long pause, and then he drew a deep breath. "I don't know. We've never spoken of that, either. Not in so many words. She is happy now, and that is a blessing."

Hilary glanced at Mrs. Walker. She was quiet tonight, perhaps cowed by Davenport's high-handed interference that morning. Or maybe she was apprehensive about meeting the famously haughty Westruthers.

Who could blame her? Hilary's own nerves jangled.

When she entered the drawing room at Montford House on Davenport's arm, she tried her best not to show how intimidated she felt. At least she was familiar with some of the faces now, and Rosamund gave her an encouraging smile. Cecily greeted her cordially enough, but Hilary guessed Davenport's sister still reserved judgment on her brother's fiancée.

Then there were the Westruther men. If Hilary were not well practiced in the art of hiding her emotions in company, she might have gaped at the wealth of masculine good looks on display.

Viscount Lydgate was a golden-haired Adonis, very precise in matters of dress. Yet he was the reverse of effeminate. He shared the same strong, determined line of jaw as the rest of his cousins and there was a shrewd alertness about his clear blue eyes, as if he was on guard for trouble, ready to respond in an instant.

She noticed that Lydgate sported a fading bruise beneath his eye that looked to be the same vintage as Davenport's own.

The Viscount bowed over her hand. "As you see, Miss deVere, I bear the marks of your betrothed's handiwork. Haven't shown my face on the town in days."

Briefly Hilary met Davenport's eyes. His eyebrow quirked up and he grinned at her, making her feel the most unaccountable glow in the pit of her stomach.

"He does seem to enjoy hitting people," she said to Lord Lydgate.

"Perhaps you might cure him of it," said Lydgate with his flashing smile. "We should all of us be grateful, eh, Beckenham?"

Lord Beckenham loomed up beside them like a monolith. Good Heavens, he was as tall as Davenport, with a face like a handsome granite sculpture. Dark and sober, with kindness in his eyes, Beckenham said, "That our cousin is even here tonight must be due to your offices, Miss deVere."

"Mine?" She laughed. "I did nothing, I assure you. Lord Davenport is anxious to make sure my debut is a success and means to enlist His Grace's support. But it was all Davenport's idea."

The two men exchanged a glance that seemed to communicate volumes, but the volumes might have been written in Greek, for all Hilary could tell.

Was it so very significant that Davenport should join his own family for dinner? His cousins seemed to indicate that it was. Was he so desperate to marry her off to someone else that he'd alter his habits to achieve his aim?

A lowering reflection indeed.

The atmosphere was casual—or as casual as it could be in such a grandly appointed house—with Rosamund standing in as hostess. She directed Lydgate to take Mrs. Walker in to dinner, while Hilary found herself going in on the Earl of Beckenham's arm.

"I trust you are enjoying your stay in London, Miss deVere?" Beckenham inquired in a deep, resonant voice that conveyed a sense of rock-like stability she responded to immediately.

"Yes, indeed." She was beginning to enjoy it now that all the terrors of being sent home were behind her. The company tonight was not half as daunting as she'd expected.

With a smile, she added, "I went shopping today in Bond Street. You can have no notion how entertaining it was."

"You forget I lived with Rosamund and Cecily for many years," he replied. "I believe myself to be thoroughly conversant with the joys of shopping."

She recalled Davenport's assertion that his own talents

ran more to *un*dressing a lady and blushed. "Then you are well ahead of most men in understanding," she said. "It will stand you in good stead for marriage, my lord."

A shadow passed over his face. "As you say."

He studied his wine glass for a few moments. "Miss deVere, I realize we've only just met and it is not my place to interfere. But may I counsel you to caution? Lord Davenport has been going through a . . . difficult transition, shall we say. He has not yet adjusted to all of this." He waved a hand, as if to indicate their surroundings, but Hilary knew he meant more than the family and Montford House.

"I am aware that Lord Davenport has a certain reputation, my lord," she said, choosing her words carefully. "However, he has been all that is kind and generous toward me."

According to Davenport's lights, it was true. She wasn't entirely certain why she was so quick to defend him, however. Beckenham did not mean to be spiteful or cruel.

Beckenham sipped the ruby-colored claret and set down his glass with the precision that seemed to characterize his movements. "It seems to us as if a different person returned to us from the grave. You would never think it to observe him now, but Lord Davenport was a scientist before his disappearance, wrapped up entirely in his work."

A scientist? *Davenport?*

Her astonishment must have been evident, because Beckenham answered her unspoken question. "I don't wonder at your surprise. The change in him has us all in a puzzle. A quandary, you might say."

She'd suspected there was more to Davenport than a charming noble ruffian, but a scientist? Hilary couldn't wrap her mind around that concept.

"What could make any gentleman alter his ways so drastically?" she said.

Beckenham's dark eyes met hers. "I don't know, Miss deVere. One hopes he comes to his senses soon, before he is barred from good society altogether. There are only so many transgressions one can commit, even when one is an earl."

Beckenham's attention was claimed by Rosamund then, and Hilary digested the conversation, allowing herself to be served buttered asparagus spears by a liveried footman.

When the footman withdrew, she caught Davenport watching her. He sat diagonally opposite her, too far away to have heard her low-voiced conversation with Beckenham.

Yet, his jaw was set and his eyes flashed. Was he angry at her? How could he be?

She looked down anxiously at her table setting. Had she used the wrong cutlery? She knew the rules of table etiquette inside and out. Besides, she'd made sure to mirror Rosamund's actions so as to be doubly certain.

To her right, the Duke of Ashburn murmured, "My dear girl, what *have* you done?"

"I?" She gave a start, then followed the direction of his gaze toward Davenport's glowering face. What indeed? "Why, nothing, to be sure."

Cecily's husband had eyes of such unusual golden hue they appeared almost feline, perceptive and penetrating. He leaned toward Hilary. "Can it be that your fiancé is jealous?"

She forced herself to look down at her meal. Deliberately, she cut into a spear of asparagus.

"Lord Beckenham and I were conversing like two rational dinner companions. Why should Davenport be jealous?" she said a little breathlessly. The asparagus rolled, refusing her attempts to stab it with her fork. "There's no reason for him to be jealous."

"No reason in the world," Ashburn said, and laughed softly.

"Tell me, Miss deVere," he added after a pause, "what would induce a lady so virtuous and sensible as you appear to be to shackle herself to a rogue like Davenport?"

Despite the trend of her discussion with Beckenham, she'd been unprepared for so direct a question and was taken aback.

Recovering her poise, she said, "It was my mama's dearest wish that Lord Davenport and I should be wed one day. And besides," she said, her brow furrowing, "Lord Davenport has many good qualities."

"Such as?"

"Well, he can be lively company, and he's kind. Oh, and he is chivalrous on occasion." She gave a spurt of reminiscent laughter. "Even when he doesn't mean to be."

That Davenport's native shrewdness was accompanied by a powerful intellect made her feel off balance. She would need time to absorb the implications of this new dimension Beckenham had described.

Ashburn set down his knife and fork to regard her. "I see."

She abandoned the asparagus for the moment and sipped her wine. "Your Grace, Lord Beckenham has marked a vast change in Davenport since his return. What do you think? Do you happen to know the cause?"

There was a long silence while Ashburn contemplated her. Conversation buzzed around them, laughter, clinking of china and cutlery.

Finally he said, "Miss deVere, when a man loses his purpose in life, he can go one of two ways—fall into a fit of melancholia, or run headlong into dissipation. Overindulgence in vice, while deplorable, is often a sign of inner turmoil."

Inner turmoil. When she'd first met him, she would have sworn Davenport was as three-dimensional as a paper doll, with no inner workings whatsoever. How prejudiced and wrong she had been. On closer acquaintance, she'd realized his flippant good humor was just a façade. Tonight she'd discovered he possessed hidden depths she'd never dreamed could exist.

Would she ever discover the truth about Lord Davenport?

* * *

After dinner there was no time for the gentlemen to linger over port or for the ladies to gossip over tea in the drawing room. Everyone climbed into their carriages and moved off to their various destinations.

Having handed the ladies into his carriage, Davenport turned to find Beckenham at his elbow.

Beckenham said, "A novel experience, seeing you behave yourself, Davenport. And in such a worthy cause, too. Is your tongue sore from licking Montford's arse yet?"

"All but growing calluses," he acknowledged with an insouciant grin.

His big, sober cousin had practically monopolized Honey at dinner. As Davenport had predicted, the two of them got on like a house on fire.

"Are you going to Lady Arden's?" Davenport asked. If Beckenham did, it would be the first time he'd set foot in a ton gathering outside Montford House for years.

"Good God, no," said his cousin. "You know how I abhor such stuff."

Becks wasn't so enamored of Honey as to break his drought and follow her to a soiree, then. Davenport relaxed a little.

"I've asked Miss deVere if she'd care to see the sights of London," said Beckenham casually. "She said you vowed you'd rather stick needles in your eyes than visit the Tower and the Royal Exchange."

Davenport made himself shrug. "You're a beggar for punishment, Becks. What next will you do? Escort her to Almack's?"

"I might at that," said Beckenham, with an uncharacteristic grin. "You can't do it, after all. You're banned from Almack's, remember?"

The smugness with which Beckenham made that remark set Davenport's teeth on edge.

All sorts of threats ran through his mind. *Keep your hands off my betrothed or I'll make you the last castrato in England* was uppermost among them.

Before he could voice the words, his cousin touched his hat with one fingertip in what was, for Beckenham, a jaunty salute. "'Night, Davenport. Look after Miss de-Vere this evening, won't you, old fellow?"

Gritting his teeth, Davenport watched his cousin stroll off into the darkness.

He turned to climb into his carriage, only to find the steps had been pulled up, the door shut.

"Hey!" Davenport slapped the flat of his hand on the black-lacquered panel of the barouche.

Lydgate stuck his stupid fat golden head out the window. "Sorry, Davenport. This one's full. You'll have to go in Montford's carriage." He turned his head to call up to Davenport's coachman. "Drive on!"

Without a glance in Davenport's direction, his own bloody coachman whipped up the horses and left him in their dust.

*   *   *

The evening went on in much the same vein. Davenport's cousins took Honey under their collective wing, introducing her to a stream of eligible men.

Despite that fright of a hairstyle, Honey attracted buckets of admiration, as he'd known she would. The party was a crush. He couldn't get near her for most of it.

Not that he tried particularly hard. This was what he'd wanted, wasn't it? An opportunity to hand her off to a worthier man.

Yet when he saw that it was Gerald Mason and Ashburn she now conversed with, enough was enough.

Mason had the scientific practice and respect of his peers that Davenport had once possessed, then lost. He was damned if the fellow would get Honey into the bargain. Hell, the awkward scientist had nearly tripped over his tongue salivating after Lady Maria only the night before. Now he'd set his sights on Honey.

Davenport started over to them to claim his betrothed.

"Lord Davenport." The dulcet tones of Lady Maria reached his ear.

He was tempted to ignore her, but while he paused, debating with himself, her hand shot out to catch his arm in a pinching grip.

Davenport turned without troubling to hide his irritation. He was in no mood to deal with Lady Maria now.

"Lord Davenport," she repeated with a hint of steel in her dulcet voice. "I must speak with you a moment."

"My lady, now is not the time and here is not the place," he said, quickly brushing her hold from his arm.

She licked her lips, and it struck him that she was nervous. What did she have to be nervous about?

Lady Maria's family was affluent. Their pedigree was quite as old and illustrious as the Westruthers'. She did not exhibit the least sign of infatuation or genuine feeling for him. The truth was, she didn't know him well enough to have fallen deep in love, in any case. They'd barely spoken beyond trivialities and spent any time alone together groping each other madly.

She was a beautiful girl. Even so, he wondered why he'd taken the risk or the trouble. Too much time on his hands and not enough good honest work, Beckenham would have said. Perhaps Beckenham would be right at that.

"Name a time and a place, then," she said quickly when he made as if to turn away.

What he saw in her eyes made him uneasy. He'd been wrong about Lady Maria. She wasn't nervous; she was desperate.

"Are you in some sort of trouble?" he asked her, with a quick glance around to make sure they weren't overheard.

Her lips pressed together and her eyes grew bright. "I—I need to speak with you alone."

It could be a trick. Most likely, it was. Only a handful of days ago she'd done her best to lure him into a compromising situation so her father might discover them together and demand that he marry her. If he agreed to meet her in private, the same result might occur.

He grimaced. "My dear girl, I'd wanted to break this to you gently, but it seems I have no choice but to tell you now. I am betrothed to another lady, Maria. That is why I will not meet you anywhere alone."

Her hand flew to her mouth. The stark panic that pinched her features startled him. Despite her machinations to entrap him, he had a strange impulse to help her. He wasn't stupid enough to offer assistance at the expense of his own liberty, however.

He tried another tack. "Is it something you might tell your father, perhaps? . . ."

"*Betrothed?*" she whispered. She'd turned as white as

her gown. "To whom, pray? What lady in her right mind would take *you* for a husband?"

"That is not your affair." He didn't feel quite as sympathetic toward her as he had before. With a touch of indignation, he added, "You didn't seem to mind if we were found together at the Middletons' ball."

"You are perfectly right," she said in a vicious undertone. "I was insane to even think of letting you touch me. I cannot imagine why I did."

He might have reminded her that she was the one who'd done most of the touching and that she'd started it, but that would be ungentlemanly and he didn't want to cause a scene. Instead, he made her a careless bow in what he hoped was a final farewell.

Beneath his nonchalant demeanor, he seethed. And the more he examined his reaction to Lady Maria's scathing words, the angrier he became. Not with her, but with himself, for expecting to be treated as the man he'd once been. When would he learn?

Lady Maria had schemed to entrap him into marriage, all right. But he'd wager the reason she'd chosen him wasn't a flattering one. She'd an ambition to become a countess, perhaps, but she was a noble lady of beauty and fortune. She could reasonably expect to wed a far more respectable, more eligible gentleman than Davenport. Why, then, would Lady Maria blatantly pursue a man she despised?

By Jupiter, he wasn't piqued, was he? He didn't even like the girl. Damned if he'd waste any more time speculating about her.

He realized that he'd lost sight of what Honey had been up to. Even while maintaining a proper distance he'd managed to keep an eye on her all evening, but the interlude with Lady Maria had occupied his full attention. He scanned the crowd. Where was she?

His irritation flared anew when he saw her surrounded by admiring gentlemen. She was too dashed pretty, even with that startling hair arrangement, to be left alone. Where the Hades was her chaperone? That's what the woman was here for, wasn't it? To guard her charge against unscrupulous bounders?

That his brother-in-law and Gerald Mason hardly qualified as bounders scarcely crossed his mind.

Honey looked so earnestly up at Ashburn that for a telling second Davenport's hand clenched into a fist. He wanted to floor his sister's husband, then seize Honey, hoist her over his shoulder, and carry her off.

The urge startled him as much as the unwonted violence of his emotions. He needed to get hold of himself or he'd be in danger of creating the kind of scandal that would leave him no choice but to marry the chit. That was an outcome neither of them desired.

The reflection didn't stop him making a determined beeline for his faux fiancée.

* * *

Hilary experienced Davenport's regard all evening in a hot prickle of awareness at the nape of her neck. Each time she glanced in his direction, he was watching her. The unwavering constancy of his attention made her feel as if he and she were the only people in the room. In the world, for that matter.

Conversations faded into silence, noise and movement blurred to shadow. It was just she and Lord Davenport in that salon, staring at each other from a distance, a current of heat crackling between them.

When had she changed from finding him the most infuriating, irritating man alive to feeling this unmitigated yearning for his presence above all others?

The only thing that pulled her out of this strange trance was hearing his name spoken aloud.

The redheaded Mr. Mason seemed to have trouble suppressing his resentment against Davenport. "To think that for years, that charlatan was worshiped like a god by scientists and laypeople alike. You should have seen the way even ladies who knew nothing about chemistry used to attend his lectures in droves. Byron was nothing to it. And look at him now, if you please. A laughingstock. A blot on the copybook of the institution."

Ashburn said soothingly, "You mustn't let it distress you, Gerald. After all, Davenport's folly and misdemeanors—scandalous though they were—do not reflect on you."

"Such a waste," Mr. Mason muttered. "A waste of a brilliant mind. He didn't have to make up those claims, you know." He frowned. "Yarmouth agrees, and he should know, shouldn't he? I cannot understand it. To this day, his motives are incomprehensible to me."

"That's because your character is quite different from Davenport's," said Ashburn.

Hilary turned her head sharply to regard him. Somehow, she didn't think Ashburn meant that as a compliment to his brother-in-law. It seemed disloyal for him to speak of his wife's brother in that vein. She'd not have believed it if she hadn't heard him herself. He'd seemed to display a sympathetic and nuanced understanding of Davenport's situation at dinner that evening.

Davenport moved toward them and she sought some method of changing the subject so he wouldn't overhear her companions' disparaging remarks. A lady in blue silk waylaid him, she saw with relief.

A most exquisitely lovely lady, Hilary thought, watching them. That tempered her relief, somewhat.

With his back to her she couldn't see Davenport's expression, but there passed a look over the woman's face that made Hilary's eyes widen. The look was desolate, appalled, furious all at the same time.

Had Davenport hurt this young woman?

They exchanged more words; then he bowed and strode toward Hilary, cutting through the crowd. The others who had joined their circle instinctively moved aside for him when he approached. She didn't blame them, considering the fierce look on Davenport's face.

"Your servant, Miss deVere." He bowed to her, then nodded in the gentlemen's direction. "Gerald. Ashburn. No doubt the two of you have been wringing your hands over me."

"Not a bit," said Ashburn easily.

"Excuse me," said Mr. Mason. He turned on his heel and stalked away.

"You'll find Lady Maria on the terrace, I daresay," Davenport called after him.

To Ashburn, he said, "Mason making trouble, is he?"

"I handled it," said Ashburn. He inclined his head. "Will you excuse me, Miss deVere? I see my wife trying to claim my attention."

The glare Davenport gave the other men in the vicinity made them disperse like spillikins. "I suppose I can guess the topic of conversation before I arrived."

An uncharacteristic bitterness tinged his tone.

"I confess, I didn't understand what they were talking about." Hilary paused. "Why did you never mention you are a scientist?"

He shrugged. "I keep forgetting you have not been privy to all the gossip. It was quite a scandal, even amongst the ton."

"He called you a charlatan." She'd believe many things of Davenport, but not that. She did not believe he would lie or cheat. There must have been some mistake.

He stared down at her and for a moment she thought he

wouldn't answer. "I must show you the gallery, Miss de-Vere," he said, holding out his arm. "Lady Arden owns a collection of Canalletos that you might enjoy."

She wasn't sure about this. She ought not to go anywhere alone with him. Merely talking with him too long would set gossiping tongues wagging.

"Come with me, Honey," he said in a low, intense voice that thrilled down her spine. "I want you."

She gasped. Her gaze flew to his. "What, here?"

"Yes. Here." His dark eyes burned into hers. Her breath grew choppy and the knowledge of what he intended heated her blood, made parts of her tingle with anticipation.

"But I—I can't." What he wanted was wholly out of the question. The consequences if they were caught did not bear thinking of. Even now, she risked her reputation speaking so long and intimately with him. She glanced around, to see if anyone might have overheard his outrageous suggestion.

"I know of a place we can go," he said.

That made her think of all of the other ladies he must have lured from parties like this. Oh, yes, he'd know all the discreet little alcoves where one might dally in seclusion.

"Of course I cannot go anywhere private with you," she said. "I have too much care for my reputation."

His regard was so intense, she thought it might burn a hole through her beautiful new gown.

"Don't," she said softly. "Don't look at me like that. Everyone will see. They will know."

"What, Honey? That I had one taste of you and now I'm addicted? That I can't sleep at night for thinking of ways to be inside you?"

"You must not speak to me like this," she said in a stifled voice. "We are not truly betrothed, remember? In a month, we will never see one another again."

At that reminder, the shutters closed over his expression.

His wariness made her angry. "Ruin me, my lord, and you forsake your own liberty. I think it's clear that one more false step will have us at a church with Lord deVere's pistol to your head."

"Do not pretend you would relish that prospect any more than I," said Davenport coolly.

She only wished he were correct on that point.

But he didn't press her again. The mere talk of marriage with her had put a damper on his ardor, it seemed. She'd rejoice in the circumstance if it didn't give her such a queer, hollow sensation in her stomach.

Denying him made her feel irritated and prickly and somehow thwarted. She wished he'd not had the opportunity to proposition her. The exchange had almost ruined her evening. If Mrs. Walker had done a proper job of chaperoning her, this wouldn't have happened.

Where was her duenna? "Do you see Mrs. Walker anywhere?" she said to Davenport as she scanned the crowds.

"Last I saw, she was in the refreshments parlor. I suppose you want to find her, do you?" He blew out a breath and she couldn't tell whether it was exasperation or some stronger emotion. "Come along, then."

* * *

Mrs. Walker was drunk. Being well-versed in various manifestations of inebriation, Davenport knew the signs. Judging from Honey's stupefied expression, she did not immediately comprehend what ailed her chaperone. Probably just as well.

The woman sat alone on a low cushioned bench with her head lolling against the wall behind her and a glass of champagne tipping precariously in her slackened grasp.

A soft snore rose to greet them.

"She's asleep," said Honey, blinking. "Good Gracious, how could anyone take a nap in the middle of a soiree?"

"Well, it is past midnight," said Davenport. "Perhaps the lady is exhausted from the rigors of the day."

He thought it best not to disillusion the poor girl. Honey would take a pet if she knew Mrs. Walker was sozzled. Then she'd fall into another fit of despondency about the vagaries of her relatives. He didn't like it when she did that.

"Ma'am?" said Honey. "Mrs. Walker?"

The lady opened her eyes, blinked, then closed them again. With a vague bat of her hand, she slurred, "Go away."

"Oh, dear Heaven, she is *intoxicated*!" Honey's voice rose on the last word, making her clap her hand to her mouth and glance around to see if anyone had heard.

Fortunately, no one paid the least heed to them. They stood in a small, shadowy alcove flanked by potted palms. The perfect place for a lovers' tryst, in fact. Davenport wished Mrs. Walker far away.

"Best leave her be," he suggested, offering his arm. "I'll escort you home if you like."

Instead of taking his arm, Honey gripped his wrist in a determined hold. "We cannot leave her. What if someone else discovers her like this? What if Lady Arden or the duke . . . Oh, good Heavens, how awkward that would be."

Releasing him, she bent over the lady and patted her cheek. "Mrs. Walker, it is time to go home."

The hand that clutched her glass shot up in the air, spilling the remnants of champagne. "Brrring me another!"

"You have had quite enough champagne, I should think," said Honey tartly, trying to pry the glass free of those clutching fingers.

"Perhaps you ought to leave this to me, Honey," said

Davenport, eyeing the rising tide of pink in her cheeks. Once she got her back up there was no saying what she'd do.

She lifted her chin, a militant sparkle in her eye. "Mrs. Walker is my kinswoman and my responsibility, not yours." Sparing him a glance, she added, "Would you be so good as to procure me a glass of water, my lord?"

"Of course." He went in search of a footman, thinking that a pot of strong coffee would be more beneficial to Mrs. Walker at this moment. Or had Honey sent him off as an excuse to be rid of him while she used some un-orthodox ruse to sober up her relative? She must have gained quite a deal of experience with her brothers over the years. He found himself curious as to her methods.

Upon his return, however, Honey was no closer to waking Mrs. Walker than she'd been before. She took the glass with a murmur of thanks and sipped it. Then she squared her shoulders, marched over to her chaperone, and dashed the remaining contents of the glass in her face.

Mrs. Walker came to life as if woken from the dead, gasping and whooping. Davenport winced with fellow feeling. He'd received similar treatment that morning at the Grange.

"There." Honey set down the vessel, took her chaperone's damp face between her hands, and spoke with a cut-glass clarity designed to penetrate the fog surrounding Mrs. Walker's brain.

"Mrs. Walker, we must go home now. You are going to get up and walk with us through the salon, into the hall, and out of the front door without speaking, stumbling, or casting up your accounts on someone's shoes. Now. Do you think you can you stand?"

Mrs. Walker's head bobbled.

Taking that as an affirmative, Honey nodded also and

expelled a forceful breath. "Right. Lord Davenport, please take Mrs. Walker's other arm, if you will be so good."

Between them, they helped the chaperone up. She reeled a little and Davenport feared for his footwear at one point, but once she had her balance Mrs. Walker became a trifle more cooperative.

When they reached the hall, Davenport called for Montford's carriage to be brought.

"But won't the duke need his carriage?" said Honey.

"It will return in plenty of time for him, never fear," said Davenport. He planned to take Honey home in his own carriage and he had no intention of sharing that journey with a lady who was three sheets to the wind.

"Leave her to me now," he said to Honey. "You go and make your excuses to Lady Arden. I'll see that Mrs. Walker is helped to the carriage."

"Yes. Quite." For a moment, those white teeth worried at her underlip. Then she squared her shoulders. "I'll say she's been taken ill."

Watching her hurry off, Davenport had to pause to admire the self-possession that saw her sobering up an inebriated chaperone before confronting her rather daunting hostess. He only hoped her ladyship was as favorably impressed with his protégée as he was. Lady Arden's support could mean the difference between social success and failure.

Mrs. Walker leaned heavily against him and muttered something into his lapel. He blew a waving ostrich plume from her coiffure out of his face and grimaced as he steadied her and maneuvered her to the door. He'd been an idiot to believe dressing Mrs. Walker would solve Hilary's problem. Fine feathers did not necessarily make fine birds. Not when the bird in question drank like a fish, at any rate.

Having deposited the lady in the ducal carriage and sent her home, he girded his loins and went to hear the verdict. The Duke of Montford and Lady Arden were powerful players in the Beau Monde. Their support was critical to Honey's success.

Ruefully he admitted Honey had been right to spurn his suggestion of a quick tumble upstairs. The mere suggestion showed a lack of respect he hadn't felt or intended.

She'd managed to work her way under his skin in the most baffling manner. So much for being the logical scientist. His reactions to her seemed to bypass his brain.

Seeing that Honey was engaged with his cousins at present, he moved to where Lady Arden and Montford stood together.

Lady Arden, commanding in bronze satin, greeted him with, "A very pretty-behaved girl. You are to be congratulated, Davenport."

"I confess myself wholly taken by surprise," Montford said. "That is not to say a Westruther couldn't look a great deal higher for a wife, but . . ."

The duke spread his hands in an eloquent gesture. The unspoken sentiment that Honey was better than an actress or a tavern wench or, even worse, Davenport's cousin Bertram stepping into his shoes hovered in the air.

It helped when people had only the lowest expectations. One could rarely disappoint them.

"We positively must secure Almack's vouchers for Miss deVere," said Lady Arden.

Montford raised his eyebrows. "You aim high, my dear."

The lady smiled serenely. "It will be a welcome challenge. Oh, I'm not saying it won't be difficult, but I shall endeavor. Bring Miss deVere to call on me tomorrow, Jonathon, and we'll plan our strategy."

* * *

Davenport handed Honey into his carriage, which he'd managed to have brought around before Lydgate could again commandeer it. "I sent Mrs. Walker home by herself," he explained as the door shut behind them with a decided snap. "I want to talk to you."

"Then you did wrong, sir." Her breathing came faster. His gaze dropped to the tops of her breasts, so enticingly displayed by her new gown. "What do you have to say to me that cannot be said in front of Mrs. Walker?"

"Only this," he said huskily. He pulled her to him and kissed her.

He'd expected protests and recriminations, but her hand settled on his coat lapel, then gripped it, drawing him closer.

A renewed passion surged within him at this encouragement. He sank into her, pushing her back against the velvet cushions in the corner of the banquette seat.

Her mouth was like warm, wet silk, clinging to his, sliding against his, giving back everything he wanted and more than he'd expected.

She was such an innocent and he was a bad, bad man to do this to her in a moving carriage with her house a short distance away. Yet he couldn't stop himself any more than he could have stopped a comet hurtling through the sky.

The carriage halted far too soon. He lifted his head to listen. They weren't at Half Moon Street yet, surely.

Honey's labored breathing beneath him made him look down at her. She was all wild-eyed and soft lipped from his kisses. A rosy flush stained her delicious skin from those pretty breasts to the roots of her badly arranged hair.

"I adore you," he breathed.

Her eyes glowed like stars; then her lashes lowered with unconscious coquettishness.

The carriage still wasn't moving, so he reached over to lift the blind and look out of the window. A snarl of traffic had halted them. Apparently many of Lady Arden's guests had left at the same time and now there was nowhere to move until the bottleneck at the end of the street dispersed.

He let the shade fall shut.

"It appears our carriage ride will take longer than I'd thought."

* * *

Dazed, Hilary had no time to reflect or puzzle out what he meant by the comment. He shifted to sit beside her, scooped her up, and plopped her down on his lap.

The bulge in his trousers made itself evident then, nudging her leg in the most insistent way. The memory of having him inside her the previous night made her shiver.

"What if someone opens the door?" she whispered, already trailing soft kisses down his upturned face. Over his temple, down the hard line of his cheekbones, along the uncompromising jaw.

"They won't." His hand slid down her leg to her knee. Hooking underneath, he lifted her leg, maneuvering it until she sat astride him as a man might sit a horse.

She kissed his earlobe, accepting his certainty because it suited her. And because she suspected his servants were trained not to interrupt him when he had a lady alone in his carriage.

Boldly she slid her tongue along the outer shell of his ear. He shuddered, moving his hips beneath her.

"You like that," she whispered.

"If any part of you touches any part of me, I like it, Honey."

She drew back to regard him. Every time she looked, he grew more handsome. How could that be?

She moved her hands from his shoulders to frame his face, holding it steady while she kissed him deeply, possessively, as he'd kissed her.

The carriage lurched forward, rocking them together so that he nudged against her sex.

His hardness made her gasp. His hands at her waist urged her against him, again and again, rough fabric against smooth wet, sensitive flesh. The dampness between her legs must be soaking into his trousers, but he didn't seem to care.

He thrust his fingers between them, beneath the layers of her gown. He touched her so expertly she was nearly maddened by it. Her control—what was left of it—slipped from her grasp. On another shuddering gasp, she kissed him passionately, wildly, grinding her mouth against his.

"Inside me," she panted. "I need you."

"Yes." His dark eyes held none of the merry wickedness she'd seen there before. They seared her with fiery intensity.

With quick, jerky movements, he freed his member, found her entrance, and thrust, pulling her down over him at the same time.

The shock of that powerful invasion made her give a choked cry. His hands gripped her waist as he thrust and thrust, over and over with powerful, uncompromising strokes. She might have held the higher position, but he dominated her completely, possessed her with a strength and raw sensuality she had only guessed at before.

Her hair tumbled down around her ears as she strained to keep up with him, all her senses focused on the feel of him inside her, stroking inside her in exquisite torture.

Her eyes popped open in surprise as she felt that tightness upon her again, increasing bit by bit, but not quite . . .

there. She whimpered in greedy longing and a hint of frustration, tightening her hold on his shoulders, her springy locks falling forward over her face.

Davenport gripped a hank of her hair and pulled her head down to him so his lips slid across her cheek. In a raw, husky tone, he uttered the most obscene phrase she'd ever heard, hot breath in her ear as he pumped harder into her and she shattered, convulsing around him, gripping and milking him, taking him with her over the brink.

CHAPTER EIGHTEEN

After that, Davenport cajoled Honey into letting him sneak up to her bedchamber for a more leisurely session of lovemaking. In Mrs. Walker's state of inebriation she wouldn't have noticed an orgy going on in her house, but Hilary still made him climb up to her, for fear of the servants.

When they were spent at last, Honey raised herself on one elbow and looked down at him.

"You never told me why you disappeared from London," she said, investigating his chest with one curious, trailing fingertip. "How did that come about?"

He grimaced. "You really want to know?"

At her nod, he tried to decide how much to tell her and where to begin. He hadn't confided in anyone save Ashburn. Cecily knew, but only because Davenport had given her husband permission to tell her. The story seemed to belong to another lifetime.

At last, he said, "I disappeared to escape various government agencies and . . . others who were hounding me."

"Why? What had you done?" Apprehension showed in her face. No doubt she feared he'd done something unforgivable. She was right to be wary of his past, but not for that reason.

"Oh, nothing illegal or even immoral, on the face of it," he assured her. "Ashburn told you I was a scientist, didn't he?"

She nodded.

"I'd invented a kind of explosive that . . . Well, it doesn't matter what kind of damage it could cause or how it was made. I was stupid enough to make my breakthrough known to the wrong people. The military and arms manufacturers alike wanted to exploit the invention. Not to mention the French."

He gave a sour smile. "Well, of course they did. I was so bloody naïve, flush with the excitement of discovery, the military value of an explosive didn't occur to me. 'Think of all the people we could maim and kill in one fell swoop,' they said. 'Think of the profits.' When I realized the frenzy my Promethean hubris had caused, it was too late. The gods were already punishing me."

"So that is why you disappeared." Her palm smoothed over his rib cage in the most distracting way. "Did they imprison you? Were you incarcerated all that time?"

He clasped her hand, held it against him, threading his fingers through hers. "No, no, nothing like that. But I don't doubt they would have locked me up, and worse, if I hadn't acted first. I feigned my own death, burned down my laboratory. The story was that I'd died in the fire. Ashburn aided me. I would not have survived without him."

"Ashburn?" She stared at him. "I had the impression your brother-in-law is no great supporter of yours."

"Did he call me a charlatan? A disgrace to the Royal Institution?" He gave a snort of laughter that contained no mirth. "It's due to Ashburn that I was able to return to my old life at all. He used his influence to discredit my work, you see. He branded me a braggart and a poseur, made me a laughingstock."

He'd resented Ashburn's actions, though he'd agreed there was no other way. A part of him still resented them. Intellectual arrogance died a hard death, it seemed.

She thought about that. "So no one believes you were capable of inventing anything," she said slowly, her fingers returning the clasp of his. "You cannot go back to your work for fear they'll realize the truth."

He didn't like the pity he saw in her eyes. "One person wasn't convinced," he said. "Someone has been following me, presumably trying to discover if it was all a hoax and I'm secretly trotting off to my laboratory every night instead of amusing myself in the stews. Months of leading a hedonistic, pointless existence hasn't convinced him otherwise."

"Following you?" Her gaze darted to the window, the hand that held his tightening. "Might they have seen you climb up here?"

"I've been extremely careful," he said. He'd taken pains to be seen leaving her house in his carriage tonight before doubling back. The night before, he'd lost his shadow before approaching the house.

But it was too late to hide their association altogether. The man who followed him would know they'd traveled together to London.

"You may be sure that he and his masters aren't concerned about my amorous interests, in any case," said Davenport. He hoped to God that was true.

She thought that over for a moment and seemed to accept it. He tried not to feel nettled at the relief that made her shoulders drop a little and the air expel from her lungs with a soft whoosh.

"What do you plan to do about all of this?" she said finally.

A good question. The business had gone on for far too long. He'd told himself he'd let it go on because sooner or later the powers that be would lose interest in him. The truth was rather less flattering, he thought now. He'd been too sunk in apathy to care.

"You needn't worry. I'll deal with it." And to his surprise, he meant it. "But now . . ." Lazily, he drew her to him and kissed her slowly and thoroughly. "I want very much to deal with you."

Her breathing hitched as he rolled with her, his long legs tangling with her slim, dainty ones. Her hair spilled over the pillow around her head like whirls of syrupy sunlight. He stroked it back from her brow, picked up a curling tendril and ran it through his fingers, kissed the silken skeins of it, and let it fall. Her scent filled his head, dizzying him as he stared down into her eyes.

She smoothed her palms over his shoulders, regarding him gravely. There was an open, trusting expression on her face that he'd never seen there before. He caught her hands and pinned them down on either side of her head.

Her breathing quickened as he bent his head to hers. When he fastened his mouth over her crushed-strawberry lips, she sighed and surrendered.

He angled his head, kissed her slowly, deeply, using his tongue to coax hers into play. A tentative touch rewarded his efforts. At his murmur of encouragement, she licked into his mouth a little more boldly, her body twisting restlessly beneath his.

A soft moan escaped him as his cock brushed the wet curls between her thighs. The urge to drive into her grew insistent, but he'd only just begun. He released her hands and moved down her body.

Davenport paid her breasts their due, worshiping them, first with his touch and then with his lips and tongue. Honey's hand stroked his head in a tentative benediction, and a wave of possessiveness broke over him, unsettling in its strength.

There was no stopping himself then. He gripped her hips and entered her with one smooth, deep stroke. Even as she gasped at the sudden invasion, he ran a hand down her thigh and hitched it higher, driving ever deeper, until he lost all concept of the two of them as separate beings.

At the height of his passion, he was only dimly aware of her stifled cry, of her body shaking violently beneath him, of the hot, wet flesh that surrounded him, contracting in a pulsing rhythm. He was too far gone, mindless, wrapped in the intensity of his own pleasure.

He barely had the presence of mind to wrench away from her when his crisis came.

* * *

After what seemed like hours of intimate exploration, they fell into a daze of sated exhaustion. Davenport's hand settled, heavy and warm on her breast. Hilary all but purred at how good it felt.

He moved over her once more, giving her nipple the odd, desultory lick that sent a dart of bliss arrowing down her body.

"Why can't I resist you?" She sighed, spearing her fingers through his hair.

She was cursed with a fatal weakness for this man. Every time she thought he'd loved her until she couldn't take any more, he proved her wrong, reawakening her desire.

Silently he laughed, hot breath flowing over her wet nipple, setting her whole body tingling. "Honey, you can't resist me because I know your secret."

That sentence was punctuated by another slow, firm lick that made her stomach tighten and her sex clench.

What secret? "I'm almost afraid to ask."

His tongue traced around her aureole, tantalizing her

in between his words. "That whatever prim exterior you might show to the world, you're a naughty, wicked girl inside."

A bolt of excitement speared through her. "I'm nothing of the sort," she managed. "I can't imagine why you should think it."

His mouth closed over her pink, distended flesh and sucked, making her melt into the mattress.

"You know why I think it?" He kissed his way up her décolletage, pausing to nip her chin on the way, and finally reached her mouth.

She took the bait, too curious to feign disinterest. "Why?"

Those dark eyes laughed down at her. Then he kissed her on the nose. "You love it when I say dirty words."

The mere idea revolted her. "Are you mad? I do not."

"So you have that, too." He rolled away from her and put his hands behind his head in a pose of purely masculine satisfaction.

"I wish you would stop speaking in riddles." She gave a huff and drew the sheet up over her breasts. Her loins ached in frustration.

"Oh, it's quite common among straitlaced females—or so I'm told." She heard the smirk underlying his matter-of-fact tone. "Coupled with the desire to hear me whisper filthy suggestions in your ear, you choose not to believe or accept that this is the case."

"It is *not* the case, I'll have you know." She was almost certain it wasn't. Surely only courtesans and other wantons would enjoy such treatment.

"You may say what you like, Honey. I know differently. You have no idea the satisfaction it gives me to be the only man who knows it."

He was so smug. She narrowed her eyes at him. "You

are talking nonsense to be provoking. I won't listen to you."

He rolled toward her again and propped his head on one elbow and plucked the sheet from her breasts, feasting his gaze on her. "Shall I prove it, here and now?"

Heat flooded her belly. "No, because I *don't* like it and you must stop this right this minute. It's insulting and—and in any case, you're wrong."

He regarded her with a glint of challenge in his eye.

"We'll see, shall we?" was all that he said before he took possession of her mouth once more.

* * *

Despite having enjoyed Honey's sweetly rounded body several times the night before, Davenport begrudged every minute Beckenham spent in her company today. Why had he been so stubborn as to refuse to take her to see the sights of London himself? He was only giving Beckenham more opportunity to show what a superior fellow he was in every respect.

"You are quite medieval, you know," said Cecily, who sat flipping through a stack of what appeared to be old scandal sheets. "She won't return any faster simply because you keep watching for her out that window."

She pulled one scandal sheet closer. "Gracious, did you know that Lord H.-F. is rumored to be bringing a suit against Mr. L. for criminal conversation? That must be Lord Howell-Fotheringay, must it not? But who, I wonder, is Mr. L.?"

"Who gives a fig?" said Davenport. "Howell-Fotheringay is a brute and his poor lady deserves all the criminal conversation she can get."

Cecily put down her paper and stared at him.

"What?" he said, frowning.

"You are snappish today, besides pacing about like a caged tiger. Hilary is with Beckenham, Jonathon. She's as safe as can be."

"That's what you think," he retorted. "Beckenham's a dark horse, mark my words. It's the quiet ones you have to watch."

"Beckenham, a dark horse? That's the most ridiculous thing I ever heard."

She reached over and selected another printed sheet and settled back to read. "Anyone would think you were jealous."

Of course he was damned well jealous. His throat felt tight and hot whenever he thought of Honey alone with Beckenham.

"I should have insisted Mrs. Walker accompany her." Not that the hard-drinking matron was in proper frame to undertake such an excursion.

Really, the woman was not a satisfactory chaperone by anyone's definition. Mrs. Walker's lack of vigilance had come in handy for his own nefarious purposes. Now he realized her shortcomings would be equally welcome to any other man hopeful of getting Honey on her own.

"They are in an open carriage," said Cecily. "They are visiting tourist haunts, surrounded by hundreds of people. What on earth could Beckenham do to her, even if he were so inclined? Which, I promise you, he is not. Whatever he might have said to provoke you, you must know he's still eating his heart out over that dreadful creature."

Cecily curled her lip and Davenport pitied Georgiana Black if she ever crossed his sister's path. Beckenham was Cecily's favorite person in the whole world. Anyone who trampled on his tender feelings would answer to her.

Davenport wasn't convinced, however. Honey was the first respectable female Beckenham had taken an interest in for years, if the others were to be believed. Worse, if Davenport *were* to choose a suitor for her—which he had no intention of doing—Beckenham's name would be top of the list.

He yanked aside the curtain to peer out again into the street.

"About time," he muttered as Beckenham's curricle drew up at the door.

For an instant Honey's face tilted up to the sky and Davenport saw her cheeks were becomingly flushed. He hoped the fresh air and sunshine gave her that particular radiance and not Beckenham's silver-tongued flattery.

That Beckenham was neither silver-tongued nor particularly given to flattery was beside the point. You never knew what a man was capable of until he met a woman he fancied. Look at Davenport, about to trundle off to Lady Arden this afternoon to plan a young lady's debut.

Beckenham didn't come into the house but merely saw Honey to the door. Though Davenport did his best to squint downward to see how they looked when they parted ways, the awning obscured his vision.

"Oof! Shut the curtains, do." The plaintive cry came from Mrs. Walker, who stood on the threshold, putting her hands up and turning her head away from the sunlight that shafted in through the window.

Davenport inspected the damage. Mrs. Walker clearly still suffered ill effects from last night's roistering. She couldn't call on Lady Arden in that state.

He'd anticipated this and brought Cecily with him to take her place.

He turned to the window to make sure Beckenham had left. Before he let the drapes fall, a flash of movement across the street caught the tail of his eye.

He made himself step back from the window. He didn't want to show that he'd seen the figure loitering, watching the house.

But he'd caught a glimpse of a man with a narrow, pointy face like a weasel and knew he wasn't mistaken.

* * *

Hilary wondered if Davenport regretted his insistence on accompanying her to Lady Arden's that afternoon. He'd been taciturn and inattentive, a frown creasing his brow.

"Don't mind my brother," said Cecily as they set off for Lady Arden's town house. "He's jealous that you had such a pleasant drive with Beckenham today."

The bait failed to get a rise from Davenport, but that didn't seem to bother Cecily. She expanded on her theme, wondering aloud if Davenport might challenge Becks to pistols at dawn over the excursion.

Hilary regarded him doubtfully. On the one hand, the notion he might have been jealous made her a trifle giddy. If he was jealous, it meant he cared about her, at least a little, didn't it? But that didn't explain his present abstraction.

He was no better when they sat down to tea with their hostess.

Lady Arden was saying, "I do not pretend it will be a simple task to procure vouchers for you, my dear, for the patronesses particularly despise your guardian. Lord de-Vere has offended them on so many occasions, I've lost count."

Hilary winced, but Cecily put her hand over hers and pressed it. "Never mind about Lord deVere. We all of us have relatives we'd consign to the Outer Hebrides if we could."

"Isn't that the truth?" muttered Davenport with a meaningful glance at Cecily. So it seemed he was paying attention, after all.

Lady Arden smiled and waved a hand. "Yes, never mind

that, my dears, I will find a way. Jonathon, you must keep your distance from Miss deVere, at least until she is sent the vouchers. Lydgate here will escort her to Almack's, of course."

Davenport's brows slammed together.

Fearing he'd punch his cousin in Lady Arden's drawing room or do something equally shocking, Hilary said quickly, "Why cannot Davenport escort me, Lady Arden?"

"I can't," he said. "I've been banned."

"Banned from Almack's?" Hilary repeated. "Whatever for?"

"That's quite all right," said Lydgate, his blue eyes alight with wicked laughter. "I don't mind squiring Miss deVere to a few balls."

Whatever the joke was, Davenport didn't seem to find it amusing. "Been getting in some sparring at Jackson's lately, Lydgate?"

The viscount looked innocent. "Why should I need boxing practice to attend Almack's?"

"You might need it sooner than you think," said Davenport. "Next time, you won't have Beckenham at your back."

"Now, now, children," said Lady Arden, holding up a finger. "Enlivening though all this masculine braggadocio might be, let us return to the subject of vouchers for Miss deVere."

She turned to Cecily. "I believe we ought to set our sights on Lady Sefton and Lady Jersey, don't you? Maria Sefton is a kind soul and she is a great friend of mine, so I don't anticipate too much trouble there. Lady Jersey can be . . . difficult, but she is not nearly as proud as Mrs. Drummond-Burrell."

Cecily said, "I can ask Ashburn to use his influence with her."

"That would be welcome, but it might not be enough."

She tapped her fingertip to her lips. "Lady Jersey has a soft spot for a rake. . . ."

They all looked at Davenport.

"Jonathon," said Lady Arden, "on second thoughts, I might drop a word in Lady Jersey's ear that you are courting Miss deVere and wish to settle down. If I promise her that you will come back into the fold and behave yourself if Miss deVere is granted vouchers, she might consent to give you another chance."

For once, Davenport's expression was unreadable. Seconds passed and Hilary wondered if he'd even heard what Lady Arden said.

"Jonathon?" said Cecily.

He shook his head. "No. Miss deVere is perfectly capable of securing those vouchers on her own merits."

"But my dear Jonathon, with your help—"

"Out of the question, ma'am. I do not go on bended knee to anyone, particularly not to Lady Jersey. Besides"— his gaze flickered to Honey and away—"we agreed, did we not, to keep the betrothal a secret. Lady Jersey is known as Silence for a reason. She'd never keep such a juicy tidbit to herself."

Doubt twanged at the edge of Hilary's mind. His arguments sounded logical, and yet . . .

Was it unreasonable of her to wish he'd thrown caution to the winds and laid this sacrifice at her feet?

Of course it was. She'd be spinning air dreams to believe him capable of such a selfless gesture. She would have to do this on her own, then. Or at least without his help.

So be it. That was what she'd always planned, wasn't it? She'd come to depend on Davenport, she realized, a foolish and dangerous habit to acquire.

"We shall mount our final attack at Montford's ball," said Lady Arden. "That's a week hence, which gives me time to lay the groundwork." Her eyes sparkled. "If we can bring this off, it will be a triumph, my dears."

Hilary thanked the others profusely for their help in establishing her in society. She only wished the task didn't provide them with quite so much of a challenge.

CHAPTER NINETEEN

Davenport wove his way through the detritus that littered the dark London back alley. The cobbles beneath his feet gleamed in the moonlight, slick with rain and refuse. The stench of open drains and rotting food permeated the air.

At his approach, a tangled mass of rubbish scuffled and seethed. With a screeching chatter, three rats broke free of the rubbish heap, scattering in different directions. One flowed over Davenport's boot, tail twitching.

He wasn't concerned with rats. Tonight he hunted a weasel.

He feigned a drunken stagger as the vermin scampered off into the shadows. He wanted the man who followed him to think he was vulnerable. The man might get cocky and, therefore, careless. Mustn't overdo it, though. Even at his worst, he rarely allowed himself to reach the staggering stage. He hadn't bragged when he'd told Honey he carried his liquor well.

The weasel shadowed him tonight. Davenport had sensed him immediately he'd set foot out of his house, although the fellow was damned good at staying out of sight.

He'd let the fellow shadow him all this time, faintly curious to see what might come of it and not caring enough about his safety or his future to eradicate the nuisance for good.

But when the man began stalking him outside Honey's home in broad daylight, no less, the bastard had gone too far. It was time to be rid of this menace, once and for all.

To that end, Davenport had made his usual rounds, which began with dining at his club, then degenerated steadily in respectability as the night wore on. Culminating in this reckless sortie into the rookeries to attend an exclusive but exceedingly nasty gaming hell.

He found the nondescript door and gave the correct knock and the right password. He was admitted by a burly red-haired individual who went by the name of Rusty Nail.

"Evening, Mr. Nail," said Davenport. "Anyone interesting?"

"The usual, my lord. Rawling dropped a cool thousand in one sitting last week."

"Oh?" Davenport surveyed without much interest the motley collection of hardened gamesters who had gathered in the large salon. Ordinarily, he found the mixture of risk and calculation involved in games of chance stimulating, but he had other fish to fry tonight.

Hazard was the name of the game here, and the grim, quiet air of desperation attested to the fact that this was not a club for the faint of heart or the slender of purse. The establishment catered to the Quality and thus provided excellent refreshments, but unlike other such places, it barred women from the cardroom. Not even the lightskirts who might entertain a gentleman to various exotic and perverse activities upstairs were permitted to distract these committed gamesters from the tables.

"Sir." Nail held out his hand to take Davenport's coat. Davenport didn't remove it. Instead, he dropped a purse of coins into the man's palm.

"I need you to do something for me," he said.

Nail, who survived in his trade by being several times sharper than he looked, cocked a wary eyebrow.

"I'm not asking you to cut anyone's throat," said Davenport. Though he rather fancied Nail would do just that if the price was right.

"Someone is lurking outside this club. Could be an informant for the magistrate. Could be it's someone who has a more personal interest in my movements. Either way, I want you to flush him out."

He explained the plan to Nail, who grasped his role immediately. Calling for another heavyset employee to take his place at the door, Nail headed out into the night.

Davenport moved easily through various rooms before slipping out the back way and stepping into an even more noisome alley than the one from which he'd entered. He walked toward the front entrance of the club, where the weasel no doubt loitered.

He didn't have long to wait. There was a muffled shout and a pelter of quick footsteps heading toward him.

Davenport flattened himself against the wall, waiting until the large figure of the weasel ran full tilt toward him.

He was fast, Davenport would give him that. With a flying tackle worthy of a Cambridge playing field, Davenport cannoned into the weasel and brought down the fleeing man.

He rolled the weasel over but only landed one good punch before the glint of moonlight on blade told him the fellow was armed and striking.

The downward thrust would have shivved Davenport between shoulder and neck, but in the nick of time he caught the weasel's wrist in a vice-like grip. The man was strong and cunning and clearly at home with a knife.

Davenport's face was set in a grimace of effort. He ground out, "Who sent you? Why are you following me?"

A feral smile twisted the weasel's thin features. He didn't answer, just renewed his effort to bore down on the back of Davenport's neck with the knife.

On a sudden furious surge of strength, Davenport forced the weasel's arm down hard on the ground, banged it once, twice, on the hard cobbles, finally making his grip spasm open. The blade clattered to the ground.

Davenport wanted to beat the fellow to a bloody pulp. He had to make sure this foul worm never so much as looked at Honey again. But he needed to know who'd sent him and why.

Davenport scooped the knife up and hauled the fellow to his feet. He muscled him to the wall and pinned him by his throat. Nose to nose, he spoke clearly, "You'd better start talking, because men like me do not bleat to the authorities when men like you bother them. They crush them like bugs beneath their feet."

He eased the pressure a little from the weasel's neck to let him talk.

Hoarsely the man said, "Someone will send you a message. No 'arm will come to the little lady if you cooperate."

A red haze washed over Davenport's vision and his grip tightened involuntarily on the weasel's throat.

The fellow's foot shot out to kick him in the shins. He clawed at Davenport's wrists, fingernails gouging. "Kill me and you've got nothing," he gasped hoarsely. "And another'll take my place, sure as check."

"You so much as look at the lady again and I'll gut you," ground out Davenport.

A faint, hoarse cry came from outside the club. Davenport heard it, but he didn't let it draw his focus from his captive.

The man sneered, his teeth an uneven white flash, and jerked his head toward the club. "Stuck your mate like a pig, I did. You Quality, you're all the same. Don't give a toss about the feller back there bleedin' out in the gutter, do yer?"

For the first time, Davenport noticed the dark, irregular patch on the weasel's coat. The sweet stench of blood was on him, too.

Bloody hell. Davenport glanced back along the alley, seeking the large shape in the gloom.

That second of inattention was enough. With a twisting, wrenching motion, the weasel got free.

Cursing viciously, Davenport let him go. He raced along the alley and fell to his knees beside the big porter, who was lying on the stones clutching his side with a dark pool of blood around him.

On a string of oaths, Davenport bent to half-lift the man from the noisome ground, supporting his torso. Giving a sharp shout for assistance, he took out his handkerchief and did his best to stanch the wound.

"You need a doctor," he said to Nail, his heart pounding. There was a sick roil in his stomach. Dear God, what had he done?

"Just a scratch, guv'nor," gasped Nail. "I'll be . . . right as a trivet. . . ."

The big man sagged in Davenport's arms.

*   *   *

Dawn crept across the sky as Davenport walked home from the aftermath of that terrible night. He was covered in blood and the unidentifiable slime of the cobbles on which he'd knelt to help Nail. He reeked of those substances, but the scent that filled his nostrils, seeped into his brain, was the clammy stench of fear.

That bastard had threatened Hilary. His Honey.

How could he have so underestimated his opponent? He'd never dreamed that after months of following him that passive and silent shadow would lash out with threats against the woman he . . . Against Honey, a gently born lady who had nothing to do with any of this.

How could he have guessed the fellow would be so good with a knife?

And Nail. God Almighty, if Nail died, it would be his fault.

The burden of that guilt weighted his shoulders even while the need to get to Honey quickened his steps.

But he couldn't go to her in this state, at this hour. His body was filthy, and there was a growing stain on his soul. As soon as he'd taken care of Nail, Davenport would send someone to make sure Honey was all right and stay there until he could arrange for a replacement. He'd post a guard around the clock to keep her safe.

The weasel had said Davenport would hear from them. The implication was that there'd be a demand, that if he didn't meet it they'd harm Honey.

He ground his teeth until his jaw ached. He'd hand that bloody formula to the Devil himself before he'd let anything happen to her.

But no, he realized. He'd be damned if he'd do either. He was going to find the bastard behind all of this and he was going to destroy him. And he'd take great pleasure in crushing that vicious weasel beneath the heel of his boot.

In the meantime, he needed to fight the instinct that made him want to guard Honey every minute of the day and night. If they saw how important she was to him, their plan to use her would gain strength.

He ought to end the pretense of their betrothal. Too many people knew of it already. There was no guarantee the news would remain within their family circle. De-Vere, for one, had an interest in making the engagement public in order to force Davenport's hand.

He hissed out a breath. Honey hadn't secured those

vaunted Almack's vouchers yet. It went against the grain
with him to deny Honey her heart's desire. He'd just have
to make sure his family stood by her, even if he couldn't.
Better for her if he stayed away. Hadn't Lady Arden said
as much before she'd come up with that crackbrained
scheme to reinstate him with the patronesses?

Inside him, cold rage howled like a blizzard. He loathed
the idea of hurting Honey, but it had to be done. He had to
make a break with her. Not forever, just long enough for
him to find and deal with the man responsible for threat-
ening her. Even if the weasel's employer wasn't deceived
by his ruse, Davenport had to do everything in his power
to protect her while he dealt with this new menace.

He hoped to Hell it would be enough.

* * * *

Hilary scarcely set eyes on Davenport for days after their
call on Lady Arden. That lady had appointed herself in
charge of Hilary's debut and kept her busy from noon
until the small hours with social calls and carefully or-
chestrated appearances at various balls and parties.

Mrs. Walker seemed happy to be relieved of responsibility, but Lord deVere was not so sanguine. He was,
however, no match for Hilary's steely-eyed mentor.

Lady Arden gave Lord deVere a fine trimming when
he stormed in one day to protest her usurpation of his
kinswoman's authority.

"My dear sir, Mrs. Walker is a vulgar, low-minded
drunk," she said succinctly. "Worse than that, she has
execrable taste. You ought to thank your lucky stars I've
taken your ward in hand, let me tell you."

DeVere blustered and ranted, but he failed to cow Lady
Arden, nor did she allow herself to be provoked into losing her temper by his high-handed ways. Hilary could

only watch, openmouthed in astonishment, as Lady Arden deftly routed the irascible baron.

"Men are simple creatures, easily handled if one only knows the way," confided Lady Arden as she oversaw several alterations to the gowns Hilary had ordered from Giselle. "Lord deVere has always had a *tendre* for me, you know, which makes it child's play to get him to do as I wish."

She smiled that secret, feminine smile Hilary had seen on Cecily's and Rosamund's faces at various times. How wonderful it would be to have that kind of power, she thought.

A feeling of utter inadequacy stole over her as she tried to reconcile the heat and urgency of Davenport's lovemaking on the night of Lady Arden's soiree with the utter dearth of communication from him since their visit to her ladyship the next day.

At first, she'd wondered if he'd met with an accident, but one of his cousins or Lady Arden was always with her. Surely they would give her such news if that were the case.

He seemed to have taken Lady Arden's warning to heart. If he wouldn't assist her by reforming himself and pleading with the patronesses for mercy, he should not be seen with Hilary while her chaperone angled for Almack's vouchers.

It seemed out of character for him to docilely do Lady Arden's bidding. He was far more likely to turn up everywhere like a bad penny, if only to tease her. And would such considerations have prevented him from stealing up to her bedchamber at night?

The nights were colder without his big body beside her, his laughter warming her from the inside. Gracious, how could he have become so essential to her happiness in such a short time?

Perhaps Trixie was right. Once a man had what he

wanted from a woman, he lost interest. She bit her lip. No. That couldn't be true. No matter how he tried to show the world he was a care-for-nothing, she knew he cared for her. He might not love her, but he wouldn't cast her off without a word.

Something was wrong. Something had gone awry the afternoon they'd gathered at Lady Arden's, but she could not put her finger on it.

The agony of going over and over the last day she'd seen him, trying to interpret every word and gesture, made her head spin. She tried to put him out of her mind. Yet, with his family surrounding her, the evidence of his generosity to her everywhere, and his name never far from someone's lips, he was always in her thoughts.

Ah, who was she fooling? He would have dominated her mind if she sailed alone to Gibraltar.

She recalled the beautiful young lady who had accosted Davenport at Lady Arden's soiree. Later she'd discovered the girl's identity. Lady Maria Shand, Lord Yarmouth's daughter. Her stomach churned at the thought of Davenport with another woman. It didn't bear thinking of, yet she could contemplate little else.

"Rosamund," she said, "what do you know about Lady Maria Shand?"

Rosamund's head jerked up in surprise. Her lovely eyes cooled. "I only know that you need not worry about her."

"Oh?" her voice scraped. "Is—is there a reason I *might* be worried?"

Shrugging, Rosamund looked down at her work. "She tried to get her claws into Davenport a while ago, but he was clever enough to realize what she was about."

"I see." Hilary hesitated, burning to know how far it had gone before Davenport saw through the girl. "She seems so . . . virtuous."

"My dear, you will soon learn that in society looks are

almost always deceiving. Lady Maria is the reason Xavier and the other cousins kidnapped Davenport. The plan was to send him back to his estate, but it seems they didn't get that far."

"Why his estate?" said Hilary. "Did they actually think he would stay there?"

"They hoped being there might bring him to a sense of his responsibilities. Then, too, his attitude to Lady Maria was such as to lead us to believe it would be a case of out of sight, out of mind. He was bored, Hilary. Lady Maria was a fleeting fancy. A diversion, nothing more."

Was that what she'd been? she wondered dully. A diversion, easily forgotten when something new and shiny came along?

"You don't look quite the thing today, my dear," said Rosamund, changing the subject deliberately, Hilary thought. "Are you not sleeping well?"

Rosamund had taken to embroidering a series of garments for the baby who would arrive in the summer. She set the tiny, exquisite stitches with such swift precision, Hilary was frankly envious. Was there nothing Rosamund could not do?

"I suppose I'm not accustomed to the noise of London," Hilary said.

She refused to admit she lay awake in the dark night after night, her body restless and her heart aching. For Davenport.

Everything she'd ever wanted was within her grasp. Respectability, a sense of belonging. Almack's, for Heaven's sake! But it all seemed hollow without him.

One thing had changed. She no longer expected or even wanted that quiet, kind, gentlemanly husband she'd yearned for. The suitor of her dreams seemed weak and bland as milk against the full-bodied potency of Davenport.

How foolish of her. How utterly perverse. She would have danced with joy at her good fortune if she'd known a month before how far she'd come. Now it wasn't enough.

She wanted more. She wanted *him*.

As well wish for the moon as pine for Davenport's love.

"Finished." Rosamund snipped off a thread, then folded the garment neatly and set it aside.

She lifted her face to the sunshine that poured through the drawing-room window. "This weather ought not be wasted. Shall we take a stroll in the garden, Hilary? Some fresh air might do you good."

Hilary refrained from saying fresh air could do nothing to improve her mood. She forced a smile. "That would be very pleasant."

Before they could rise, the knocker sounded. Moments later, they heard a heavy tread on the stairs.

Rosamund's brows rose. "I told the butler I was not at home to visitors. It must be—"

The door opened, cutting off her prediction.

Davenport erupted into the room. "Rosie, I need to—"

On seeing Hilary, he pulled up short. Whatever he'd been about to say to Rosamund died unspoken on his lips.

His face was haggard, as drawn and tired as Hilary felt. When he first set eyes on her, he lit up. Equally swiftly, the expression was gone, leaving his features curiously wooden.

"Ah, excuse me, my dear. I didn't know you had company."

Rosamund laughed at his sudden formality. "Hilary is not *company*, Jonathon. But now that you're here, perhaps you might lend me your support. Your betrothed requires fresh air and exercise. I, on the other hand, require a nap."

She stifled a small yawn—Rosamund even yawned elegantly—then blasted Davenport with her dazzling smile.

"Would you take Hilary for a turn about the garden, Jonathon? It would allow me to enjoy my siesta without feeling I am neglecting her."

Reddening, Hilary cut in. "There is no need. Indeed, Lord Davenport obviously came to speak with you on a private matter, Rosamund. I'll go."

She snatched up her shawl and reticule, but the strings of her purse had tangled themselves in the fringe of the sofa cushion and she had to stop to work them free.

A sudden sheen of tears blinded her. Her fingers fumbled and her cheeks grew hotter still. If only she had a tenth of Rosamund's poise, she could leave with her dignity intact.

"On the contrary. I'd be happy to walk with you, Miss deVere," said Davenport. His voice held a tinge of laughter, no doubt at the confused ineptitude of her struggles with the reticule. That made her want to hit him.

When she finally disentangled her belongings and moved toward the doorway, he held out his arm. She hesitated but then took it, sweeping a glance upward beneath her lashes at him as they moved out of the room.

He was so startlingly handsome. Whenever she looked at him, she suffered a shock of awareness, one that burned through her body, setting off tiny sparks in secret places. Memories of his caresses flooded her. How utterly humiliating that simply looking at him should make her cheeks flame.

Amusement at her confusion had softened the drawn lines of his face. If she were in the business of lying to herself, she might have detected tenderness in that gentling of his expression.

But his neglect this week gave the lie to such sentiments. Unless he'd been laid up with a fever the past few days, he had no excuse for failing to call on her or at least send her word that he'd been detained.

She stole another glance at him through her lashes. Whatever he'd been doing, it hadn't allowed him much sleep.

She squeezed her eyes shut. If he'd spent the past week in drunken debauchery, she didn't want to know about it.

Suddenly it occurred to her that of course, that was it. A leopard didn't change his spots no matter how gently he purred. Faced with the prospect of turning respectable for her sake, he'd immediately taken the first opportunity to prove himself unworthy. He'd gone straight to the Devil.

Well, it was time for her to put an end to this charade. If that meant the withdrawal of his family's support and Lady Arden's as well, so be it. She couldn't remain tied, even as a pretense, to a man who only sought to escape.

* * *

Davenport fought to get himself under control. This was far more difficult than he'd thought it would be. He hadn't expected to see her here. Hadn't yet prepared for this meeting.

He'd tried lying to himself, tried making excuses to put off the final blow, but the truth was plain. He needed to put an end to the pretense of an engagement. So many people knew of it already, he couldn't gamble on the truth (or the truth as his relations knew it) failing to become public.

He was no nearer to finding his nameless enemy than he'd been on the night Nail was stabbed. Nor had he received the threatened demand.

He'd come to tell Rosamund of his decision and to beg her to stand by Honey even if he could not. When he'd seen Honey there, at home in Rosamund's drawing room, he'd been so overjoyed he'd made a great effort not to stride across the room and snatch her up in his arms. It might be a long time before he could hold her again.

The sweet confusion Honey had displayed over her recalcitrant reticule only served to remind him how dear she was to him, how much he'd miss her when he'd done what he must.

They maintained uneasy silence until they emerged into the small garden at the back of the house.

He led her to the rose arbor, where he dusted the seat for her with his handkerchief and stood while she sat and made a project out of arranging her skirts.

She'd untied and retied the ribbons of her bonnet twice before he said, "At least here, we have a modicum of privacy. What would you wager against my cousin's watching from an upstairs window?"

She shook her head. "Rosamund would not do that."

He gave a disbelieving snort and nipped a full-blown pink rose from the trellis that arched over their heads. He looked down at its miraculous shape, the perfect, soft petals of it, pristine and somehow innocent until bruised beneath careless fingers or trampled underfoot. With a twist to his mouth, he plucked those petals, one by one, and tossed them aside. The breeze caught them, lifting and whirling, until they fluttered to the ground some distance away.

Resentment knotted in his throat. The bright spring day seemed to sear his retinas, until he was blinded to everything but her. He longed to lay her down in the soft, scented grass and make love to her with every part of his body and a whole, untarnished heart.

He couldn't. He'd viewed the problem from every angle, driven himself crazed with calculating ways and means. But he was no closer now to discovering the mastermind behind the threats Weasel Face had uttered than he'd been at the beginning.

He was still waiting for that communication they'd promised him.

Maybe that was it. Maybe they wanted to drive him mad with waiting. All part of the torture.

Oh, he'd find the bastard, all right, but would that be too late for Honey? Was it too much to hope that if he cooperated they wouldn't see the need to involve her? He'd do anything to keep her safe. As it was, he'd set men to guard her, day and night.

She must have grown tired of waiting for him to continue, for she said apropos of nothing, "Lady Arden has mounted a plan of attack to win the support of the Almack's patronesses, but she is disappointed in your refusal to help, my lord. You never did tell me why you were banned from Almack's."

He frowned. "I don't remember. But that's not important. Listen, Hilary, I must tell you something."

He tried to breathe, but there was no air out here at all, fresh or otherwise, though the breeze stirred the curls at her nape. He wanted to press a kiss to that spot, feel her responsive shiver beneath his lips, hear her sigh. Inhale her violet scent.

She stared up at him, her eyes shadowed. "What did you just call me?"

"I beg your pardon?"

"Not Honey," she whispered. Then she nodded to herself as if that confirmed something she'd known all along.

She clasped her hands in her lap and looked at him straightly. "Perhaps I ought not to let you stand there, wondering how to phrase it so as not to hurt my feelings, my lord. It is high time, is it not, that I gave you your congé? You have served your purpose, after all."

He blinked. "That's not what—" Only it was. It was.

"Do not try to dissuade me." She waved a hand. "I realize you've developed certain tender feelings for me. That's only natural given our . . . nocturnal activities. I believe with men it is always so. They so often mistake the physical act for something deeper, poor creatures. But pray, do not regard it. I am sure we shall both find satisfaction elsewhere."

He was too dumbfounded to respond.

She stood and shook out her skirts with the air of shaking *him* from her life.

Suddenly the frustration, the turmoil, all of it, bubbled over. Savagely he said, "Shall we kiss and part, then, my dear?"

He gripped her arm and yanked her toward him. She gave a hiccupping sort of gasp and stared up at him with wide, fawn-like eyes.

A small, choking sob burst from her, before he set his lips to hers.

Her rigid body seemed to stiffen further, but he didn't take that for rejection. He merely deepened the kiss, sliding his tongue along the seam of her lips. With a soft, agonized cry, she melted against him, flowed around him. She filled his senses with the scent of violets, the sweetness of her mouth, the petal softness of her skin.

He lifted his head and tugged at the ribbons that secured her bonnet beneath her chin, pushed the confection off. Then he held her close, burying his nose in her bright curls, calling himself every kind of fool. He *had* come here to break with her, but he hadn't found the courage or the necessary ruthlessness to do it in the callous manner he'd intended.

He couldn't deal her the blow she waited for every time she made a connection with someone. Every time she fought to make her world secure, someone knocked that security out from under her.

He knew, deep down, that she'd acted out of a need to strike first. She cared for him; he felt it in her kiss, in her bittersweet surrender.

He'd come here to break with her, but she'd done his

work for him. He ought to take her at her word rather than kissing her and calling her a damned little fool.

"My sweet, foolish Honey," he murmured into her hair.

But he was the fool. He was far too stupid and weak and selfish to do what he needed to do. Ending it might not have made any difference, but at least he would have known he'd done all he could.

Now . . .

He raised his head so he could look into her face. Her eyes, a little dazed, stared back at him in dawning confusion.

"I won't let you go," he said in a voice thickened with passion. "I can't."

She blinked. Her lips, deeply pink and a little puffy from his kisses, formed a whispered question. "What do you mean?"

He took her by the shoulders, ran his hands up and down her forearms. "I stayed away to protect you, Honey. But I can't go on doing it. I need to explain."

He led her back to the seat to sit by him while he told her an expurgated version of the night in the alley.

She turned pale when he mentioned the threat against her, but she remained composed enough until he reached the end of his tale.

"I'll find the man responsible," he said, "if I have to comb England to do it. In the meantime, men I trust will guard you against harm."

Agitated, she laid a hand on his arm. "Oh, but you must not! It is too dangerous. Davenport, do be careful."

He covered her hand with his. "I am taking care. But they will contact me again, and when they do, I'll be ready. I won't make the mistake of underestimating them next time."

"Enlist your cousins' support," she urged. "They are capable men, powerful, too. They can help you find him."

He'd considered it, of course. The notion of asking for help, even of Ashburn, was abhorrent to someone who'd survived on his wits alone for so long.

But he'd been self-indulgent and stupid to have held on to his pride when Honey was in danger. How much better could four of them cover the ground than Davenport alone? Plus the Duke of Montford. The duke had connections everywhere.

It was time to put pride aside for Honey's sake.

"Yes. I'll do it. In the meantime, it would be best if you and I pretend our engagement is no more. I don't want the blackguard getting wind of it."

She lowered her gaze. "Yes. I—I understand. That would be best."

He looked down at her with a twinge of unease. "You've taken this remarkably calmly."

Perhaps the terrible news had not yet sunk in. The weasel had threatened her, for God's sake! He'd knifed a man in the belly.

She gazed up at him, her eyes bright with tears. "You will find him and stop him. I know it." She made a helpless gesture. "Oh, it is crackbrained of me, but I—I don't fear a deadly assassin nearly as much as I feared losing you."

She couldn't mean it, not really, but his heart blazed with joy.

"You *are* cracked, my sweet. Deliciously, wondrously insane." But he said it with a strange catch in his throat, as he caught her to him and kissed her with a passion and a hunger and a desperate, mad hope that he could keep her safe with him forever.

CHAPTER TWENTY

I see your Mrs. Walker takes her cue on interior decoration from the Prince Regent," observed Cecily as she entered Hilary's bedchamber.

Weeks ago, such an observation would have mortified Hilary, for the ton decried Prinny's garish interiors. But she had weightier things on her mind today than Mrs. Walker's questionable taste.

Frustration gnawed at her, but she could do nothing to help Davenport except keep herself safe. She rarely left the house except to attend her evening engagements. There was always a Westruther cousin with her on these occasions. They guarded her most faithfully and she gleaned news from them of Davenport when she could.

He never came near her. Probably to keep up the pretense that she was nothing to him. In her opinion, it was too late for that, but he'd been adamant. He didn't want to take any chances.

They'd announced the end of their betrothal to their respective families. She'd endured an hour-long harangue from Lord deVere over her broken engagement that had sorely tested her composure. DeVere only let her remain in London because she assured him she was on the brink of being admitted to the hallowed assembly rooms of

Almack's. And, she suspected, because now that Lady Arden had taken her under her wing, he needn't go to any trouble for her.

"Scrubbed up well enough, haven't you?" said deVere, eyeing her up and down. "Maybe you'll catch a husband yet."

She didn't want to catch another husband. She wanted Davenport with a ferocity she'd never felt about anything or anyone before.

Now Hilary smiled at Cecily's quip about the décor. "Mrs. Walker's aesthetic is an acquired taste. I admit, I have yet to acquire it, but one never knows."

Cecily chuckled. She removed her bonnet and set it down, then stripped off her gloves. "Show me what you will wear at Montford's ball."

Trixie hovered in the corner, awestruck at standing in the same room as a real-live duchess. Hilary gave her an encouraging smile. With a start, Trixie brought forth The Gown.

Giselle had refused to consider stark white for a young lady of Hilary's coloring, no matter how appropriate the hue might be for debutantes. This gown was a shade the modiste called *beurre,* a buttery cream, overlaid with a robe of the finest ivory net, embroidered all over with tiny gold leaves.

"Ahh," said Cecily. "Ravishing! Giselle has outdone herself, has she not? I'm so glad Davenport took you to her. She is a genius."

Cecily opened the drawstring on the reticule that dangled from her elbow and drew out a ruby velvet pouch. "I brought you something."

A single strand of lustrous, creamy pearls spilled onto Hilary's dressing table. Cecily picked it up and held it against the gown. "Yes. Just the thing. I have the earbobs and a bracelet to match and combs for your hair."

"Ohh," Hilary breathed, touching the smooth, cool pearls with tentative fingertips. "I've never worn anything so fine."

The warm glow in her chest expanded to fill her. She met dark eyes that reminded her so much of Davenport's it made her heart ache a little. "Thank you, Cecily. I shall take great care of them."

"They will be yours when you marry Davenport," said Cecily. "I simply liberated them a little early from his strongbox."

Guilt punched Hilary in the solar plexus. She ought not wear the Davenport jewels. Not under false pretenses.

"You took them without Davenport's knowledge?" she said, trying for a neutral tone.

Cecily blinked in surprise. "Oh, no. In fact, he asked me to choose something for you."

Hilary digested this, hardly knowing what to think. "Hasn't he told you of our decision not to wed?"

"Yes, but that is nonsense, so I didn't listen." Cecily waved a hand in dismissal. "You two are perfect for one another, and when you have both stopped being stupid and miserable, you'll see it."

There didn't seem much point arguing. Hilary wished Cecily might be right, but in her heart she knew Davenport didn't truly love her. He liked her. He liked bedding her. His chivalrous instincts were roused because she was in peril. For one, brief moment in the rose arbor, when he'd held her in his arms and kissed her, she'd hoped . . . But he didn't love her.

"How is he?" she asked.

"He is . . . distracted, short-tempered, and altogether impossible," said Cecily. "And yet, in some way I find difficult to put my finger on, he is more himself than he has been since his return."

Conscious that Trixie overheard every word, Hilary

said, "I daresay it was a big adjustment after so many years away."

"Yes," said Cecily slowly. "I'm coming to realize how much of an adjustment it has been."

Hilary darted a glance at Davenport's sister. Had he confided in her about the latest development?

With a glance at the waiting maid, Cecily seemed to shake off her thoughtful mood. "We shall speak of that anon. Right now, we need to think about your hair."

Tapping her fingertip against her lips, Cecily ran a speculative gaze over Hilary's coiffure. Trixie had proven herself a quick learner with deft fingers and an eye for the styles that suited Hilary's face.

Despite the importance of looking her best at Montford's ball, impatience skittered down Hilary's spine. For once, she didn't wish to discuss frills and furbelows. She wanted to know about Davenport.

"You have remarkably pretty hair and you should make the most of it," said Cecily as she circled her, viewing her from every angle. "Something loose, I think. Simple, yet sophisticated."

Hilary looked doubtfully at her maid, who raised her eyebrows and blinked in response.

"Sit, sit!" Cecily made a shooing motion toward the dressing table and Hilary obediently sat. "I'll show your maid how it's done." She smiled at Trixie and beckoned. "Come along; I won't bite."

Hilary blushed and protested at Cecily so demeaning herself as to arrange her hair, but Cecily waved away her objections. "I like doing it," she said.

When Trixie had perfected the coiffure Cecily showed her, Hilary ordered tea for them in the upstairs parlor.

"Thank you for showing my maid that style," said Hilary, handing Cecily her cup. "It is perfect."

"You don't have any sisters, do you?" said Cecily. "Well,

neither do I, of course, but I lived with Rosamund and my other cousins at Montford House for years. She and I were forever creating our own coiffures and practicing on one another."

Cecily rolled her expressive eyes. "Imagine growing up side by side with such a beauty. Intolerable! The only thing that saved me was that I'm so dark. If I'd been fair like Rosamund, I should have eaten my heart out with envy."

Hilary laughed. "I doubt that. I've rarely seen sisters closer than the two of you. Why, you complete each other's sentences."

"Only when we are in company. When we are alone together, we don't need to finish our sentences at all." Cecily sighed. "It is a pity Rosamund is so adorable. I wanted to loathe her when I first arrived at Montford House."

She sipped her tea. "Oh, but I was an angry child. I spent so long being furious at Jonathon for leaving me—as if dying was his choice. Ironic, isn't it? I never knew how close to the mark I was. I was only beginning to reconcile myself to his death when he was resurrected."

"It must have been a shock." It was bad enough for Hilary when he'd announced his identity. Imagine if one thought one's beloved brother died and he later returned.

She regarded Hilary shrewdly as she set down her cup. "Has he told you how that came about?"

"Yes, he has," said Hilary. Tentatively, she said, "And now he is in danger again."

"Only this time," said Cecily with a grim little smile, "he has the might of the Westruthers at his back."

* * *

Davenport mulled over his notes again, tamping down his impatience. The scene of Xavier's library was wholly different from when he'd been there last.

Papers were scattered everywhere. His cousins came and went, delivering pieces of intelligence gleaned from sources high and low throughout London. Davenport was the obvious one to receive and collate the information, piecing fragments together like a jigsaw. But the enforced lack of physical activity made him edgy and frustrated.

He needed to be a hundred places at once. Kicking that weasel-faced villain's head in and forcing him to spill his guts about who'd hired him. Interviewing lowlife villains and hired cutthroats, scientists, apothecaries, intelligence officers, and military officials.

Visiting Nail, who even now languished at death's door after the weasel had stabbed him in that alley. Davenport had insisted on hiring a nurse and calling in an experienced doctor, but both professionals had shaken their heads. They must wait and see.

He was bloody well sick of waiting.

He wanted to be with Honey. He wanted to see her triumph at Montford's ball, then take her away and do unimaginably wicked things to her body.

He needed to *do* something, not sit here behind a desk.

But the task of finding the instigator of the weasel's activities was too large for one man. He'd been forced to delegate. They'd all used their various connections among the military and the government; even the Duke of Montford had lent his efforts. All of them drew a blank. Ashburn had met with universal derision when he'd raised the subject of Davenport's invention with various members of the Royal Institution.

Such attitudes could be feigned, of course. However, Ashburn's subtle suggestion of significant monetary reward for a man who could synthesize such an explosive as Davenport had claimed to do didn't meet with more than tepid interest.

No one thought it could be done safely. And even if it

could, why risk one's own reputation following in Davenport's erratic footsteps?

Beckenham strode in, closely followed by Lydgate, who wore full evening dress. Hell, what was the time? Davenport glanced at the clock and shoved a hand through his hair. He'd be late for Montford's ball at this rate.

"Managed to identify Weasel Face," said Lydgate, tossing the sketch Davenport had made onto the desk in front of him. "It wasn't easy. Name of Silas Ridley. It didn't help us, on account of he's flown the country."

The expressions on his cousins' faces told him the reason his quarry had fled.

"Jonathon," said Beckenham quietly, "Nail is dead."

The words crashed through Davenport, and a blistering obscenity broke from his lips. His throat burned like fire. "Because of me."

"He's dead because a villain stuck a knife into him," said Lydgate impatiently.

The memory of that villain's sneering mouth telling him he'd stuck the porter like a pig haunted his dreams.

"No." Davenport snatched up the sketch of Ridley and crushed it in his fist. "If I hadn't involved Nail in the business, he'd still be alive."

"You trusted Nail to handle himself," said Beckenham in his grave, sensible way. "He was a professional villain, just as Ridley was. You paid him handsomely and he took the job."

Davenport set his teeth. "Much good the money will do him now."

"He knew the risks," said Lydgate. "He accepted them. He accepted the same risk every time he went to work in that hell. Life expectancy among porters at that place must be a year at the outside."

Lydgate spoke with the authority of a man who risked

his life in his line of work as a matter of course. But each time, Lydgate knew what he was getting into.

Even Davenport hadn't realized what he was up against in Ridley. He might be reckless with his own safety, but he had no right to be reckless with anyone else's. He'd held the burly porter's life too cheaply and this was the result.

"You will, of course, provide for his family," said Beckenham.

"Already done."

A vicious fury overtook him. Bloody Beckenham, always meeting his obligations, never putting a foot wrong. And Lydgate, so coldly ruthless beneath the smooth façade of a Bond Street beau. All three of them in this room were privileged and wealthy, with the power of life and death over far too many people. It had been this kind of callousness he'd sacrificed his life's work to guard against.

He turned on them both, snarling. "Oh, yes, I can toss money at them. That makes it all nice and tidy, doesn't it? A man's dead, a woman widowed, and their children can never have their father back, but I may buy my way free of guilt with a sum that most men like us would spend on their annual handkerchief bill."

Beckenham flicked a glance at Lydgate, as if signaling him not to argue further.

Davenport turned his back on them rather than see pity or, worse, bewilderment in their eyes.

There was a pause. Then footsteps. A large hand settled on Davenport's shoulder, gave it a brief squeeze.

"Get out, will you?" Davenport's fists clenched, but even he knew his guilt and shame couldn't be erased by physical violence. "Just leave."

* * *

"Davenport's not coming, is he, Rosamund?"

Hilary tried to swallow her disappointment, but it was too sharp and jagged to choke down. She'd hoped . . . What had she hoped?

That when he saw her exquisitely gowned and elegantly coiffed the scales would fall from his eyes. He would instantly declare his love, go down on one knee, and propose in truth this time.

It hurt to know how laughable that fantasy was.

"He said he'd be here," replied Rosamund, fanning herself languidly, as if she hadn't a care in the world. "Lydgate hasn't arrived yet, either, so don't panic."

"Do you think he's found the man who has been following him? Do you think he intends to confront whoever is behind this tonight?"

Rosamund shook her head. "They would have sent Griffin word." She blew a breath through her pursed lips as if she needed to relieve tension. "My dear husband is spoiling for a fight. They all are."

At least the men of this family were exceedingly good at fighting. Rosamund's husband was a colossus of a man who used to win money in prizefights at local fairs. And of course, Hilary knew Davenport's capabilities. Rosamund's brother, Xavier, Marquis of Steyne, was rumored to have killed a man with his bare hands.

Hilary didn't know whether to believe that. Having met the enigmatic marquis, she rather thought it might be true.

Lady Arden came upon them, brimming with excitement. "My dears, I have happy news. Lady Sefton is all but persuaded. She told me she thought you a very pretty-behaved young lady, Miss deVere, and that you had an air of modesty she found most pleasing."

"Well, and so she is a pretty-behaved young lady," said

Rosamund with a warm smile at Hilary. "We did not need Lady Sefton to tell us that."

"Still," said Lady Arden, holding up an admonitory finger. "We are not over the final hurdle yet. Lady Jersey will attend later this evening, I hear. Mark my words, she will be the tougher nut to crack."

"My lady, you go to so much trouble on my behalf," said Hilary. "Indeed, I thank you."

"Oh, tosh," said Lady Arden with a smile. "As I said, I enjoy a challenge." She craned her neck a little. "Ah, I see Lord deVere bearing down on us. I shall head him off at the pass while you ladies make your escape. We do not wish to emphasize *that* connection any more than necessary tonight."

She sailed off through the crowd like a warship into battle.

Hilary and Rosamund threaded their way through the guests to the other side of the room, where a group of chairs ranged against a wall.

Rosamund sank down on her chair with a small sigh of relief.

Hilary wished she might feel more enthusiasm for Lady Arden's news. But what did Almack's matter when she was so afraid for Davenport all the time?

Where was he?

Davenport had more important things to think of than attending a ball; she knew that. They were no longer betrothed, and he was trying to stay away from her for her own good.

Foolish of her, but those considerations didn't make her feel better.

"There is Lydgate now," said Rosamund on a note of relief. Her brows twitched together and her fan stilled. "But Jonathon is not with him."

Hilary's heart bounded into her throat. "Oh, I shall go mad, I think."

Lydgate strolled up to them in time to hear her. His brows rose. "There is no cause for alarm, Miss deVere. Davenport is hale and hearty and shortly to arrive." He assessed her. "What you need is a drink. Champagne. That's the ticket. I'll get you some." He grinned down at Rosamund. "Feeling the heat, Rosie? Lemonade for you, I think."

"Oh, yes," said Rosamund. "That *is* what I need. Thank you, Lydgate."

Despite her brothers' hard-drinking proclivities, Hilary had never so much as tasted champagne before. She'd been careful to only drink lemonade or a few sips of wine when in company so as not to give the impression she was one of *those* deVeres. She couldn't imagine anything worse than falling into a stupor like the one to which she'd seen Mrs. Walker succumb.

Tonight, however, she no longer cared about all of that. When Lydgate pressed the glass into her hand, she took a tentative sip and repressed a sneeze when the bubbles tickled her nose.

"Treat that with respect," said Lydgate, laughing at her reaction. "It's a fine drop."

"Montford never stints when it comes to champagne," agreed Rosamund.

"The only thing he does stint on is my quarterly allowance," Lydgate muttered. "He's a positive miser when it comes to doling out *other* people's money."

"Poor Lydgate," teased Rosamund. "Are you short of cravats? Have you been reduced to using ordinary blacking on your boots instead of champagne?"

Hilary took another appreciative swallow of the fizzy wine. "This," she said positively, "ought not to be wasted on shining boots."

Lydgate had hit the mark. The champagne was just what she'd needed. As she made her way through the glass, she became conscious of relaxation slowly spreading through her body. The strict guard she usually kept on her tongue seemed to melt away. Rosamund and Lydgate seemed entertained by her chatter. For the first time that evening, the future didn't look so bleak.

Even when Lady Maria Shand promenaded past on the arm of her partner, Hilary didn't feel the slightest barb of jealousy.

Her glass had been empty for some time and Hilary was hoping for more when Davenport came in. His head turned sharply, as if he'd scented her on the wind. In blatant disregard of his resolve not to draw attention to their association, he made a beeline for her.

Her senses heightened instantly. Heart pounding, she set down her glass and rose at his approach.

He was so vividly handsome, everyone else in the room seemed to fade beside him. Her heart did a slow, hard tumble in her chest.

She loved this man. When she saw the toll the past few days had taken on him in his drawn face, she wanted to take him in her arms.

She loved him. There. After all of her struggles against it, she could finally admit that to herself.

He leaned down to kiss Rosamund's cheek, then bowed to Hilary. "Miss deVere, would you care to dance?"

His dark eyes burned into hers, fierce and tortured and somehow pleading at the same time. Even if she'd wished to spurn him, she could not resist the need to give him everything he desired.

She placed her hand on his arm and allowed him to lead her to the floor. A waltz. It was a waltz and she went into his arms as easily and inevitably as if she were coming home.

How difficult it was to keep the proper distance when she yearned to hold him tight, to kiss away the trouble on his brow. She wanted to take him inside her and harness all the passion and fierce longing she saw in his eyes.

"I—I thought you might not come," she said.

A quirk of the lips briefly lightened his features. "What, and miss your triumph? I wouldn't dream of it."

"What is it?" said Hilary. "Has something happened? You look . . ." *Desolate. Furious. Lost.*

"Let's not speak of it now," he said. Leaning in, until his mouth almost brushed her ear, he said, "Honey, I need you. God, I need you so much. Let's get away from here."

On a gasp, she tilted her head back to stare. "Now? But . . . but we can't." Gracious, Lady Jersey would arrive soon. How could she possibly face the patroness of Almack's after doing . . . *that* with Davenport?

"Tonight," she said softly, so no one would overhear. "Later, in Half Moon Street."

"I can't wait that long. Can you?"

There was no wicked glint in his eye now. Gone was the laughing cavalier who shrugged life's cares from his shoulders as easily as if they were a cloak. He was a man in pain with a great burden to bear and Hilary's heart would need to be made of stone for her to deny him.

Her heart was his already.

"I have no right to ask; I know it," he said huskily into her ear as he whirled her down the room. "But I want you so much I'm aching for you. I'll die if I don't have you. I want to be inside you, feel your hot, wet—"

"No, stop!" she hissed. How could he say such things in the midst of this elegant crowd?

Her body trembled, his urgency feeding her own. "But how?" She darted a glance around her at the crowd of dancers, spinning down the room. "Where? It's impossible. Even you could not seduce a lady in the middle of a ball."

With a laugh that seemed to ring hollow, he said, "My dear, sweet Honey. You should know me better than that by now."

CHAPTER TWENTY-ONE

Following Davenport's directions, Hilary had escaped the ballroom on the pretense of finding the ladies' retiring room and instead made her way to a little-used parlor on the first floor.

The parlor seemed to be a music room, with a harp and a pianoforte and a group of chairs. An elegant chaise with serpentine scrollwork on the back stretched languidly in the window bay.

Her heart pounded against her ribs. What she was doing now jeopardized everything she'd striven so hard for. But when she'd glimpsed Davenport's pain, she couldn't deny him. More than that, she wanted him with a desperation that equaled his. A thrill shivered through her body.

Minutes ticked by. She wondered if something had prevented him from coming.

Finally, the door she'd left slightly ajar opened and he walked in.

He didn't see her at first, for the pianoforte lid obscured most of her form from that angle. After one swift glance around, he leaned his shoulders against the wall, his face drawn. His chest heaved and his throat worked, as if he found it difficult to swallow.

A wave of sorrow swept over her. He seemed so desolate, so alone.

Considerations of propriety, virtue, even plain common sense seemed paltry and trivial when the saucy pirate who had so tormented her on the journey to London could seem lost and broken.

"Did you think I would not come?" she whispered, stepping out of the shadows and moving into the circle of light cast by the candle he held.

His head jerked up. "I thought . . ." He blew out a breath. "It took me some time to get away. I thought you might have given me up and left. Or done the sensible thing and stayed clear altogether."

"You thought I'd desert you when you needed me," she corrected softly. Now she knew he needed *her* and not simply physical release. Knew with a simple, clear conviction she was loved, even if he wouldn't admit it. Nothing else mattered to her now.

He needed her because she cared for him. He needed her because there was no one else who understood.

She thought of the way his family rallied around him. Perhaps they had tried to understand him, but he'd pushed them away, repelled them with his flippant charm. Davenport's careless veneer was a tough one to crack.

She put a hand up to touch his cheek. "Tell me," she whispered. "Tell me what made you look so haunted just now."

He caught her hand and pressed his lips to her palm in a passionate kiss that scintillated down to her toes. "I thought you weren't coming," he said.

No, it was more than that, but his lips cruised down her forearm to the sensitive skin inside her elbow and she almost lost her train of thought.

Oh, dear Heaven, how could she tempt his confidences if he did this every time they were alone?

"Something is troubling you," she whispered." I want to know what it is."

He was drawing down the puffed sleeve at her shoulder, tracing a sinuous path with his tongue. "Honey, we'll talk about it later." He kissed along her clavicle. "Right now, I'll go up in flames if I don't have you. Talking can wait."

And when he pressed a burning trail of kisses across her décolletage she knew that neither of them was in a fit state to discuss anything sensibly now.

"We have to be quick," he muttered, taking her mouth as he maneuvered her backward, toward the chaise longue.

Before she knew it, she lay down on the slender couch with her skirts pushed up to her waist. Davenport stretched over her, one knee planted between her body and the chair back, one foot on the floor.

She could not well imagine a more compromising position. "What if someone comes?" she whispered with a quick glance at the unlocked door.

"They won't," he said. He kissed her urgently, freeing himself from his pantaloons, sliding inside her.

He let out a groan of need, but he paused and seemed to brace himself, holding the urgency of his desire at bay. Jaw clenched, he slid inside her, set up a steady, tantalizing rhythm that made her whimper softly and lift her hips to urge him on.

He reached down between them and with a rustle of fabric found the most sensitive part of her, teasing it, stroking it in exquisite counterpoint to his thrusts.

She met her peak with a sharp cry.

"Shh." He covered her mouth with his and gave her what she'd craved all along, a strong, deep stroke that made her stifle a moan of pleasure in her throat.

When he reached his own crisis he gave a sharp, guttural groan in the side of her neck. Shudders rippled through his body, violent and wrenching.

They were still joined together when his breathing finally calmed. They stayed like that for some time, his face nuzzled into her neck, the weight of his big body pressing on her in a way she found immensely satisfying.

"Ah, I'm a deadweight. Sorry, Honey." Slowly, he withdrew from her and took care of them both with a handkerchief.

She didn't know how she would right her appearance so as to return to the ballroom. This had been a reckless, wanton act, but she couldn't bring herself to regret it.

He took her hand and helped her to a sitting position, then sat beside her with his arm around her waist. Turning, he pressed a kiss to her forehead. This time, it wasn't patronizing or a careless gesture. His kiss told her she was cherished.

"What happened tonight, Jonathon?"

He blew out a ragged breath. "A man died because of me."

Her stomach churned. No wonder he'd looked like death himself when he'd walked into the ballroom.

"Tell me."

So he did. He told her all of it, and if she hadn't already been crazed with worry for him, this incident brought home the full gravity of his situation, the immediacy of his danger.

"You came to the ball anyway," she said, in wonder.

"I needed you," he said. "Being with you was the only thing I could think of that would keep me sane."

He took her hand and pressed a passionate kiss to her palm.

She put her arms around him and kissed him with a poignant sense of desperation and a tiny tinge of hope.

"I didn't mean all of the things I said in the rose arbor," she whispered.

He bent his head to press his brow to hers. "I know."

"Jonathon, I love you. I love you so much it hurts. I never thought love would feel like this."

He drew back to search her face, the strangest expression on his own. She read denial in those dark eyes, repudiation in the twist of his mouth.

The expression swiftly vanished, to be replaced by . . . what? Pity? Compassion? Oh, dear Heaven, that was even worse.

Hilary felt as if her heart had caved in, like a derelict house receiving its death blow. She tried to pull away from him, but he held her fast as everything crumbled to dust inside her.

"Wait. Honey, I—"

The door flung open, to reveal the unmistakable figure of a woman.

Lady Maria Shand.

"Damnation!" muttered Davenport. He released Hilary as if she were made of live coals. Even while she acknowledged the wisdom of his action, the alacrity with which he made it struck another blow.

Despite his quickness in disentangling himself, there was no way to make this rendezvous appear innocent. Only a simpleton would have failed to understand what had just transpired between them. Whatever else she might be, Hilary suspected Lady Maria was not a simpleton.

Their unwelcome guest stepped into the candlelight. "Davenport, you are so predictable. You always pick the music room. I wonder why that is."

"What are you doing here?" Hilary had never heard Davenport sound so cold.

Lady Maria's clear blue gaze flicked over them. "So it

is true. My father said it was, but I didn't believe him. You *are* entangled with this deVere female."

"What does your father know of it?" Davenport's voice was sharp.

"Oh, merely that you escorted Miss deVere all the way from Lincolnshire to London without a chaperone. That you spent a night on the road as husband and wife."

A feline smile spread across her features. "I have enough ammunition against you to create a scandal that will sully Miss deVere's good name from here to Edinburgh."

All the blood drained from Hilary's head. She was ruined. Her recklessness had finally caught up with her. She was guilty as charged and could offer no excuse except love. Love did not qualify as a defense in the court of the ton.

She waited for Davenport to speak, to find the way out of this mess. She could only think of one.

Davenport sucked in a breath. He didn't so much as glance at Hilary.

"Miss deVere has done me the honor of accepting my hand in marriage." The words came out smoothly, but without any inflection of happiness or warmth.

"So she's the one," said Lady Maria. She gave a scornful laugh. "Good God, Davenport, are you mad? A country mouse without style or beauty to wed a Westruther heir? And a deVere into the bargain."

Hilary stood and drew herself up. She was shaking with hurt and fury, but she'd die before she allowed this spiteful wretch to see it. "I may be a deVere, but at least no one has ever accused me of vulgarity, Lady Maria."

"*Oh!*" The astonished affront in those ice blue eyes made Hilary want to laugh, despite the ache in her heart. "Davenport, are you going to let her speak to me like this?"

"Yes," said Davenport simply. "You cannot conceive how much I enjoyed that."

He made a sweeping bow. "And now, if you have quite finished being vulgar, my lady, I have to inform you that you are also de trop."

"Oh, I'm going," said Lady Maria, her cheeks flying spots of color. "You, Miss deVere, are about to be ruined. I shall tell the world what I've seen tonight, the things my father knows about you. Let's see who will be called vulgar then."

Lady Maria swept from the room, leaving Hilary in a state of shock. The house of cards she'd built with such painstaking care was about to be set aflame.

Davenport stayed only to take her hands in his. "It will be all right, Honey," he said. "I'll make it right. She won't talk. You will not have to marry me."

It was as if he spoke to her through a wall of ice. Cold flooded Hilary until she wasn't sure if she could move or speak. She felt herself nod in acknowledgment when she really wanted to scream denials, to cling to him and never let him go.

He lifted her freezing hands to his lips and pressed a kiss to them. Then he bolted after Lady Maria.

Fingers shaking, Hilary tried her best to put herself to rights. It was all she could do at this moment, when planning one step beyond the present seemed a feat too taxing for her frozen brain.

Her hands dropped to her sides. What was the use? Her gown was crushed, hair a messy tumble, shouting her disgrace to the world. Even if she were adept at arranging her hair, there was no looking glass in the music room to assist her.

Trixie was in the retiring room with the other maids. If only Hilary had thought to ask Davenport to send the girl up to her, she could at least get herself out of this place without appearing to the world as the fallen woman Lady Maria called her.

Suddenly she knew she couldn't wait for Davenport's return. She didn't have the courage to sit here and listen to him explain to her that he didn't love her, that he'd always said he wouldn't marry her, that he didn't intend to do so now.

Lady Maria would spread the news of her ruin far and wide. Davenport had no power to stop her. By now, everyone at the ball downstairs would have heard of her disgrace. She thought of Lady Arden's excited anticipation of procuring her vouchers for Almack's and a bitter smile twisted her mouth. There would be no Almack's for her now.

She regretted that her behavior would embarrass Lady Arden and the Westruthers, who had accepted her and vouched for her. They'd have no choice now but to turn their backs.

When he discovered she'd rather be ruined than wed Davenport, Lord deVere would wash his hands of her, throw her to the wolves. He was only interested in his dependants if he could use them as pawns in his bid for power and wealth. She was damaged goods now. Her brothers had never bothered with her. She could only hope they wouldn't eject her from their household altogether when the gossip began to fly.

Trixie might help her, but she was a trained lady's maid now. It would be selfish to make her return to the Grange and step back into the role of housemaid.

The only person Hilary deVere could depend on was herself.

The old loneliness yawned ahead, more frightening now because it seemed utterly final. But she couldn't think of that now. She must not think of it.

She'd have to escape the house without anyone seeing

her, leave London as quietly and swiftly as she could. Without her presence to fuel it, the gossip about her liaison with London's most infamous rogue would die a quick death. In a matter of twenty-four hours, she would be gone.

In a month, a fortnight, even, Hilary deVere might never have been in London at all.

* * *

Davenport caught up with his quarry on the staircase, gripped her upper arm without hesitation or apology, and drew her into the shadows on the landing.

"Take your hands off me," she hissed. "If I screamed you would be in a pretty mess, would you not?"

"But you won't scream, Lady Maria, will you? Because I know your secret."

That made her chin jerk up. "Secret?" She essayed an unconcerned laugh. "Whatever can you mean?"

"I mean the babe you carry in your belly," he said grimly. "The one you were so desperate to pass off as mine."

She turned white to the lips and he knew he'd guessed right.

In that moment, he understood. All of the determined pursuit, the attempts to seduce and entrap him. She'd been desperate, and she'd seen him as an easy mark. The newly resurrected Earl of Davenport. Reckless, foolhardy, randy as hell, without too many scruples left. Certainly ready to take what she'd offered.

She'd have succeeded, too, if she hadn't shown her hand too soon. He shuddered to think of their future together if they'd been forced to wed. And he *would* have married her if society had demanded it. He would never have abandoned her to her fate.

Now that he understood the sheer panic that had driven her to such devious lengths, he could find compassion in his soul. Perhaps he might help her if she'd let him.

"Who is the father?" he asked gently.

She covered her face with her hands. "I cannot tell you. I cannot! And anyway, he would never marry me." She gave a bitter laugh. "He *cannot* marry me. He is already married, a fact he told me *afterward*, mind you."

He sucked in a breath. "The man ought to be horse-whipped. Does your papa know?"

Vehemently she shook her head. "Oh, dear Heaven, of course not! He'd turn me out of doors. Why do you think I did what I did?"

This was a problem she'd faced alone. He had to admire the steel in her, even if he resented the solution she'd found to her problem.

He thought of Gerald and the longing looks he cast Lady Maria when she wasn't aware. "There is one who I think would count himself honored to wed you."

Indeed, he wondered why she hadn't sought the easier target. Had Davenport's wealth and status been sufficient lure to turn her back on one who truly cared for her?

"You mean Gerald." Her voice shook on a sob. "Oh, but how could I deceive him so? He is a good man. I—I couldn't do it."

Davenport couldn't fail to draw the obvious conclusion. That she'd chosen him precisely because he *wasn't* a good man. Well, she'd been correct on that score, hadn't she? He'd come very close to obliging her.

"You made a mistake," said Davenport, gently now. "If you tell him the truth, perhaps Gerald will be more understanding than you know."

"He loves me," she said, her whole frame trembling. "He might marry me. But how could I do that to him? How could he accept a child that wasn't his?"

Remembering the stark longing on Gerald's face, Davenport thought the poor fellow might take her on any terms. In fact, he rather thought confession would be good for Lady Maria's soul and place the pair on a more even footing. That she'd balked at treating Gerald the way she'd treated Davenport meant there might be hope for them yet.

He said, "Perhaps that is a chance you must take. But whatever happens, Lady Maria, you may rest assured that I'm at your service. If Gerald can't find it in his heart to marry you after you tell him the truth, then I'm sure something can be arranged."

Short of marrying her himself, that was.

She gazed up at him, wonder and a good deal of shame in her eyes. "All along, I knew. I tried to fool myself that you deserved to be deceived, that you were just like all of the other rakes who take cruel advantage of such innocents as I was. But you're not, are you, Davenport? You never were."

She bit her lip and turned her face away. In a suffocated tone, she said, "Pray accept my apologies, my lord. I behaved badly. So badly that I cannot conceive how you should forgive me or wish to help me. But . . . I thank you. And I . . . I wish you happy with—"

Tears choked her and she couldn't go on.

"Not at all," he said, patting her shoulder gingerly and glancing about for means of escape. "Why don't you, er, dry your eyes and tidy up? I'll see you back in the ballroom."

He needed to get to Honey and reassure her, do whatever he could to dispel the grave trouble he'd seen in her face. Surely she couldn't think that he cared for Lady Maria? Not after all he and Honey had been to each other.

He climbed the stairs again, knowing that the forthcoming conversation would be the most important of his life. If he messed this up, he might as well blow his brains out.

Every instinct told him that convincing Honey to marry him was not going to be easy after that scene with Lady Maria.

By the time he arrived back at the music room, he was wound so tightly he could barely breathe. He opened the door and peered through the shadows, inserting his index finger into the space between his collar and his neck. Why had he tied the damned thing so tightly? It was strangling him.

"Honey?" He moved farther into the room, but he could tell even before he did so that the room was empty.

Honey had gone.

CHAPTER TWENTY-TWO

For many moments, Davenport stood like a bloody pillar of salt in the doorway to the music room, unable to move or think for the conflicting imperatives that crowded his brain.

Had she returned to the ballroom without him? Perhaps she'd gone to find Rosamund to beg her to take her home.

"My lord! I've been looking for you everywhere." A footman, out of breath, caught up with him as he entered the ballroom and handed him a paper. "This was delivered here half an hour ago."

"Thank you." His thoughts filled with Honey, it took him a second or two to focus on the note.

When he read Gerald's hasty scrawl, he uttered a blistering oath that made a passing matron give him a shocked stare.

As he crushed the paper in his fist, he muttered an apology to the lady and scanned the crowd, hoping against hope to see Honey.

He found Rosamund, but his cousin hadn't laid eyes on Honey.

"I thought she was with you," she said under her breath,

the sharpness of her tone belied by the society smile. "Don't tell me you've lost her."

"If she comes back to the ballroom, keep her with you," he instructed her. "Don't let her out of your sight."

He lost valuable minutes in his search. Mason was in grave danger, if he only knew it. And now Honey was missing, too.

An inquiry of the butler told him Miss deVere hadn't called for her cloak or for a carriage to be brought. Nor had anyone see her leave. Perhaps she'd gone to the ladies' retiring room to freshen up. He scrawled a message and left it with a footman to be delivered to her.

Davenport questioned Mason's sister, then inquired of several people whether Yarmouth had been seen at the ball. He couldn't find Beckenham, but there was no time, so he left him a message with a linkboy who loitered outside, then he bolted through London streets until he found a hackney cab.

He didn't know what he'd find at Mason's laboratory, which was situated in the attics of an old house on Upper Wimpole Street. He hoped he wasn't too late.

He paid off the driver and drew out his pistol, hoping to God he wouldn't need it, that Gerald hadn't been quite as foolish as he suspected.

The front door stood slightly ajar. A bad sign, one that had Davenport moving silently through the poky hallway, up the stairs to the second floor, where Mason kept his library.

A board creaked on the landing. Davenport froze. He listened, ears straining, but the only sound he heard was the faint ticking of a clock.

Back against the wall, he peered around the doorframe.

"Damnation," he muttered, releasing the hammer on his pistol and pocketing it. He was too late.

Heart pounding and a sick dread in his stomach, he strode over to Mason, who was slumped over his desk.

"Gerald!" Davenport put fingers to the man's neck and detected a pulse.

Relief washed over him in a heady rush.

His hand came away sticky with blood and he saw the spot where Gerald had been struck. It was still bleeding, which meant the culprit wasn't far.

Perhaps even in this room—

A flash of movement caught the tail of Davenport's eye. He snatched up the closest thing to hand, which happened to be the ink pot, and flung it in his attacker's face.

Even spattered with blue ink, Davenport recognized the face instantly.

Ridley.

Rage raced along his veins like fire, roared in his head. Without pausing to draw his pistol, he launched himself at the killer.

Ridley's knife bit into his skin, slashing a long gash up his forearm, but Davenport made the sacrifice to get close enough to wrestle for the weapon. His hand clamped over Ridley's wrist as they hit the floor, rolling, scuffling in a struggle for supremacy. The fight was silent, bloody, and brutal, but Ridley was simply a hired thug. Davenport had righteous fury on his side.

The pistol fell from his pocket and skittered across the floor. Ridley's attention was caught. His gaze tracked the weapon, and the distraction was all Davenport needed. He pinned Ridley to the floor in a wrestling move he'd perfected at Cambridge. A vicious smash of Ridley's wrist on the bare floorboards made him let go.

The knife dropped to the floor just out of Ridley's reach.

There was a flare of fear in Ridley's eyes as Davenport

loomed over him. Then he curled his lip. "You don't have the guts to finish the job, do yer? Useless toff."

"This is for Nail, you bastard," Davenport snarled. He drove his fist into the man's sneering face.

The urge to keep hitting him even after the man lost consciousness was so strong, Davenport exercised a severe effort of will to stop. He wasn't here to kill Ridley, satisfying and just as that might be.

Quickly he ripped the man's coat open and searched inside it. No pockets. Inside his waistcoat, then. Grimacing, he slid his hand between the man's waistcoat and his graying shirt.

Paper met his touch. He whisked it out and unfolded it with trembling fingers.

By George. Gerald had got it.

The method for synthesizing the nitroglycerine. The reason Davenport had been hounded and forced into hiding was all here on paper. Gerald had cracked it.

He checked over the workings and frowned. Then he shoved the paper in his own pocket and searched for something to bind Ridley's hands and feet.

* * *

"You're a damned fool," said Davenport, handing Gerald a soaked washcloth to bathe his aching head. "More of a fool than I was. At least I had the excuse of youth. Don't you know why I had to disappear? Because of that damned formula. And now you've gone and replicated my work they'll be after you."

As briefly as possible, he'd told Gerald the truth of his feigned death and reappearance, only to discover that his friend and rival had guessed most of it already.

Gerald winced as he pressed the wad of cloth to the back of his head. "It was always a competition between us. Yarmouth played on it; I realize that now. But you won this time, Davenport. You got the girl."

Davenport's brows twitched together. "Do you mean Lady Maria?"

Gerald nodded.

"Don't be daft, man. She doesn't care a button for me."

In fact, he was almost certain now that if Gerald could accept another man's child as his own and marry the chit they'd have a reasonable chance of happiness. It wasn't his place to tell Gerald about the babe, however. He'd leave that to Lady Maria. Sadly he doubted the girl had the wit to realize how lucky she was in having Gerald's heart at her feet or the courage to pick it up.

Gerald grunted, shifting in his chair. "That's not what it looks like to me."

"What does Lady Maria have to do with this?" Davenport gestured to the paper in his hand.

"Yarmouth," Gerald touched the back of his head and hissed. "He promised me he'd approve my suit if I succeeded where you failed."

"It's not in your line of work," said Davenport. "Why did he choose you?"

A grim twist to Gerald's mouth told Davenport that if he'd ever harbored illusions about Yarmouth he didn't have them any longer. "At the time, I was flattered. Now, I think he chose me because if I was tied to his daughter I'd be under his control."

"What changed his tune?"

Gerald shrugged. "I started thinking with my brain instead of the contents of my trousers, began asking questions. Yarmouth didn't like it. But I was stupid and jealous of you with Maria. I let him goad me into admitting I'd solved the problem."

A scuffle at the door made Davenport snatch up his

pistol. He cocked it with deadly purpose and trained it on the opening door.

Hilary stumbled into the room, her neck held in a harsh grip by Yarmouth, the man Davenport now knew was his enemy.

Davenport's quick reflexes nearly had him pulling the trigger on his own sweetheart. Thank God some instinct had stayed his hand. His hand shook. His body went first hot, then cold before his mind kicked into gear, his senses sharpened to a deadly point. There was no room for error here.

Fear stiffened Honey's features. She was white as death. That she wasn't dead or maimed or injured was no thanks to him. Where the hell was Beckenham? He was supposed to have been watching Yarmouth.

"What's he doing here?" Davenport ground out with a glare at Gerald.

Mason swallowed hard. "I sent him a note, too. I thought the three of us could come to an arrangement."

"Apparently, you were wrong." God, he could kill Gerald for being such a fool. What had he sought to achieve by bringing them all together? A pity he hadn't realized the full extent of Yarmouth's villainy before this.

But then, even Davenport hadn't been certain. Not until Lady Maria had betrayed knowledge about his journey to town. Yarmouth could only have come by that information one way: by having Davenport followed.

"Put the gun down, Davenport, there's a good fellow," said Yarmouth. Even with a pistol to a lady's head, he smiled benignly, like a vicar at a tea party.

With Honey held so close against Yarmouth's bulk, the pistol was useless anyway. Davenport released the hammer and complied, placing the weapon carefully on the desk, within reach if he needed to dive for it.

Even in these circumstances, Yarmouth's mouth stretched in that wide, urbane grin Davenport found so irritating. He glanced over at his henchman, bound and gagged on the floor. "I see I was right not to trust Ridley with this. He is usually such a reliable tool."

"Not so reliable, after all," said Davenport with a glance toward Ridley, who lay helpless on his back in the far corner of the room. "I'd lay you odds he'll testify you hired him to kill the porter at that club. I'm sure the Duke of Montford could arrange for leniency on his sentence in return for—"

Davenport moved even before the report of Yarmouth's pistol shattered the air. Hilary cried out, her instinctive recoil wresting her free of Yarmouth's slackened grip. Davenport shoved her aside, dealing Yarmouth a blow to the guts that doubled the man over. Groaning, he slid down the wall.

Between wheezes and gasps and fruitlessly squeezing the trigger on his now-spent pistol, Yarmouth still managed a sneer. "Where's your evidence now, Davenport, eh?"

"Right here," said Davenport, moving to crouch over Ridley. "You missed."

He'd banked on Ridley providing a difficult target, lying flat on the ground. Not that he'd weep real tears over the man's demise, but he'd prefer that Ridley spill his guts in a signed confession and implicate Yarmouth in the business first. Ridley might get his sentence commuted to transportation if he laid information against his employer, but he wouldn't entirely escape justice for killing Nail.

The man was awake now, and his fury and fear at being gagged and bound showed in his ferocious glare and reddened face. But Yarmouth's pistol ball had missed him and buried itself in the floor a yard or two away.

Having assured himself Ridley was unscathed, Davenport moved quickly to Hilary's side. "My dear, are you hurt?"

She flinched from his touch. "No. I am unharmed."

She glanced at him and away again. There might not be pain in the rest of her body, but there was a world of pain in her eyes, and he thought he knew which particular villain was responsible for that.

He'd failed her. He'd led her into danger of the gravest kind. She probably thought he'd abandoned her back at Montford's ball, too.

There was no time to dwell on that now. He needed to get Honey away from here. But how to do it when he had so many loose ends to tie up? He couldn't trust Mason with Ridley or even Yarmouth, come to that.

But Yarmouth wasn't finished. He smiled groggily at Gerald, who had looked on with his mouth opening and closing like a fish throughout. "Just out of curiosity, do you still wish to marry my daughter, Mason? You see, I'm inclined to look favorably on your suit. With or without the solution you promised me."

He gave a dramatic shudder. "When I think of the profits that you're letting slip through your fingers . . . You could be set up for life, man! You could support my daughter in grand style, never have to work again."

Gerald pressed his lips together and didn't deign to answer.

"You can give them your blessing before you stand trial," said Davenport dryly.

"But you'll have to tie the knot quickly," continued Yarmouth as if Davenport hadn't spoken. He made a moue expressive of distaste. "You see, Gerald, the stupid little bitch went and got herself with child."

"*What?*"

Mason's furious exclamation split his ears, but Davenport fixed his attention on Hilary. Her pale face had turned ashen. Her eyes seemed hollowed out, like a starving waif. Those golden-brown eyes turned in his direction with an expression so broken, he almost went to his knees.

"And of course Davenport won't marry her," Yarmouth added, malice dripping from his tone as he struggled to his feet. He still clutched his midriff, but his vigor was returning.

"The babe isn't mine," said Davenport, addressing neither Gerald nor Yarmouth but Hilary. "Honey, you must believe me."

Gerald's anguished voice rent the air. "She doesn't believe you, and neither do I!"

Davenport heard the ominous click of a pistol being primed. *His* pistol, the one he'd left on Gerald's desk. A glance confirmed it. Gerald pointed the gun at him.

"Put the pistol down, Gerald." As he spoke, Davenport took three cautious steps to the side, but the pistol in Mason's hand tracked his movements and he dared not try anything for fear of him pulling the trigger. "Honey, lie down flat on the floor."

He didn't look to see whether she obeyed him but kept his eyes on the weapon.

"Gerald," said Davenport in a calm tone with a hint of warning in it. He swallowed hard.

His vaunted recklessness, the gaming, the women, none of that had been an act. When his life's work had been stripped from him along with his reputation, he'd ridden hard and fast to the Devil and told himself he'd enjoyed every minute of it. The Earl of Davenport truly had not cared whether he lived or died.

Until he met Hilary deVere.

Now, as he faced the real prospect of death at the hands of a man he used to call a friend, life became a precious gift, indeed.

Honey. He must not die leaving things like this between them.

Struggling for calm, he said, "Gerald, you must believe me. The babe cannot be mine."

"Well, of course you'd say that," scoffed Yarmouth. "What man wouldn't, staring down the barrel of his own pistol, eh?"

"Shut up! Shut up, both of you!" yelled Gerald, spittle flying. He was red in the face, and the hand that held the pistol in an inexpert grip trembled. A more dangerous man with a weapon than Ridley, in many ways.

"I'll shut his mouth for you," muttered Davenport.

"Allow me," said a feminine voice so stripped of emotion that he barely recognized it as Hilary's. She raised a heavy carved bookend and brought it down hard on Yarmouth's head.

"Bravo," said Davenport, when he'd recovered from the astonishment of seeing his dearest love brain his greatest enemy.

There was no opportunity to take advantage of the diversion, however. Gerald's agonized rage had narrowed his focus to Davenport and Davenport alone. He would not be distracted.

It was a risk, but Davenport raised his gaze from the pistol to meet Gerald's eye. Slowly, succinctly, he said, "Gerald, I give you my word as a gentleman, I never compromised Lady Maria. The child she is carrying is not mine."

The absolute sincerity in his tone seemed to confuse Gerald. His chin quivered, but his hold on the pistol remained firm. "Why should I take your word about anything?"

Why indeed? Davenport fell silent. Hadn't he taken pride in renouncing all claim to the title of gentleman?

"Because I do," said Hilary quietly, moving to stand next to him.

"Dammit, Honey, get down," he said. "You're making yourself a target."

Then he registered the meaning of those three words she'd uttered. Did she truly believe him? Or did she simply say that to calm Gerald?

Either way, she ignored his order, homing in on the man with the pistol. "In fact, Mr. Mason, I *know* Lord Davenport is not the father of Lady Maria's child, for she told me so herself."

"You? She told *you*?" demanded Gerald. "But—"

"Yes," said Honey, lying through her teeth. A slight tremor in her speech betrayed her fear, but that was the only sign of discomposure she showed. "If you don't believe me, why not ask her yourself?"

She let that sink in, then went on in that precise schoolmistress voice of hers that he knew so well. "And I do not mean to criticize, sir, but the gentlemanly code would forbid that you shoot an unarmed man in cold blood. After all, solving this kind of dispute is what affairs of honor are for, are they not? You should rather request Davenport's seconds to wait on yours. Moreover . . ."

She rattled on in the same instructive tone for so long that Davenport thought his eyes might cross if he weren't so terrified on her behalf.

It seemed to have the same stultifying effect on Gerald, for he passed a trembling hand over his face, as if tried beyond endurance. Even with a pistol in his hand, he was too polite to contradict or interrupt a lady.

"Of course, if you still wish to shoot Lord Davenport, I'll stand aside," continued Honey amenably. "But if you've decided to be sensible, perhaps you might oblige me by releasing the hammer on that lovely pistol. Yes, that's it," she said encouragingly as Gerald numbly complied with her request. "My dear Mr. Mason, I do believe you ought to sit down. You look a trifle faint."

As competently as if she'd handled firearms all her life—which, knowing her upbringing, perhaps she had— Honey removed the pistol from Gerald's now-slackened grasp and expertly released the hammer. She handed the weapon to Davenport without so much as glancing at him.

Only when Gerald finally slumped into his desk chair again did she sink to her knees on the floor, her chest heaving as shudders of relief racked her body.

Before Davenport could recover from the fourteen heart attacks he'd suffered while Hilary talked Gerald into submission, Beckenham strode in, his usually precise appearance somewhat the worse for wear.

"Where the hell have you been?" demanded Davenport. "You were supposed to watch the bastard."

Beckenham's brow was creased with worry. "I saw him go into Montford House, but he didn't come out again, and I'd no reason to suspect what he was up to until the boy gave me your message and I went in search of both him and Miss deVere. Yarmouth must have smuggled her out through the back garden. It took me a great deal of time to pick up the trail."

He glanced around. "I got here as quickly as I— Miss deVere!" He crossed to Honey, who was still on her knees, shivering.

Struggling out of his coat, Beckenham knelt beside her and put it around her shoulders. As Davenport should have done. As he would have done if Beckenham hadn't got there first.

The warmth seemed to thaw Honey from her shocked state. She turned her face into his big, dependable shoulder and wept.

Watching them, Davenport felt as if someone had stabbed him repeatedly in the stomach and ripped his entrails out for good measure.

"*Gerald!*" Lady Maria Shand stumbled onto the scene.

"What the Devil's she doing here?" said Davenport, snapping out of his piteous abstraction.

Beckenham shrugged. "I passed her on the stairs."

"Oh, Gerald, my darling! You are wounded. How can this be?"

Lady Maria hurried over to her injured swain. Gerald had started to protest that he wasn't badly hurt, but he seemed to think better of it as her delicate hands fluttered over him and her blue eyes gazed earnestly into his.

Davenport watched Hilary deVere seek safety in the shelter of his cousin's arms. A great hole gaped inside him. It burned with cold intensity, like frostbite.

"Honey," he said in a voice that barely scraped through his vocal cords. "I need to talk to you, away from here. Let's go down."

He could tell she wanted to deny him, but she had never been a coward. She moved ahead of him, out the door.

A brave woman, his Honey. Facing down a man with a pistol. That took courage of no mean order. He was still furious with her for doing it, but he couldn't help but worship her at the same time.

He loved her. The blinding simplicity of this fact nearly made him miss his footing on the stairs. He'd had to face near death, both hers and his own, to realize it, but now that he had, he needed to make her his.

He led her downstairs to a disused parlor and lit a candle there with hands that were not quite steady.

After all that had occurred, he wasn't certain she'd forgive him. She'd told him she loved him but that seemed a lifetime ago.

He hesitated, not knowing where to begin. Afraid to begin, if the truth were known. What he started she might finish, annihilate him with a word.

A resolve solidified within him. He wouldn't let her deny him. Not now. Not when he'd finally woken to his own stupidity. What he wanted was clear now, no longer colored or obscured by the past.

He wanted to be with Hilary deVere forever.

The longing to hold her swept over him, but she stood by the window, her arms crossed in an attitude of self-containment. He couldn't quite stomach the prospect of her rejecting any physical overtures he might make.

He forced himself to say the words. "I love you, Honey. Will you be my wife?"

The flimsy curtains fluttered around her in the breeze. Moonlight streamed in, adding silvery highlights to her golden hair.

She didn't speak for many moments. His heart seemed to have migrated to his throat and it beat so hard, he wondered she couldn't hear it.

The silence stretched until he said, "Honey, please answer me. Will you be my wife?"

She opened her lips and he braced for the blow. "I'm afraid I cannot marry you, my lord."

He'd expected her answer, but that didn't lessen the pain of hearing it. "Why not? I know I did something or said something wrong back there in the music room, but if you'll just listen to me—"

She shook her head. "I'm afraid I cannot marry you because you are not good enough for me."

Was that all? "Well, of course I'm not good enough for you. Ask any of my family. Ask Becks up there. But I love you, damn it, Honey. And you said that you loved me."

She tilted her head to the side. "I don't think you do

love me, you know, Davenport. Though I give you full credit for retrieving the slip you made back there in the music room."

"Slip?" Now he was confused.

"You thought you could make all right with Lady Maria. What you forgot was that even if the silly female could be brought to keep her mouth shut about our . . . liaison, she is not the only one who knows of it. After tonight, everyone will expect you to do the right thing, make an honest woman of me. The only way to save my reputation is to sacrifice your freedom. And you'll do it, won't you, Davenport? Because here's the secret I know about you." She lowered her voice to whisper. "You're no true scoundrel at all."

She'd put pieces of the puzzle together. They fitted, but they didn't show the true picture. "It's not like that."

Her eyes were bright with tears, but her voice remained steady. "I saw how you looked when I told you I loved you, Jonathon. It wasn't the expression of a man in love who had just discovered his feelings were returned."

That piece of truth rammed him in the gut like a fist. He stared at her, knowing the situation was fast careering out of his control, powerless to stop it. "I hadn't realized then. I didn't know—"

"You told me I needn't marry you. Those were your words before you ran after Lady Maria to shut her mouth so we would not be forced to wed. I find it difficult—impossible, really—to believe your sentiments can have altered so greatly in the space of a few hours."

"But they have, damn it! Or at least, they haven't changed, I just didn't recognize them until now. Honey, you needed to have the choice. I didn't want you committed to something you might later regret. That's why I needed to keep Lady Maria quiet."

"Really?" He was making such an abysmal mess of

this, her skeptical expression held a tinge of pity. "I'd told you I loved you only minutes before. It seems to me that you were the one whose precious freedom was at issue. You were terrified of committing yourself. That's why you wouldn't even try to procure vouchers for Almack's, isn't it?"

"Oh, now I've heard everything. What has Almack's got to do with us?"

She jabbed a finger at him. "You claim you don't remember being banned. As if it doesn't matter. As if having those doors closed to you is so insignificant it slipped your mind."

"It did," he protested.

"*I don't believe you.* You are a coward, my lord. Afraid to fight for what is most important. Worst of all, you are afraid to love."

He eyed her warily and wondered if her recent brush with death had turned her into some sort of goddess with powers beyond mortal ken and no hint of mercy in her soul.

She went on, remorseless. "Your colleagues in the scientific world shunning you, the Almack's patronesses barring their doors against you. Your own cousins taking you into the country and dumping you in a barn. All of that mattered to you, Davenport, or you wouldn't have committed such ridiculous excesses until now. You deny the hurt because you're too proud to admit you need these people. You need society. You need your family. You need your work." She took a deep, unsteady breath. "You need me."

"Honey, that's what I've been trying to tell you. I love you. I need you. You have to marry me."

"No, Davenport," she said gently. "You are simply trying to make the best of a bad bargain. And I won't let you."

"That's not it at all." He took a long, unsteady breath

and attempted to make order and sense of the roiling mass of feelings inside him. For someone so adept at employing words to charm and beguile, he'd never been good at using them to express deep emotion. They were so new and raw and tender, these emotions, it caused him physical pain to strip away all the flippancy that he'd used to protect himself all these years.

But he would do it for her.

He swallowed hard. In a voice deepened with passion and hoarse with desperation, he said, "Honey, you are my sun. You're the heat that warms me and nurtures all the good things inside me, the light that drives out my darkness. I was lost, aimless, spinning into oblivion until I met you. You pulled me into orbit around you. In serving you, protecting you, striving to be worthy of you, in *loving* you, I've found my true path."

He searched her face for some sign that she understood, but her eyes—those glorious, gold-flecked eyes—did not relent. They simply filled with tears.

"You must not say those things," she said, squeezing her eyes shut as if to block out his words. Tears slid down her cheeks. "I simply *cannot* . . ."

She shook her head vehemently, catching her lip between her teeth. She opened her eyes again. "It is too late for this, Jonathon. Far too late."

"No! No, it can't be." Davenport strode forward, intending to pull her into his arms. Something he ought to have done immediately. She could never resist him physically, and he wasn't above taking unfair advantage of that fact.

She warded him off with a sharp wave of her hand. "Don't! Don't touch me, I can't bear it." In a tone of near despair, she cried, "Oh, why can't you just let me go?"

He'd reached for her, but now he let his hands fall by his sides. He felt as if he'd been gutted like a fish. He'd laid open his insides for her inspection and she'd spurned them without hesitation. Pain, jagged as a fisherman's blade, cut through him. He took a ragged breath and realized there was nothing left for him to say.

Beckenham chose that moment to poke his head into the room, causing Honey to turn her back, wiping surreptitiously at her eyes with the back of her hand. "If you want to take Miss deVere home, Davenport, I can clear up here."

When a tense silence greeted him, Beckenham's dark gaze flicked from one of them to the other. "Oh. Sorry." He cleared his throat awkwardly. "I'll go."

"That's quite all right, Lord Beckenham," said Honey, turning with a brilliant smile and only the slightest hint of dampness on her cheeks. "I'd like you to take me home, if you would be so good. Lord Davenport must attend to his business here."

Beckenham cocked an eyebrow at Davenport for confirmation.

After a long pause, Davenport nodded. It was his responsibility to see that Yarmouth and Ridley got their comeuppance.

More important, he needed to stop digging a bigger hole for himself with Honey. He needed to find a way to convince her he was in earnest. He *had* to convince her. The alternative was unthinkable. He'd just discovered he couldn't possibly live without Hilary deVere.

"I'll send Lydgate over with the magistrate," said Beckenham, offering his arm to Honey. "Yarmouth won't stand trial, of course, but Xavier is already working on the problem of what to do with him, I believe."

Adding clairvoyance to his other alarming qualities, Davenport thought. He watched with agonized frustration as his Honey smiled at his dependable cousin. Thanking him for his kindness, she tucked her hand into Beckenham's arm and left.

All the light left with her, it seemed. Not even in the darkest hours of his exile had he felt so alone.

* * *

Hilary was too shattered to speak once they left Mr. Mason's house, and Beckenham did not press her. The terrors of the past few hours seemed to fade into insignificance when compared with the agony of her final talk with Davenport.

The pain was too great for anyone to bear. How would she go on without him? Worse, how could she stop wanting him, even when she knew she'd made the right choice? Hadn't she known all along how dangerous it was to fall in love with such a man?

She might have put on a brave face with Davenport when she rejected his proposal, but now she confronted the reality of ruin, the contempt of everyone she'd ever respected and admired. She dreaded facing anyone who belonged to that world. Cecily and Rosamund would be crushingly disappointed in her. Not to mention Lady Arden and the Duke of Montford. None of them would ever speak to her again.

What an idiot she'd been. She ought to have considered all of this before she'd fallen into bed with Davenport. What had he said once? It was his job to seduce her and her job to stop him. She'd failed at her duty quite miserably, had she not?

But she hadn't succumbed to his outrageous charm, nor had she fallen in love with a handsome face. It was his innate kindness, his understanding of human foibles, and his readiness to forgive them in others that had undone her resolve.

He'd never judged her lacking because of her family or where she lived. He'd poked gentle fun at her insecurities, inviting her to laugh at things that once had so intimidated her. He'd defended her with his words and, when necessary, with his fists. He was a hero in the unlikeliest of all packages.

That's why it killed her to hear those precious words on his lips. He'd said he loved her, and it seemed to her that he said it more easily each time. He'd almost convinced himself it was true. But he hadn't convinced her.

Now she must do what was best for both of them and leave London for good.

As Beckenham's curricle drew nearer to Half Moon Street, she wondered if even the vulgar Mrs. Walker would turn her out of doors once she heard the news of her disgrace. That seemed a prospect too humiliating to contemplate.

With a dull sense of inevitability, she said, "Lord Beckenham, would you take me to my brothers' lodgings, please? They're in Jermyn Street."

* * *

When all was finished with Yarmouth and Ridley and it became clear that Gerald and Lady Maria had resolved their differences, it was far too late to do anything but go home.

Before he left, Lady Maria assured him she'd said nothing to anyone about "that other matter," by which he took her to mean that now she was happy with Gerald she no longer sought to make everyone else's life a misery.

Hilary's reputation was safe. He meant to make damned sure it remained so by marrying her as soon as he could get her to actually speak with him again.

He wasn't fool enough to make any further attempts tonight. Or this morning, as it now was. When his business was finished at Mason's house, he went to find Beckenham.

They said confession was good for the soul, but it certainly wasn't good for one's amour propre. When Davenport finally divulged why Hilary might choose to hide out with her brothers rather than return to Mrs. Walker's or Rosamund's house, Beckenham's response had been worse than a fist in the face.

Davenport was treated, at great length and in painstaking detail, to all the reasons he was less than dirt beneath Hilary's dancing slippers. Every one of which he already knew.

"Why don't *you* marry her, then?" he demanded of Beckenham, giving voice to the jealousy that had been gnawing at him for days now.

"I?" said Beckenham, his brows knit. "You believe I have an interest in Miss deVere? I have a kindness for her, of course, but that is all."

He appeared bewildered by the accusation, as if when it came to love he was not even in the running and no one could expect him to be.

Cecily was right. Georgie Black truly had ruined Beckenham for all other women.

For the briefest of moments, Davenport's heart lifted. But no matter what Beckenham felt or didn't feel, that didn't change the essential facts.

Honey wouldn't have him because she didn't believe he truly loved her. She thought he acted from chivalry. Chivalry! Now that was rich.

* * *

The following morning, Davenport dragged his aching carcass up to the rooms Hilary's brothers had hired for the duration of their London stay and banged on the door. Hilary's brother Tom answered the door on Davenport's third knock.

"Oh. It's you." Tom leaned his significant bulk against the doorframe and crossed his arms.

"I don't want to fight." Davenport held up his hands in a gesture of peace. "I just want to see Miss deVere."

"You're too late," said Tom, stifling a yawn. "Ben's already taken her home."

"*What?*" Turning away, Davenport raked a hand through his hair. He swung back and said, "Did she leave anything for me? A note, a message, anything?"

The other man appeared to think about this question carefully before he said, "No." The door slammed in Davenport's face.

His first impulse was to drive all the way to Lincolnshire to plead with Honey to take him back, but he made himself stop and think. He used to be good at thinking.

He was a coward, she'd said. Afraid to love.

He kicked at a stone that lay in his path. He wasn't afraid to love. He loved her, didn't he? Of course he did. The seesawing emotions he'd experienced in the last few days had to be the product of either insanity or love and he wasn't quite ready for Bedlam yet.

He adored her. He'd told her he loved her. It hadn't been an easy feat to force those particular words past his lips but he'd done it. Yet it seemed that wasn't enough.

He needed some perspective, which he wouldn't get haring off after her as soon as he could saddle a horse. He needed perspective, and he needed help.

And he knew just where he might find both.

Sighing with a mixture of inevitability and apprehension, he wrote to Cecily, Rosamund, Lydgate, Beckenham, and Xavier, requesting their presence at a council of war. On second thoughts, he sent for Lady Arden and the Duke of Montford, too.

CHAPTER TWENTY-THREE

L etter for you, miss."

"Thank you, Hodgins."

Hilary watched the manservant depart with a twinkle in her eye. Ever since she'd persuaded her brothers to purchase a new suit of clothes and give him the official title of butler, she'd noticed a marked improvement, from the way Hodgins carried himself to his manner toward her.

Hilary had made other changes around Wrotham Grange. The large pack of dogs no longer roamed the rambling mansion at will but was confined to the library, her brothers' domain.

Since their recent sojourn, Tom and Benedict had developed a taste for London and were home less often, which suited her. Presumably, her stipulation that they might entertain women only when she was away from home might have had something to do with that.

She kept herself busy with setting the household to rights, even persuading Tom to fund the most urgent structural repairs.

There wasn't a moment in the day she wasn't conscious of the ache of loss. An ache that turned sharp and jagged when she knew for certain she wasn't carrying Davenport's child.

She ought to send up thanks to Heaven. What a calamity that would have been.

There was nothing to do but carry on and make the best of her situation. Her notoriety did not seem to have spread to this corner of the world, so she grabbed at overtures of friendship from locals with both hands.

Her London stay, brief though it had been, had taught her much. She liked to think her experience with Davenport had mellowed her; she no longer minded everything she said and did, nor did she judge others as harshly. She, of all people, knew about fallibility now.

For the first time, she had friends. True friends, who she trusted would not abandon her if news of the stain on her reputation ever spread as far as Lincolnshire. She wanted to think these good people's friendship underscored the falsity of what she'd found with the Westruthers. She had not heard from any of them in a month. They must be snubbing her on account of her disgrace. She'd expected as much.

Yet her heart was not so cynical and refused to feel disillusioned. She still believed she'd found something special with Davenport's family. It hurt when they abandoned her, but she understood the reason.

Using the knife in her desk, she slit open the letter Hodgins had handed her. Two smaller cards enclosed in it fluttered to the ground. The letter was from Cecily and it read:

Dear Hilary,
   Davenport strictly forbade us from writing to you before now, so do forgive our silence, won't you? We were monstrous put out that you ran off without a

*word, but if my dear brother was being his usual
Infuriating Self, who can blame you?*

*Only now we are in a quandary. Lady Arden
procured these vouchers for Almack's, as you will
see. . . .*

With a gasp, Hilary scooped up the two cards that had
fallen free from the letter. The topmost one bore a blotchy
red seal and the signature "M.S.". It read:

Ladies Voucher
Deliver to:
Miss Hilary deVere
Tickets for the Balls on Wednesdays in *April,* 1819

There was one Wednesday left in April. . . .

"What's the matter, Miss Hilary?" Trixie asked. "You
look like a goose run over your grave."

"Yes, quite well, thank you," said Hilary absently.
Dear Trixie. How she'd stare to hear they were bound for
Almack's!

She looked at the other voucher and saw Davenport's
name scrawled in spiky black ink.

"He did it." Wonder filled her as she read the voucher
over and over.

"He *did* it!" She jumped up and grabbed Trixie's hands
and danced her in a vigorous jig around the room.

When she let go, Trixie put her hand to her bosom, her
cheeks flushed, eyes bright. "Does that mean we're going
back to London, Miss Hilary?"

At the mention of London, Hilary's initial flush of elation gave way to caution. She tried to calm herself, but the
butterflies in her stomach thrashed about with gay abandon.

"I don't know. Wait, let me see. . . ."

With a shaking hand, she snatched up the letter again.
Greedily she devoured the rest of Cecily's missive:

*You will be pleased to know that the Trouble we
anticipated from a Certain Quarter is no longer a
threat. You are free and, indeed, welcome to return
to us at any time. You should not have run away,
dear Hilary. If you were better acquainted with the
Westruthers you would know that when we set our
minds to something, we* always *prevail!*

*If you choose to attend the subscription ball next
Wednesday, I do beg of you to bring Jonathon's
voucher with you and meet him outside Almack's at
ten o'clock, for they close the doors at eleven sharp
and do not admit anyone after that time.*

*My brother could, of course, call for you in Half
Moon Street, but where would be the fun in that? A
rendezvous is so much more romantic, don't you
agree? Just do not get yourself kidnapped again!! I've
heard quite enough gnashing of teeth from my male
relatives over that incident to last me a lifetime.*

*In closing, let me remind you, my dear, of our
family motto:*

"To a valiant heart, nothing is impossible."

Be valiant, dearest Hilary. . . .

Yours, etc.

Cecily

*P.S. Rosamund says she will not speak to you
ever again if you do not return to us this season.*

*P.P.S. Beckenham desires me to add that only
your presence can make Davenport the least bit
bearable, so would you please come at once.*

Something inside Hilary burst open and she laughed
and cried with the heady relief of it, blotching Cecily's

letter, until she was wrung out and spent. She hadn't realized the true weight of the anxiety that had built and built
inside her over her damaged reputation and the place she
had lost among the affections of the Westruthers.

And Davenport! The greatest rogue in London had gone
cap in hand to the Almack's patronesses and won his way
into their good graces once more.

She wondered what he'd done to demonstrate his
change of heart.

Hilary bit her lip. Had he done it for the right reasons,
though? She hoped he didn't see it as some sort of test he
must pass to win her. She trusted that by the end of the
process he'd understood she wanted him to reclaim his
place in society for his own sake, not for hers.

Almack's.

She'd finally achieved her dream. Or part of it, anyway.

Smiling, and without even a twinge of regret, she took
the voucher with her name on it, gave it a quick, smacking kiss, and threw it on the fire.

* * *

Davenport took out his timepiece and gazed at it for the
hundredth time.

Five minutes to eleven and still no sign of her. Everyone knew that even the Duke of Wellington could not
enter Almack's after eleven o'clock.

Where the hell was she?

He'd moved Heaven and earth and everything in between to secure those vouchers for himself. He'd matched
wits with Lady Jersey, played the prodigal son with Lady
Sefton, dallied innocently with Countess Lieven, waltzed
with Princess Esterhazy. He'd even expressed humble con-
trition for his misdeeds to Mrs. Drummond-Burrell,

which had been a tricky business as he truly had no recollection of what they were.

He'd worn knee breeches this evening, for God's sake!

He couldn't even go inside to drown his sorrows in the piss-weak claret cup they served because Cecily had persuaded him to send his voucher to Honey as proof of his sincerity.

She'd probably laughed herself sick and tossed it in the fire.

He'd waited almost an hour for her to come, feeling like a damned fool holding the little posy of violets Rosamund had insisted he bring to pin to her gown.

Hilary hadn't even arrived in London when last he'd checked today. Mrs. Walker had no expectation of seeing her, and her brothers were as close as oysters on the subject.

A nearby clock began to strike the hour.

A sick feeling of dread flowed over him. He crushed the posy between his palms, rendering the air sweet with its scent, then let it fall. Then he leaned against the rail in front of the most exclusive club in London and rubbed his face with the heel of one hand.

On what must have been the fifth strike of the clock, someone tapped him on the shoulder, then thrust some sort of card under his nose.

"Sorry I'm late," a feminine voice—*her* voice—said, "If you want to go inside, you'll have to hurry, I expect."

He looked up, hope breaking over him like spring sunshine after a bleak, endless winter. He seized Honey, swung her around and around, then crushed her to him, kissing her as if he might never stop.

"I love you," he said to her in the shadow of Almack's as the clock struck the ninth chime. "Quick, if we hurry we can make it through the doors in time."

She was smiling, her eyes glimmering with tears. "I don't want to go in there, Jonathon. Not tonight."

For a bare, crazed instant he couldn't decide whether to shake her or howl. All the trouble he'd gone to for those vouchers over the past month—for nothing! The calls he'd paid, the endless cups of tea he had drunk. At Beckenham's behest, he'd sat in the House of Lords again, and wasn't that just a barrel of laughs?

He'd even taken the first, tentative steps toward reestablishing himself as a chemist, assisting Gerald in his work.

But with sudden, belated insight he realized what he ought to have known all along. That dear, fey face with the harlot's mouth stared up at him, willed him to understand it, to understand her.

Ever since they'd met, her sole ambition had been to attend Almack's. What woman didn't want to go there?—as Xavier had cynically remarked.

But for Honey, the frills and furbelows and fancy parties were not important for their own sake. To Hilary de-Vere, Almack's meant acceptance. All she'd ever wanted was to belong.

He stared down at her, suddenly serious. "You belong with me, Honey. Tell me you know that it's true."

Her face lit like the fireworks at Vauxhall. "Yes," she breathed. "Yes, Jonathon. I know it. I do."

He hugged her to him and held her tight and kissed her lips, her eyelids, her nose, her brow. He buried his face in that silky, glorious hair and inhaled her unique, dear scent.

"Violets," he murmured shakily, making her laugh.

Then he drew back to look at her with a mix of tenderness and awe and humble gratitude for his good fortune. "I'm a fool, Honey. It was never about Almack's, was it?"

Shaking her head, smiling through her tears, she reached up to touch his cheek. "I love you, Jonathon. Take me home."

Read on for an excerpt from Christina Brooke's next novel

The Greatest Lover Ever

Coming soon from St. Martin's Paperbacks

Georgie rattled the doorknob, knowing it would be hopeless. What in Heaven's name was the wretched man up to now? A quick glance around showed no other possible means of escape. She had better search the room for weapons.

She discovered nothing of practical use in the sparsely furnished chamber—not even a fire iron with which to brain her host should he try to ravish her.

The minutes dragged by; she realized how foolish it had been to suppose she could rescue her sister from this kind of peril. Ten to one, Violet enjoyed the festivities, happy as a lark, watched over by her companions. While Georgie was imprisoned in a boudoir by a lecherous marquis with a grossly overblown opinion of his charms.

Fools rush in, indeed. Hadn't Marcus always complained of her impetuousness? It seemed she still hadn't learned her lesson.

The key turning in the lock made her stiffen, her heart bounding into her throat.

She moved as far from the bed as she could manage. Not that it would make any difference to Steyne, but it made her feel better. She snatched up the Chinese vase from the mantel, tested its weight. Too delicate to do any damage and probably priceless into the bargain. She set it down again.

But the tall, dark-haired figure who entered was not Lord Steyne.

It was his cousin, her former fiancé. Marcus Westruther, Earl of Beckenham.

He stood there for what seemed an age, silhouetted against the doorway. She couldn't see his features clearly in the shadows but she didn't have to. They were as sharp and clear in her mind's eye as they had ever been in the flesh.

For several moments, the shock of seeing him again suspended her faculties. Her lips parted but no sound came out.

Emotion flooded her chest, a swirling mass of reactions that could not be separated into constituent parts. The strength of it made her light-headed.

What could she say to him? She'd avoided a meeting between them for years, and now, to see him in such fantastical circumstances . . . Could anything be more disastrous?

Ought she simply tell him the real reason she was here?

Could she trust him? Instinct told her yes. But why on earth should he help her, even if she told him her troubles? He'd washed his hands of her years ago.

She'd rejected him as a husband, dealt a severe blow to his pride. As far as Beckenham was concerned, there could not be a more unforgivable crime than that. Particularly for a man who prized honor and loyalty above all other qualities.

So she waited in the silence. She would follow his lead. He was the injured party, after all.

Her awareness of him was so heightened that the mere tilt of his head as he studied her made her heart zing about her chest like a firework. She heard nothing but her own breathing. The unruly hitch in it seemed to echo in the silence.

He moved into the room, then closed the door. "I hear you've been looking for me."

His deep voice resonated through her body, stirring the embers of a fire that had long lain dormant. *Yes, but never in my wildest dreams did I think you'd be here.*

She didn't answer. Oh, God, it was awful and humiliating and . . . and *wonderful* to see him. She hadn't laid eyes on him since that dreadful night when she'd released him from the engagement. Almost by tacit agreement, she'd lived in Town while he'd largely kept to his estate. She'd heard he'd attended Lady Cecily Westruther's come-out ball in London last season, but of course she hadn't been invited to that auspicious event. Most pointedly not invited.

And now here he was, with her. In a quiet bedchamber in the midst of a raucous, licentious party. But it didn't feel as if they stood in any kind of oasis here. It felt like the eye of a storm.

Her mouth dried as he reached up a hand to loosen his cravat, flick it open, and pull the long strip of linen from around his throat. Then he walked over to the washstand, where a pitcher of water and a basin stood as if ready for guests.

"Take your clothes off," he said to her over his shoulder. "I'll be with you in a moment."